Blythe

John E. Kramer

Freedom Forge Press, LLC
www.FreedomForgePress.com

Blythe

by John E. Kramer

Published by Freedom Forge Press, LLC

www.FreedomForgePress.com

Copyright © 2017 by John E. Kramer

www.BlytheBook.com

All Rights Reserved

ISBN: 978-1-940553-07-8

Cover by Don Wilson
© 2017 by Don Wilson

Dedicated to my wife, Holly.
Every good story is written for a single person.
This story was written for you, my Love.

One of mankind's greatest sins is inaction in the face of injustice.

Blythe

Acknowledgements

The author wishes to thank and acknowledge all those who helped make this nearly two-decade-long labor of love a reality. Let me thank in a special way Chip Mellor, my once-boss and always-friend, who encouraged me throughout this effort, and who graciously created a sabbatical system that allowed me to write most of this work. Thanks, too, to four gifted editors: Matthew Berry, Matt Cavedon, Ann Fischer and my brother, Peter D. Kramer. Thank you to Don Wilson, for his artful cover design; you remain a maestro of the graphic design world. Thank you to my publishers, Val Muller and Eric Egger; may you and Freedom Forge Press continue to inspire the world around us. I acknowledge a homily heard years ago that inspired the passage about the loaves and fishes recounted to the best of my recollection and expanded upon in Chapter 31. And, finally, thank you to my kids, Robert and Alina; you each inspire me in your own way to keep the faith and to make this world a better place.

Part One

John E. Kramer

Chapter 1

He drifted like a sick shadow between dark homes, dragging his feet over the familiar cobblestones. No one witnessed the specter that passed their doors and floated a paltry shadow across their curtains. All good people were asleep at that hour.

This figure had no business being twenty years old—not in his emaciated form. A dying ninety, one might accept, but twenty is still a growing age; an age for filling out, not for wasting away.

There was something queer about him that invited torment. Even the summer wind that swirled about him couldn't resist. It lifted the cuffs of his pants to expose pale, bony ankles. It caught the tail of his shirt, tossed it about, then billowed it in a gust to accentuate its emptiness. The wind shot out through his collar, tossing his hat to the ground, giving away the thin but wavy hair and withered form that left little room for imagination as to the underlying anatomy. He reflexively reached out to retrieve what was his, but the wind rolled the hat away from him, just out of reach. All the while, in the surrounding darkness, whirlwinds caught odd corners of eaves and shutters, haunting him with moans of confession and regret.

Hardened by a life of this kind of taunting, he stopped suddenly as a man does when he realizes his life has been a rehearsal for just such a moment. He stood as if caught from behind by the elbows. With an air of dignity, he straightened himself to send a message to the circle of invisible tormentors surrounding him that he would not play their games anymore. At last he was above it all. He let the hat roll on and disappear.

The young man stood there and dared the wind to return, but when it did not, he relaxed into his stooped and spent posture, pressing his shoulder for support against the stucco wall of a humble valley home. He stood there for a long while gathering his strength staring blankly in the ambient light at the cobblestones before his feet when at last he realized: He knew these stones; he knew them best of all.

He shuffled out a few steps into the lane so he could face the house he had left in anger two years before. The door, nearly hidden in the recessed entryway, appeared weathered and formidable. He studied it, lost in his hurtful memories, unsure of whether to knock when—up the lane from where he had come—came the faint, deep moaning of the wind. There was nowhere left for him to go.

With skeletal knuckles, he gently—too gently, perhaps—rapped. A puff of wind tossed the hair he had just tried to straighten, exposing a red tattoo cross all sides of which were equal in length. He let his hair alone now and was about to knock again, this time more forcefully, when two hushed voices from beyond the door made his hand draw back. They bickered at each other as they approached until one could finally be understood reprimanding, "How am I supposed to know until I open it?"

A forgotten window beside the door sprang into existence in yellow light. The knob rattled and turned and a shaft of light cut through the open crack. A solitary eye, a shock of salt-and-pepper tasseled hair and the hints of an aged face appeared. The woman's unseen mouth barked, "What is it?"

Before the visitor could answer, the other disembodied voice, this one of a man, asked in an urgent whisper, "Who is it?" to which the woman at the door hushed, "I don't know!"

The solitary eye returned to the man who had disturbed her sleep. She demanded again, "What is it you want?"

The young man stepped more clearly into the light and watched the eye for some sign of recognition. There was none.

Finally, the stranger spoke in a weak but unmistakable voice, "It's *me*."

The whites of her eye suddenly became more visible and her mouth fell agape. The unseen man's voice impatiently implored more loudly this time, "Who is it?" as the door swung open to reveal a gaunt figure with deep-set eyes staring back at him.

Disconcerted by a thousand ancient fears rolled into an instant of darkness, of strangers, of a midnight knock at the door, of uncertainty, of age, of death, the man asked more humbly, "Who are you? What is it you want here?"

Without turning back to answer him, the woman's voice gently cracked, "It's your son…come home," and as she said this, she raised her arms to the stranger who stepped forward into her embrace, leaving his own arms at his side.

The man of the house remained where he was, awestruck in horrible silence looking at his wife and his withered son. With her eyes still tightly shut and tearing, the woman reached out and closed the heavy wooden door. The harbinger had come home.

Blythe

Chapter 2

In a trance that held no emotion or wince of pain, she drove the sharp point of the ornate gold ring deeply into her arm's tender underside.

Suddenly, violently, Blythe shook from the neck up. Her smooth jaw line of porcelain skin clenched into rolling knots of tense muscles. The rush of adrenaline and pain was there now. And when she heard her mother's chair scrape against the hardwood floor in the kitchen just below her bedroom studio, shame was there as well.

No matter. The cut was made.

Blythe pinched a fine paintbrush from the tripod's shelf and dipped the tips of its hairs into the pooling burgundy mass. The surface tension broke, releasing a trickling, tickling stream that circled her slender arm and dripped with a metronomic beat onto her smock. Tiny red novas formed where they struck the white cloth.

Blythe never flinched. Her palette of flesh held steady. She made sure only the tip of the brush became damp and dark. She worked quickly, streaking dozens of strokes onto the vertical canvas, adding accents to the tiny crests of ocean waves beneath the setting summer sun as those reclined at picnic watched from a grassy cliff. It was all the work needed. The painting was complete.

With the rain now ended, the last patch of sunlight finished its crawl through the back window of her room across the floor and up the wall until it shrank to a thin line then disappeared entirely. For the past hour, the heavy smell of her mother's cooking crept under her bedroom door and permeated the room, triggering Blythe's subconscious countdown to dinner.

She sat back to gain some perspective on the work while unconsciously pressing her forearm hard against her ribs to stop the bleeding. She blurred the line of the horizon where sea met sky. Likewise, the coastline was blended into a continuum from water to land except where those most distant rays of light came ashore; there, she left a vivid contrast.

Her concentration was broken by her father's heavy steps across the kitchen floor and his muffled voice, having been just awakened from his late-afternoon nap. His rising told Blythe the meal was now set on the table. Soon she would be pulled back into the same food, the same conversations, the same patterns it took everything in Blythe's will to free herself from as she escaped into her art.

"Dinner, dear," she mumbled absentmindedly, rubbing patches of the canvas with her thumb, followed an instant later by her mother's trill up the stairs, "Dinner, dear!"

Blythe tossed back her long brown curls that fell about her face in carefully arranged disorder. She sank her brush into a glass of murky water. She untied her smock, folded it in half to hide the stains, then dropped it into a basket her mother would collect later that day in another never-ending cycle of domesticity.

Blythe twisted her forearms, meticulously examining their battle scars. She tore a thin piece of parchment from a sheet purchased for some artistic effort and stanched her latest wound. She rolled down her ever-present long sleeves as she walked over to her windowsill to light the large half-consumed candle that rested there. When she returned, the thick wick would give off a warm and steady light and dispel the darkness, which she feared every bit as much as she did when she was a child. For now, in the twilight, however, the candle competed with the world's glow making the room darker for the competition. At least there would be no darkness upon her return, she consoled herself.

She opened the door and made her way past her parents' bedroom door. The drip, drip, drip from a leak in the room's ceiling set the cadence for her own rhythmic bounces down the stairs to the kitchen, not in beat with the drops, but in that space of time in between when the drops were landing. "Here she comes," she muttered under her breath just a second before her mother sang the same words.

"The pot's nearly full," Blythe announced, taking her customary seat between her parents.

"Duffy," her mother scolded. "Haven't you called Danny to fix the roof? It'll be the death of us."

"It'll be the death of you; it's on your side," he chided.

Blythe watched as he bit off a big piece of buttered bread then pointed at her mother with what remained in his hand. "Besides," he said, "I have too much hanging over my head to be concerned with what's hanging over your head right now."

"You'll promise to call on him tomorrow?" Iris asked.

"Absolutely, absolutely," he replied.

"Grace," Iris announced.

At the utterance of the word the three heads bowed, one still chewing. They said, "Bless us, oh Lord, and these Thy gifts, which we are about to receive from Thy bounty, through Christ, our Lord. Amen."

Duffy was the engine, slurring the prayer along. Iris applied the brake with her slow, thought-filled words. They were so used to battling each other for control of that prayer that neither noticed how for years Blythe merely sat silent, not so much as moving her lips.

"It would be nice if you slowed down every now and then," Iris suggested.

"Many things would be nice," Duffy quipped with a wink, popping the remains of the crust into his mouth.

"You've been in a rare mood these past few weeks," Iris said. "To what do we owe this treat?"

"Clean living," he responded simply.

Blythe looked at her mother then at her father's paunch and burst out laughing. He, too, looked down and laughed. "My prosperity," he said, quite satisfied, and patted his belly.

"Prosperity?" Iris laughed, looking at her own spread. "May I call it that, too?"

"I'll call it your beauty rings."

"Beauty rings, indeed," Iris scoffed. "I would like to know what's gotten into you."

"I'm telling you, it's clean, honest living. Honest," he insisted. "Haven't you noticed how well things are for us all? It's a blessing, I tell you. A blessing for right living."

"How was the painting today, dear?" Iris asked.

"Finished," Blythe answered. "I'll show it to you when we're done."

"That would be lovely," Iris replied and hummed as she continued her meal.

"My little hummingbird," Duffy glowed, looking at his daughter, pointing with his fork to his wife.

Blythe carelessly twirled a white rose she had plucked from the humble arrangement taken from her mother's garden then glanced up to see her mother glowing back at her father. Occasionally she lifted the bloom to enjoy its perfume.

Iris turned her attention to the collection of recipes that sat on the table next to her plate. It was a cluttered mess she assembled over the years. Blythe marveled at the sudden focus and quiet intensity that took hold of her mother as she flipped through the notes, anticipating the next meal she would make for her family.

At supper's end—at least for the ladies—Blythe handed her mother the bloom, which she carefully pressed between the pages. The two women ascended the stairs. They passed the drip, drip, drip, prompting Iris to call down, "It's nearly full, dear." Duffy's response was the sound of his utensils on his plate.

The twilight's afterglow long since gone, the candle's radiance illuminated the painting's vibrant colors, its decadent swirls of clouds blending to blue sky blending to bluer seas with wind-tossed white caps catching the burnt yellow and red of the setting sun. Iris's eyes fell to a grassy cliff where she and her husband and their only child once shared a picnic.

"It's just as I remember it, too," Iris whispered, unwilling to spoil the moment by speaking at full voice.

Behind them, Duffy lumbered up the stairs murmuring indistinct curses about the ceiling and the rain and the nearly full pot.

From her youth, Blythe had made furtive mental studies of her mother's face and she did so again as Iris held her chin and nodded with approval at her daughter's work. She saw a distance now in her mother's eyes as Iris pulled herself away and walked to the window looking out into the darkness, the candle's yellow glow softening her doughy, lined face.

"Stay there a moment," Blythe pleaded, startling her mother.

Iris froze.

"Stand there and think again what you were just thinking," Blythe directed her. "Lift your chin a little. Now a little more. To the left. Right there. Now look out and, again, think what you were thinking just a moment ago and take yourself back there."

Her mother tried to regain what she imagined was her natural appearance keeping her eyes looking out to infinity. Blythe snatched a torn piece of parchment and a chunk of charcoal. With scribbles uninterrupted even by her father's splash of curses from the room next door, she placed herself within the artist's aura that vanishes faster than light flies, but, when seized upon, makes time and light and everything else stand still.

"There," she exhaled. Her mother exhaled as well.

Blythe stood beside her mother and held the paper down low tilting it toward the available light so they could look together for the first time on what she created.

"You have a gift, my dear," Iris whispered. "Thank you for making me beautiful." She kissed her daughter's high brow.

Blythe heard her father lumbering back up the stairs and the resonating clang as he dropped the pot at the foot of the bed where the drip, drip, drip echoed loudly in its hollow vessel. The burly, balding man entered the room, his once-red hair now pure and uninterrupted white. He breathed heavy from the labor of walking up the flight as he placed himself just inside his daughter's door. Blythe swept past, leaving a kiss on his cheek then bounded again down the stairs between the leaky ceiling's three-count rhythm.

He turned and extended his arms to hug her, but before he knew it, she was gone. With a look of wonder and his arms still outstretched, he turned back toward his wife who was only just looking up from the sketch. "Did I tell you we're living right?"

She chortled.

"What's that you have there?" He struck a match against the wall and lit a pipe that he pulled from his worn shirt chest pocket. He then lit a nearby candle. Duffy took the image from her and held it as far away as his arm would allow, tilting his head back for added distance.

"It's me," Iris whispered up at him in wonder.

"I know beauty when I see it," he said examining her face, his head still bent back. He stooped forward and kissed her forehead then wrapped her up in his great arms. They rocked for a long while until she patted him on the belly and laughed disparagingly, "Your prosperity."

As they turned to leave, Blythe's new painting caught her father's eye. "Hmm," he complained.

Iris stooped in the man's shadow picking up the laundry. "What is it?" she asked.

"Just like in her life—no boundaries. Air mixed with water, water with land, land with air. Life has lines, Iris. It has boundaries. She refuses to recognize them."

"Isn't art supposed to reflect the artist?"

"It's supposed to reflect reality," he corrected. "We draw lines, then we live within them. Otherwise there are consequences." He handed her the candle and gathered the clothes from her arms.

"Consequences," she laughed. "And lines," she continued. "Explain those things to the young."

"Still," he said, his eyes never leaving the work, "it has beauty. We are blessed, Iris," he said, blowing out the candles so the only light remaining came through the door from down below. "We are indeed blessed."

Chapter 3

The party was over, but no one would admit it.

For long hours this youthful group celebrated into the tired early morning hours. Work and obligation loomed close, but they were too joyous to care. No responsibility, no worldly concern could drag them down. They were young and therefore immune to time, immune to nature, immune to the excesses of the night. Nothing they did could carry a consequence.

Old Lucre's store was full, as always, but this being somewhere between midnight and dawn, the valley's older populace, who filled it during the day, had long since retreated to their homes, ceding to the younger set who took over the place within hours after sunset.

After walking alone for the better part of the night, Blythe made her appearance.

Pressed in amid the crowd, a hand gently pulled Blythe's arm from her side. She winced at even so light a touch as the confident-yet-tender grip exerted. Blythe yielded, allowing herself to be led without resistance as she ducked and wove among the jostling bodies trying to catch a glimpse at who took her along. The throng parted enough for Sylvia, a plain but true star among Blythe's constellation of friends, to turn and whisper into Blythe's ear, "Parissa's on the prowl."

Sylvia pressed her forearm for emphasis, but Blythe ignored the pain.

"Where is Aaron?" Blythe asked.

"They're downstairs. She goaded him into a rodellé. She's been after him all night. You better hurry before she eats him alive."

"I trust Aaron," Blythe said.

"But do you trust Parissa?" Sylvia asked.

Blythe kissed her friend on the cheek and walked off.

Loud shouts and songs and the noise of wagering preceded Blythe as she descended the stairs.

She passed a stranger who asked another, "Won't Lucre shut us down for the noise?"

A young man replied, "Not a chance. He only comes down from his room when there's work. You see anyone working here?"

Crowded around a room, dozens of friends, and friends of friends, and strangers in various intoxicated states broke out into song until the lyrics were exhausted or forgotten in fits of laughter.

Darwinian battles between young men raged in many forms, but chief among contests was an intimate yet physical duel of controlled combat called a "rodellé," an ancient competition whose goal was simply stated yet difficult to achieve; pin the challenger's knees to his chin. Such a position could be achieved only through an unpredictable combination of brute strength, opposition fatigue and forced contortionism. The use of weapons in a rodellé was considered bad form, as was biting or striking an opponent. Harm—inflicted intentionally or otherwise—lost one favor. And favor, in this generation, was social currency. It could not be inherited. It could only be purchased through individual merit.

Tables and chairs and all things fragile were set aside as spontaneous rodellé broke out from room to room throughout the night. Some rodellé were quickly settled. Others, in rare cases, continued stubbornly for an hour or more. But in the end there was favor: favor in victory, favor for a noble battle lost, favor in honorable competition.

In the center of the room, two men, stripped to the waist, were locked together and tumbled about. Blythe could tell by the broad, muscular back hunched over its opponent that Aaron was, as usual, having the better of his challenger.

"Blythe," a confidant hissed to Parissa, as Blythe brushed by her shoulder to walk deeper into the room. Parissa's onyx eyes, which had been transfixed on the battle, caught Blythe as she passed then just as quickly returned to the fight so as not to have been seen noticing her rival's entrance.

"Pin! Pin! Pin!" the crowd chanted until soon thereafter Aaron's opponent gave way and was left as a humbled heap on the floor. Aaron stood and raised his hands above his head in victory. Blythe held herself back as Parissa rushed to him with a drink. She wrapped her arms around him following his lead as he turned and drank the cup dry in one well-practiced motion. This little dance ended with Aaron facing Blythe, still panting for air with a great smile on his face, his blonde hair disheveled. Parissa's lips pressed hard against his sweaty, slick neck. Everyone fell silent in tense anticipation of what might happen next. Even strangers picked up the cue and stopped cheering; their hands remained raised to their open mouths while their eyes turned to Blythe, who stood alone above the onlookers sitting on the floor circling the challengers. In this expectant stillness, Parissa refused to release herself. She tossed her long black mane and held Aaron tighter, working her lips up and down his neck, sucking his earlobe, pressing her hips hard against his.

Blythe and Aaron's eyes remained locked on each other.

Finally, Aaron announced plainly, "Blythe."

Parissa flicked her hair again and corrected him, "Parissa."

Blythe stated calmly, "No, it's Blythe."

Parissa feigned surprise and swung around, but kept her arms around her prize. Without ever looking at Parissa, Aaron absently handed her the cup she had given him in victory and slowly swept her aside with one arm. Never losing Blythe's eyes, he reached his other hand deep into his pocket and pulled out a gold band, more ornate than any of the eight others that adorned her fingers. With the crowd still mesmerized, he held it up at arm's length between his thumb and middle finger and closed one eye until the ring formed a perfect circle around one of her eyes. She closed the other eye and looked back at him with a broadening smile. With her head bowed and that sheepish smile still on her face, Blythe sauntered towards him gracefully extending her right arm, raising her wrist then lowering her ring finger until it plunged into the band, fitting snugly into place. As the crowd exhaled and returned to animation, she tucked herself into his arms and rested her cheek on his chest. She closed her eyes anticipating the completion of the embrace as he lowered his chin and pressed it against the top of her head, gently kissing her crown.

Only Parissa, who skulked across the room, remained riveted on the couple. Even as Aaron held her, Blythe stared down Parissa as the other partygoers, finally feeling the hour, herded slowly up the stairs to return to their homes. Parissa glowered at every eye she met as she joined the exodus. All gazes darted away from her stare, except Sergio, who winked as he remained in Lucre's basement.

Blythe's attention shifted to Sylvia, who alone fought against the tide of bodies streaming out. Sneaking behind Sergio, she traced her fingertips across his narrow shoulders then playfully presented her hand to him as he turned. He bowed nobly before licking it from knuckles to the wrist. She pulled away from him in disgust.

The room quickly emptied. Sylvia, Sergio and Aaron set about cleaning up the party-worn surroundings without a word to each other, while Blythe rested on a throne of boxes Aaron had constructed for her. She watched as they worked. Cups and clothing were picked up and piled in separate stacks, one to be cleaned or discarded, the other to be retrieved later—if at all—by shy, young ladies who had regained their sobriety. As the three applied themselves to the task, Blythe sat there quietly and admired her new ring.

"Aaron?" she asked lazily. He stopped to give her his full attention. She loved the way everyone in the valley looked at her, even the jealous ones. She delighted in each affirmation that no one could help but appreciate her, even if only on a superficial level. That delight was Blythe's sustenance. But she especially enjoyed Aaron's gaze, which was made unique by its confidence. She would tolerate that look from no one else. Blythe continued in her idle tone, "You're not ambitious, are you?"

Aaron returned to work, refusing to answer her.

She held the ring up high to inspect it. "A great man would have all my fingers covered in gold by now. He'd have me dressed in gold."

"You want a great man?" Aaron asked.

"Yes," she said.

"Then find a good man," he suggested.

She said, "But you are a good man, Aaron. I want a great man. I want you to be a great man, to be my great man."

"You don't see a secret that hides in plain sight, Blythe," he grunted, stacking one heavy box upon another.

"Oh, a lecture!" she chided.

"A fact," Aaron said. "Greatness—lasting greatness—never comes to anyone who seeks it. The pursuit of goodness leads to greatness, but the pursuit of greatness, whether by a man or a nation, leads to ruin."

"You don't understand your own potential."

"And you don't understand the danger of your desire. I'm telling you that the secret—the irony—to getting and keeping all you want is that you have to work for something less than that end; by seeking something shy of your mark…just simple goodness…you will get more than anything you can dream of. If you want greatness that will last, you cannot get it by seeking greatness. You can only get it through going after what is simply good."

Blythe rose as he spoke and circled him as he passed. She said, "You only say that because you have no ambition." She pushed him back into her throne then leaned over him, her hands pinning him in. "I can give you ambition," she whispered seductively. She drew in closer. "I can make you great."

He darted past her and said, "I have no interest in being great." He knelt before her, collecting what he had dropped.

"But you have greatness within you," she countered. "I see it."

"If you see that, you're seeing a result but not the cause."

"What is the difference?"

"You can only see the end you want but not the way to get there. You want us to be better than everyone around us…richer…more powerful…greater."

"What's wrong with wanting that?"

"It is the wanting that is what's wrong."

"You're making no sense."

"You want a home?"

"Yes."

"Goodness. You want to be well-provided for?"

"Of course."

"Goodness. You want my lifelong love?"

"I expect it."

"Goodness. And when you put all those simple, good things together, you get greatness in life, greatness in a family, greatness in the world. What I'm trying to tell you is that good men build; great men destroy. They destroy because they try to control something other than themselves and that always leads to destruction."

"Maybe I am talking with the wrong brother," she complained. "Maddox seems more inclined to…."

"Maddox!" he dismissed. "Oh, there is greatness! A great user. A great obscene…."

"Have I struck a nerve?" she interrupted innocently.

Sergio chimed in, "You've struck his core…a man's pride."

Blythe asked, "Don't you want this valley when your father passes it on? He owns most of it. Do you want Maddox to rule you or do you want to rule him?"

"I want to rule nothing…no one," he said.

"Maddox does."

"And so does Blythe?" Sylvia asked.

Blythe smiled and returned to her throne.

Sylvia mimicked her walk, swaying over to sit on Sergio's knee, but he moved it at the last moment, catching her under her arms just before she fell to the floor.

"Maddox," Aaron laughed in disgust as he stacked books back on a shelf. "Maddox, who shows no self-control, should control others? And my father…the man who balances his books with shrewd calculation of both money and men, who issues no idle threats to those in any way in his debt…holds his son—that son—to no account. My father stokes his ambition, feeds his recklessness, and everyone must pay for Maddox, everyone but Maddox himself. Damn it!" Aaron exclaimed.

"What is it?" Sergio asked.

"A book is missing," Aaron said looking over the rows of neatly bound volumes. "It's *The Crooner.*"

"Was it a green, bound book?" Sylvia asked.

Aaron answered excitedly, "Yes. Where is it?"

"I saw who took it," said Sylvia. "I hate to tell you, but it was Maddox. He plucked it from the shelf just as you started your rodellé then went upstairs."

"Damn him!" Aaron burst out. "You know who'll be blamed."

"Maybe your father won't notice," Sylvia comforted.

"Not see this missing tooth?" he responded in disgust pointing to the gap.

Blythe continued, "So Maddox should have the valley and everything else your father leaves behind instead of you? Why would you let him have it when you know he'll only abuse the privilege?"

"Neither of us will inherit the valley," Aaron answered.

"What makes you so certain?" Sergio asked.

"My father despises anyone getting the better of him, of even the smallest part of him. He knows anything given to Maddox will be squandered or taken from him by men who resent what he's been given. My father couldn't bear losing all he's hoarded like that. Maddox will get more than he needs but less than his due. And he'll quickly lose that."

"And if it were given to you?" Blythe asked.

Aaron sat on the arm of Blythe's throne. He looked up the empty stairs for a moment. "I won't accept what's not his to offer," he said.

"Ha!" Blythe laughed and pushed him off to his feet. "You take his pay!"

"And you wear the rings his money buys," Sergio interrupted.

She faced Sergio. "But I'm not deceiving myself by pretending I'm above taking what's given me."

Aaron cleaned up the party's last remnants and said, "I take what I earn from him…nothing more."

"Oh, how noble," she mocked. "So you leave Old Lucre more to own and Maddox more to waste. What difference does that make?"

"It makes a difference in the way men look at me," Aaron said.

"He's right," Sergio said with a great yawn. "They look at Aaron with respect. I've seen the way men like your father look at Lucre when they don't think anyone is watching. They hate him for grabbing everything in the valley. They know that they've given up too much to him, but he can play on their fears. He poses as their savior with one hand on their shoulders while the other fishes for loose change in their pockets. And just when they think they know better, when they have him all figured out, he whips them into some new frenzy and finds a way to capitalize on the moment to take even more from them. They know Aaron is not like his father, taking a bigger and bigger piece of what they earned each day because he's lucred them."

"Lucred them?" Blythe asked.

"Taken advantage of someone worse off than you," Sergio explained as he stretched out on a small bed in the corner of the room. He yawned to Aaron, "Isn't that what your father does?"

Aaron nodded solemnly and concluded, "I take only what I earn. It makes a difference in how I look at myself."

"I don't trust Lucre for my own petty reasons," Sergio confessed.

"And what would those be?" Blythe asked.

"He makes no sound when he laughs," Sergio said, his eyes closed now.

Aaron guffawed. "He's right! All these years it's bothered me, but I never knew why! He shakes and he quakes and his eyes light up, but he doesn't make a sound. It is laughter without life."

"It's an affront to those of us with a sense of humor," Sergio yawned.

"And what else?" Blythe asked.

"He whistles too well," Sergio said, curling up on his side and using his hand for a pillow.

"Too well?"

Sergio let out another great yawn and observed, "Any man who whistles so perfectly has spent too much time alone. The better a man whistles the fewer friends he has."

Blythe watched as her friend Sylvia sat first on the corner of the bed where Sergio now slept. As the conversation continued, she cradled herself in his arms and soon drifted off to sleep along with him. To see how Sylvia pursued him without so much as a response on his part frustrated Blythe beyond speech. "Love is supposed to be an echo," she thought. "A call and a response."

Blythe shook her head. "Then I am talking to the wrong brother. You have no ambition."

Aaron studied her face for a moment. "Perhaps you do belong with Maddox."

Blythe walked up to him and clenched his muscular forearms until she nearly pierced them with her nails. "You're better than him, Aaron," she said. "I know you are. But he always gets the best of everything. I want you to have your share. I want us to enjoy it. Don't you deserve it? Don't we deserve it?"

Aaron pulled himself free then wrapped his hands around her forearms. She winced from the shooting pain and suddenly he melted; tears welled in his eyes. He released his hold. He took her by the shoulders and whispered disappointed, loud enough for only her to hear, "Not again, Blythe? Not again?"

She didn't answer. She returned to her throne and turned her hands like a Persian dancer to admire the accents of new morning light that caught the nine bands. Only her left ring finger remained bare.

Aaron stopped again to look at her. "Gold is cold," he said. "The only warmth it has we give to it."

"Isn't that true of everything?" she asked.

He took her right hand and pressed her palm against his chest. She slowly pulled it away.

"Meet me at the bridge tonight?" she whispered with excitement.

"At the bridge," he agreed. He kissed her hand then released it.

Aaron admired Blythe as she swayed up the stairs smiling back at him one final time before her eyes rose above the stairwell's ceiling. Her fingers danced again down low below her waist to accentuate the many rings before they, too, disappeared.

From his resting place Sergio declared, "Blythe and blithely; who would have guessed the words were opposites?"

Aaron nodded, still looking up the stairs. "I wish she had the sweet confidence of her looks."

Chapter 4

A young man, dressed in a crisp white shirt and dark red pants waited casually, leaning against a home's elegant façade. His shirt, unbuttoned to his sternum, revealed a muscular physique wrapped in perfect olive skin. Maddox studied him as he approached and asked the young man, "Did you forget something?"

Notté revealed a handsome smile then pulled out a tan leather-bound book he had tucked into the back of his pants.

"What is it?" Maddox asked.

Notté said, "One of many books, but unique like every other. Still this man is not satisfied to have only one alone." He nodded toward the tidy home they stood before.

"Nor even one at a time," Maddox added.

They both smiled.

Notté knocked and continued to study the book in his hands.

"What are you thinking?" Maddox asked.

"How many books does a man need?"

Maddox shrugged. "Some men need no books; every word they ever felt they needed was printed from the beginning in here and here," he said pointing to his head and to his heart.

"There is a comfort with that certainty."

Maddox continued. "Then there are others like our friend inside, or you or I, who can read for a lifetime, collect book after book trying to fill that emptiness…to understand what's missing in our lives, but we never will succeed."

Notté agreed grimly. "It is either there or it is not."

Maddox concluded, looking at his volume, "We press our hands against them, we rub their spines trying to learn through osmosis and hope to feel something move between the covers. But we never will, really. We just collect titles."

"So we collect or we are collected?" Notté laughed. "Who gives a damn? So long as we enjoy ourselves before they put us on a shelf to gather dust. Let him take me in," he exclaimed, pounding hard on the door with his fist. "At least for a while we belong to someone. For a time we belong somewhere."

They both laughed again.

A distinguished looking man—tall, lithe, with fastidiously arranged salt-and-pepper hair and a meticulously trimmed mustache to match—opened the door. He leaned out and looked up and down the street, pulling down sharply on the points of his green, velvet vest to straighten out the slightest crease. Satisfied no one was looking on, he stepped aside to welcome in his guests.

"What have you got for me?" he asked excitedly.

Maddox entered first, handing him his green, bound volume.

"*The Crooner,*" the man said, impressed. "Very nice. And you, my friend?"

Notté handed him the tanned leather edition with no words on the cover. The only thing that appeared was a red cross of equal sides. "I'm not familiar with this one," the man said.

"Don't worry," Notté assured him. "It will grow on you."

Chapter 5

He moved with a flourish he could never defend when others mocked him.

It was not in his nature to fight, nor was it in his nature to change.

It was his unfortunate fate to live in an age and a society where such differences were beaten out of the standout.

The long hair always gets cut first.

His mother didn't mind. In her eyes, the recurrent beatings were merely his peers' ways of trimming off his flamboyant edges so he could better fit in when he grew into a man. His father was quiet on the issue, as he was with everything. It was his mother who decided all matters for the household, as she had decided when his parents married, when they had a child and on all decisions in their lives, great and small.

But this young man's sails would never be trimmed to someone else's satisfaction. He knew and accepted that, as sure as he knew he wanted nothing more than peace from others—the peace he felt for them in his own heart when he wasn't being beaten for his eccentricities.

Unwilling to be anything but true to his nature, he drew deeper and deeper into himself and endured what he had to endure until one day someone of an equally kind heart drew to his side; someone like him who desired nothing more than peace but who had also been cast aside and castigated for being different.

One found the other and became a duet, who joined with others to become a quiet foursome, and an invisible symphony of friends formed to offer the harmony of acceptance and affection that could be found nowhere else. For once, there was that perfect tranquility in his heart that he always knew existed but had eluded him.

But nothing in this world is perfect.

One kind and faithful heart led him to another, and to another that was less kind and less faithful, and down the social circles he continued until he found himself far from his home in a place he did not want to be. It was not his choice to be there, but his choices led him where he was; everyone around him a heart-scarred transient searching for an oasis none would ever find.

And so it was with bitter irony that he made his way home once and for all and looked into the fear-struck faces of his once tormentors, this impossibly thin man earning a wide berth as he passed. He never once dreamed he could inspire fear in any of them. The best he wished for from them was to be left alone. At last, but too late, he earned his wish.

Chapter 6

"No, Aaron. You can't leave," Lucre responded in his typically frugal staccato. "Business comes before anything—before everything."

"I've worked all day…alone," Aaron protested.

"Alone?" Lucre bellowed. He swung his great shoulders around to face his son, his head bowed on a stout, strong neck. "Then who was that man behind the counter? Who carried as much stock up from the cellar as you? Who opened an hour before you came down?" Aaron's father raised his nose for defiant emphasis each time he asked, "who?"

"I'm not talking about you…," Aaron began.

"I know who you're talking about," Lucre spat back. He swept his hand to settle his thick hair, so black it appeared to have a tint of blue. "Maddox isn't your concern."

"He should be yours."

"Don't think he isn't," the bull of a man paused, his dark, pupil-less eyes settling disquietingly on his son. The lack of definition in Old Lucre's eyes made them appear thoughtless to the uninitiated, but fiery to those who knew him well. "How I deal with Maddox is my prerogative. He's my business, not yours. Now finish piling those potatoes."

Aaron returned to his work. The dust from the potatoes Aaron stacked high rose like incense smoke in the nearly flat angles of sunset light that crossed the room. Caught in a daydream, he paused a moment to watch the tiny specks rise as he traced his fingers on the tubers, then tossed them more feverishly to get the job done. The dull, rhythmic thuds punctuated Lucre's exotic warbling. These sounds alone passed between the two men, but no words.

Old Lucre looked up from his ledger as he closed it with a crisp slap. Looking at his son, he snorted, "Our chronic silence, Aaron," then paused again to gather his thoughts. "I make no apology for expecting more from you than your brother. If I expect more, it's because I know I can count on you."

"But Maddox told you yesterday that he would be here today," Aaron said. "If anyone else broke his word to you, you would never forgive them. You would never work with them again. Why is Maddox so different for you?"

"Because he's mine," Lucre said.

"But if I ever did that, you would…," Aaron began

"You wouldn't."

"But if I did," Aaron started again.

"Aaron," Lucre paused, exhausted from the day. He looked down at the closed book. "Aaron, you are just going to have to trust me. I know you resent how soft I may seem on Maddox, but if I were any harder, he would break. Don't think I don't know what goes on with him. I know more than you know…more than I care to know. But understand, I won't break anything I've taken years to build."

"But look at what you're building," Aaron pleaded.

Lucre bowed his head and swept his massive hand again across his thick hair. The bull was tiring. "He needs my help, Aaron. And I have to give it to him. There are a lot of things you don't understand, but believe me in this; I'm doing what I have to do to help him. He needs my help for just a little while longer then I know he'll be all right."

"But look at what he does when you help him," Aaron insisted. "He only becomes worse. He uses everything and everyone around him, and he's never called to account. He wastes what we earn."

"He is being called to account, Aaron. In ways you couldn't

imagine, he is being called to account," his father assured.

Aaron replied, "Oh, spare me."

"I've said enough," Lucre said, sliding the book under the counter. "Get back to your business. You've finished the potatoes. Good. Now sweep the floor, clean up the stock, and then take an inventory of what we need to add to the shelves. You'll need to wash the windows, too, and run over to Iris's to give a count of loaves we'll need for tomorrow. After you get done with that, you may go with Blythe, if you have any energy left within you." He laughed, silently shaking his shoulder as he walked out the front door leaving a fading tune as he whistled away.

Old Lucre was gone but a few moments when Sergio vaulted through the open top of the Dutch door, clapped in midair, and landed smartly on the ground, posing with his head held high and his fists resting daringly on his hips.

Aaron leaned on his broom and surveyed his friend, as if expecting the display. "They'll make a statue of anyone these days," he said unimpressed, then returned to his sweeping.

"Come on!" Sergio said excitedly. "It's nearly dark. Do you want to surprise Blythe, or is she going to beat us to the canal?"

Aaron said, mimicking his father's staccato, "Business comes before anything—before everything."

"So coined Lucre," Sergio said.

"So followed Aaron," Aaron exhaled. He again took on his father's frugal dialect, "Finish the potatoes, sweep the floor, clean the stock, inventory the shelves, wash the windows, order the bread, then—if you have any spirit left in you, ha, ha, ha—find Blythe and make love like I wish I still could."

Undaunted, Sergio clapped his hands again and spun around on the ball of his right foot, his arms outstretched, the personification of joy. As he did so, he peered out the open top of the door. "Many hands make light work!" he exclaimed, vaulting out the door. In a moment the half door slowly swung open with Sergio standing beside it at attention. He announced as a courtier, "Lady Sylvia."

Sylvia glided in and raised her hand to Sergio, who took it and licked it as he had before at the party. She shrieked in disgust; her entire body shook. She dried her hand on her skirt and swung her other hand at Sergio, just missing his nose. She offered to Aaron, "This fool here tells me you need some help?"

"Sylvia," Aaron said in a tone of genuine appreciation. "You couldn't be sweeter. I have everything to do, but it's my work. I won't ask for your help."

"You're not," she said. "That sprite already has. Now do you want to see Blythe or not?"

"Of course," Aaron admitted.

"Then direct me," she ordered. "What can I do?"

At Aaron's suggestion, she tended to the windows.

"And you!" Aaron ordered to Sergio. "Quit dancing around and straighten those shelves."

The little man sprang to an aisle. With Aaron's back turned, he picked up three apples and juggled them for Sylvia's amusement. He then added another, and another, and another until six red orbs followed a frantic circle around his face. Still pressing hard on the broom, Aaron turned and saw his friend's play and yelled in disgust, "Sergio!"

All six apples and the juggler himself tumbled to the ground.

Sylvia laughed and clapped. She walked over, helping Sergio to his feet. She cautioned Aaron, "You shouldn't frighten him like that. He has a weak little heart."

Sergio responded in his own defense with a fawning look up to his protector, "Weak, perhaps. But it's full."

Sylvia looked passionately into his eyes and dipped him backwards. He closed his eyes, anticipating her kiss as she dropped him back onto the apples. Aaron burst out laughing as he and Sylvia returned to their work.

Sergio slipped to his feet in time to see Kagetsu float silently across the store's threshold. The pallid beauty of her face set off by her dark hair and serious mien held Sergio hunched and dumbstruck, with half-crushed apples still dripping from each hand.

"Can I help you?" he asked with unusual seriousness.

Sylvia, still washing the windows, answered without turning, "You can stay out of my way."

Kagetsu looked at him silently as she approached. He stood taller. She turned down the aisle before his, drifting up and down the pathways, never leaving Sergio's sight.

"If there is anything...," Sergio began again with hushed enthusiasm, recapturing Kagetsu's dark gaze over her shoulder at him. Her attention made him fall strangely silent again.

"There is one thing," Sylvia declared, turning towards him. "You may escort me to...," She looked at his captivated face and followed it, for the first time recognizing Kagetsu's presence.

The disjointed conversation made Aaron turn, too. "Kagetsu," he said warmly. "I didn't hear you come in. Is there something you need?"

"Anything?" Sergio solicited. He beamed in her reflected glow, his eyes transfixed on her long, delicate fingers that traced themselves across the many items on the shelves, but which never settled on any single one. Sylvia looked down at her own stubby and soapy hands, and angrily whipped the suds off of them. She turned her back on them and returned to work.

"There's nothing I need," Kagetsu said. "Sometimes I like to come in here and hope that something will pull me in."

"But nothing ever does," Aaron observed.

"That is my fault, not yours, Aaron," she admitted, completing her orbit of the store and drifting towards the door. "You have everything here one could want, but there is nothing I need. Until tomorrow?" she asked Aaron.

"Until tomorrow," he confirmed, as did Sergio in a reverent whisper.

Sylvia let her rag splash down into her bucket. "That's all for me," she said.

Sergio, spellbound by the empty door, didn't move.

Sylvia looked at him and declared, "She has all the warmth of moonlight."

Sergio did not respond.

Sylvia crossed his path and snapped her fingers to reanimate the young man. Jolted back, he scratched his nose with a hand that held the wet and sticky apple remains and looked at it curiously, as if questioning who had put it there. At last his thoughts returned to the room around him and he silently went back to his work straightening up the shelves.

"I hope you finish soon, Aaron," Sylvia said, giving him a peck on the cheek. She looked over at Sergio and continued, "He won't be much good to you. Kagetsu pulls his heart like the moon pulls the ocean."

"I thought it was women who were governed by the moon?" Aaron jested.

"A myth." She smiled. "When it comes to love, men are the lunatics. Women are solarists; we are as steady as the sun."

"Well, be patient," Aaron counseled. "Sooner or later it will be your turn to shine."

"Maybe it will," she said. "But no woman wants to live in another woman's shadow."

With that, she left.

"Sergio," Aaron scolded. "How could you treat Sylvia like that?"

"I know, I know, I know, I know," Sergio cowed. "It's not so much Sylvia as Kagetsu. For heaven's sake, the heart has four rooms. Can't two be filled by different occupants?"

"Not if you want to keep the whole heart happy," Aaron answered.

Sergio said, "But I'm worried whether there'll be any room left for me."

"A full heart has more room than an empty one."

"So Blythe has left you room?" Sergio asked.

"Blythe!" Aaron remembered, looking out at the dim sky. "It's nearly dark. She'll beat me to the bridge for sure."

Sergio once again glanced out the door. "A savior reigns!" Sergio exclaimed. "Who is the one man on earth who would do anything for you?"

"You?" Aaron asked, unsure of his answer.

"Think again!" Sergio laughed.

"Augustus!" Aaron responded.

Sergio dashed back out through the top of the Dutch door as he had first entered. In a moment, the half door swung open slowly and Sergio regally strode back in announcing, "May I present, the colossus Augustus."

In walked a man who, by looks alone, could have been mistaken for Aaron; tall as Aaron, muscular and blonde, he walked in past Sergio and stood before Aaron.

"Augustus!" Aaron cheered. "Will you do me a favor?"

Augustus nodded.

"I have to finish my work here, but I'm supposed to meet Blythe under the bridge. Sergio and I have a plan to scare the wits out of her, but I'm stuck. Is there any way you could clean up the stock, make a quick list of what we need on the shelves, then order three dozen loaves from Iris for tomorrow? I may still have just enough time."

Without speaking a word, Augustus walked over to Aaron and took the broom from his hands. He put his hand on his friend's back and pushed him toward the still-open door, and began sweeping.

"There is a friend!" Aaron exclaimed to Sergio, then shot out the top of the door as Sergio had done.

"There is a man who loves you," Sergio said to the departed Aaron, then bowed in appreciation to Augustus.

Augustus merely looked up and smiled, never stopping his work.

Sergio slowly pulled the door open, gave Augustus a quick salute and dashed on his way.

Blythe

Chapter 7

"You comfortable?"

"Mmm-hmm."

"Cold?"

"Always. But I'm warm for now."

"Here is a blanket for your feet. Dear gawd, what have they done to you?"

"I just need a little rest, Pa. I'm so tired."

He didn't want to stare at his son, but he couldn't help himself.

"I'm just as much to blame as anyone."

"Do you hurt?"

"Not when I'm cushioned like this. It's like lying on a cloud." He looked to his father and said, "You told me not to go with them. You warned me."

"I don't care about that now. Your arms. They're still tore up."

"Serves them right; they're to blame. All because of one needle. I had no idea…"

"I shouldn't have said anything."

"How could you not?" He looked down at his arms. "I don't even feel like they're mine anymore. I'll cover them. I'm cold anyways."

"You sleep."

"I need sleep."

"I'll be right here."

Chapter 8

"Hold on, Aaron!" Sergio exclaimed in a hushed grunt. "It's slipping!" The hundred-pound boulder fell from their hands and landed with a muffled thud in the newly plowed field.

"Come on," Aaron urged. "One more good haul and we're at the bridge. Let's finish this."

"The only thing finished after this will be my back," Sergio complained, straining with his friend to lift the massive stone. They scurried sideways across the field like a couple of battling crabs. The two hunched creatures crept beneath the canal's ancient wood and rock bridge and dropped the boulder at the water's edge.

Sergio collapsed, his legs splayed out. He rested up against the rock and gasped for air, but Aaron would not let him pause.

"Get up," he ordered. Sergio started to complain, but Aaron cut him off, "She'll be coming. Let's not waste everything we've done by getting caught. Help me swing this into the canal. Then you can go."

"Into the canal?" Sergio objected.

"That's what I said. Follow my lead."

Begrudgingly, Sergio rolled over on his stomach and rose.

"We'll rock it and toss it in on three," Aaron instructed.

The two pressed their heads together as they worked their hands beneath the stone.

"Ready?" Aaron asked.

"Ready," came the reply and they lifted with everything left within them.

Aaron called out as they cradled the rock back and forth, "One. Two. Three!" launching the orb upward, making it disappear for a moment in the shadow of the bridge. It nearly skimmed the underside of the boards before continuing downward on its path, splashing halfway across the stream.

Both young men remained bent over for a long while, unable to speak. Aaron rested his hand on Sergio's back. "Thank you, Sergio," he panted. "Now get out of here."

Sergio asked, "But how will you scare her with the stone in the middle of the water? I thought you'd hide it above then let it splash when she arrived."

Aaron straightened up, his head ducked slightly under the boards. "Every night," he began, his chest still heaving, "Blythe and I meet here beneath the bridge." He nodded up the canal, "For weeks now I've been diving under the water up there by the willow. I hold my breath as long as I can and pull with the current to get downstream without coming up for air." He paused again to catch his breath. "I can make it beyond the bridge. But I want to spring up right here as she waits for me and scare the life out of her."

"So why the rock?" Sergio asked.

Aaron said, "Until yesterday, I couldn't reason how to come up at just the right place. In the daytime, I can see the shadow of the bridge, but Blythe and I always meet here at night. I needed some marker."

"That's why we couldn't use a smaller stone," Sergio said.

"Exactly," Aaron answered. "I didn't think of it until yesterday when my father had me stack potatoes. When I traced my fingers on them I watched some dust rise straight up in the sunset light. I did the same job tonight and saw how the dust rose again. I knew this had to work. I'll trace one hand along the bottom of the canal. Once I touch that stone, I'll know where to shoot up and take her by surprise."

Sergio laughed, "A woman like Blythe and you waste your time with potatoes and games."

"Played well and with the right woman, games are love," Aaron said.

"I play games to avoid love," Sergio said.

"Or so you think."

"Meaning?" Sergio asked.

"You feel nothing for Sylvia?"

"Of course I do," Sergio said, as if in pain. "But Kagetsu…. Have you ever seen her walk, Aaron? She doesn't walk; she floats. I've never seen her feet touch the ground."

Aaron said, "The right dress and the wrong desire can hide any woman's more pedestrian qualities."

"Haw, haw," Sergio brayed. "Easy for you to say when you have your heart's desire. Aaron and Blythe, the king and queen of the valley!"

"And you as the jester," Aaron said, framing his friend in his outstretched hands as if in a painting.

Sergio slapped Aaron's hands down. "More of your pranks."

"What am I supposed to do?" Aaron asked. "Ignore her?"

"You used to."

"That was early on. You know as well as I that the only woman a man ignores is one he's just met and wants to impress or one he knows well and wants to avoid."

"Remaining cordial to the rest," Sergio finished the thought.

"It's every man's nature. I play little games with Blythe to remind her she's always in my thoughts. She understands more deeply what that means."

"Or so you hope."

"Men live on hope," Aaron said.

"And die on confirmation."

Aaron pushed his friend out from under one side of the bridge as he departed in the other direction, and said, "Let's move before she sees us." Aaron walked upstream along the bank. He called out, "Go back through the woods so Blythe doesn't see you. I'll let you know how it goes."

Every few moments, Aaron turned to see if Blythe approached. The path she would travel cut its way up from the valley's trees across an open field before reaching the bridge then disappearing again into deep woods on the other side of the water. This opening allowed Aaron a chance to see at least a faint view of her as she made her way to their meeting place.

He circled to the far side of a willow that stood back from the bend. There he undressed. The cool night air tightened his skin. Aaron glanced out from behind the tree in time to see Blythe sneak beneath the bridge.

He lowered himself to the cold, slick grass and mud that banked the canal. Slimy squirts of mud bubbled up between his fingers as he steadied himself with the palm of his right hand. A cold coating of earth covered his thigh and hip as he turned on his side and slipped without a splash into the water. The canal's walls were shear and dropped off quickly to their full depth. Aaron allowed himself to submerge completely and pulled hard underwater against the current to keep pace with where he entered. He broke back through the surface. The shock of the brisk stream forced him to exhale in an exclamation—a sound he only afterwards hoped hadn't carried downstream. Aaron pumped his powerful legs, reaching for the depth of the canal he knew was just beyond his length, even stretched out as he was.

Removed from the valley lights and smoke, a dome of stars sparkled brilliantly where they weren't outshone by a waxing gibbous moon. As he approached the bend, he stretched out and floated on his back, staring up in wonder at the magnificence.

Downstream, Blythe crouched beneath the bridge, her arms wrapped tightly around her legs with her chin resting on her knees. She leaned back against the stone edifice for support. Blythe began to hum, but the moment the sound reached her ears and broke the silence, she stopped for fear that someone else might hear her. She hated these moments alone under the bridge before Aaron arrived. Isolated in the darkness, she was a tense coil ready to spring at the slightest uncertain sound.

Waiting to hear the song Aaron sang as a comfort to himself and as a warning to her as he approached, she kept her eyes wide on the stream but remained conscious of everything around her. The light played upon the little eddies and ripples occasionally tossing up a sparkling diamond here and there. She heard the gurgling of the water as it churned past and lapped against the sides of the canal. Rarely, a fish would slap the surface, reminding her that these were living waters, a life spring to her valley home.

Such considerations filled Blythe's mind in the split second of time it took Aaron to break the surface and rise like some hideous water monster. She thought to herself, "What a large fish," but as the image continued to grow, and, along with it, the massive watery sound of the being, she became acutely aware that this was no mere fish. This was something much more serious, more threatening.

Her entire body sprang to life, launching her up and around the corner as she heard the awful, hideous sounds of the creature rising from the cold, dark, deep water. By the time she was around the corner and running for her life, the echoes of her scream still resonating, her mind began to register the sound of Aaron's laughter along with his splashes from beneath the bridge. She bounced and spun around, flailing her arms in hysterical anger mixed with self-reproach at having been tricked. Her terror had spiked but was already dissipating. Her anger, too, began to recede.

As she stood in the field beside the path, Aaron poked his head out from around the bridge. She could hear him still laughing.

"Are you coming back?" he asked.

She stood silently staring at him, her arms crossed over her chest.

He held his naked arms outstretched to her and said in a gravelly voice, imagining what sound a water creature might make if it were able to speak, "Blythe forgive Aaron. Aaron sorry for frighten." She laughed but moved no closer toward him as he continued, "Aaron no frighten again."

"Blythe know Aaron lie," she said, mimicking his voice as best she could. She walked to him.

With her arms still across her chest, Blythe rammed herself into his arms, knocking him back a few steps. "You're a fool," she said.

"Fool loves Blythe."

"Fool loves water," she replied, taking a half step back then pushing against him with all her might. He flew backwards and made a tremendous splash. Again, he burst through the surface in laughter, only this time she joined in it with him. He treaded water and splashed her as she ducked beneath the bridge and began to disrobe. Aaron swam under

Blythe

the bridge and called over to her, "Aaron need Blythe," causing a trill of laughter to trickle out from the darkness. He repeated even louder, "Aaron need Blythe!"

"Shhh!" she scolded him. "Someone will hear you!"

He grumbled, "So far from village. Blythe, Aaron safe here. Blythe, Aaron much alone."

Stripped to her skin, Blythe took two running steps and launched herself out over the water, for a moment hovering suspended above him, one leg back, the other forward with both arms out wide. She landed in front of him, sweeping her arms forward, burying him in her wake. Aaron recovered quickly, wrapped his arms under hers and spun her around. He plunged his lips onto her neck. She felt the underside of her tight, warm breasts pressed up high against his cold skin and his cool forearms flashing out waves of chills against her smooth back.

"Oh, oh! It's cold," she protested.

He raised his mouth to her ear long enough to whisper, "You'll get used to it soon. It's beautiful…and so are you."

"Shhh!" she ordered.

"What is it?"

She swam to the side and clung low to the bank. She waved him over. Aaron swam up silently behind her and surrounded her, digging his own hands into the dirt on top of hers. He began to kiss the back of her neck.

"Stop," she ordered. She whispered, "Someone's coming. I heard a voice."

Two approaching voices grew out of the night. Aaron and Blythe recognized them as their fathers' as the men made their way down the path back toward the valley floor.

"He's been busier than I expected," Duffy said.

"He has the easiest task in the world," Lucre responded. "Leading the corrupt to corruption."

Duffy laughed, "You take liberties you shouldn't and you'll find your liberties are taken from you, I suppose."

"That's right," Lucre said. "Sin sells itself. I'm surprised he's only as far along as he is."

Duffy asked as they clomped across the wooden boards dropping dust and dirt on those below, "So where does his game end?"

Lucre answered without hesitation, "With his own destruction, I imagine. That's the only way these things end. Evil feeds on itself. What can survive that?"

As the two men continued their conversation across the span, falling dust found its way to Blythe's nose. She began to sniff, only taking in more of the fine powder.

"No!" Aaron urged her. "Don't do it!"

Unable to control herself, she began to take in tiny, forceful fits of air.

"Don't!" he pleaded. "You'll give us away!"

"I…I ca…I can't…." and with that she took in a great breath of air offering half the sound of a sneeze as Aaron dunked her before she could release it. The muffled explosion let out a thousand bubbles to the surface. Aaron tried to control his laughter as Blythe fought him to break free.

The stomping on the bridge above halted as Aaron clutched her head and brought her up, whispering instantly in her ear, "They've stopped!"

"What was that?" Lucre asked.

No one moved. The only sound was the gurgling of the canal.

After a long pause, Duffy broke the stalemate by proclaiming it to be the stream then said, "Well, I'm glad for what you're doing, but glad I have no hand in this."

"No hand in this?" Lucre asked incredulously. "Don't you dare try to skirt your blame for this."

"My blame?" Duffy shot back. "I didn't start this. You know that as well as I."

"No," Lucre agreed, "You didn't start this, but you did something just as bad; you kept quiet. You didn't say a thing and let Henry spread like a virus among this valley."

"What was I to say?" Duffy pleaded. "To whom could I have spoken? It was something entirely beyond my control."

The men continued on their way.

49

At last, Aaron announced, "They're gone now."

Blythe growled, "You nearly drowned me!"

"I'm sorry. I had no choice."

Holding her with one arm and stroking through the water with the other as he kicked forcefully against the weight of the stream, he brought her out into the center, coming even with the stone. He rested on it, leaning into the current to keep steady, but no longer kicked.

"Can you touch bottom from here?" she asked.

His hands descended her back. Her knees rose in excitement. He cupped her cheeks, squeezing firmly and said pensively, "Yes. Yes, I think I can."

She yelped out of surprise when he grabbed her and splashed him saying, "The bottom of the canal? You can stand on it? You never could before."

Unwilling to give up his secret, Aaron let go the stone and allowed him and Blythe to drift downstream. Blythe broke free and swam to the edge of the canal. She raised herself up out of the water in one smooth, sensual motion. Aaron swam close and sidestroked in front of her admiring what he imagined he could see.

"Coming ashore?" she invited, leaning forward. He raised his arm towards her. They locked their hands firmly on each other's wrists. He raised one foot and dug it hard against the canal wall to raise himself, then leaned back as far as he could go. The force of his movement lifted Blythe unwillingly to her feet and launched her again over the water as she let out another yelp.

They laughed and played and splashed each other before finally settling once again on the stone where they rocked rhythmically against the stream, her legs wrapped around Aaron, stretched out, pulled along by the current. She leaned back to an angle that cut her resistance to the competing pressures pushing her forward and carrying her back. She was buoyant. The moment was effortless. As she reached back in graceful delight, her hand struck something dense but fleshy. In that moment, she felt the tangle of hair among her fingers.

"Something hit me!" she shrieked, extracting herself from Aaron's embrace.

He laughed and said, "It's just a rock. I put it in there with Sergio earlier this evening."

Blythe was on shore, wrapped up again against the stones in a huddled ball, her arms wrapped around her legs. "No!" she insisted. "It wasn't a rock. It gave when I hit it with my hand."

"Don't be foolish," he began, "You probably just hit a...."

His words froze and sent a chill through the air that made Blythe shiver.

"What?!" she shouted, crawling over to her clothes and throwing them on hastily. "What is it?!"

Aaron had knocked something, but it wasn't the stone. He plunged his hands down and felt around, stretching his neck to keep his head above water. The fingers of his right hand meshed with another bony hand just as he felt something hard and unyielding hit his crotch. He let loose an uncharacteristically high-pitched scream of surprise and took in a mouthful of water as he slipped off the stone. Combined, the two experiences caused him to wretch as he struggled to breathe, to keep his head above water and to free himself from whatever cold thing it was that held his hand in the blackness.

Blythe screamed again and rose to hide around the corner of the bridgehead. Aaron struggled to raise his hand, still kicking and pulling to keep his head high. There was no way he would allow himself to be submerged, never to return to the surface.

His right hand reached higher and higher out of the water trying to extract itself. As it did, a gaunt, pale arm rose with it. Aaron had seen a skeleton before, but what he pulled from the water didn't fit his memory. Even in the darkness he could tell this wasn't simply bone that transfixed him, but still it was so similar. Aaron's gaze followed the emaciated arm downward from its starved wrist to the pod of a swollen elbow and down farther. So much of the terror within him ordered him to stop pulling, still his hand continued to rise in hopes of being free.

Aaron didn't consider his own mouth, half-submerged and filled with water, as a bulbous forehead rose up, followed by a nose, out of which he could hear water trickle, and a mouth slung far open within breathing distance of his own face. The apparition and Aaron emerged like two dance partners, one from this world, one fresh from the grave. The lead partner kept his head thrown back in a pose of frozen laughter as Aaron pulled them higher and higher. They circled around in the stream's pull and tug.

Aaron at last became aware of Blythe's shrieks of pleadings, "Let him go! Let him go!" as she clutched tighter to the bridgehead for reassurance. Aaron was unsure if she was calling out to him or to the being that refused to release his hand.

With his free arm, Aaron sought to push the thing away, but that only raised its head to equilibrium, setting it erect for one moment in mute horror, jaw slack, eyes open but rolled back. Suddenly it drooped forward without restraint, slapping the water and filling Aaron's mouth with its backwash.

This was too much for Aaron. As he coughed violently to clear his mouth, he lowered both his hands and pushed mightily on the thing's chest. The force of his shove lifted the being half out of the water and tossed it back through the air to the bank where it made a sick, hollow, slapping thud against the mud of the canal wall. It stuck there, its left arm remaining outstretched, reaching into the air skyward. Aaron looked on, captured in revulsion as he watched the wasted corpse slide down for just an instant then splash face-first into the watery darkness.

Then everything went still.

Both he and Blythe wondered if what they had seen was real. But they knew their minds were too objective to play any such games. They each knew what they had seen.

Aaron sprinted up the stream in a wide circle around where he imagined the corpse's reach might be. His hands dug into the canal's edge as he hoisted himself out and continued over to Blythe. He crouched beside her and covered her as he looked back to the stream to make sure the thing wasn't crawling out after them.

From the water, an arm reached out as if giving a final wave, a final call for help as the current rolled the body over. Something in that act made Aaron see the being as something different than a terror; he realized that if he didn't act at that instant, whatever or whoever that was would be lost, forever.

Aaron stood up abruptly. Blythe stared up at him.

"What? Is it back?"

Aaron didn't look down at her as he dropped her hand. He ran at full speed toward the bank then plunged headlong into the canal.

Blythe again pressed her palms against the cold, real stones of the bridgehead. Unable to restrain herself, she rose and hurried over to where Aaron had disappeared looking farther and farther downstream. There was no fear in her, only the deepest pleading to see Aaron rise again.

Out from the water some twenty paces downstream Aaron at last reemerged with an arm wrapped around the chest of a pale and rigid naked form.

"Help me pull it out!" Aaron called.

Blythe ran down and wrapped her delicate hand entirely around the bony wrist of the arm Aaron extended to her. She leaned back on her heels expecting the effort of pulling to be a struggle, but there was hardly anything at all to lift, the dead man had so dwindled. The body flew out of the canal and landed with his head face down in her lap.

Horrified, Blythe scrambled backwards to escape its imaginary clutches, letting the dead man's face drop into the flat grass and mud, his arms spread wide.

Aaron hoisted himself onto the bank and laid there on his back exhausted, his hand resting on the body's thin calf with the understanding that if the thing moved, even slightly, he would sense it. Blythe negotiated a far circle around the dead man and crouched beside Aaron's chest, underneath his free arm. She stared over him and began studying the corpse.

"Are you all right?" she asked Aaron.

"I'm fine," he said. After a moment, he craned his neck to get a better look. "Whoever he was, he must have starved to death. You can count all his bones."

Blythe stood but didn't move from her spot. "He must be an old man," she said. "He's nearly your height, but my God, Aaron, he's wasted away. The poor thing."

Aaron turned over, resting on his side. He practically closed his fingers in a circle around the man's ankle and traced it up in a nearly unbroken ring to the man's knee.

"Don't touch him," Blythe cautioned.

"I've already danced with the poor devil. If he's got something, I'm

Blythe

sure I've got it by now."

"Don't force fate, Aaron. Please let him go."

Aaron did.

"What's this here?" he asked. He crawled to his knees and held his face close to the man's foot. "It's a mark."

"Like a birthmark?"

"Like a brand…here on his heel."

"Aaron, please don't touch him," she pleaded.

"I just want to see what this is. It's raised. It's some sort of cross. And what are these dark spots?"

"Aaron, don't touch them!"

"I won't. But what are they?" He bent in close examining the dozens of dark patches that dotted the man's entire body. Although Aaron couldn't discern color, they appeared to be some sort of ulcer bubbling up in weeping openings from the skin. His blind hand felt the ground until he found a twig.

"Aaron, don't!" Blythe said. "If not for your safety, for his dignity."

"Blythe, I can't hurt him anymore than he's hurt now. I want to understand what this is. What happened to him?" He pressed the twig beside a few of the sores trying to give them some dimension, never pressing directly into the wounds.

"Please, Aaron, let him be. You don't know what it is or who he is or what made him die. You could get it just by touching him."

"Blythe, I took in a mouthful of water that was in his mouth. Trust me, if it is something contagious, I've already got it."

"You don't know that. Now please," she said as she reached down, laid her hand on his shoulder and guided him to his feet. "We'll tell my father what we've found and he'll take care of him. He will be able to tell us what happened to him."

They stood silently above the dead man with their arms wrapped around each other studying the entire length of him and across his outstretched arms. As they did so, the stream churned on behind them, pumping its way down through the hills, into the heart of the valley, the lifeblood of all who lived there.

Chapter 9

Sergio rarely if ever walked. He sprang. He ricocheted. But that particular morning, Sergio inched his way down the alpine path into the valley and the village.

Despite his best intentions to sleep in his own bed, he found himself simply too tired to travel home from the bridge. Instead, he knelt beneath a cluster of pines and swept together a little crib of needles that served admirably as a bed until the first beams of fierce, red sunshine struck his face and coaxed him to rise.

With pine needles in his matted hair, Sergio walked like a little child roused out of a deep sleep. He cupped one hand and rubbed his eye while his other arm flopped about. Every step was a spastic lurch and halt, lurch and halt that shook his whole body.

Parissa giggled at him as he passed the gazebo in the center of the village circle. He opened one eye and looked over to where she rested.

"Hard night?" she asked.

"Hard isn't the word for it. Exhausting."

"At the bottle again?" she asked.

"I wish. The stream. Playing silly games with Aaron."

"And where is he now?"

Sergio looked at her through one squinted eye and asked, "Where is he always?"

"With Blythe?"

He pressed his finger to the tip of his nose and sat beside her.

"Look at you. You're a mess," she said, plucking pine needles from his hair and clothes while he sat, his eyes closed, appreciating the pruning with a satisfied smile.

"You're adorable," she said. She gently traced her hand across his cherub cheek, sweeping down along his jaw. She let her fingers end with a flourish of tickles behind his ear. The surprise of the sensation made his eyes flutter open and he looked at Parissa as if for the first time. He could see his own reflection in her dark eyes. To his surprise, she was already smiling warmly back at him having leaned forward within the range of intimacy. He blinked again and his mouth fell open slightly, unsure of what to say.

Her eyes closed and her head tilted to the side. He instinctively responded in kind and placed upon her lips the most perfectly cushioned kiss. He held it for a long moment, savoring its warmth, its pressure, its taste, its smell, and, most of all, its surprising source. He had always been dubious of Parissa. She, for her part, always treated him with naked contempt.

"You've won her over," he thought. "You are amazing."

Not wanting to feel her release, he ended their embrace with a gentle pucker and slowly withdrew. With his eyes still shut, he playfully nestled his nose next to hers and placed infinitely more tender kisses on each of the raised corners of her mouth.

He looked back at her, dazed. "I never felt you cared for me," he whispered.

Parissa again swept her fingertips behind his ear and drew him close, kissing him. She whispered, "I don't."

He looked at her even more puzzled.

She released him and rose without another word, her smile remaining. She walked down the gazebo steps and off in the direction of her cottage never looking back.

As he rested his head against a pillar and watched her walk away,

Kagetsu passed beneath him. She glanced up with a smile laced with censure.

Panicked, he called out, "No! No, wait! It wasn't like that!"

She turned away and continued gliding away.

"Kagetsu," he pleaded. "Kagetsu, please!"

She stopped and walked back to him in retrograde, floating up the stairs. Sergio moved over to offer her the place Parissa had vacated but Kagetsu refused to accept it.

"Sergio, you owe me no explanation," she said in her sweet but characteristically aloof way. "You're under no obligation to me."

"But Kagetsu, I want to be…with all my heart, I want to be."

"With all your heart?" she asked, raising her glance to Parissa.

"I do," he said. "I swear to you, I do. Don't you know how I feel?"

"Sergio," she said sweetly. "You love to love. You love to be loved. You love to be in love."

"Yes," he said. "But with you! I feel everything for you."

"And for Parissa?"

"She was a distraction!"

"And for Sylvia?"

"She's a friend!"

"And for Michelle and Marta and Nadia?"

"A daydream! A peccadillo! A curse to me now!" he assured her. He jumped up and extended his hands to her, but she withdrew hers and clasped them gracefully in front of her. "If you would be mine, I'd never so much as look at another woman."

"Open your eyes," she said softly. "Open your eyes and you would gain my respect."

"Open my eyes? To what?"

"Whom do you see me carrying on with?" she asked. "Or hear about me meeting?"

He looked around studiously, his hands still extended towards her. His eyes darted about the empty streets as if trying to find one individual among an invisible teaming crowd.

He haltingly concluded, "There is no one."

Blythe

"And why is that?" she asked.

"Because there is no one you love?"

She corrected, "Because there is no one I wish to love, Sergio."

His hands at last relaxed.

She said softly, staring off in the direction Parissa had disappeared, "Sergio, how many women have you been with?"

"I…."

"Exactly," she said. "Either you've had so many you can't remember or you've had so many you don't want to answer out of embarrassment."

He stood there mute.

"I don't want to be added to that history…to be tied to everyone you have tied yourself to…to be just another name in a list of names," she said. "I want more for myself than that."

"But…." he objected.

"Say another word and you've lost even my friendship forever. Sergio, there is too much risk…too much risk in love. Every day, men and women promise their hearts then give their eyes and minds and spirits to someone or something else. I've seen it."

"But love remains," he insisted.

"The hope of love remains," she said. "Love is a lie people believe because it is more comforting than any truth."

"Oh, Kagetsu, you couldn't be more wrong," he said, raising his hands out to her again. "Love is the truth everything else hopes to become."

"Leaving you bitter when it fails," she said.

"Leaving you better because you're closer to the truth," he said. "Kagetsu, you're adrift out there. I see it. Don't you see that love is the confidence that you are not alone even when you are by yourself?"

"That's a sweet wish, but I won't have it. I won't lie to myself." She dared him sweetly, "Show me the perfectly faithful man in love."

"Perfection?" he laughed. "Is that what you expect? Perfection?"

"Not perfection; perfect faithfulness. If love is everything you say it is, you should be able to point to someone…anyone…in perfectly faithful love; someone whose heart has never been tempted."

"But perfection isn't the point," he argued. "To be tempted is to be human. Love is love because it overcomes temptation."

"But if it were love, it wouldn't be tempted," she said.

"Just because you admire a pool of water doesn't mean you're going to take a swim."

"I would rather live faithfully with myself than unfaithfully with another."

"But…." he began.

She held up her hand and he fell silent. "You may think you love me, Sergio, but I think it is something lower than that. I want more than that or I want nothing at all."

Kagetsu took one step back and left him. Sergio instinctively reached out to her but couldn't muster the words to call her back. He turned away and paced the length of the gazebo.

"I want more than that or I want nothing at all," he heard a woman's voice repeat followed by a deep, sincere laugh.

He looked around. He was alone.

"What can you see in someone so cold, Sergio?" the voice asked.

He cocked his head to get a better perspective on where the voice was coming from. He launched himself over to his left and bent over the railing.

"Sylvia!" he exclaimed. "Have you been there this entire time?"

Sylvia sat on the ground with her back to the gazebo's trellis skirt. She bent her head far back to look up to him, her face beaming, smooth and radiant in the early morning sunlight. Sergio reached down an arm and lifted her to her feet. Sylvia spun around as she stood and walked backwards away from him. As she dusted herself off, she advised, "Remember what happened to the little boy who couldn't make up his mind on what he wanted, Sergio."

"What was that?" he asked.

"He ended up with nothing," she said.

She stopped and addressed him, her hands on her hips, "Sergio?" She waited for his response as if to make sure he was listening.

Finally, he replied, "Yes?"

"Love is like any other decision in life; you make a choice, then work to make it the right choice."

"I don't understand," he said.

"You will," she said turning and walking away. She called back to him, "Before you've alienated every woman around you, choose one… choose one you like, and soon enough you'll find that she's the one you love. We're not all just friends and distractions."

* * *

Blythe and Aaron stormed through her parents' front door and into Iris's kitchen.

"Is father back?" Blythe asked breathlessly.

Iris looked over her shoulder at them, her hands buried wrists-high in bread dough. Stacks of breads and muffins were piled around her. She asked reflexively, "How do you know to ask if your father is back when you haven't been here to know he was out?"

She turned back to her work.

Aaron blushed but Blythe persisted, "Iris, we need him. Is he here?"

"The study," Iris replied. Blythe darted for the closed door at the far end of the kitchen. "But you shouldn't disturb him," Iris cautioned. "He's been up half the night."

"He's in the study," Blythe dismissed disparagingly, bursting through the door with Aaron close behind. "How can you study when you're asleep?"

"Study?" a startled Duffy asked with a worried voice as he sat up in his chair, roused out of a deep sleep. He asked worriedly, "What do I have to study?"

Aaron began, "We were up by the canal…."

"Were you?" Duffy interrupted with sudden focus. "When?"

Aaron recalled Duffy and his own father crossing over the bridge while he and Blythe swam below. Unwilling to reveal what he had heard, Aaron cautiously continued, "Late evening. We were swimming downstream of the bridge when Blythe struck something in the water."

Blythe continued, "We were about shouting distance from the

bridge when I reached out and hit something hard. Duffy, it was a man who drowned or…."

Aaron interrupted, "He was some old man, but neither Blythe nor I recognized him. He mustn't have been from the valley. Duffy, he looked terrible…just wasted away."

"Wasted, you say?" Duffy asked absently as he rose to his feet. "Were you able to get him out of the water?"

"We were," Aaron said. "We brought him upstream and laid him near the bridge. As you go up, he'll be on the near bank to the left of the path. The poor man. There was nothing left of him."

"Father, you're smiling," Blythe observed, dumbstruck.

"Oh, it's something else entirely, Blythe," Duffy said, catching himself. "I'm sorry. I was just recalling my dream. So you got him out of the water. Good, good. I'll go up and take a look right now. Let me wash up."

There was a knock at the front door, which Iris answered. They could hear her welcoming sing-song, "Oh, Maddox! Here for your father's order?"

"There was something else," Aaron offered, stopping Duffy at the study's door.

Duffy asked, "What is that?"

"He had some kind of tattoo or brand," he said. "On his ankle."

Blythe added, "It was a cross. Aaron said it was raised."

Aaron concluded, "And he was covered in sores…. dark, open sores all over him. At first we noticed them on his back and then we rolled him over."

"Who did?" Duffy asked, alarmed.

Aaron asked, "Who did what?"

"Rolled him over? Who touched him?" Duffy demanded. "The two of you?"

Aaron said cautiously, "No…I did. Is there a problem?"

"No, no, no," Duffy deflected, "It's just evidence. I don't like to hear anyone touching any evidence before I've had a chance to look at it first. If you ever find another one, Aaron, don't touch him any more than

Blythe

absolutely necessary. You've got to be careful about these things."

"Find another?" they both asked, dumbfounded at the suggestion.

Duffy caught himself again. "Of course you won't," he said. "But when you come on any place where there is a death or where a crime may have happened, you want to leave things undisturbed. It's common sense." He concluded, "It's evidence."

"He is evidence," Blythe corrected. "He was a man."

"Yes, I suppose you're right, dear," Duffy admitted. "He is evidence."

Duffy suggested to his daughter, "You've had a long night, dear. Go upstairs and try to get some sleep? I'll take care of this from here."

He kissed her on the forehead and hugged her tightly. Still in her father's arms, Blythe reached back to Aaron and they squeezed each other's hands before she climbed the stairs. Duffy continued, "Aaron, I would appreciate it if you would come with me to show me exactly where this body is and share any other details you can remember."

"Of course," he answered.

Duffy asked, "Wait here for a moment. I need to ask Blythe's mother something."

Aaron agreed. As Duffy left the room he closed the door behind him.

Duffy quickly waddled across the kitchen past Iris to the front where Maddox waited.

"Good!" Duffy said in an urgent hush. "You're still here. Listen to me. Aaron and Blythe found a body up near the bridge…just to the left on the near bank. You and your father better get up there now and get everything cleaned up or this whole thing is going to explode. You understand?"

"Who was it?" Maddox asked.

"Hell if I know," Duffy shot back, "But if you don't get up there now, everyone in the valley is going to know about this, and if they do, you know what that means for you. Now go!"

Duffy pushed him out the door. Satisfied Maddox was on his way, he returned to the kitchen as Aaron opened the study door. Duffy took a half hop to make it to Iris and surprised her from behind with a passionate kiss on her cheek and a bear hug.

"Duffy!" she exclaimed and dropped three loaves of bread on the counter.

Duffy said, "My work here is done! Aaron, let's get going. I'll get my hat."

"What was that you asked Maddox?" Iris called to him.

"Maddox?" Duffy asked quizzically. "I didn't even know he was here. You probably heard me talking to Aaron."

"But...." Iris began.

"Now, now, now. I've got work to do," Duffy said, waving his arms dismissively as he returned to his study, "I can't stay around here gabbing."

Iris walked out into the tiny entrance hall but immediately returned. "He's gone," she declared entirely befuddled, her arms filled with bags holding a dozen loaves of bread.

"Who's gone," Duffy asked, returning to the room.

"Maddox," Iris answered.

"You and Maddox!" Duffy erupted. "What is it with you today?"

"But he was just here," Iris continued, cowed. She said to Aaron, "He was here to pick up your father's order."

"Look, Aaron," Duffy offered. "I know your father will raise hell itself if he doesn't have his order first thing in the morning. Let's take those loaves over on our way. Whoever it was you found up there isn't going anywhere from what you've said."

As they made their way to the door, Duffy absentmindedly patted his shirt and pants and asked, "My field book? Where are my papers? I'll need something to write on. Hold on Aaron, I'll get them."

Duffy waddled once more across the kitchen and up the stairs to his bedroom.

"Aaron," he called out, as he descended the stairs with an empty bucket of water. "I'm going to need to dump this first. It will just take a moment."

Iris smiled at him and cooed, "Oh, before it was even full! Thank you, dear."

"Absolutely, absolutely. Anything for you," he said, giving her a

Blythe

peck on the lips as he passed.

He returned to the room, empty bucket in hand and once again ascended the stairs. On his return to the kitchen he exclaimed in frustration, "My papers!" and again launched himself back out of sight. Duffy disappeared for quite some time before finally returning and leaving with Aaron in tow.

* * *

Notté turned over and squinted toward the window. The curtain was drawn, but he could tell by the intensity of the light creeping around the edges that the day was well under way. He glanced first around the room at the many musical instruments and accoutrements that were laid about, then back across the bed to the young man lying next to him.

"You certainly were a prodigy," Notté whispered audibly as a compliment to his latest partner who remained asleep. "You played well and long and with passion."

Notté glided out of bed without disturbing his slumber. Silently, he picked up his clothes that had been strewn about the room. In moments he had gathered all but one of his shoes. He looked around the back of chairs and under the bed, but it was nowhere to be found. At last he paused then reenacted how he had undressed. A smile crossed his face.

He tiptoed around the bed and stood beside the armoire. He reached far above his head and felt about the top, at last locating the mislaid shoe.

He cradled his bundle of clothes close to his chest to free his hands then picked up a violin and bow that sat on a small table next to the bedroom door. He fumbled to open the door and walked out into a great room that was arranged as a chamber where his acquaintance instructed and held recitals. Notté effortlessly bent in half above a narrow, elegantly upholstered couch and dropped his clothes in its corner.

He returned just outside the bedroom door and shut it carefully.

Notté strutted to the center of the music room with the exaggerated steps of a ballet dancer walking to the center of a stage, the violin in one hand and the bow in the other. He bent deeply forward and extended his arms down low, stretching them out. He rose up, continuing the warm up, making himself into an enormous arc that raised him to his toes, hips thrust forward, his back bowed, shoulders arching even farther backwards, and his arms stretched high above him farther back clasping the instrument by the neck with the bow still firmly in the other hand. He let out a great, silent yawn and bounced back erect to the balls of his feet.

Notté lifted his hands into place. He paused for just a moment, the bow suspended above the strings, anticipating the first note. His face held a serious intensity. Soon the room was filled with deep, sad, profound and haunting music. He moved with the tune he played—the naked form with naked notes that glided and sometimes swirled about back and forth between the light and the dark. "Pathos," the music's undertone seemed to whisper. "Pathos. Pathos. Pathos. Pathos. Pathos."

At last, Notté lightly pressed the very base of the bow against a solitary string and pulled out the most exquisite note that grew infinitesimally thinner and more refined. It seemed to cling to the air with the knowledge that its life was brief then—gradually, imperceptibly—it disappeared.

What was left was the ghost of music, the memory of a note.

Notté strode over to the couch and laid the instrument down. He picked up his clothes, article by article, and dressed without disturbing the pervasive silence he had found, disturbed then restored.

He cracked open the front door, letting in an abrasive abundance of light. Notté pulled back his head in protest, allowing a moment for his eyes to adjust.

He gracefully spun around the door, closing it behind him. It was still too bright to see, so he blindly but cordially smiled and bowed to the conversation of two women as they passed before him, holding his pose until they passed.

He paused for a moment and set his face to the sun taking in the warmth until he was certain the ladies were gone. His eyes still strained, he winked glances up and down the lane to be sure he was alone. The smile fell from his face, leaving a sickened and angry visage. Quickly he pulled a small knife from his pocket, opened the blade and traced a small cross of equal sides on the lintel. Just as quickly, the knife returned out of sight.

Blythe

Notté made his way unsteadily down the few slate steps but soon regained his form and strutted his way back up the village paths.

He was a tired vanguard. He had performed his duty with skill and pleasure, but it was time to return home. Steadily he climbed up and up, out of the village and into the open land that surrounded it.

As he crossed the bridge, he turned and glanced without emotion or hesitation down at a pale and wasted corpse that lay beside the canal. It held his eyes as he continued on across the span. Once he reached the other side, he began to do a little dance. He swayed forcefully in one direction and then the next, holding his hands high and tight and tough against his chest. It was clear he danced to a tune he knew well: one that became a part of him through the reinforcement of habit and the habit of reinforcement; one that inspired the cruelest combination of indifference and calculation the more it was considered, the more it was sung, the more it was danced to. It was a song impossible for anyone possessing human empathy to conceive. It was a song that delighted in destruction. It was a song of Henry's strain.

Part Two

Chapter 10

"What a pity for a groom to be sick on his wedding day," Iris observed.

The dapper groom stood drawn and weary before the gathering.

Duffy quipped, "Take it as a final act of rebellion. It is his body's last stand, begging him to reconsider."

"Duffy!" Iris reproached. "Be kind."

"What?" he objected. "It must be a shock to his system considering the life he's led."

Iris said, "We should be happy he turned away from that life to something more…more…natural."

"One can hope," he said. "Oh, the times I'd have to come to this place when one young poof or another would get out of line. You wouldn't believe the things that went on right here in this room."

"I'd rather not think about that," Iris said sitting up straight. She lifted her hands, which she had been sitting on out of habit. She wiped her palms gently on her dress and said, "He's settling down now. Let's be happy for him."

"Let's indeed," Duffy said. "At least this should be the end of any trouble I have with him."

Maddox passed by Duffy and Iris to take a seat in front of them.

An impromptu guffaw escaped Duffy before he could hide his shock at the young man's presence at this event. Maddox's eyes darted from the sniffling groom to Duffy in a contemptible glare. It was a look that pushed the pudgy man back in his seat and forced him to lower his focus into his lap. Iris sat wide-eyed at the exchange. She contained herself just long enough for Maddox to turn and sit before she begged to know, "What was *that*?"

Duffy pursed his lips and shook his bowed head saying without words, "Let it pass."

Blythe sat at Duffy's other side continuing to stare off around the room, examining all the books that lined the walls from floor to ceiling, volume after volume. Every once in a while she met the startled glance of another member of the gathering who sheepishly looked away, as if caught doing something he shouldn't have been doing. Normally, such looks fueled Blythe, but not on that day; on that day she was alone and empty in the room. She sat with her arms across her stomach; her thumbs carelessly stroked her covered forearms and occasionally pressing down hard against them.

"What a collection," Duffy commented snapping her back into the room. "What I wouldn't do with a collection like this."

"Read it," Blythe responded with ennui.

Her father gave her a confused glance.

She didn't need to turn to know the befuddled expression on his face. She explained, "That's what you wouldn't do with this collection— read it. You have an entire room of books at home but you've never opened one."

"But it's comforting to have them around me in case I ever want to read," he responded, satisfied with his answer. He returned to examining the room in appreciation. He repeated, "What I wouldn't do with these."

The groom caught Maddox's eye. He showed the palms of his hands and looked around the room with a shrug to ask the young man in a signal, "Where is he?"

Maddox broke off any eye contact. He never turned around to see if the groom's preoccupation was in the room. He knew he wouldn't be.

At that moment the entrance doors swung open and brilliant light flooded in. Every head, except for Maddox's, turned to see the silhouette of a podgy woman dressed in a gown that glowed around the edges from the sun's beams. The light and her veil conspired to obscure any details of her face until at last she took a step forward and paused, and then another step. Haltingly she entered the room walking between the orderly rows of seats. Her shoulders shook with uncontrollable little sobs of joy as she turned one way and then the other. Sylvia and Sergio were among those to whom she gave a glance of wondrous disbelief as she swept by in her solitary procession.

Sylvia cooed to Sergio, "She's finally found someone. Gwendolyn always said she would make a wonderful wife, but she never thought she would have the chance."

Sergio shook his head slightly. "Seems like a bit of an odd match. He never showed much interest in her, let alone any woman. And I didn't think she was seeing anyone at all."

The groom's face was haggard as he watched her approach. His eyes were deadbeat as he looked down to her. His lips clung to an ailing, designed smile. It would not be an exaggeration to say he had the bearing of a prisoner who had suffered much at the hands of his captors but who, at last, witnessed his liberator's approach. Such was the manner he conveyed as he stood at the top of the aisle on a small raised platform looking down at her. It was a look of sick relief, of exhausted triumph that he had made it this far. His years as a single man were closing and everything about him clearly stated that it was none too soon.

The couple faced each other and locked hands. Without releasing their clasp, they turned to the gathering.

"Welcome to the day neither of us thought would ever arrive," the groom began.

"We're a little surprised ourselves," a man's voice responded from the back of the audience and the room rolled with laughter.

"We are, too. We are, too," the groom responded in good nature. "We thank you all for coming here as our special guests. Gwen and I decided to throw out convention...no surprise there," he adlibbed

Blythe

soliciting more laughter from his guests. "Rather than follow a traditional ceremony, we decided to each read a selection from the works you see around you that best summarize how we feel about the other and about this day. Neither Gwen nor I know which passage the other has chosen, so I'm sure we will enjoy the surprise as much as you, if not more. You will be pleased to know, this ceremony will be brief."

The gathering murmured in appreciation.

To triumphantly conclude his remarks, the groom stated, "Afterwards, we invite you all to join us for the reception to end all receptions."

He turned back to his betrothed. "Gwen, shall I go first or shall you?"

"You," she said hastily, then added as a nervous afterthought, "my…dear." She let out a little giggle of excitement at the sound of the words and looked out on the crowd in surprise that she had been able to manage them.

"Very well," he said.

He strode to a small table and lifted half of a white cloth that covered two books. He returned to Gwendolyn then opened the green-bound volume to the page marked with a white ribbon. The groom said in a voice that spoke more to the crowd than to his future wife, "I shall read from a work I have just acquired. It, better than any other piece, tells you how I feel right now, Gwen. This is from a work called *The Crooner*."

Lucre, who sat in the front right corner of the assembly, looked across at Maddox. It was a certainty that Maddox felt the pressure of his father's glare, but the young man was literally and figuratively unmoved by the intuition. He refused any pressure to turn. Lucre craned his stare back across the room to Aaron, who was already looking squarely at him. Aaron's face flushed to match his father's bright, red, angry tone.

The groom began, "And little by little there was a happy emptiness: a void he had longed for, but could never feel in the honesty of his youthful heart. The heart was still true, but older now. And at last he felt for sure there was no desire in it, save for one—for his one."

He gently closed the book and looked up to his fiancée.

Fat tears streamed down Gwendolyn's cheeks as she looked at him then out to the crowd as if to ask them if they heard what he said.

He rested the book on the table then returned with a gentle kiss on her cheek. She wiped her cheek and he wiped his lips. Another wave of little nervous giggles sprang forth from throughout the gathering at the couple's responses.

Gwendolyn squeezed his hands before releasing them. She walked to the table where she uncovered a tanned leather-bound book with an even-sided red cross die stamped on the cover. As she returned to him, he looked down at her selection and chuckled with ironic recognition. He looked at Maddox who stared blankly back.

Her voice wavered nervously as she began, "I don't even know the name of this book," she said, turning it around as if somehow the title would appear where it had not been before. "But the passage I chose describes the mystery with which you and I so quickly came together," she said in a voice audible to nearly her groom alone. "I hope you like it… dear."

She looked at him with a quivering smile and cleared her throat with all the force of a man. The groom winced slightly, but his smile returned, tinged with sweet patience. She stood there for a moment to regain her composure looking quickly out again at the audience with a nervous shrug that once more asked, "Can you believe I'm doing this?"

She read, "Be on guard if it gives you comfort, for all the difference it will make. I am patient and ever-watching. I live for that moment when you think yourself safe. It is then I will steal in and surprise you, when you thought you would be forever left alone and untouched by the mystery that sweeps in those around you. Hidden in love's plumage, I will descend upon you. Mankind's greatest desires—to love and to be loved—will find my way into you.

"Reason with such a power.

"It cannot be done.

"Predict its course.

"It cannot be done.

"Stifle its drive.

Blythe

"It cannot be done.

"I will conquer with that force that conquers all. Your heart is not safe from me. So long as there is love, I will find you. So long as there is love, I will make you mine."

After Gwendolyn returned from the table, all that remained of their ceremony was their exchange of rings and a concluding kiss. Had the groom not faced the back of the room in their embrace, someone might have noticed that his eyes never closed as long as their lips touched. Without emotion, he stared blankly to the back wall.

Despite the rain that the red sunrise had forecast, the festivities afterwards were, just as the groom had promised, the reception to end all receptions. Cross-sections of the valley citizenry who rarely, if ever, came together, gathered in celebration of this union. "Those Troublesome Ones," as Duffy called them, clung together as packs of young men disassociated with the rest of the assemblage. Questionable friends of the groom who remained a mystery to the bride, they laughed louder, drank deeper, and looked out with more hostility than any others.

These were juxtaposed with the companions of the bride—women of stout character and stout ankles. There were dozens of them who, by common exchange, knew everyone else's foibles better than their own and who exercised a remarkable and regular proficiency for pointing out these faults. With craftsmen's precision, they put themselves in the company of those they wanted to disassemble, then went to work with a subtle stream of questions and statements that stripped away any defense the individual might have had. Sooner than later they exposed the very quality that that person most hoped to hide. For a sparkling moment, whichever one of these priestesses guided the inquisition rhetorically held up that fault and turned it around on display for all to see. They did this so they could—with equal public attention and personal magnanimity—graciously forgive that person for their transgression. In so doing, these women felt they walked a path to grace for they were by their own accounts good, decent and, above all else, forgiving women.

To her credit, Iris never engaged in such social critiques. Perhaps because she didn't judge, she found herself the hub of all their exchanges; she was the one with whom the others gathered in twos and threes to share their stories. Whenever there was only one woman alone in her company, however, the conversation never steered to salacious denigration. Instead, they cooked up more simple discussions of families and such as they cooked up simple foods in her kitchen.

The valley men assembled were like men everywhere at such events; they were preoccupied with not being preoccupied about their day-to-day concerns. They dulled themselves not only with food and drinks but with the conversations they had shared as many times as they had gathered. Whereas the women conversed on an endless list of subjects, each one—without ever stating it explicitly—measuring social standing, conversation among the well-acquainted men was ritual bent on avoiding any certain conclusion about anything or reaching definitive conclusions about everything. Mostly, though, it was always a conglomeration of the same putdowns and praises—the greater the putdown, the higher the praise.

Men generally speak so they do not have to listen; most would prefer to stand around silently, but one or another makes the mistake of raising a question that must be answered or making a statement that must be supported. In the instant that follows, men assess each other, usually with remarkable accuracy. Most are found to be about equal with another, a few are considered better, others are found to be worse—these are the ones who inevitably speak the most. Nothing bores a man more than listening to another man he considers beneath him.

For what seemed an eternity, Sergio remained cornered by a man most considered far worse than themselves. Bunting was his name, and he had not stopped talking for the five drinks Sergio had excused himself to fetch in hopes of somehow breaking free of the man. Sergio consumed them with an even more fervent hope of somehow making this man disappear. Escape seemed hopeless until Kagetsu's passing inspired him to push beyond his captor.

Kagetsu passed by, as always, cool and silent, with a radiance that waxed and waned to suit the introspection of her mood. Sergio drew in closer and closer, looking for an opportunity to speak.

75

At last she stood alone and surveyed the room. Sergio approached.

"May I get you something to drink?" he asked. "Some wine? Maybe a draft?"

"Neither," she said, barely recognizing his presence.

She walked off and stood in front of a table between two seats. Sergio pulled out a chair and motioned for her to sit.

"I'll stand," she replied, still not looking at him.

"That's fine," he said pleasantly. "I will, too."

"They have plenty to eat," he laughed. "Too much to choose from, really. May I fix you a plate?"

She offered coolly, "I'm not hungry."

It was a breaking point for the little man.

"Choose!" he yelled.

The party stopped and looked at him.

Sergio protested, at once maudlin and wildly furious, "For God sakes choose something...anything!" he said. "What are you? A statue? Are you above any human need?"

In the entire room, Aaron was the only person in motion as he made his way to his friend.

"Kagetsu," Aaron began, putting his arm around Sergio's shoulders to lead him away, "forgive Sergio. He was born breach; from the very start he wanted to make an ass of himself."

Without thinking, Sergio returned to the corner from which he had come. Bunting continued their conversation as if it had never stopped while Sergio stared deeply into his drink, emptying it, then stared into the emptiness. He looked around the room in an unfocused sweep for Kagetsu, but could no longer find her. So his eyes sank back into where his longing had begun. He looked into the bottom of a glass that began to fill with his tears as Bunting, unaware, continued his monologue.

Father Philip filled the void in the room by lifting two glasses and tapping them together. Soon all in the room respected his signal and gave him their attention. He returned the glasses to the table and looked warmly at the couple. He said, "Bruce, first let me welcome you back to the valley. Wherever it was that you had been for the past many weeks, it is clear that you found there a new outlook, one that has led you to reassess your life and to welcome the unity of marriage. May God bless you and your new bride."

The party applauded.

"And Gwen," he continued. "Gwen, it is clear from the beautiful expression upon your face that you have your heart's wish. May you always be thankful to the God who heard your heart and who blessed your husband with someone so wonderful. Let us all bow our heads for just a moment. Dear Lord, bless this union that was entered into today. Keep Bruce and Gwen ever-faithful, ever-loving, ever-blessed and ever-bound to each other in their joy. Amen."

Duffy stole in behind Aaron. He asked, "Still seeing ghosts?"

Aaron responded sullenly, "It wasn't a ghost, Duffy. It was a dead man."

Duffy taunted him, "Since when do dead men rise and walk away? Or would Father Philip be better able to answer that question?"

Aaron responded, "Should I tell Father Philip you are now a skeptic about both God and men?"

"There's no need for that," Duffy retreated, looking to see if the good Father could be in earshot. "I believe what I see and I didn't see any sign of a dead man. Now do I lie, or do you?"

"Dead men disappear since Blythe and I saw one and you didn't," Aaron said. "My word has always been good with you, Duffy. And I gave you my word on what I saw. Why wouldn't you believe me now?"

"Oh, I don't know," he said, enjoying the moment. "Maybe because there was no trace of a man where you said you saw one? Aaron, play whatever game it is you're playing, but leave me out of it."

Duffy was positively giddy.

Aaron shook his head and walked away. He bumped into Sergio who excused himself from Bunting and clasped onto Aaron.

"Thank you!" Sergio exclaimed.

Aaron turned back to see Bunting standing alone. He said, "I'm sorry I didn't get to you sooner."

"He's death."

"He's worse," Aaron said. "He's a bore."

Aaron leaned up against the wall. He stuffed his right hand into his pocket and pulled out a smooth band of gold ornamented only with tiny gold beads that encircled the two edges. He held it up for inspection.

"A wedding ring?" Sergio asked in disbelief.

"She has a ring for every finger but the one this was made for," Aaron said. "This will complete the set. Aren't you going to wish me luck?"

Sergio said, "I wish you sanity and restraint."

"Coming from you, that's better than luck," Aaron replied.

Sergio asked, "When are you going to ask her? Now?"

"No," Aaron shook his head. "I thought I might, but she's not herself today."

"She's too much herself."

"Careful," Aaron cautioned.

"Am I wrong?" Sergio said. "She's in her own world today. I wonder what she thinks about in those times."

Aaron paused for a moment, then shuddered.

"What?" asked Sergio.

"She told me once that when she's in a mood like this, it's like being in a coffin with the lid closed." He shuddered again as if freeing himself from a cobweb that caught him by surprise and may still have a spider somewhere on him.

"You and tight places," Sergio smirked.

Aaron said, "I think she described it that way just so I wouldn't ask any more questions."

"So if not today, when will you ask her?"

"When it's right. I'll know when it's right. We have all the time in the world."

Blythe broke from the crowd and brooded towards him. He stuffed the ring back in his pocket but kept his hand there to maintain a casual air.

"My father still thinks we're lying," she said.

Aaron asked incredulously, "Why would anyone play games about seeing a dead man? What could we possibly have to gain?"

Blythe responded in a disinterested manner, "I have no idea." She nestled into him. She rubbed her head against the side of his face and his collarbone as if marking him as hers. Sergio, ever the faithful friend, ignored them both and looked out at the crowd.

Across the room, Parissa laughed a little too loudly as she leaned to within inches of Duffy's face. As she laughed, she flicked her hair and looked around at the many men who looked at her out of the corner of their eyes. She paused momentarily at one or another, and then returned her unnaturally full attention to Duffy. She continued to look up at him with smiling eyes that seemed to sparkle all the more in their manufactured rapture. She looked up adoringly at his steady stream of chatter. Entranced by her attention, Duffy talked more and more.

"It's interesting." He paused. "For all the power I have, it hasn't changed me. Oh, sure I get offers from people you wouldn't believe because they think I can give them something. But I rarely take them up on them. It wouldn't be proper."

"What could you give me?" she cooed.

He blushed even deeper and remained lost for an answer that would not provoke a slap.

Although they could not hear exactly what was being said, the women around Iris carefully studied how her husband and Parissa spoke; each woman enjoyably assumed the details. Iris was too caught up in her disappointment to hide the hurt from her face. It was that look that Sergio followed to Blythe's father and on to Parissa.

"Blythe?" Sergio asked. "It looks like your father needs to get your mother a fresh drink."

Blythe turned and saw Parissa holding her father's arm and wildly shaking her mane of hair in laughter. Blythe pushed off Aaron's chest as if it were the wall and walked over to them.

Duffy laughed to Parissa, "These young poofs think I don't have it anymore. But I've got everything I always did, and more. Absolutely, absolutely. Watch this."

Duffy bellowed to a nearby violinist, a young man dressed in a brightly colored vest, "Quit trying to win the groom back with that kind of playing! You've lost him. Play something a man and a woman can dance

Blythe

to!"

The young man never missed a note as Parissa and Duffy laughed themselves silly. The melody soon finished, but Duffy did not. He egged on the artist again, "Play something a man feels for a woman!"

The musician sniffled from his cold. He looked squarely at Duffy's crotch and played a smooth descending scale of notes musically emasculating the man of authority with a tune that could imply only impotence. Duffy lunged toward him just as Blythe arrived and flung herself between them. She got up in her father's face and said, "Mother needs a fresh drink."

Duffy reluctantly lowered his glare from the violinist to Blythe. He looked back up at the young man and called out defiantly before turning away, "How lucky for you, poof."

Blythe rolled her eyes at the young man after she sent her father on his way. She scanned the room unsuccessfully for Parissa until she looked to Aaron. Parissa leaned into him as she had to Duffy, inviting his attention with her deep looks, flirtatious laughs, and flinging hair.

Unlike when she flew to her father, Blythe slowly, purposefully walked to Aaron. She studied him to see how he reacted to Parissa's advances. As Blythe passed the clutch of older women around Iris, she heard one of them cluck, "Poor Blythe's hands are full keeping that girl off her men. They don't seem to be helping her much."

Blythe maintained her deliberate pace as she walked past the laughing Aaron on her way to the door. She said, "Aaron, good luck with Parissa. Not that you need anything more than a pulse to attract her." She asked Parissa, "Or have you lowered that standard, too?"

"Blythe," Aaron called out, but he knew she would not stop. To pursue her would be fruitless. Their friction could only be resolved in another time and in a more private place.

Parissa still sparkled up at him.

He looked down on her in disgust. "Why?" he asked.

"We are fate, Aaron," she said. "You don't know it yet. But you and I are fate."

"Fate is what happens when you surrender," he said, shaking his head as he pushed past her. "I don't own any white flags."

"I've got something white you can wave," she offered.

He left Parissa only to come face to face with his father.

"About *The Crooner*...." Aaron began.

Lucre held up his hand. "You don't have to explain. I put two and two together and got Maddox. Enough said about that. I've got some business I need your help with. I've purchased Bruce's collection."

"His library?" Aaron asked incredulously.

"His entire collection," Lucre told him. "He'll be going away again for some time he said and he won't have any more use for books."

"But you don't read," Aaron said.

"No. But I buy and sell," Lucre said. "I already have two purchasers who'll divide the lot."

"And a pretty profit for you?"

"A man should never apologize for success, Aaron," his father advised. "I'll need you and your strong friend here to pack them up and get them ready."

"But Sergio can't pack up books. They're too heavy for . . ." Aaron began to object on Sergio's behalf until he turned around to see Augustus at his shoulder, nodding his approval.

"Then tomorrow it is," Lucre concluded and walked amid the guests.

"Looks like I made work for you again," Aaron apologized to Augustus, who only shrugged off the suggestion.

Behind them a commotion of voices raised as the bride and groom made their way out.

"Where did they say they'd be off to?" Aaron asked. "Oh, that's right," he remembered. "Bruce muttered something to Maddox about taking her to some kingdom."

Chapter 11

He was the quintessential man's man—tall, rugged, capable. He was the go-to man regardless of who was in need or what the issue was at hand. He was a sure and steady peg in the wall on which everyone could hang their heaviest burden and feel assured it would be handled well.

And yet, the puzzle of his bachelorhood remained a burning question for all who considered such gossip. Which woman would finally win his heart and his hand?

Those who asked such questions missed half of the equation— the male half, where the answer could be found. Many answers, in fact. And often. Always with discretion. Always in well-held confidence so no scandal ever emerged. Until that turn of events that turned the equation from addition to subtraction. One lover died. And then another, and another. Many more were sick, and soon he, too, joined that list.

And just as with all his confidential friends, he, too, soon withered and died in isolation. One case alone among a mountain of other cases, each in isolation. It would not be until much later, when connections could be made and conclusions could be drawn…conclusions even involving this man's man.

Chapter 12

Ever since returning from the reception, Blythe sat before her easel posed as an artist angrily unwilling to work. Brush in hand, she refused to look up at the empty canvas, her arms and legs crossed, her shoulders and head turned away from what one might presume should be her focus.

A decade's worth of refining artistry surrounded her. Each piece hung in the chronology of its completion, lovingly preserved by a mother who could ill-afford the expense of each frame, but who insisted on it nonetheless. Iris revered the beauty her daughter could create, beauty Blythe knew her mother felt but could not express in the limited vocabulary of life's experiences accumulated with such a pragmatic man as Duffy. Iris's palette was limited to flour and water and yeast, and golden browns.

Blythe hated having her work around her as she started a new painting. She felt closed in by each piece, but knew their practical effect was to drive her deeper into herself, from there to extract something truthful and filled with beauty, even as her consciousness felt quite the opposite.

Before she could raise the brush that was still damp with her blood, Blythe heard the front door slowly creak open then shut without her father's customary thud that rattled all of Iris's precious knickknacks. It was her mother returning early—and alone—from the reception.

Having sat contorted and still for so long, Blythe moved stiffly. She rolled down her sleeves, tenting them so they wouldn't catch on the still-fresh wound.

Blythe turned her head to listen more clearly as her mother laboriously climbed each step—one, then another, then another, then another—the heavy feet expressing for Blythe how heavy her mother's heart must feel. The sight of Duffy and Parissa's public flirtation and her mother's cowed and pained expression remained vivid for Blythe. She wished her father could be in the room with her just then, that she could make him hear how his wife slowly creaked up the stairs, her spirit sapped, walking like an old woman because he made her feel old. Blythe wished to force him to listen, to make him regret how he drained the strength of the woman who loved him better than any other person could.

"She loves you more than you deserve to be loved," she wanted to scream at him.

As Iris reached the landing, Blythe heard the muffled thump of her mother dropping a stack of laundered clothes at her daughter's door. Blythe knew Iris was retreating to her bed, but for both their mutual sake at that needful moment, Blythe didn't want to give her mother that option. She called out, "Mother?"

Blythe heard Iris pause, unsure of whether to just ignore the call and continue to her room, or to respond. It was the moment of indecision Blythe needed to change her mother's path.

"Can you come in?" Blythe asked uncertain whether she had any consolation to offer. She heard her mother stoop with great effort and retrieve the pile of clothes.

Iris slowly entered. Half hidden behind the door, she bravely lied, "I thought you might be asleep," to explain her unusually quiet ascent up the stairs. "I have your laundry here. Shall I leave it on your bed?"

"Thank you," Blythe responded.

Iris said with faux cheer, "I know we have a rule about not seeing your paintings before they're finished, but I can tell by the colors left on your smock this time that there's a lot of that deep red. There were no other colors on it."

Blythe silently put down her brush.

Iris picked up a smock, "The other colors quickly wash away, but that dark red stains the deepest."

She turned a sleeve inside out and began rubbing the little spots that remained, holding it out for her daughter to see. She said, "It bleeds right into the cloth. It leaves its marks on the inside where only you and I know it's there. The best I can do is scrub them to light pink, but they are permanent, I'm afraid. They've become part of the fabric. You should be more careful with that color."

Blythe suggested weakly, "You shouldn't try so hard to wash it away."

"That's not in a mother's nature, Blythe," Iris said. "A mother wants everything like new for her child."

"I guess some things can't be washed away," Blythe said softly, still straining to find words that could restore her mother's spirit. In the awkward pause that remained, Blythe blurted out before she could consider the propriety of her question, "Why do you think Aaron doesn't ignore Parissa when she acts like that?"

Iris had been on her way to the door but stopped. Her back to her daughter, she gazed absently toward the many paintings and responded, "I suppose it's because she makes herself available...because she's beautiful and young and she shows an interest in him, Blythe."

"But how is that different than what I offer him?"

"Well," Iris began heavily, "I suppose those are mostly the reasons your father was so taken by her."

"But father...." Blythe began defensively before her mother silenced her by holding up one hand.

"But for a young man like Aaron," Iris continued, "Parissa would also be new...someone who would offer the attraction of something different for him."

"And for men, new is better?"

"They get old and tired in their comfortable routines that they

Blythe

demand we create for them, but expect us to remain forever new, dear," Iris said, seemingly losing what little reserve of energy she possessed. She looked out the back window into the rain, resting her hand on the bedpost for support. The rain pot in her bedroom played a symphony of notes with all the drops it caught.

"Please, dear," Iris instructed maternally without even looking back at Blythe, "Don't chew your nails."

Blythe lowered her hand from her mouth, never realizing it had risen there in the first place.

"We grow older, Blythe," Iris said. "And when your father or Aaron do what they did tonight, well, that just makes us older, and so it feeds on itself. The more their eyes wander, the older we get, and the older we get, the more their eyes wander."

Blythe presumed, "And the younger they feel."

"For a short time," Iris answered. "For a short time they recapture some youth. But in time the guilt of those distractions ages men even more quickly than it does us. Everyone loses. No one is left better by those distractions."

Iris tried to maintain her brave face and laughed. "The worst part is, you get older and the Parissas get younger."

There was an awkward pause until Iris concluded, "I know Aaron loves you, Blythe, but he's young. Any man's head would be turned by the kind of attention Parissa gave him. It doesn't make it right, but that's just the way most men and some young women are. She has nothing on you, though, dear. Don't ever forget that."

"Thank you, Mother. That helps," Blythe said sweetly, hoping her own consolation would console her mother.

After Iris disappeared into her room for the night, Blythe went to work, madly mixing colors on the palette and spreading them about the canvas with a broad brush. Sweeps of paint became gowns and suits flowing in the motion of a dance while off to the side in more muted tones, sat a solitary doughy figure slumped over a table with the impression of a glass in her hand. And to the other side of the dancing couples was a more slender figure, whose body faced the dancers but whose head bowed away from them looking down at her upturned hand which punctuated her gracefully extended arm. The two women looked away from the lithe figure at the center whose hand rested on the arm of a portly man. The focal point of the painting, their heads were tossed back in laughter oblivious to dark edges of sorrow that grew out of the painting's outer frame.

The painting was perfection. It flowed effortlessly from Blythe's brushes to convey everything that had transpired only hours before.

She examined it, but there was no appreciation for what she had created. It was too close to how she felt.

As her eyes drifted across the canvas and rested for a moment on each of the characters, she absently reached out and took a palette knife in her hand. She scraped the canvas nearly clean, until only a cartoon of the original image remained. She then spread out a copious stock of white pigment and even as she studied the various images, she began spreading out wide swaths of white across the still-tacky paint covering each and every detail until her mother's bowed head and Blythe's own hand were the only impressions that remained. She drenched the brush one final time in the white island and with two strokes back and forth took away her mother's pain and then, with two more, her own. What only moments before had been her finest work was now the foundation for something else; the hurt she had felt was transformed into white canvas on which she could create anything she chose. It was entirely within her control.

Or so she hoped.

Through the drying white veneer, hints of colors began seeping back to the surface. The effect of her whitewash was not to forever obliterate the scene but instead to merely scumble it, the vivid colors repressed as if caught in a fog.

Never considering whether or not her mother was asleep or would in a moment reenter her studio room, Blythe raised her sleeve and pinched open the sores that had begun to coagulate. Across the muted tones, Blythe traced fine ribbons of her blood, adding somber shadows to her own self-portrait, casting a lengthy drop shadow at her father's and Parissa's feet, and finally, creating a sad triangle of darkness beneath her

Blythe

mother's bowed head and between her two outstretched arms.

Just as with the memory of the evening, the painting would not allow itself to be destroyed.

Blythe bowed her head on her arms and cried inconsolably and in silence.

Chapter 13

Robed in white, Father Philip haunted the corner of the village green, nearly imperceptible in the shade of the oak's low-hung limbs. He looked out at the valley's youth who had drifted there throughout the night for their trysts and who remained spent and still, men atop women, men with men, women nestled into women, women clung to men.

Here was Sunday morning in the valley.

He whispered to himself, "Ecstasy without joy."

Philip's face held no fascination, only pity that they had wasted themselves when he knew life could offer them something better. He stood there, unsure if he could speak any words to get through to them.

Without a conscious effort to seek them out, words formed in his mouth. Unable to restrain them, he bellowed, "Professing themselves to be wise, they became fools!"

All were startled awake, certain they had heard something, but unsure what it was. Had they heard a voice shouting over them, calling down to them?

Giving their anxious sputtering time to spread, Father Philip repeated from his concealment, "Professing themselves to be wise, they became fools!"

They were each suddenly aware of their own nakedness. Even the boldest hurriedly stood and dressed.

Father Philip confidently strode out among them. As he did so, he pleaded in a kind voice, "Please, stay. Listen. I have something that each of you should hear."

One young girl hastily made her way to the green's fringe.

"Stay!" he yelled in her direction.

She froze.

Then he asked more sweetly after she stopped, "Please, stay."

The girl sat down where she had stood.

He continued to walk to the center of them and said, "The words I just called out to you weren't mine. These were Paul the Apostle's words. Maybe you've heard of him. Paul was speaking about the youth of another valley—Rome—in another time. But ask yourselves: Does this apply to me; could Paul have been talking right now to me? Take just a moment to listen to what I have to say, then, if you want, leave. I am not here to stop you. But I think you need to hear this."

To his astonishment, they stayed.

Without the aid of a Bible or notes, Father Philip recited the passage in a strong but caring voice, "While claiming to be wise, they became fools and exchanged the glory of the immortal God for the likeness of an image of mortal man or of birds or of four-legged animals or of snakes. Therefore, God handed them over to impurity through the lusts of their hearts for the mutual degradation of their bodies. They exchanged the truth of God for a lie and revered and worshiped the creature rather than the Creator, who is blessed forever. Amen."

Out of the habit of religious training, a few of those gathered responded out loud, "Amen." Those who did not, looked at them quizzically. Father Philip could see that the ones who spoke, however, did not act ashamed of their spontaneous response. Instead, they looked stoically up to the speaker giving his words that much more validity.

It was to Philip's great fortune that at that precise moment, the sun came out from behind a cloud making his robe so white that those gathered around him had to close their eyes from the intensity of the reflection. He watched as they closed their eyes and listened to his words as he continued. "Therefore, God handed them over to degrading passions. Their females exchanged natural relations for unnatural, and the males likewise gave up natural relations with females and burned with lust for one another. Males did shameful things with males and thus received in their own persons the due penalty for their perversity."

"Listen to what Paul is saying," he urged, then continued with the passage, "And since they did not see fit to acknowledge God, God handed them over to their undiscerning mind to do what is improper. They are filled with every form of wickedness, evil, greed, and malice; full of envy, murder, rivalry, treachery, and spite. They are gossips and scandalmongers and they hate God. They are insolent, haughty, boastful, ingenious in their wickedness, and rebellious toward their parents. They are senseless, faithless, heartless, ruthless. Although they know the just decree of God that all who practice such things deserve death, they not only do them but give approval to those who practice them."

He paused to look at them. His eyes swept them and studied each face or bowed head as they passed. "These are Paul's words to the Romans. Did you know Rome is a valley like we are in? This valley is Rome. These words were written for you. I have no doubt that last night you had ecstasy here on this green."

He could hear some laughter at the bluntness of his words, at a priest's willingness to acknowledge so openly such a topic. It held their attention as he continued. "You had ecstasy. But you had no joy," he said with profound sorrow on their behalf. "I can see some heads nodding in recognition of what I just said. Last night you had the intensity of physical feeling, but it was momentary; there was nothing lasting to it; there was no lasting joy involved in what you did. Now you have a hollow, empty feeling…a feeling that you are unclean."

He paused to let the words sink in. "You can have sex, and have ecstasy and have joy. But not like this. You can't have joy doing that in a place like this and not in that way. But you can and should have sex. And enjoyment. And joy. And you will only have it in the right time and place and with the right partner. You've heard these words before. You may not have wanted to believe them last night or you may have been talked out of them, but I know that you believe them now."

More heads bowed in recognition of what the priest was saying.

"Let me invite those of you who want to, to stay," he said. "The rest of you—who want something better, deeper, more filling, more joyful—come, follow me. I'm going to the church on top of this hill where the congregation is gathered waiting to welcome you. Don't be frightened," he said quickly, so as not to lose them. "They are not there to judge. I've already spoken with them. They are there to offer you hot and cold cloths to clean your hands and faces: to wash last night off of you, for good. They are also there with food and drinks, but most of all they are there to welcome you back to a place that is God's house, a place of forgiveness, a place of joy. I've spoken to them and they genuinely want to share that joy with you. Those of you who wish to stay here, stay. The rest, come with me!"

He walked his straight and purposeful line without looking back, hoping perhaps one or two would follow his way. As much as he wanted to turn around to see if anyone followed his lead, he knew he could not look back; to do so would be a sign of doubt. He did not want to become like Lot's wife, turned into a pillar of salt. He told himself as he walked, "To win them, you must believe that you've already won them."

At that moment, however, he heard some young girls laughing. He had not made it twenty steps, and he could hear them laugh.

"Perhaps they are laughing at me," he thought. "No matter."

He continued up the hill.

He listened intently for the sound of other feet on the cobblestones he walked, but he could not hear any. He continued climbing up in the direction of the church.

Back up the hill, Father Philip approached the church. He was certain he had heard at least one set of feet behind him, but there was no talk, no whispers, nothing to give him any confidence that so many as two people had taken up his offer.

He reached his hand out, opened the door, then stood to the side to welcome whomever it was who followed him. His face illuminated as Sergio walked by, followed by Sylvia and another dozen young people.

"Welcome," he said to each as they entered. "Welcome."

Once they were all gathered inside, he walked in. The church was silent as the regular congregation and the new entrants nervously surveyed each other.

"Do we have those hot and cold cloths ready?" Philip called out.

Some of the women sprang into action. The congregation parted to let them through. Those with the hot cloths helped the guests wash their faces then their hands. They were followed by another flock of women with cold cloths who silently did the same as everyone watched. Father Philip could see little joyful tears escape from one and then another of the youthful gathering at the comforting, refreshing sensations.

"Do we have some breakfast for these people?" Philip asked. "They must be hungry."

From the side aisles of the church, men and women came forward with warm plates of food and silently handed them to each of their guests. Then, plates were passed throughout the congregation so the guests would feel comfortable to eat as the others did.

While they were eating, Father Philip stood in the center of the congregation that filled the pews and each aisle. He said in a warm, public voice, "Let us take a moment to thank the Lord for this day, for this meal, and for the blessing of these young people who have decided to come here to find the peace of forgiveness and God's joy. Our Father, thank you for the many blessings of this day. You created the darkness and the light and have taught us that we are the children of the light. Bless all gathered here and bless this food, which we are about to eat. Let it strengthen our bodies, and we turn to you to strengthen our souls against the temptation and snares of this world. Be with us always, and let us always be with you."

All responded, "Amen."

As they ate, Father Philip took his place again in the center of the church. Again without the aid of any text, he recited a passage from Luke's gospel.

"A Pharisee invited Jesus to dine with him, and he entered the Pharisee's house and reclined at table. Now there was a sinful woman in the city who learned that he was at table in the house of the Pharisee. Bringing an alabaster flask of ointment, she stood behind him at his feet

Blythe

weeping and began to bathe his feet with her tears. Then she wiped them with her hair, kissed them, and anointed them with the ointment. When the Pharisee who had invited him saw this he said to himself, 'If this man were a prophet, he would know who and what sort of woman this is who is touching him, that she is a sinner.' Jesus said to him in reply, 'Simon, I have something to say to you.' 'Tell me, teacher,' he said. 'Two people were in debt to a certain creditor; one owed five hundred days' wages and the other owed fifty. Since they were unable to repay the debt, he forgave it for both. Which of them will love him more?' Simon said in reply, 'The one, I suppose, whose larger debt was forgiven.' He said to him, 'You have judged rightly.' Then he turned to the woman and said to Simon, 'Do you see this woman? When I entered your house, you did not give me water for my feet, but she has bathed them with her tears and wiped them with her hair. You did not give me a kiss, but she has not ceased kissing my feet since the time I entered. You did not anoint my head with oil, but she anointed my feet with ointment. So I tell you, her many sins have been forgiven; hence, she has shown great love. But the one to whom little is forgiven, loves little.' He said to her, 'Your sins are forgiven.' The others at table said to themselves, 'Who is this who even forgives sins?' But he said to the woman, 'Your faith has saved you; go in peace.'"

Father Philip looked seriously about the room. "There is no place here today for conflicts or guilt, only celebration. The first thing we did upon entering today was to cleanse ourselves. We are all now in a state of grace. Let our actions to each other show that. Today is the day of the clean start."

Chapter 14

Augustus and Aaron labored on in their rodellé with neither possessing a distinct advantage and, as in all their earlier tumbles, with no one else in sight; Aaron flaunted his prowess, in wrestling and otherwise, before any available audience, but Augustus, as with other facets of his life, kept his skills to himself, exercising them only for his own satisfaction or for that of his closest friend and only companion, Aaron.

At last, Augustus, with his hands gripped together over Aaron's chest, lowered his elbows locking Aaron's arms to his side. It would not provide the definitive pin each had sought, but it secured a stalemate that made it impossible for Aaron to move his arms. His legs had been long-since immobilized.

Aaron was trapped; his panic set in.

Those frantic moments—when Aaron realized freedom was an impossibility, when claustrophobia found its form—turned him into something wild, something irrational, something inhuman.

As if they were somehow distinct from his form and not already part of him, he consciously pleaded with each group of muscles, starting with his shoulders and finishing with his feet, to somehow help him break free. Augustus could feel the rapid and steady descent of Aaron's pleadings as parts of his foe's body shook fiercely to wiggle free. Still imprisoned,

Aaron's entire body convulsed wildly, screaming to himself in the silence of his thoughts that he must be free. He strained everything within him in revolution and in terror to free himself from Augustus's grip. But he could not.

He let out a shrill, exasperated shriek of surrender. This was a sound Augustus had grown accustomed to in their challenges. This signaled the end of their match.

Although it was true that Aaron had never lost a match between them, he had never beaten Augustus. The best either of them could muster, it seemed, was a draw: a mutual agreement neither to victory nor defeat with neither able to pin his opponent's knees to his chin. Augustus, however, always had the better of the match. Aaron, inevitably, ended up contorted and unable to move, though he was not technically defeated. Their rodellé bouts stretched on longer and longer but always ended in stalemate, with Aaron on the defensive.

Just as he had always done at these moments, Augustus flung the sweaty and twitching Aaron beyond arm's reach, beyond where Aaron could lash back at him out of captivity's reflexive hatred.

Augustus, battle weary, dropped to a crouching position, then rolled to his back, spent and splayed on the dusty hardwood floor of Old Lucre's basement.

"I think you toy with me," Aaron admitted. "I think you could pin me in no time or snap my neck if you wanted, but you play with me."

Augustus didn't respond. He remained on his back looking up at the bare boarded ceiling, his sides heaving for air.

It was early evening, but this being summer, the full light of day strained to make its way in through the dirty windows.

Up the stairs, the door opened and Old Lucre called down, "You down there, Aaron?"

"I'm here," he said.

"What are you doing down there?" his father asked.

"Augustus and I were in a rodellé."

"When there's work to be done?" his father bellowed. "Get your shirts on and get up here."

Muttering under his breath, Aaron rose and followed his father's order, helping Augustus up as well.

Aaron and Augustus plodded up the stairs and into Old Lucre's shop, their hair and clothes still disheveled from the tussling. A few people, including Sylvia, milled around the low aisles filling the small baskets they carried over their arms. Maddox read quietly behind the counter. He gave them a disinterested glance as they entered.

Old Lucre stared over at the two young men with a look of reproach. He pantomimed to them to tidy up, straightening his own hair and quickly pulling his shirt down neatly. They obliged.

"Aaron, I'll need you upstairs for a moment," Old Lucre said. "Augustus, you and Maddox mind things here."

No sooner had Aaron and Lucre left then Notté strode in, his long black hair curling and tumbling over the collar of his unbuttoned white shirt that seemed all the more brilliant against his dark skin. He tucked his thumbs into the front of his dark red pants as he surveyed the room.

Maddox looked over without changing his expression of boredom then returned to his book. Neither in any way acknowledged the other.

Notté crossed his arms and strolled up the aisle next to Sylvia, nonchalantly taking in the shelves both figuratively and literally as he slipped little items into his baggy pockets.

He pretended not to see one of the valley Hens as he stole up next to her. He followed her closely, stride for stride, letting her maintain a slight lead. Apparently lost in his thoughts, he refused to look at her as she stopped and glanced over her shoulder to see who followed her so closely. At that precise moment, with Notté's eyes still fixed on the contents of the shelves, he let his arms swing down loosely, his hand gently tracing her behind.

He swung around to her in shock as she let out a little exasperated cry. Notté quickly and profusely apologized, "Scuzé, scuzé!" holding up his hands to signal he meant no offense, that the contact was every bit as much a surprise to him as it was to her. His sincerity told her that perhaps she shared in the blame for their accidental encounter.

The Hen looked up from his taut, exposed chest to the endearing,

Blythe

bewildered expression on his face. Flushed, flustered, and perhaps a little flattered, she gave him an understanding, uncomfortable laugh to ease his concern.

More importantly for Notté, Sylvia guffawed not so much at the perceived innocent affront as at his entire manipulation of the scene. How Sylvia reacted wasn't important to Notté; it was that she reacted. Each understood that everything he had done since entering Lucre's was entirely for her benefit. He turned down her aisle and flashed a well-rehearsed, befuddled smile. Notté strolled up right behind her then turned away in sudden disinterest—perhaps too sudden, he thought, in his well-trained style—toward the shelf opposite from hers.

"You've got quick hands," she said without turning around.

"I didn't see her there," he objected.

"I'm talking about what you stole."

"Does it bother you?" he deflected. "What is in my pants…does it bother you?"

She blushed a little at his awkward phrasing but went beyond it. She turned toward him and said, "It should bother you…taking what isn't yours."

"I take what I like," he responded casually, making sure as he turned that their arms rubbed ever so slightly.

Sylvia stared contemptuously at the transparency of his effort. She turned and walked away.

Coming up behind her, he whispered, "You are not interested?"

Just at that moment, the Hen walked by, evidently lost in the expanding memory of their accidental interplay. She smiled warmly at him, unaware of or unconcerned with his closeness to Sylvia. It was a look he reciprocated out of habit, even going so far as to spin himself around to watch her as she passed so they might continue their flirtation. He stopped everything to give the Hen his full attention. She drank it in.

As soon as she moved on to pay for her goods, Notté turned away. The moment he was certain she could no longer see his expression, a look of dismissive disgust filled his face, a look he was only slightly aware of until he found himself suddenly face-to-face with Sylvia, who scrutinized him. Upon seeing his telling look, she became his mirror, offering him the same disgusted expression.

Notté quickly smiled, trying unsuccessfully to recover…to casually throw off how he had looked as nothing telling, as nothing important. His smile tried to convince her, "That expression was merely how I feel about her, you understand, and you really can't blame me for feeling that way. Look at her. And look at me. Can you imagine what possible interest I would have in such a woman? But you are special because you understand why I had to smile and how I truly feel about her…and about you at whom I am now smiling sincerely."

His smile tried to sell all of this.

But Sylvia would buy none of it. She looked at him and laughed.

"What?" he asked, offended.

She said, "You flash your teeth like an animal—to mask your weakness."

Notté's facial cast changed again. He recognized she was unrecoverable.

"I'm sorry," he said with perfect sincerity. "I didn't know you like women."

Sylvia looked up at him, dumbfounded at his remark and how suddenly he had turned on her. She tried to correct him, but he raised his hands to stop her.

"It's all right," he said. "I wouldn't want such a plain cow anyway."

Notté casually strolled away.

The suddenness of his transformation left Sylvia stunned; his arrogance left her breathless. Certainly she had no interest in him, but for some reason he stirred in her the need to defend herself. As she stood there blinking, all she could utter with everything swirling around in her mind was the beginning of a thought, the first word of which escaped her lips before she could scare up even one more word to follow it. "You . . ." she trailed off.

He turned back to her and in the same hushed, drawn-out tone responded like a cow, "Mooooo."

She remained frozen by his rudeness.

Blythe

But that was not the end of it; transformed again, he sprang back to her. He leaned in close to her face and growled.

Sylvia questioned herself. Was she sure about it? Had he actually growled?

He had. Staring directly into her eyes, he let out a growl that was low, fierce and certain.

In a flash, Notté snatched something from her basket. What it was she didn't see. Despite his closeness, he gave an extra little lunge, his face darting directly at hers, nearly striking their noses. As he did so, he snapped his teeth so they came together with a crisp click.

Sylvia recoiled in the knowledge that the person standing before her was capable of anything; there was no predicting him. He was confident she could not bring herself to look around for help. She did not dare take her eyes off of him. He made her senseless with fear.

He slowly leaned in again, forcing her to lean back. She blinked quickly with revulsion and uncertainty, half expecting to be mauled by those beautiful white teeth he had a few moments before displayed in a smile. Her lips drew back and her chin fell as if hoping to guard against a quick snap at her neck.

Notté studied her with a closed-lip smile and bright, inquisitive eyes. Clearly, he liked the effect he was having on her.

Then, without warning, Notté spun on his heels. He slipped whatever it was he held in his hand into his pocket and was gone.

Sylvia stood there for a long moment, as if still seeing him before her, as if, somehow, he was still present right there despite the fact that she sensed him leave in her peripheral view. As she slowly awoke to the realization that he had left, she became aware of how rigid every muscle in her body stood. She felt as if an invisible cast covered her entire body. She tried to move. The best she could do was to shake.

Three aisles away, Augustus stood up from his work stocking the lower shelves. He looked over at Sylvia's trembling profile. Making his way over to her, he gently took her by the arm and walked her to the counter. Still in a daze, she let Augustus unload her items, which Maddox added to the ledger.

Maddox looked at her and asked Augustus, "She finally realized how much my father is gouging her?"

Augustus only shrugged and continued unloading her things.

Sylvia didn't speak. She began to break down as Augustus gathered her purchases and carefully placed them in a bag. He guided her to the door, swung it open, and escorted her away as Maddox looked on.

Lucre and Aaron pounded down the stairs.

Lucre called out on his descent, "Augustus, I'll need you and Aaron to go to Bruce's to pack up his books."

Rounding the corner into the room, Lucre surveyed the store for Augustus. "Augustus?" he called out.

"Not here," Maddox answered.

"Well, where is he?" Lucre asked.

Maddox did not look up as he responded, "He walked out without saying anything."

"Well, no surprise there," Lucre said. "Aaron, find him and get his help. Even with him, you'll be lucky to finish tonight. Bring the entire collection here to the basement when you're done. I've got two buyers coming."

Aaron asked, "Why would Bruce suddenly sell everything it took a lifetime to collect?"

"He has different priorities now, I suppose," Lucre answered in a tone that struck Aaron as uncharacteristically melancholy for his father. "Other things are more important than a pile of old books."

"Oh," Aaron said, presuming some memory of his mother must have filled his father's mind. "He's a married man now."

"Yes," Lucre answered absently. "I suppose that, too."

"Well, you'll get him and Gwen a good price for them, I'm sure," Aaron reassured his father. "It will be a nice gift for their return."

"They won't be returning, Aaron," Lucre said. "They've…they've decided not to. I'll miss her especially. She was a dear one."

"Well, it's not like they can't return someday," Aaron said.

Lucre stared at Maddox who continued reading. Something in the man made him enraged. He shouted at his son, "Why don't you make

Blythe

yourself useful!"

Unfazed, Maddox looked up at his father, his placid expression never changing. He turned a page and returned to his reading.

Aaron was surprised by the sudden anger of the exchange, but not by Maddox's response or by his father's lack of follow through. As much as he would have liked to see his father throw Maddox off of his stool and lay him out with one of the big man's fists, he knew that would not happen.

Aaron asked, "So if he's given you his entire collection to sell and he's not returning, where does the money go?"

"He gave me instructions, but they are none of your concern, Aaron," Lucre snapped. "Why don't you be off and find Augustus? Your business is to pack the books with that friend of yours and bring them back here."

"But…." Aaron objected.

"It was his decision," Lucre snapped again. "He gave me the books and told me to sell them for whatever I could get for them, and that is exactly what I'm going to do, keeping *The Crooner* for myself," he said, pointing the words at the unresponsive Maddox.

"Will he help?" Aaron asked, looking at his brother.

"Does he ever?" his father responded.

Aaron shook his head and went on his way to find Augustus.

Chapter 15

It wasn't solely the surface-stinging, bone-deep pain of the open sores scarring his body that made him lay still and silent in his bed; it was the heavy recognition that no one—not one person in his life—was left to raise him for even one dignified moment out of so pitiful a state. No one survived to clean the filth in which he lay or to momentarily break his fever's spell with a cool cloth to his temples. All those he had known and loved in his life were dead. He saw each of them die one by one before him, providing a thousand unwanted lessons about the slow-motion and unstoppable assault that soon awaited him. Ignoring those daunting insights, he extended complete kindness to each as they suffered in their last hours, a kindness he wished someone could reciprocate. His once-proud and manly frame wasn't even a memory anymore. Translucent skin draped over angles of bones, and veins pulsed visibly along his temples even as he rested. It was the only movement in the room, but that, too, would be stilled within the day.

Chapter 16

No one had seen Sundar for weeks before Aaron learned of his return. Excited to see his friend and hear about his latest adventure, Aaron suggested to Augustus that they stop by Sundar's on their way to pack Bruce's library.

"Knock again," Aaron suggested as he cut across the lawn to a front window. "Augustus," Aaron said as he stared in. "The place is empty."

Augustus walked over to see for himself. Each room that they could see was completely cleared out. They looked at each other in disbelief.

"You heard he came back, right?" Aaron asked.

Augustus nodded.

Aaron continued, "Did you hear anything about him leaving?"

Augustus shook his head.

Aaron looked back in the window and said, "This is bizarre."

"He's gone," said a voice from behind.

Duffy walked toward them from the street. He said, "You missed him by about a day. What a tragedy."

"What happened?" Aaron asked.

Duffy said, "Sundar came back very sick. Do you have any idea where he's been?"

Both young men shook their heads.

Duffy continued, "No one knows. But wherever it was, he caught something that clogged his lungs. His parents cared for him, but he died within a few days. I know he was a friend of yours. I'm sorry."

"He's dead?" Aaron asked. "Sundar is dead?"

Duffy said, "It is a tragedy, Aaron, but it happens."

Aaron asked, "Duffy, could this be connected to that body Blythe and I found up at the...."

"Aaron," Duffy cautioned. "Don't bring that up again. You and I went all over that place and didn't find so much as a dead flower. Let it go."

Aaron looked at him with perfect frustration. "Duffy, I'm telling the truth. There was someone there. Your own daughter says there was someone there."

"Absolutely, absolutely," Duffy laughed. "Hence my skepticism."

Aaron continued, "Whether you believe it or not, there was. Could that be connected to Sundar?"

"Aaron, we're treating Sundar's death like any other death in any other similar circumstance," Duffy said. "Death happens, Aaron. Your friend lived pretty wildly. And this wasn't the first time that he went missing for a while. You know that better than I do. We have to just look at this as a payment for all his hard living."

Aaron asked, "What was it?"

Duffy said, "His parents said his lungs just filled up and he couldn't breathe anymore."

"Pneumonia?" Aaron asked.

"I suppose," Duffy answered. "They were with him and said he didn't suffer too much at the end, if that helps you at all. He went quickly."

Aaron and Augustus stared at the grass and shook their heads trying to understand all they had just learned.

As they walked away from the home, Aaron asked, "Where did all their furniture go? And all their art? And where did Sundar's parents move?"

Duffy shrugged, "Well, that's none of my business, Aaron. All I know is what they told me. I can't tell you anymore."

John E. Kramer   108

As they parted, Duffy called back to Aaron and Augustus, "You two were always the straight ones in that bunch you run with. You work hard and you're good fellows. I'm not saying what happened to Sundar could happen to you or anyone else, but there is no reason not to be a little careful. Stay close to your family and to your work and I'm sure you won't have trouble like your friend here. Who knows where he was when he caught whatever killed him. Don't mess around like Sundar did. This valley needs good men like you."

With that, Duffy turned and walked briskly away.

"You both are a couple of good young men," Aaron mocked under his breath. "This valley needs men like you."

As they walked on, it began to hit home for Aaron.

"Sundar is dead, Augustus," Aaron said in disbelief. "He's dead. I don't even know what that means."

They walked over one of the many bridges that crossed the canal and, just as they had done each time they crossed since they were children, they picked up one stone each and dropped them in. They watched the tiny ripples form and grow, get carried along in the slow-moving water then vanish beneath the span. All traces of the marks they had made disappeared silently and forever.

When they reached Bruce's home, the impeccably maintained Tudor exterior showed splashes of mud along its base from the recent rainstorm.

"That would have driven Bruce batty," Aaron laughed, pointing it out to his friend. "Let's take a couple of buckets out here when we're done and clean that off for him."

Aaron reached into his pocket and pulled out the key. Along with it came the ring he carried for Blythe. It caught Augustus' eye.

"Someday soon." Aaron smiled.

They worked for many hours until all that remained was a final bookshelf that filled the back wall of the rear room. Unlike the other walls, which had a window here or there, this was a solid wall of books, owing to the earthen embankment that lay behind it.

"Weighty thoughts in heavy volumes," Aaron grunted, as he

Blythe

stacked a full box on top of another. "My back is telling me that there is no such thing as a little light reading."

He turned back to the shelf.

"What's this?" he asked. He opened a small and familiar book to the first page and read aloud, "Ex libris Aaron Lucre. Maddox must have lifted it from me and given it to Bruce. Well, one good turn deserves another," and he set it aside to take home.

Aaron began his work from the left side of the shelf, Augustus from the right. Box after box they raced each other to see who could reach the center first and pack into the other's territory. Aaron had won the competition on each of the previous shelves and finally he wondered whether Augustus wasn't having a little fun at his expense, letting him win and consequently shoulder most of the work. Regardless, Aaron was so competitive he would take any victory he could find.

Having cleared the center shelves, Aaron reached up to the next top shelf to begin boxing another column of books when the entire section removed itself from the wall and began toppling over on him. Aaron would have been crushed if not for Augustus' reflexes. Hearing the first creak and looking up to see the shelf tipping out, Augustus lunged at Aaron and knocked him across the room and into some boxes, then, at the last possible moment, he pulled in his legs to get them out of harm's way. The entire section of bookshelf with all its heavy contents crashed to the floor. When they stood up to assess the damage, Aaron and Augustus were stunned to find a passageway revealed.

They peered into the darkness.

"Where do you suppose it goes?" Aaron asked.

Augustus shook his head as he squinted to look deeper into the tunnel.

The knob on the front door rattled and the door creaked open. Aaron and Augustus looked at each other, then at the hole. Old Lucre called out in his staccato, "Well done, boys. You finished?"

"Just about," Aaron called back. He stood to one side of the section, Augustus to the other. They lifted it with ease and placed it back where it belonged, its back wall covering the passageway entirely. All that remained of the mishap was the pile of books that lay tossed about the floor.

Old Lucre stepped into the room where they were already back at work.

"When these are boxed, leave them here," he instructed. "The second buyer's men will take these right where they are; the first already picked up the ones you stacked in my basement. Good thing, too," he said. "Looks like we'll need the room with everything we have coming in."

Aaron and Augustus looked at each other as Old Lucre scanned what they had accomplished. Neither of them liked the sound of that.

Blythe

Chapter 17

Kagetsu rose up the hill toward the church. Until her chance passing on the green when she overheard Father Philip's invitation—a plea meant for others—she had never before been inside the church. Having found it a welcoming and contemplative place, however, she returned often for evening services.

On her ascent, Notté pulled alongside her, matching her pace.

"Good evening," he said. "You go to the church, as well?"

She bowed to him with a polite smile, the straight line of her shiny black bangs dipping even with her eyes as she watched him. Kagetsu continued silently on her way.

"This hill is murderous," Notté said. "You make it look easy, how you glide."

Again, she turned and smiled, but Notté, having a careful eye for such details, recognized that she offered a slightly more shallow bow. He held his tongue until he considered speaking an absolute necessity.

Notté gallantly extended his hand to help her up the steep stairs.

"You've been cut," she observed, seeing a deep scar that crossed his palm.

He pulled his hand back reflexively and kept it cupped by his side. "A childhood accident," he explained self-consciously. "I forget it is there…

until someone reminds me."

Kagetsu reached the first step and daintily extended her hand for his.

"I'm sorry," she said in a sincere, even tone. "I did not mean to make you think of it."

Notté sheepishly extended his injured hand, opening it only when it touched hers. Even then, he made sure it remained palm down. They climbed the stairs in silence then turned to enter the church.

They reached the door at the same time as Duffy. He opened it for the couple and let them through. The portly man smiled warmly to Kagetsu but studied Notté as he passed.

"Good evening," Duffy said, to engage the young man. Notté kept his eyes forward on Kagetsu and gave Duffy a little inaudible grunt of thanks as he walked by.

Kagetsu walked through the entrance hall and into the nearly empty nave. A few gray-haired Hens dotted the pews here and there on the right side. She slipped into a pew all the way at the front, hidden behind a pillar.

Notté peeled off and remained in the entranceway, letting Duffy pass him by. The valley peace officer surveyed the young man's back as he passed. Duffy walked all the way down the center aisle and turned left until he reached the sacristy door. He knocked. Father Philip beckoned him in.

Father Philip said as he put on his robes, "What may I do to help you, Duffy? You have not been in here before as I recall."

"No, this is my first time back here," he said. "I always wondered what this room was for, but never really gave it much thought."

"Well, which is it?"

"Which is what, Father?"

"Which is it?" Philip asked. "Did you always wonder what was in this room, or did you never give it much thought?"

"Never given it much thought, I suppose." Duffy laughed nervously. "Funny how you can visit a place every week and not even think about an entire part of it. I guess since I never came back here, I just put it out of my mind."

Father Philip was used to listening carefully to others' words in the confessional and elsewhere. Spoken words always said more than written ones, he felt.

"So what is it you need?" the priest asked as he dressed. "I have a Mass to start in a few moments."

"I just have a brief question, Father." Duffy paused to consider the best phrasing.

"Don't think too much about it, Duffy," Father Philip advised impatiently. "Just let the words form themselves. What is it you want?"

"I was wondering, Father. What if...and this is just a question... what if a man knows of something but he keeps it to himself?"

Philip asked, "Well, knows of what? What kind of a thing?"

"Suppose he knows someone who is bad...who is doing bad things, and suppose he knows that something bad might happen to that person if he...or she...continues doing that bad thing, but I don't tell them and that bad thing happens to them. Would I...would someone get punished for keeping my mouth shut?"

A bell in the church rang, signaling the beginning of the service. Father Philip could picture the five gray heads who had just risen to their feet and turned their eyes to the other side of his door. In no less than five seconds he was expected to emerge from the door as he had punctually for every Mass of his ministry.

"You say these people are doing bad things?" Father Philip asked hurriedly.

"Yes," Duffy answered.

"And these people know that they are doing bad things, but they continue to do them nonetheless?" the priest asked, straightening his robe and only half-considering the question before him.

"Yes, Father," Duffy said. "That's what they're doing."

"Then they are going into the situation with open eyes and open minds, Duffy. We should point out to these people that what they're doing is wrong, but people must be responsible for their own actions. Right?"

"Right, Father. Absolutely, absolutely," Duffy answered, thoroughly relieved. He patted down a crease on the priest's shoulder.

Blythe

"Now I have to go," Father Philip said. He looked down at his robe and asked about the garment, "Do we have this straight?"

"Absolutely, absolutely," Duffy responded to the priest's advice.

Father Philip walked out, his robe askew.

When it came time for the gospel, Father Philip had been lost in thought for quite some time. The little gathering had recited its "Alleluia," anticipating the gospel, and remained standing on their aged and tired legs for many minutes, hoping the priest would soon make his move. It was a long, silent time before the priest finally realized all eyes were fixed on him.

Father Philip speedily rose and read the gospel. He then concluded by calling out well-rehearsed passwords and receiving the appropriate response from the congregation, signaling the time for his homily.

It wasn't until then—when he looked out on the parishioners— that he realized he had stared for so long up at an ornate stained-glass window of Jesus as the Good Shepherd, that the radiant image of his Lord dressed in a flowing, intensely red robe through which the vespertine sun poured—that he recognized the image had been burned onto his eyes; that exact image became superimposed upon each individual standing before him as he looked upon them.

He paused to smile at the imagery. The congregation smiled back.

He looked out on the dwindling congregation and felt a little sad. Just as he took in a breath to continue, Aaron and some other young people he had seen that Sunday morning on the green noisily tramped into the church and filled its back pews; nearly a dozen of them following Aaron's lead. He and the priest gave each other appreciative nods and suddenly Father Philip could not contain his smile.

"Normally it is you confessing to me, but right now I want to confess something to you," Father Philip continued. "When I was sitting up here before—before the gospel—and you waited for I don't know how long for me to walk over here to recite the gospel, I was transfixed by one of our magnificent stained-glass windows: that one, with the Good Shepherd on it," he said.

One of Aaron's compatriots let out a bleat that echoed through the church. Each of the Hens' heads whipped around as if they were owls—

their shoulders barely budged. Kagetsu also turned, though more slowly, to see who it was that would disturb the priest in his own church. On seeing who it was, she turned back around, unimpressed.

"That's okay, ladies," Father Philip quelled the Hens. "You are all welcome here," he called out to the back pews. When he felt he had things back in hand, he said, "I bring this up—the window of the Good Shepherd—because having looked at that beautiful image for so long, with the sunlight illuminating it so brightly as it does, I now have the image of Jesus superimposed on all of you. I am not only seeing you, I am seeing Christ on you…Christ in you…I am seeing Christ as you."

The ladies sat up straighter in their seats and smiled approvingly at each other.

He said, "But as I look at this image, I want to warn you of something. I want to warn you of that very image I now see on you. Jesus was certainly a good shepherd to his people, but, despite the sound I heard earlier from one of my friends in the back, you are not sheep."

He let the words echo off the back stone wall of the church and echo all around them. "You are not sheep…You are not sheep…are not sheep…not sheep."

Upon hearing the echo, he said it again and let the words thunder throughout the church. "You are not sheep…You are not sheep…are not sheep…not sheep."

When the words had died down, he continued. "Despite all the people out there who would demote you to an object, who would reduce you to animal form, you must guard your humanity…guard your humanity…your humanity…humanity.

"Yes, we are created by God with free will, and we can choose to accept or reject Him; we can choose to do what is wrong—what we know in our hearts is wrong—but properly exercised, we must use our free will, use our reason to consider the consequence of our actions and fight within ourselves to do what is right, to do what is just, to do what is good not only in God's sight but in our own.

"The purpose of faith together with free will is to elevate man, to make him a purposeful creature…not a sheep but a free and thinking

117

Blythe

creature capable of achieving greater things than he would absent the knowledge of his Creator. If what you believe does not achieve that end, then it is mere superstition or worse yet, it is a cult of destruction and death. What makes a cult different from a religion? In a religion, God sacrifices himself for his followers. In a cult, the followers sacrifice themselves for their god. True faith operates under the assumption that people are free but not free of accountability. They must reap what they sow. Said another way, you will get what you deserve, but that doesn't have to be a bad thing. That can be a heavenly thing if you believe and let your actions show that you believe. You are accountable."

He looked out on them. The image of Jesus had long since disappeared; these tangible people remained.

"These are the things that make you better than sheep," he said. "These are the things that make you men and women. Don't let faith make you a follower…make you a sheep," he said quietly. "Let faith make you a person."

Father Philip looked up and around at the stained-glass windows that ringed the upper reaches of the church. They all turned dark as the sunlight retreated below the surrounding hills.

"It is night now," he observed. Everyone gathered there looked up and around to see that there was no more light left in the windows. "This is when the world most needs our light, when the world needs the illumination and strength that comes from faith. It is easy to be brave in the day. Only a liar says that he is not afraid in the dark.

"Let me share with you a little poem I wrote some years ago. It explains, especially to our young friends who've just joined us, the effects of faith on darkness in your life, but also how fragile and vulnerable that light is if it is not carefully guarded. The forces of darkness are relentless. They want you to fail—to be blind. Even as darkness shrinks away and hides its face from the light of our goodness, it seeks a way to snuff out that inspiration before it can grow and be shared and be strengthened. It will use your seeming invulnerability as a means to defeat you. But remember; so long as there are lights out there, faith will be preserved, men and women will find their way, lighted by belief. The darkness that we find so rightfully threatening, the darkness that always seems to win, will lose. I call this little poem, 'The Match.'

From the match's first strike
Darkness retreats.
Like all things born of strength
Light finds conceit.
A breeze snuffs out the flame.
All darkness cheats.

"Darkness cheats, my friends," he repeated. "That is why we need as many lights of true faith as we can find to corner it, to expel it. We are the light of the world. Now let us act like it.

"God bless you all. Amen."

Blythe

Chapter 18

He knew by the panicked look in his own eyes that his end was near.

He saw that look in others before their end, and, while it was still within his power, he wanted to avoid that same miserable destiny. He had suffered enough pain and humiliation, enough anxiety and isolation, and he knew from the death of all his friends what lay in store for him in the weeks ahead if he allowed himself to linger in life. He wanted none of it.

He set a stack of boxes high up in the room with a vaulted ceiling, then tied the rope firmly around the exposed beam, more than a full story above the hardwood floor.

His only worry was whether his skinny body still carried enough weight to snap his neck when the rope went taut. He wanted an instant death. He didn't want to suffer another day, least of all dangling at the end of a rope struggling for air for who knew how long.

He slipped the noose around his neck, set the knot so it rested right below his left ear, then tightened the slack. He loosened it a bit to avoid the discomfort of the rope's coarse fibers against his skin. He laughed that that should be his response—not willing to endure a moment's discomfort in the seconds before he would end it all by his own hands.

He took in one last deep breath and, knowing he might talk

himself out of this fate if he delayed, he kicked away the stack and left the world with one quick snap.

Chapter 19

"There is a tension in your work that makes it so alive," the collector said to Blythe. "What is it?"

Iris could not contain herself and proudly chimed in, "She pours her lifeblood into each piece."

Iris turned from the smiling collector and glowed at her daughter but was bewildered by Blythe's injured expression. Since she was a little girl, Blythe's right eye would wander ever so slightly to the outside. When she was being punished, that imperfection only accentuated the little waif's vulnerability beyond anything her mother could restrain herself from consoling. At those moments, no matter how angry Iris had been, she could do nothing but sweep the just-punished child into her arms and hug her so hard her daughter could barely breathe. Iris would dry Blythe's tears as her own flowed uncontrollably and without consideration. It was that same vulnerable expression—of someone who already hurt so deeply receiving yet more suffering—that Blythe gave Iris, all for saying what? That she poured her lifeblood into her work?

Embarrassed, Iris averted her eyes, which settled on the hamper. The red stains. Iris realized; they were not paint.

As Blythe regained her composure and explained what she saw in her own art, she glanced every now and again to her mother, each knowing exactly what the other thought. Neither dared to look long at the other but when their eyes met, as they did time and again, they darted away as the collector continued on and on about how magnificent Blythe's style had become.

"She has the eye for it," he said, as Iris again focused on that ever-so-subtle shift in her daughter's right eye, making her want to wrap up the girl, hold her, ease every pain Blythe felt, inside and out. It was all Iris could do to restrain herself.

As the collector settled on the pieces he would purchase, he asked Blythe again, "That seascape? Is there no way I can talk you into selling that one, as well?"

"That is a gift to my parents," Blythe apologized and watched Iris's expression transform from preoccupation to a moment of joyful surprise. For a moment, Blythe made her mother forget their mutual hurt.

Blythe and Iris wrapped with great care each purchase, tying them all together with twine. As he tucked them under his arm and made his way to Blythe's door, he met Duffy, who tramped heavily up the stairs and stood blocking the doorway, a half sandwich in his hand.

"Took the best of them, did you?" he asked the collector.

"I'm afraid not," he admitted looking back with disappointment to the seascape. "That one is being held for you."

"For me?" Duffy said, his mouth filled with food and his words filled with surprise.

"Blythe's given it to us, dear," Iris informed him.

The collector excused himself and Duffy stood aside. Iris followed him down to show him to the door and as she did, she called to Duffy, "The pot is nearly full again."

Duffy rolled his eyes at Blythe. He walked over to examine again the painting that was now his. "What a day that was," he recalled. "And there! Look there! Do you see that crag in the rocks?"

Blythe said, "I do." She pointed out the obvious, "Father, I painted it."

"Do you remember how your mother and I begged you not to go out there? But there you went, out as far as you could go, and then you sat down on the very edge and let your feet hang over. Oh, you nearly killed your mother on that day."

Blythe laughed, her eyes turning to two crescents arched between her high cheekbones and the lush brown of her eyebrows, as he continued, "Always the intrepid one. Always having to put yourself on the edge to prove that you're fearless."

The door downstairs closed. Iris called up, "Duffy? The pot?"

Duffy stuffed the rest of the sandwich in his mouth as he gave one final look to the painting.

"It's beautiful," he mumbled and kissed Blythe on her forehead leaving little crumbs behind that she quickly wiped away.

As her father left, Blythe sprang down the stairs between the rhythm of the drops.

"I'm going out for the evening, Mother," she said to Iris as she passed. "I'll be with Aaron."

Before Iris could assemble into words the many thoughts that crowded her mind in a confused and cluttered web, Blythe was gone.

Hearing the door close behind her, Iris reassured herself, "We must talk tomorrow. There is always time to talk, tomorrow."

Chapter 20

He sat in the chair of his room as he had for the past many hours; arms and legs widespread, luxuriating in the open space around him. He had been cramped and crowded for so long he could do nothing but spread out like a root-bound plant that finally burst free of its potted constraints.

For the first time, he understood viscerally the deeper meaning of a poem an old teacher once required him to memorize:

> *The limits of our freedom are best defined*
> *By a system of justice whose sight is blind*
> *To which side of the verdict is imposed:*
> *Are we the encloser or are we the enclosed?*

From within an imperceptible crack in the wall behind him, the subtle hints of a mist crept silently into the room. Unlike mere vapor, it didn't dissipate; rather, it held fast and accumulated into a small form. The tiny stack of cloud appeared, took in the room, then collapsed in on itself, evaporating into a swirling circle spreading outward and then disappearing entirely, like a dust ring that forms and disappears when a rock falls to the desert floor.

From behind a panel where the fog unfurled itself, two men shot from a hidden recess and grabbed the resting man so furiously by the hair that they nearly snapped his neck. They were on him in an instant, holding him fast on the floor.

"You know the rules," said a third, as he emerged from the passageway.

"I'm not going back!"

"You don't have much of a choice now, do you?"

"I'm not! I'm not going back there!" he screamed, desperately trying to free himself.

He felt the cool sensation of the braided leather straps slip over his hands, their loops tightening around his wrists making him aware of the shape of bones he had never much considered as he fought to squirm free.

"The rules are simple enough. You went out and stayed out without bringing someone back. It's the Mournex for you."

The first two men hoisted their quarry to his feet. They pulled back the panel in the wall and began to make their way through the dark passage when the captive collapsed in a futile effort to stop them. When the stabbing pain of being dragged by his backwards arms set in, he screamed for them to stop. He screamed again and promised to stand and walk with them if they would just let him stand.

"Oh, that pain is nothing compared to what you're in for," the third man assured.

Chapter 21

Aaron could not believe his eyes. There, in his father's basement, where Bruce's books had been, were all of Sundar's possessions. Intricately carved elephants, mahogany tables inlaid with exquisite scenes plotted out in alabaster, religious trinkets that Sundar had once reverently displayed, all stacked in a hodgepodge in his father's basement.

Aaron vaulted himself up to his father's room above, three stairs at a time. He burst through his father's door without knocking. There was Old Lucre, sitting behind his desk, hunched over his ledger. He looked up with his furious flat black eyes, but it was no matter; Aaron was beyond intimidation.

"What are you doing?" Aaron demanded.

"What does it look like?"

"First Bruce's books and now everything of Sundar's?" Aaron fumed. "What are you doing to these people?"

Old Lucre slapped his ledger closed and stood over his desk. "What are you accusing me of?"

"These men...."

Old Lucre scoffed, "Men!"

"These men disappear and if they come back at all, they're at death's door. Then you sweep in, take everything they own to sell it off.

What are you doing? What are you doing to them?"

Old Lucre stormed across the room. He had never struck either of his sons. With his size, and his expert ability to bully, there was never a need. But Aaron had crossed a line with him. He shoved his son back against the wall. "I've done nothing to them. I've done everything within my power to help them."

Aaron wouldn't hear it. He said, "So taking everything they own and selling it off for yourself is helping them? You didn't raise a fool."

"I didn't raise a respectful son," Lucre nearly spat. "I know that."

"Maybe the valley would like to know what you're doing," Aaron said. "Maybe if everyone knew you had a hand in what was going on you wouldn't be able to capitalize on their misery."

Old Lucre's hand shot out and closed on Aaron's throat and trapped it against the wall. Aaron choked to breathe. His father stared eye to eye with him and didn't say a word. He just studied Aaron and dared him to strike back; he dared him to try to speak. Old Lucre leaned in close and whispered, "Say a word about what you think I am doing, and I swear to God I will make you look the fool and turn you out from my house forever. You do not know anything, Aaron. Anything."

A mixture of horror and disgust filled Aaron's expression with the confirmation that his father was somehow involved in the growing mystery that was unfolding among his friends.

"You have some scheme here," Aaron choked out. "I don't know what it is yet, but I'll figure it out. And when I do, I'll let everyone know what I know."

"And when you find out everything there is to know, I hope you will. I have done nothing to be ashamed of here, Aaron. I have done everything…everything I can do to help who I can…."

"To help yourself."

Old Lucre tightened his grip again and closely scrutinized Aaron one final time before letting him go. He turned his back on his son. "You understand nothing, Aaron," he said.

Aaron hunched over with one hand on his knee and the other massaging his throat. He gasped for air and coughed hoarsely.

Finally Aaron asked, "If your hands are clean, then explain what you and Duffy were talking about up at the bridge a few nights ago."

Old Lucre had nearly made it around his desk when he stopped and slowly turned around.

"That's the first time in my life I've ever seen you surprised, Father," Aaron said, looking up at him from his hunched stance. Aaron straightened up and arched his back, his hand still on his throat. He gave a cough to clear the passageway. "You said something about someone being busier than you expected...leading the corrupt to corruption...and Duffy asked what his endgame was. You said it was his own destruction. Who's destruction were you talking about? Bruce's? Was it Sundar's?"

"And how do you know this?" Lucre asked.

"I was there," Aaron said. "I was under the bridge. I heard every word you two said."

Old Lucre turned back to his desk and sat down heavily. He took his ledger and hid it away in a drawer, then locked it up. Aaron stood there, waiting for a response.

"You don't know so much, Aaron."

"I know enough," Aaron said. "Were you involved with that dead man Blythe and I found?"

"What dead...."

"Oh, stop it, Father!" Aaron yelled. "There is no way Duffy didn't tell you. Tell me what you're doing," Aaron pleaded. "If you are not doing anything to be ashamed of, then tell me. Tell me how this all fits together. Let me help you. But if you say nothing, then I can only assume the worst."

"And why would you assume the worst of me?" Lucre asked his son. "Why would you do that rather than give me, your father, the benefit of the doubt?"

"Because of everything I've seen," Aaron protested. "These men are gone and suddenly you end up with everything they've treasured. It is yours to sell. Why? Why would they leave it to you? It makes no sense."

"Everything makes sense if you have enough information, Aaron, and you don't...you can't. I am doing no evil here. I am doing what they have asked me to do for the reason they know and I know. You do not

Blythe

need to know. It has nothing to do with you."

"But you're my father. And they are my friends."

"And it is our business, not yours," Lucre said. "I do not need you muddling this up, Aaron. I'll warn you one more time; keep your nose out of this. I won't have you sully my good name around with a lot of unfounded accusations. You have seen what I have done with those who have tried to do the same thing. Son or no son, I will do the same to you, Aaron. I will."

"But...," Aaron began.

"Aaron, I am ordering you. Keep what you know to yourself and know that I am not doing anything I have not been asked to do. I am putting no pressure on them. The arrangements we made are none of your concern. Now leave."

"Father, I trust you, but...."

"I have said what I am going to say. Now keep your mouth shut and leave."

Chapter 22

Here was Eden, a valley pressed down and overflowing with every blessing its inhabitants could desire. But it is human nature to dream, and therefore to pursue the impossible or the unwise.

They had everything.

But they wanted more.

Aaron absently strolled into the party, preoccupied with his father's warning. He walked past Blythe without a hint of recognition. He did not acknowledge Maddox, who used his father's key to open Bruce's empty home for the gathering, although neither that unintentional snub nor Maddox's indiscretion could be called surprising.

Reaching the home's back room, Aaron asked Augustus, "Have you seen Blythe?"

Augustus took him by the shoulders and turned him around. Blythe had followed him from the front door and stood behind him.

"Shall we try this again?" she asked.

He kissed the upturned corners of her tight, sarcastic smile.

"I suppose you have a ring to give me?" she asked with her head turned away and her hand daintily dangling toward his face. Aaron took her by the hand and led her out a side door that spilled out onto the dark street. Aaron closed the door behind them so they could speak, away from the party's din.

Blythe instantly reached up and wrapped her arms around his neck and pulled herself up for a deep kiss.

"Blythe," he objected, as their lips still touched. He could taste the alcohol on her breath. "Blythe, we have to talk."

"Kiss first, talk later," she stated, but he would have none of it.

"Blythe," he insisted, "this is about the body we found. It's about that, and much more."

"There is only one body I care about," she said. She grabbed him by the belt and pulled him close. She looked up to kiss him, but he drew his head back.

"Blythe, listen!" he ordered her.

From against the wall only a few steps away from them came a deep, confident laugh. Aaron's head whipped around. "Who's there?" he demanded.

Notté stepped out from the shadows and into the light that fell from the door's window. "Someone who would know to shut up and kiss that woman," he said. "Such a woman as that, and you are talking, talking, talking. What a waste," he laughed again.

Blythe laughed with him.

Aaron took a step toward him, but Blythe whined, "Aaron, don't. He was only having fun. And besides, he's right. You are talking too much."

Aaron broke free of Blythe and took two steps toward Notté, who took a quick step away. He threw up his hands in surrender. "I love, my friend. I don't fight. She's all yours."

Aaron watched Notté's shadow grow as he sauntered up the street and turned the corner toward the home's front door. Aaron swung around to Blythe then walked past her along the wall to ensure no one else was lurking there in the shadows.

Aaron asked her, "Do you remember when we were under the bridge and our fathers passed overhead?"

"And I sneezed," she said.

"And you sneezed, right. Our fathers were talking about corrupt people going to corruption and about someone headed for destruction."

"Then we found the body," she said as she nestled back in.

"We found the body," Aaron repeated. "Now think about what else happened right around then: Bruce disappears and won't return. Now, today, I found out that Sundar has died."

"Sundar is dead?" she asked.

"He's dead and his family has moved out," Aaron confirmed. "I don't know who that man was that we found, Blythe, but Bruce and Sundar were both social misfits...."

"Like us," she said.

"Well, more like our friends, but yes. And no sooner are they gone than my father takes all of their property and sells it, he says at their request. He said Bruce asked him to do it. Does any of this make sense?"

"Oh, Aaron," she said wearily. "I don't know. I can't believe Sundar is dead. How?"

"Your father said it was pneumonia."

"So my father knew? And didn't tell me?"

She nestled back into him once more and wrapped her arms around his neck again. "I didn't want any of this tonight, Aaron. I just want to be with you and to be held. I miss you during the day. I miss you so much."

"Blythe?" he asked incredulously. "What are you thinking? Haven't you heard a word I said?" He reached up and lowered her arms.

"Ow!" she cried.

"Blythe, how can you do this to yourself?"

"Because I need you and you're not there. That's how I can do this. I need something to fill me...something to give me a charge and where are you? Out looking for ghosts."

"Now you sound like your father."

"My father isn't the fool you make him out to be. My father is a good man."

"Who doesn't believe us when we tell him what we saw, and who doesn't tell us what he knows?"

"If you think there is some connection between all these things, I'll ask my father tomorrow. If he knows anything, he won't be able to lie to me. He never can when I press him. But Aaron, that's tomorrow. Can we forget about everything for tonight?"

"I...." Aaron began defensively.

"Aaron," she broke down. "I wish we had never seen that body. I don't want to think about that dead old man anymore, or about Bruce, or about Sundar. I'm tired of thinking of all of it. I want to think about you. And I want you to think about me. Can you do that, Aaron? Can you do that for me? Just think about me for a little while?" she sobbed.

"I can do that," he soothed. "Shhh. I can do that, Blythe."

Aaron looked up the street. He shook his head in frustration.

He rocked her gently in his arms kissing the top of her head then said, "Tell you what. Let's go inside for a moment. Let me get a drink and I'll meet you outside the front door. Wait for me there, and in the time it takes me to finish one cider, I'll be all yours. No deaths. No conspiracy. Just you and me. What do you say?" He kissed the top of her head again.

She whispered back to him, "I need that, Aaron. I need you. I need to be needed by you."

"I do need you," he whispered back into the top of her crown. "I do."

They walked in the side door. Notté stood in the doorway leading into the next room and he pushed back to let them by, never taking his eyes off of Blythe.

"Pin! Pin! Pin!" the spectators chanted as another rodellé concluded.

Blythe turned back to Aaron and asked, "You won't keep me waiting?"

He smiled, "A plague upon us if I do."

Blythe swayed off, looking back on him once and giving him a sweet little wave over her shoulder. Aaron turned to watch the rodellé, but was incensed to see Notté ogling Blythe.

"You better watch your eyes," Aaron warned. "And your mouth, too."

"Relax, my friend. You are a very lucky man."

Aaron told him, "I'm not your friend and don't tell me to relax."

Again, Notté raised his hands in surrender.

As they turned back to watch the match, Parissa brought Aaron a cider without him ever having asked. She added sparkle to her eyes and looked up to Notté. "Aaron, are you going to introduce me to your friend?"

Aaron took a deep drink and refused to look at him. "Never seen him before."

Taking the initiative, she offered, "I'm Parissa."

He took her hand and gently kissed it. "Enchanted," he said. "What is this game they are playing?"

Parissa responded, "It's called a rodellé." She turned to the back room. Notté slid in behind her and placed his hands on her hips. She smiled and called over her shoulder to him, "Two men wrestle and whoever can pin the other one's knees to their chin, wins. You can't hurt your challenger or else you lose favor."

"Favor?" he asked.

"Favor," she sparkled. "It shows you are a gentleman. Favor is what we ladies look for."

"Favor," he repeated. "I like that."

"Here, look," Parissa instructed. "Augustus is just about to pin that boy."

"Pin! Pin! Pin!" the entire room shouted and Augustus obliged.

"That is very exciting," Notté shouted. He twirled Parissa around and he asked her for a drink. She left him to oblige.

Notté looked over at Aaron and told him in a voice loud enough for only him to hear, "Maybe I should have a tumble with that woman of yours. I would like to pin her."

Aaron walked to the center of the back room and shouted, "Rodellé!" He pointed over to Notté. "I challenge you."

Notté strode to the center of the room as everyone formed a circle around them. The two faced off then hunched over. They slowly circled, dodged and feinted. As Notté took a step back, Aaron sprung for him and in one quick movement took him down. In no time, Notté was kissing his knees. It happened so quickly, the crowd couldn't even shout for a pin.

Aaron stood up to accept the accolades. He raised his arms over his head and turned once around. Then, to show good form, he bent over his victim to help his opponent to his feet.

Aaron looked down over Notté and asked, "Do you have anything else to say?"

Notté flashed a knife from his back pocket and cut a deep, swift arc in the air across Aaron's chest. The room's laughter turned into a collective gasp as the champion's shirt fell open. Everyone in the room froze.

Out of reflex, Aaron grabbed the would-be assassin's wrist until it nearly broke in his grip. The tension of all those present swallowed up the sound made by the falling knife as it stuck point-down into a floorboard.

Aaron pulled and lifted Notté to his feet. For a moment, they stood there silently in the center of the room, an odd couple not dancing to music that wasn't playing.

Aaron dropped his gaze to inspect where the knife had crossed him. Through the cut shirt he saw the skin was without a mark. The blade had fallen short of its target.

He slowly raised his face offering an even more menacing grin. Filled with trepidation, Notté seemed to Aaron somehow smaller than he had been before. With a wild whoop and a mighty laugh, Aaron shifted his grip to the back of Notté's collar and his belt. It was fortunate that a quick-thinking Augustus opened the side door at the last possible moment because, closed or open, Notté was going through it. Out into the darkness he flew, bruising his knees and forearms along with his pride.

As the door slammed shut behind him, a slight bank of the growing fog tumbled in across the threshold. As the breeze from the swinging door caught it, the mist rose and twisted into a miniature form standing only knee-high and for but a moment. The flimsy, disappearing apparition swung around inspecting the room as the current swept it away into the thin air from where it came, unseen by any eye.

Aaron returned to the center of the room. He paused and looked down at the knife, which remained lodged in a floorboard. All looked on him in silent awe to see what he would do. He stooped over and picked it up. Turning it over in his hands, he examined its weight and balance. He inspected the sharp, retractable blade and elegant handle on which was engraved a delicate small cross with all sides of equal length. Careful not to cut himself, he pushed the blade in, tucked the knife into his pocket and then immediately redeemed what favor he had accumulated for a fresh drink. Another rodellé began. The party resumed its fever pitch.

Parissa returned with Notté's drink and asked Aaron as he returned to the door, "Where did your friend go?"

"He is not my friend," Aaron said. "I saw him fly through the side door after you slipped away. He won't be back."

In a corner of the front room, Kagetsu stood radiant and alone. Sergio had circled her time and again, building up the courage to approach. At last, he found the nerve to speak.

"Kagetsu," he said. "I want to apologize for how I acted at the wedding. I had no right to say what I said. I hope you can forgive me."

Kagetsu smiled.

"Sergio," she said. "We may never understand each other, but we can learn to respect each other. I forgive you. And ask that if I have in some way misled you, please forgive me, as well."

Sergio beamed. "Forgive you?" he asked. He laughed at the very suggestion. "Forgive you?"

Kagetsu assessed him with a nervous smile.

He asked, "How can I forgive you when you've done nothing wrong?" He laughed, "Thank you," and again yelled those words as he left her and sprang into the back room with a little leap.

Kagetsu exhaled and drifted out the front door followed by Parissa.

Blythe paced aimlessly in the street as they approached.

Parissa chided her, "Has the sun lost its shine?"

Blythe responded, "A lesser heavenly body should not mock the sun."

"Lesser, perhaps, but heavenly nonetheless," Parissa said in her own defense. She asked, "Why are you out here when the party is in there?"

Blythe looked up without answering. "Ah," Parissa responded knowingly. "Waiting for Aaron. Well, you'll be waiting for a while. He's getting cidered."

Blythe's hand, which had played absently in her curls, slapped listlessly to her side in frustration.

Blythe

"Here," Parissa said, handing her the drink she still carried for Notté.

Blythe drank it empty then handed it back.

Parissa said sarcastically, "Oh, you are welcome." She walked over and placed it on Bruce's front step as Blythe and Kagetsu strode up the hill.

"I've always admired you," Blythe confessed. "How can you be so content by yourself?"

Kagetsu considered her question. Finally, she responded, "What can be added to something that is already whole?"

"Love? Need? Desire?" Blythe suggested.

Kagetsu dismissed her. "One masquerader under three different names."

"Four, if you count Aaron," Parissa added, catching up to them.

Blythe smirked to Parissa then turned back to Kagetsu. "Maybe they seem like masqueraders to you," Blythe said. "But they fill me."

"Blythe," Kagetsu said quietly. "Did you know that a new moon is always full on the side facing the sun?"

"I never thought about it," Blythe admitted.

Kagetsu advised, "If you want to see that fullness, it is you, and not the moon, who must change your perspective."

Blythe continued up the hill with her retinue.

A voice called out from behind them, "What a valley, where the flowers bloom at night."

As they turned, each of the ladies smiled at Notté with the secret knowledge that he had said that for her alone; he only humored the others.

Notté carefully kept his distance, unwilling to commit to one or another of them.

Kagetsu and Parissa said at once, "I . . .," then looked at the other in embarrassment. Kagetsu continued, "I am going to return to the party. She peeled off and offered Notté a little bow as she passed.

"Well, this is better," Notté said, placing himself between Blythe and Parissa, locking arms with each. "That is no party she's returning to. I know of a much better one: one that is raging right now."

"And where is that?" Parissa asked.

Notté promised to take them.

Blythe placed her free hand on Notté's arm. "Thank you for what you said before," Blythe said. Notté freed his arm from Parissa's and used that hand to cover Blythe's. Parissa crossed her arms and walked alongside them. A tight smile laced with frustration crossed her face; she had once again lost to Blythe.

"It was only the truth," Notté said. "How could that boy you were with talk so much when it was clear that talking was the last thing you needed? How could he not appreciate you—you?"

"No one appreciates Blythe," Parissa said.

Blythe leaned forward to look at her.

"I'm serious," Parissa insisted.

"Blythe," Notté considered. "I like that name. Blythe."

"Have you ever seen someone so beautiful?" Parissa asked.

"I have never," Notté assured.

"You'll never hear me say this again," Parissa admitted, "but I wish I could be half of what you are, Blythe. You are beautiful. You are confident. But even with all this, you never get the appreciation you deserve, least alone from Aaron."

"Aaron? Is that his name?" Notté asked Blythe.

She nodded.

He said, "I do not like that Aaron if that is how he treats you. You deserve much more."

Parissa continued, "All the men love Blythe and would do anything for her, but the one she loves treats her indifferently."

"That is because he takes her for granted," Notté observed. "I could tell just by the way I heard them talk. He assumes because he has her, that he no longer needs to try any longer."

Blythe asked, "So what can I do?"

Notté suggested, "Give him a reason to care…a reason to feel again for you like he once felt."

Blythe asked, "But how?"

Parissa began to suggest, "The answer is right on your . . .," but Notté cut her off.

Blythe

"The answer will come to you when you find it," he assured. "For now, let's put him out of your mind and go to that party I was telling you about. It is too nice a night for sadness. Tonight is a night for excitement."

"We're going to make this your night, Blythe," Parissa said. "We are going to give you the night you deserve."

The three walked up and over the bridge where Aaron and Blythe had found the body. Without explanation, Blythe began to cry. Notté wrapped his arm around her shoulders as he held Parissa's hand. They walked on, each silently approving the other's role.

A long walk later, the party Notté promised spilled out into a lawn. No sooner had they been there when each was handed a drink.

"Have you ever seen Blythe drink?" Parissa asked.

Notté shook his head.

"Prepare to be amazed," Parissa bragged on her friend's behalf. "Watch this."

Blythe smiled shyly up at Notté and paused for a moment to consider what needed to be done. She then drank it down in one smooth motion.

Notté looked at her with awe.

Blythe then let out a belch, which sent the three into hysterics. Notté replied, "She even does that well. What is not to love?"

He wrapped his arm back around his companions' shoulders and the three walked up across the porch and into the home. The entire house was filled with dancing, talking, laughing partygoers.

"Here," Notté suggested. "Take my drink while I get a couple more for us." He disappeared into the crowd.

"What am I doing?" Blythe asked.

"Oh, he's benign, Blythe," Parissa insisted. "Enjoy how it will make Aaron feel knowing you two were together. When he finds out, he won't take you for granted any longer. You deserve a little fun. Enjoy it. Cheers."

Each took on the same pensive expression Blythe had made before she downed that drink. They simultaneously lifted their drinks to their mouths, Parissa sipping hers while Blythe made hers disappear.

"Let me get us another one," Parissa offered. "You wait here.

Blythe obliged.

Parissa and Notté met half way.

Notté asked her bluntly, "You do not like this friend of yours?"

Parissa looked at him and responded, "Aaron is the one I want. You get what you want. I get what I want. Blythe gets what she wants…at least for now. Everyone is happy?"

"Everyone is happy," he agreed. "I'm going to have to look out for you," he smiled.

"The only difference between lust and love is if you get what you lust for," she replied. They continued on their ways.

When Parissa returned, Notté shouted to both of them, "I'm sorry, but I forgot to inform you of a little tradition in this house. Have neither of you partied here before?"

They shook their heads.

He shouted, "It is a tradition that on your first time at this home, you must take off an article of clothing with every threshold that you cross. I am sorry. This is not my rule; it is the house rules. You have already crossed two…one on the porch and the other at the front door. We can leave if you want to, but if you want to stay, that is the rule."

Parissa smiled a daring smile at Blythe and Blythe smiled back in her tipsy daze. Parissa made the first move, taking off an undergarment. Blythe clumsily took off one shoe, steadied by her friend.

"That is one," Notté shouted, "But you have crossed two."

Parissa used Blythe as a balancing post for a moment as she reached down and removed one of her shoes. Certain Blythe no longer possessed the coordination to do likewise, Parissa ducked down and removed Blythe's other shoe for her.

Blythe thanked her dear friend.

On and on throughout the night Notté took them back and forth for drinks, each time collecting the requisite articles of clothing until each was left with one last coverall.

All the while Parissa goaded Blythe and her beau, "How perfect you two are together." She stroked, "Why do you always get the best ones, Blythe?" Parissa pouted, "What I wouldn't give for him—for just one night

Blythe

with him."

In politics and passion, perception is reality. Parissa constructed in Blythe the perception that this man should not be refused anything he desired. Parissa and Notté traded tight smiles with each other as they watched Blythe slip deeper and deeper into a stupor. Parissa bore the most fascinated and vicious smile as she watched Blythe stagger into a bedroom, holding on for support to the stranger who had escorted them to the party.

Blythe crossed the threshold and disappeared into the room.

Notté closed the door behind them.

Part Three

Chapter 23

Upside down the raven flew. Down and up its wings beat; down, then up. It flashed across a tiny vision of the world, and then disappeared.

All that remained to look down upon were dark and threatening clouds that took on the appearance of firmament. Even their stormy, mossy tint spoke more of land than of air. Tapped out, these mountains of the sky shifted restlessly as they eroded, evaporating into nothingness. Their collective mass withered in a morning into scattered patches that no longer blocked the sun. These stragglers faded until one emaciated remnant fought to remain, but it too was disappearing.

In a desperate measure to survive, placing its faith in an ancient promise that what dies will one day rise again, the vapor condensed into a single raindrop and began to rise, unseen, toward the earth. For a brilliant moment, the light caught the ascending dot and transformed it into a streak of light that came closer and closer until it struck the surface of the puddle from which the world had been viewed, and obscured the once-clear inverted heavenly vision.

Everything that was known was gone.

All waited for the surface to settle, so the world could start anew.

Chapter 24

Was it day?

If so, there hung outside such a fog as Blythe had never seen. She looked about the room. Only a dim hint of light penetrated the grimy window, casting the room in indiscernible colors, muted tones.

As she lay in bed, her head reverberated with the sounds of the party that had long since ended. With great effort, she raised her wobbly self up to one elbow to look around the unfamiliar room. She was alone. She was naked.

The plaster walls were cracked. Paint peeled all about. The ceiling rotted away in the corners, water stains forming uneven concentric brown rings, a topographical map of some unknown land. The bed was nothing but a musty mattress on the floor, mildew clinging to it, and to her.

Holding a dirty sheet around her, she attempted to stand, but was too weak. Light-headed, she threw herself back on the mattress with a heavy sigh. Her bare feet remained on the cool, wooden floor.

Lying back, however, only exacerbated her dizziness. With a groan she forced herself back up again and hobbled through the door in front of her. She nestled beside a crude wooden box used as a lavatory. The cool tiles against her skin made her feel intermittently relieved and chilled. Despite every bit of self-restraint she could muster, Blythe couldn't help but wretch. It wasn't just the hangover that made her sick. It was where she was, and what she had done, and what had been done to her. Every thought and memory and assumption conspired against her weakened state until at last there was nothing more for her haggard body to release. For a long while she rested there, rocking her naked legs a little against the tiles to cool her hot skin.

When at last she felt collected, Blythe peeled herself off the floor. Without knowing who else was around, she closed the door for some privacy. Safe in the little bathroom, her ears hummed from the night before. Blythe groaned again. She stepped before a dusty, broken mirror. The room glowed gray from misty morning light that came in through a tiny lead-glass window behind her. Resting for support against the dirty basin, she gripped its sides. She leaned in and examined her face.

"Utter devastation," she said. Her glance naturally fell to the reflection of her forearms. Bruised and scarred, she looked at them coldly as she turned them from side to side examining the private damage she had done. In a trance, she raised her right hand and pressed her knuckles deep into her left arm, just above the wrist. In the mirror she watched as the sharp rings dug deeply into her slender stem until her blank expression recognized the blood that ran down in gentle streams to the heel of her hand. She flinched and examined the smear of finger-painted horror that was left.

Leaning closer to the mirror, she licked her index finger and used it to freshen up. She grimaced slightly at the taste of her own blood, although it replaced as a preoccupation the discomfort she felt over her throbbing head. Blythe bit her lip as she studied the edges of her eyes and wondered if she wasn't getting old.

Having blotted the fresh marks on her arm, coaxing them into coagulation, she walked back into the bedroom. A thought overtook her: "Aaron! I have to get to him before Parissa."

Blythe told herself that regardless of who reached Aaron first to share with him the news of what she had done, she knew…she felt confident…she hoped the love between the two of them would remain. Whichever was the truth—be it knowledge or feeling or hope—her best

John E. Kramer   150

hope lay in reaching him first.

Quickly she sorted her clothes, which were jumbled at the foot of the bed. She dressed, unable to remember undressing. Only the most vague recollection of the night before came back to her: the first party, Aaron, the walk, Parissa, the stranger, and then this house.

"Where am I?" she wondered. "What am I doing in such a filthy place?"

The hum in her head subsided. Not knowing if she were alone, Blythe quietly slipped through the door and stared around the living room. As destroyed as the bedroom looked, the remainder of the home was even worse. Old, soaked clothes were the only cushions covering couches and chairs. Bottles and other refuse lay strewn about. In the center of the room, the roof had given way. Huge patches of plaster had stripped themselves from the walls revealing the ancient ribs of rotting wooden lattice behind them.

She wondered, "Could I have been so drunk and so distracted last night to have missed all this?"

Without waiting to see if anyone else remained, she vaulted over piles of rubble and empty bottles cast about the floor. She dashed out of the once-grand, double-door entrance where all that remained was a gaping lintel, chapped with peeling paint.

Blythe ran into the front yard then turned to glance from among the weeds back at the ramshackle edifice. The two upstairs dormers, which had lost their last pane of glass, reflected no spark of life or light. A single shutter hung across one of the windows, nervously close to ripping off its one remaining bottom hinge. The porch sagged in the center. The failing house seemed to be an old, decrepit being winking down at Blythe as it smiled sinisterly at her with its toothless, dirty-faced grin. It was as if the house took some evil delight in knowing that she had come from within him. Blythe convulsed with a sudden chill that ran through her blood.

She turned wildly and ran to find her way back home; to find her way back to Aaron.

"Where are you going?" a familiar voice asked.

Something within her told her to keep running, but she didn't listen. Blythe stopped and turned to see Notté's hazy image leaning against a tree.

"What a dump," he said looking up at the ramshackle house. He strolled over to her and leaned in for a kiss. She resisted, giving him a half-hearted effort that coalesced on part of his lips and his cheek.

"So that is how it is?" he asked.

Although she was dressed, Blythe covered herself up even more by crossing her arms awkwardly around her.

"That's all right," he said. "I understand. Can I show you the way or do you know where to go?"

Blythe looked around but because of the fog could see no more than about thirty paces in any direction. "I would appreciate it if you could...."

"Not a problem," he interrupted. "We had quite a long walk here last night. Do you remember?"

She shook her head.

"If you trust me," he said, "I can show you a shorter way to where you're going."

"I trust you," she said weakly, the words convincing neither of them.

"Well, fine!" he said. Notté took her by the hand and walked back toward the house. Blythe resisted.

"Trust me." He smiled and pulled her along. "Follow me and you'll be there in no time."

They walked inside then hop scotched over the piled debris until they came to a back room. He asked, "Are you ready for this?"

She nodded.

Notté opened a closet door. The little room had no back wall—just the beginning of a deep, black passage.

"I'd rather walk the way we came," Blythe suggested.

"Nonsense," he insisted and led her in behind him. "You'll be shocked at how much time this saves. You said you trust me, right? Not too many people know about this," he said as they walked along. "But there are little passageways through the valley leading to all sorts of places.

I've studied them."

Blythe noticed that despite the depth they had walked into the capillary, somehow there was still light enough to see.

"The light?" he asked her.

"How did you know?"

"I have a gift for intuition," he said. "The walls have many minerals in them, including phosphorous. It will light the entire way. It does get a little tight coming up, so be prepared."

Up until that point, Blythe had wished Aaron could be there with her, to protect her, to give her confidence through little squeezes of his hand as they traveled. But on hearing that news—that the passage would be closing up—she knew she could never have subjected him to this. In tight quarters, she would have had to comfort him.

As Notté warned, the walls of the passageway began to close in tightly, first from the sides, forcing them to scoot sideways, then from the top, so they had to hunch and eventually crawl through a space not much wider than their shoulders. The tunnel twisted and turned, climbed then dove. Deeper they crawled, at one point, it seemed, nearly straight down into a cramped plummet that caused the loose dirt to sweep past them as they slid before it finally leveled out again. Blythe knew there was no turning back after that point.

All around them the earth seemed to pulse with sound. Blythe's ears were ringing again as they had in the bathroom, only now there was a deep, throbbing pressure accompanying it.

"That pulsing sound," she complained.

"I know," he said. "It is the closeness of the walls to your ears. It will pass soon enough. We are almost there."

Blythe continued to look ahead as she dragged herself along by her forearms, asking herself how could she have ever followed him into such a place. It was so easy at first to go along with his insistence—to trust him. But now, what was he leading her into?

"I can't go much farther," she said.

"What choice do you have?" he asked. "Do you think you are able to go back?"

Blythe

The words turned her blood cold. She would give anything to go back, to go back to last night and to be with Aaron rather than in that subterranean prison with this stranger.

"Please," she urged him. "Let's hurry."

He stopped and she struck her head on the soles of his shoes.

"What?" she asked, unable to hide the panic in her voice. "Why aren't you moving?"

All she could imagine was her greatest fear: that the passageway ahead had caved in, that it reached a dead-end...their dead end. The only option possible was to reverse their path, crawling backwards until they reached that impassible spot where their travels would end.

"This is the end," she thought. "This is where I end in some anonymous hole never to be seen again."

Her rage boiled up. How could she have put herself in this position?

She asked again, even more anxiously, "What is it?"

He paused without answering then instructed her, "If you are going to be impatient, we can wait here. Would you like that, Blythe? To wait here?"

Aaron's claustrophobia was getting to her.

"Please, no," she said, her voice catching. "No, no, no. Please go forward. Please just go. I will follow you. I'll follow you quietly. Please, let's just go. Let's get out of this place. My ears. My ears hurt with the sound. I can barely get my shoulders through. Please, let's go. Please?"

"And didn't I tell you that soon we would be there?" he asked.

"You did."

"And so you push me to go faster, like you don't trust me, like you don't believe what I told you," he said.

"I trust you. I do. Please, let's go. It's just that I want out of here. Please go. I'm sorry. Please let's just go."

Notté sighed, but did not move for many moments. Blythe poised every muscle within her to shimmy backwards, just an inch, as quietly as she could just to see if it could be done. Regardless of any obstacle she might face, she was prepared to make the effort. She did not want to upset him any more than he was already. She wanted to be rid of him. She had to know that she could go back, if it came to that.

In the instant before she made her move, Notté let out another sigh then crawled forward.

Blythe did not follow him. She rested there, her body ready to move away from him. All she had to do was let her body take over. It was already in reverse. Her will just had to let her.

Then she heard Notté stop.

The pulsing sound in the cave coupled with the palpable pumping of her own blood that pounded her ears deafened her.

"Are you coming?" he asked above the drumbeat in her head. His words were more a demand than a question.

She didn't reply.

He fiercely yelled at her again, "Are you coming?"

Blythe's body went neutral, then she inched toward him.

Notté continued on. In a few moments the passageway began to widen. Soon, they could crawl on their hands and knees, then walk stooped over, and then walk erect.

"The worst of it is over," he promised. "I was sorry to get upset with you. I knew how close we were to everything opening up, and I didn't want you to panic. I didn't want you to turn back."

She mumbled her thanks.

As they walked along, other passageways joined up with their own as it broadened. A major artery formed.

Notté stopped.

Blythe did not question him this time, although she wanted to.

Notté turned, placed his hand on her shoulder and looked around behind her, back from where they had come.

Blythe stood silent and still. She showed him that she was patient, that she trusted him.

Notté looked into the other passageways that veered off from theirs—ones they had never entered. "I am not sure we took the right passage," he confessed.

Blythe said nothing.

Blythe

Notté looked around for another few moments before concluding, "Well, these all lead this way, so it must go somewhere."

He walked off; Blythe followed him listlessly.

The pulsing in the walls remained, but it had greatly diminished. Compared to how they had just crawled, the walk became almost pleasant.

"Here we go!" he exclaimed.

Blythe ducked her head to see past him. At last there was natural light up ahead replacing the eerie iridescence that had guided them along.

"Thank you," she exclaimed.

"Just as I promised," he responded, not realizing her thanksgiving was not meant for him.

"Stay here for a moment," he directed. "Let me take a look to make sure it is a safe place to leave."

Notté walked confidently to the cave head. For a long time he looked out the entrance. To the right and the left of the opening, stairs descended into other passages. Blythe watched him look from side to side carefully studying what lay before him. She took one step to him, then stopped. She remembered his response in the tunnel when she questioned him. She did not want to upset him again.

Notté made his way back pacing carefully backwards, keeping his eyes on the entrance. He took great care that his feet should not make a sound.

"I've made some terrible mistake," he told her in a low tone.

"What?" she asked as a sudden panic arose in her.

"We took the wrong path. We're not back in the valley. We're somewhere else."

Blythe took a bold step to the opening of the cave.

"Careful, I tell you," he said restraining her shoulders. Then repeated instructively, "Careful."

Together, they walked to the opening. They peered out onto a massive piazza lined with columns beyond which were archways like the one they stood in. Throughout the open space, men drifted about, many looking gaunt and ill; it struck her that there were no women in sight. Blythe studied one emaciated form who shuffled along. She thought back to the old man she and Aaron had found in the canal. It could have been the same man.

Through the square ran a stream. Some men crouched by its side and washed themselves as guards dressed in white shirts and red pants strutted by.

"Those men are dressed like you," she pointed out to Notté.

"Ah," he observed as if surprised. "If we have to, we can blend in."

Blythe hunched over to see beyond the covered walkway that was supported by the columns. In the center of the plaza was an enormous stone tower with four open archways looking out in each direction.

As she started out, from deep within the passageways behind them echoed the most haunting howl that Blythe had ever heard. The two travelers spun around. Although it had the coarse sound of metal scraping furiously against metal, there was no doubt in Blythe's mind that that sound had been made by something living—by some living being rather than by a machine or the ground itself.

Again the distant gnashing filled the little cavern where they stood, and Blythe felt a puff of air cross over her and go out to the piazza. Whatever it was, it was coming closer.

She looked at Notté, unsure of what to do.

Without hesitation, he took her by the hand and they both walked quickly through the archway. They walked out as nonchalantly as they could manage. Having put enough space between themselves and the opening, they looked back to see a little swirl of dust pushed by the wind. Blythe thought she caught a fleeting glance of something—a man or perhaps an animal—just beyond the dim light, but Notté turned her head to once again face where they walked.

Blythe said, "Better that we are here than there," and gripped his hand.

Notté and Blythe walked around the open area. Blythe clutched his arm. Although they were dressed as everyone else, she observed how everyone they passed cut them a wide berth. Nervous looks turned Notté's way and as soon as he looked back, their heads snapped away.

"Do you know these people?" she asked.

Blythe

He looked down at her with an incredulous smile.

"How could I know them?" he asked. "I only just arrived here like you. Let's go over here where we will be less conspicuous."

Notté led her beside the tower.

"You stay here for a few moments," he instructed. "Let me get a lay of the land."

As she released herself from him, he gallantly extended his arm to her, seeming to imply that he was hesitant to leave her. She looked down at his palm and noticed the scar. Recognizing the fascination on her face, he clenched his hand into a fist and walked away without further explanation.

Chapter 25

It wasn't that Blythe hadn't waited for him that worried Aaron. He knew she would be livid when he failed to leave the party as soon as promised. What set him on edge was what Kagetsu told him the next morning; she saw Blythe and Parissa leave with that new man whom Kagetsu had met on her way to the church—the same stranger that Aaron had confronted in the alley, pinned in a rodellé and thrown out the door.

Aaron tried to convince himself, "There were other nights when she hadn't come home," only to answer, "but those were nights she spent with me."

Aaron considered the facts: the stranger wanted Blythe; he knew Blythe and Aaron were paired; he had every reason to try to get back at Aaron for what he had done to him. Trying to take Blythe away would achieve everything the stranger desired.

Aaron stood up from stocking the shelf and called over to Maddox, "Do you know anything about what happened to Blythe at Bruce's last night?"

Maddox yawned, "Since when is she my responsibility?"

"It's just that…." he looked up at his brother whose face could show no less interest. "Never mind," he said, returning to work.

Old Lucre burst in. "What did you do over at Bruce's last night?"

he bellowed.

They stared back at him.

"I just came from there," he continued. "The front door was left open, the entire block is strewn with trash, and there is a hole dug clear through his back wall. How am I supposed to sell it in that condition? What were you and those supposed friends of yours thinking?"

There was nothing for either of them to say.

"Which of you has the key?" he demanded.

Maddox answered quickly, "I don't."

Lucre faced Aaron, "Then you are cleaning up that mess by yourself."

Aaron began, "But, he…."

"But nothing," Lucre cut him off. "Were you there last night?"

Pointing to his brother, Aaron replied, "I was, but he…."

"And did you see the damage?" his father continued.

"That hole was already there," Aaron objected, at which Maddox smiled and left the room, knowing his brother had just dug himself too deep.

Lucre exploded, "Was it? When did you first notice it?"

Aaron said, "When Augustus and I were packing up the boxes. A bookshelf nearly fell on me and we saw the hole behind it."

"You and your rodellé!" Lucre shouted at him. "If you spent your time working rather than playing, you might make something of yourself."

"We weren't…." Aaron began, but his father would hear none of it.

"You're going over there now and returning that place to the pristine condition Bruce left it in," his father ordered. "I have a buyer coming by tomorrow—a friend of Bruce's—and he knows how immaculate Bruce kept that place. You will put it back as it was."

"But Maddox…."

"Don't Maddox me!" Lucre said. "I'm tired of you using him as an excuse. Now take what you need and get over there and get that place in order."

"You…."

"Not another word, Aaron."

Aaron drew in a deep breath to plead his case, but his father held up his hand, "Not another word. Go."

Aaron stormed out of the store knowing it was pointless to talk further.

Old Lucre strode over to the door to watch him go. He walked back to the center of the shop and yelled up the stairs, "Maddox!" Maddox appeared. His father said as he pulled out a leather satchel and handed it to his son, "Here is what I got for Bruce's books. This is all of it. See that it gets you in and out. Get what you can out of him. Tell him it better be something more than he had for us the last time or the deal is off. I'll have more for him when I sell Sundar's things. Now go!"

* * *

Aaron rarely flouted his father's will, but Blythe's disappearance was more important to him than his father's wrath. Aaron, Augustus and Sergio each traversed the valley moving steadily upwards in search of any information they could glean. Like Blythe, Parissa, too, had disappeared.

Aaron returned to where this whole escapade had started for him, up at the ancient bridge. He walked halfway across the span. He looked up the canal. Another storm was blowing. A stiff wind tossed about his blonde hair as he looked around. He slowly turned back toward the valley floor, piecing together what details he could remember from that night when he and Blythe last met there. All about him, the wind shook the trees and ran ripples down the water. As he faced downstream, a breeze parted the trees behind him to reveal a new addition to the landscape: a castle-like structure hidden in the greenery. Aaron surveyed the spot where he had dragged the body out of the water, then turned back around and looked up the hill one final time, but by then the breeze had relented; the castle was hidden again.

Back in the village, Aaron met Augustus at Bruce's home. His father was right; they had destroyed the place. Aaron took a close look around in disgust.

Aaron asked, "Why do my brother and his friends have to destroy everything around them to enjoy themselves?"

Augustus looked around and shook his head.

Blythe

"Drinking isn't enough for them," Aaron said. "Trysts aren't enough. Something had to be broken or ruined or dumped if they were going to feel something. Maybe that was it. Maybe people like Maddox have all been given so much...beyond what they truly feel like they are worth...that they can't feel anything anymore; they can only feel an emptiness."

He looked to Augustus for some kind of response. Still surveying the damage, Augustus nodded slowly.

Aaron concluded, "Destroying must at least lead them to feel...to feel something rather than nothing. They are missing something, that's for sure."

Aaron kicked an empty bottle and said, "Their loss; our work."

He stepped back and looked up at the face of the home. The charm seemed out of the place for him now knowing Bruce and Gwen would not return.

"We'll spend enough time here as it is," he said, and the two walked farther down the valley to Sundar's. There, too, they stood out in front of the house. Aaron considered what it meant to lose his friend, about what he would miss in life now that he would never see Sundar again.

As he prepared to return to Bruce's, he spied a figure walking by one of the windows.

"Maddox isn't going to leave another mess for me here," he told Augustus and ran to the front door.

He tried the doorknob.

It was locked.

He pounded on the door and demanded Maddox come out. To his surprise, Sundar's father, Rishi, answered. Aaron stood there dumbstruck for a moment, and then gave the man a hug. Rishi returned his affection with two awkward, uneven pats on the young man's back.

"I'm so sorry for your loss," Aaron told him.

Sundar's father excused himself and walked out the door, which he made sure was locked behind him. He searched for some words finally saying with some apprehension, "I know you and Sundar are...were close."

"I thought that you had already left. Duffy told me...."

"Duffy?" Rishi interrupted. "Duffy told you this?"

Sensing an overstep, Aaron retreated, "He said you and he talked after Sundar's…after his passing and that…."

"Then he lied to you, Aaron," Rishi said. "He and I have not spoken since Sundar returned."

They walked to the lane.

"It was pneumonia?" Aaron asked.

Rishi said bitterly, "A young man dead of an old man's illness. How old are you Aaron?"

Aaron told him, "Twenty-two."

"Twenty-two and indestructible. Sundar thought he was, as well."

Aaron asked, "How did he come down with…."

"I would rather not talk about that, Aaron. Firstly, it is quite irrelevant now that he is gone, and secondly, and please do not take offense at me for telling you, but it is none of your business."

"It's just that…." Aaron began.

"Have you ever lost a son, Aaron? Have you ever held your son, in whom you poured your life and placed your trust for the future, while he took his final breath?"

Rishi stared at Aaron.

Aaron looked down and shook his head.

Sundar's father continued, "Waiting for that…." he gasped in deeply to demonstrate for Aaron the breath he was waiting for from his son. "Waiting and praying, 'Just another breath, Sundar.' Begging for it, 'Just one more….'" he gasped in again.

"I'm sorry, sir," Aaron choked out. "You're right. It's none of my business."

Rishi sobbed beyond consolation as they walked together back into the heart of the village. As he turned a corner, Aaron said, "I'm walking up to Bruce's."

"I saw Bruce's home today," Rishi said deeply, having composed himself. "I expect that you and your brother will show Sundar's home more respect, if nothing else but for the memory of my son."

It was all Aaron could do to nod out his acknowledgement. An

Blythe

explanation would be too long and tortured, Aaron thought, "I'll let him believe what he wants to believe."

"I know this is also none of my business, sir," Aaron began, "but let me ask you before you go. When Sundar was missing for the past few weeks, where was he? Did he ever say?"

"You're right," Rishi said as he turned the corner and walked away. "That is none of your business."

"Blythe is missing, too," Aaron blurted out after him in a purposeful overstatement. He hoped the shock of those words—that another youth from the valley was missing—might play on the man's conscience and persuade him to share what happened to his son. Yes, Blythe was missing for only one night, and yes, she left with that stranger rather than taking off alone. But Aaron was willing to bluff with even so heinous a thought as Blythe's disappearance being more than a fling if it meant he might gain some knowledge to help him better understand what was happening around him. Blythe, for the moment, was bait for Aaron, but he excused that for the fish he hoped to catch. He called after Sundar's father, "I'm afraid they might somehow be related."

"Blythe?" Rishi asked brightly. "Duffy's daughter?"

"Yes," Aaron said. "When I heard Sundar was back, I expected to stop by and hear about some great adventure he had had, then Duffy told me he had died."

Rishi began excitedly, "If that is true—that Duffy's daughter is missing as well—then let me say this." He paused to consider his words, then nearly spat, "A plague upon his house for one on mine!"

Aaron looked at him horrified.

"Don't think I am being too harsh, Aaron," he continued. "For weeks I told Duffy my son was missing. I told him I thought something was wrong and pleaded for his help, but he did nothing. Because he saw my son as what he calls 'A Troublesome One,' he ignored me. He shut me out."

Aaron tried to fit this puzzle piece into place, but Rishi continued. "Do you know where the word 'justice' comes from, Aaron?"

Hearing no response he continued, "It comes from a man named

Justinian—a man from your Western world, not from my culture. It was he who said that justice is treating equals equally. But that is, at best, incomplete justice. Treating equals equally means those in power— Duffy and, yes, your father and others—get one level of justice and The Troublesome Sundars get something less."

He asked rhetorically, "So what did Justinian forget? Justice requires the application of a lesson no one in authority can remember once they take those reins."

Rishi looked at him begging Aaron to shout out the answer.

He yelled at Aaron, "It is so simple! It is found in nearly every faith, and certainly yours and mine," he coaxed. "Treating others as you would have them treat you. The Golden Rule! That is what they forget!"

"Consider this, Aaron," Rishi urged excitedly. "Consider this. If you were in a position of authority and had information that if shared would save the lives of those you loathed, would you share it?"

"Of course," Aaron said.

"Of course you would," Rishi smiled, "because they are human beings and they deserve to know. And you would hope they would do the same for you if the roles were reversed. Now let me ask you one more question. If a judgment had to be delivered against someone, perhaps even you yourself might fall under this judgment, would you not put yourself in the place of the man to be judged as well as in the place of the man's victim when rendering your decision? To deliver a truly just judgment, you must consider both perspectives, must you not?"

"Absolutely," Aaron said.

"And there is the plague Duffy may have created for himself with his own injustice!" Rishi said. "He has done both these things to my son…remained silent when speaking might have saved him and passing judgment on him without considering whether he would want the same sentence for himself and for his child. He remained the authority: dispassionate, inhuman because he did not approve of my son. If his daughter is now missing, then there is truly a greater justice at work here, and for that I will thank God. This is karma. This is a sentence from my culture's infinite justice. Pneumonia did not kill Sundar, Aaron. Unjust

Blythe

authority did."

Aaron was haunted by his last promise to Blythe, that if he didn't come right out to her he wished a plague upon himself. He asked, "Why do you say 'a plague?'"

"I am certain what happened to Sundar will not end with him," Rishi warned. "I know in my heart there was a grave injustice done to my son and somehow the heavens must make that right. They must find a proper punishment for those who refused to act. There is something evil underfoot, Aaron. What that evil is, specifically, I cannot tell you because I do not know myself. But I know there is justice, Aaron. I know there will be justice."

Sundar's father turned and left him.

Chapter 26

Along the valley wall where it met any growing hill, embankment or behind a cluster of boulders, hid myriad passageways, unknown to any of the valley's inhabitants, save for those who had ventured upon them. They were no place to enter; to go that way led to great sorrow. Yet some went in. The air was damp and heavy within its darkness. The walls rapidly constricted. Wiggling, writhing, the path was pursued farther and farther until, betrayed by the width of one's shoulders, traveling any deeper seemed as impossible as it was unwise. One begged to be free yet desired to go deeper. The point of no return was reached.

From there it was in forever, or back out to the light. Few retreated. Something in the surrounding walls' dull and oppressive pulsing drew them in to be closer to something. But what that was only those who took that passage could know or hope to know. For all those who rejected the temptations of those passageways, to even start down the paths struck their moral fiber as needlessly dangerous as they were foolhardy.

Notté and Blythe together journeyed through a similar passageway. It led to an esplanade lined with columns and archways through which ran a stream and in the center of which stood an impressive tower. Blythe remained beside that tower, as Notté had instructed her.

Notté stood in the corner talking with other men dressed as he himself was, in red pants and white shirts. Blythe watched him as he first spoke to them quietly, then gradually grew more familiar and laughed. At one point he turned and nodded to Blythe and beamed. She smiled back at him, uneasy at being the subject of their attention but in some small way hopeful that he would gather whatever information they needed to leave. He turned back to the others and he leaned in confidentially. They all laughed in an uproar.

Notté left them and sauntered up to Blythe.

"I wish I had better news," he said. She looked at him with pained eyes, thinking about Parissa. If she had not yet reached Aaron, there is no doubt that she would before Blythe could explain herself to him. Notté continued, "There is no easy way out of here."

"Where are we?" she asked.

"I can't say exactly," he told her. "It is some sort of kingdom. You see this tower?" he asked pointing above her head.

She looked up its imposing edifice as Notté told her, "The person in there designed this place, but did it in such a way that we may enter, but leaving is a different matter. That is why you see so many people about."

"We're in prison?" she asked. "You led me to a prison?"

"Calm down," he insisted. "I'm sure that is too harsh a word for it. We'll find a way out. In the meantime, those men have given us a room. You see those small windows along the base of the walls?"

Blythe turned and looked beyond the columns and between the arches to the edge of the courtyard. Down low on the walls just above the ground were dashes of openings covered with iron bars that ran the length of each wall.

"We have one of those chambers," Notté said. "Right over here near where we entered."

He began to walk in that direction but Blythe stood fast. It wasn't until he held his hand back to reach for her that he realized she was not following.

"What is it?" he asked as he walked back to her.

She confronted him under her breath, "I don't want to be here. I don't want to stay here. Why did you lead me here?"

"I may have led you through that passage, Blythe, but you followed," he said. "Wasn't there anything that told you not to go? That told you to turn back while you still could?"

"Of course there was," she admitted.

"Well, perhaps next time you should listen to that little voice rather than yelling at me." He began to walk back to their room.

She hated to admit it, but she knew it was her own ill-advised following of his will rather than trusting her own instincts that got her where she was. Blythe wished she had remembered and adhered to her mother's admonition, told to her countless times as she grew up, "She who follows another's course, finds a sure path to her own remorse."

Blythe looked around at the crowds of people who teamed about. So many of them looked gaunt, tired, sick. She didn't want to be around them. She didn't want to be here so long that she would end up looking like them. It was then, too, that she noticed, everyone else around her was a man; there were no women in sight. She caught up to Notté and grabbed him gently by the arm.

"You can charm your way out of anything," she told him. "Can't you talk our way out of here? There must be a way."

"I wish I could," he confessed. "I tried my best with them, but the best I could do for now was to get us a room. They told me we were lucky to get that with as many people as Henry is holding."

"Henry?"

"He's the one in the tower," Notté informed her. "Henry the Fourth is what they called him. They said this is his kingdom."

"Let's talk to him," she urged. "Between you and me, we can convince him we don't belong here."

"They said no one talks to Henry. No one has even seen him. They only see the effects of his work."

Blythe took him by the hand. "But there has got to be a way," she said as they walked back to the tower. "Let's just go up and ask him."

They walked around the entire base of Henry's tower, but there was no entranceway. Blythe craned her head and looked up each of the

Blythe

four sides as they went around again, looking for a way in. There was none. Each wall was a solid mass of stones all the way to the arches on the top, which were several stories above them.

She asked an emaciated and haggard man who was lingering nearby, "How do you get in this tower?"

He looked at her, laughed and shuffled away.

Blythe led Notté back to the archway where they entered and suggested, "If there is no way to enter the tower here, then there must be a place underground. Let's find it."

They walked through the archway and down curving stairs that spilled out into a hallway that ran the length of the fortress. Along each side of the hall ran door after door. Still trailing him along, she ran the length of the hall until its end, where it turned to the left. She and Notté ran its entire length, dodging and darting their heads to look into what rooms they could to find a way into Henry's tower, but they found none. Around the entire perimeter of the kingdom, not a single door led to anything more than a captive's lodging. They were back where they had begun.

She looked at Notté with a sudden awakening. "The passageway!" she exclaimed. "We can crawl back though there."

"To have your face eaten off by whatever made that sound?" he asked incredulously. "No thank you."

"But that's our only hope of getting out," she urged him.

He said, "There is no way I'll ever go back in there after that growl. It would be one thing if we knew what it was and if we had something to fight it off with. But in that tight passage…where you can barely get yourself through, never mind trying to fend off whatever beast that is… there is just no way."

"I have to get back…to Aaron," she said.

He looked at her, clearly hurt by her desire to be with Aaron rather than him, but assured her, "I understand, but I lack your courage and your motivation to leave. You are free to go, Blythe. But I am staying here. If you turn back, you'll know where to find me. I'll be around the plaza."

Notté walked her back to the beginning of the passageway and they exchanged a parting hug.

"I think you are foolish to try this," he told her.

She squeezed his hands before he walked off and said, "Better foolish and free."

Blythe disappeared into the passage. The pulsing sound returned to her ears as did the memory of that plaintive howl that had filled the cavern. No matter. She had to return to Aaron.

She returned to the passageway. Soon she crouched down low then was forced to her hands and knees to go on. The earth below her was smooth and hard, the air was thick, warm and damp. The walls continued to close in on her until they rubbed her shoulders and she was reduced to scooting along on her belly with one arm cupping in front of her and the other flailing beneath. She knew she would soon approach that place that climbed nearly straight up. If she could make it beyond there, she would be home and free.

Blythe ducked her head to make her way through. She pulled harder. Then there it was. That sound again. That haunting, grinding, moaning howl. It filled the passageway all around her. She froze still.

A puff of air crossed her face, descended past her shoulders, her back and on across her legs. Every inch of her skin became tight and prickled with fear.

She listened intently, hoping the sound was merely in her memory, that she had heard that awful cry in her mind and not in her ears.

But there it was again followed by another gust of wind. And this time it was closer than it had been before…closer than she had ever heard it. The sound grew in texture the closer it came. At first it was a scraping sound she thought, like metal on metal. But as she heard it for a second and third and fourth and fifth time, there was more throatiness to it, more gargling at the end, more viciousness at the front, lined with teeth.

The accompanying wind grew stronger and reached her sooner with every growl she heard.

She recalled Notté's words when she had suggested they climb together to their freedom. "To have your face eaten off by whatever made that sound?" he asked.

Blythe

Blythe could sense that whatever approached was only around the corner.

She lay still and lifeless, her outstretched arm drawn in as far as she could, covering her face, which lay down in the dirt. There was nothing between her and the unseen beast.

She heard it struggle to get through the passage as it came near, rubbing its back along the ceiling, its shoulders and arms scraping along the sides as it clawed its way to her.

The air became pungent as it let out a deafening roar that blew her hair flat against her head. It reached out and slapped the back of her head with its palm forcing her nose into the dirt and scratching her cheek along the hard surface. She moved her head no farther than the beast had pushed it. She remained limp.

It reached out again, this time resting its palm and fingers on her head, running its talons through her ringlets of hair, pressing the sharp tips of its nails against her skin and dragging them along as they passed her ear and circled her scalp. This sensation made the hair on the back of her neck stand on edge and turned her skin to gooseflesh. Its wide and padded palm pressed hard against the back of her head.

It sniffed intensely and exhaled, filling the air again with its foul, permeating breath, a smell of dense, putrefied flesh. Its face was so close that Blythe felt even the smallest puff of air on her forearm. It reached out with its other palm and gently covered her face. Its skin was smooth from wear, hard and calloused. Blythe dared not breathe. The tips of its long nails rested gently below her jaw line.

It moved both hands to her shoulders. Its musty stench and its coarse hair that brushed against her face tickled her nose but this time, unlike when she was under the bridge, she knew to sneeze was to die. She took little puffs of air through her mouth.

The beast pushed hard on Blythe's shoulders, trying to force her deadweight down the tunnel. She held tight with the arm beneath her. It gave another shove, but again she held fast and drove her shoulder into the ceiling as it tried to clear its way.

Blythe wasn't sure if the beast finally realized that she was either dead—and therefore not worth eating—or that its passageway was blocked beyond its capacity to open, but whichever the reason, the beast slowly retreated, scraping its awkward way backwards to its home.

Soon the sound of the animal was again far off, and the faint breeze that swept her cheek took some many moments to reach her.

"That place," she thought back to the kingdom. Despite her every desire, she knew she would have to return there. She couldn't travel any farther with the prospect of facing whatever it was that she had just encountered.

Freed from her paralyzing fear, she began her retreat back into Henry's kingdom. Laboriously she inched her way backwards until she could crawl and then crouch. Eventually, she could turn and then walk.

It was nightfall when she reached Notté. She had been so happy to leave him, now she was equally happy to see him again. Without saying a word she fell into his arms and began to sob.

It took Blythe all of that dusk to collect herself. She raised her head from his chest, sniffled one final time and looked around to the courtyard. Lights around the perimeter illuminated the open area. Blythe accepted it would be their first night in Henry's kingdom.

She rested her head on Notté's shoulder. Beside them, the stream flowed through the center of the courtyard, flat and even without the eddies it had further downstream in the valley. She studied it as she rocked there. She thought back to Aaron holding her like Notté held her. She imagined Aaron's strong, muscular arms that she needed to have enveloping her. She kissed the rounded turn of his shoulder.

"Thank you," he said softly, uttering the first words either had spoken since her return. At hearing a voice other than Aaron's, she was transported with a jolt back from Aaron's arms to Henry's kingdom.

"No way out?" he asked her.

She echoed softly, "No way out."

He gave her an enormous hug then took her by the hand to lead her toward their room. A man, perhaps twice Notté's age, broke from a little group and yelled back at his people, "It is all our responsibility to fight back! Do you want to die in here?"

His head was a mess of wild, graying brown hair, and he had a professor's paunch. His hands rested easily on his hips, thumbs forward, as he raised a hand and pointed at Blythe and yelled to Notté, "You got another one! Another jewel for your crown!"

Notté slid Blythe behind him. He asked the man, "What do you want?"

The man looked at Blythe and scoffed, "Oh, a pretty one. Wait till you see how Henry will leave you. You'll buy him a few months and he'll leave you as a bag of bones. That is all that will be left of you when Henry is done."

He snapped back to Notté, "I'm not afraid of you. I will never be afraid of you."

Notté looked back at Blythe and whispered, "He's insane. Stay behind me and be careful."

"What is that?" the man bellowed as he approached. "What are you telling her? That she shouldn't trust me?" He let out a deep laugh.

Blythe studied him, terrified. While most of him was covered in ordinary enough clothes, a dozen foul violet ulcers erupted from his neck and what she could see of his uncovered forearms. The more agitated the man grew, the deeper color they turned.

"I may be frightening," he yelled beyond Notté to Blythe, "but I am your best friend in this place right now because I am the only one with the courage and honesty to tell you that he has used you like all these captains of the kingdom use people." He motioned around to a circle of men dressed like Notté who were gathered around talking. His shouting caught their attention, and they turned to him for a moment before going back to their discussion.

"You don't have to stay with him. He'll use you like he used so many before you."

Notté looked at him nervously. "We have no quarrel with you," Notté assured the man as he sought to pass by, keeping Blythe behind his back as he walked. "Leave us alone."

"Leave you alone?" the man bellowed. "Leave you alone? Well isn't that rich! You are the savage. You are the predator, and you ask that I leave you alone," he shouted and lunged at them. Notté tripped over Blythe as he pushed her back, trying to keep himself out of the man's reach. As the man pursued them, Blythe retreated and Notté crawled backwards on his hands and feet.

"Can somebody help here?" Notté pleaded defenselessly, still backing away with Blythe behind him. "Just leave us alone," he yelled at the man.

The captains of the kingdom strode over to the madman and clamped onto him.

"Someone help!" the man shouted as he looked around for others to come to his aid. All the other captives turned their eyes away from him. They refused to acknowledge him.

He transferred his hatred from Notté to them. "You cowards! Don't you see? He knows if he makes an example of one of us, he'll terrorize the rest. Don't ignore me and hope that somehow they'll leave you alone. Show him he's wrong! Show him we are men, not cowards. For God's sake, act! Don't just stand there. Help me!"

All the man accomplished with his speech was to see more of their backs.

The captains dragged the man away toward one of the anonymous arches as he continued to yell at Notté, "Go ahead and call your men on me! They've done their worst. How many lives do you need to live for an eternity?" he yelled. "How many lives?"

Everyone in the courtyard stood and watched as the captains of the kingdom dragged the man away and out of sight. Soon his shouts faded into murmurs, then disappeared entirely.

"Let's get out of here," Notté said to Blythe as he brushed off his hands. "What is that look for?" he asked her. He insisted, "I would have protected you from him."

"On the ground?" she asked. "Walking away on your hands and feet like a crab?"

"I would have done what needed to be done," he insisted.

He led her to an arch. They ducked silently into the stairwell. It circled down to a lower hall that extended beyond dozens of doors on either side they had run past earlier in the day. They walked past a few before seeing an open door to an empty room. They darted in, and he closed the door behind them then tripped the lock, an act that didn't go unnoticed by Blythe.

"Why lock it?" she asked.

"Do you want that madman coming in?" he asked.

She didn't answer but instead turned away and looked out their opening into the courtyard. The barred opening was as high as her chin, which she rested on the framed windowsill. Notté came and stood next to her and they looked out at the many people who were gathered there.

"There is a profound hostility here," Notté observed. "We must find a way to leave this place."

"Are there any other women here?" Blythe asked.

"I haven't seen any," he said. "All the more reason to lock the door. Who knows what these men are capable of?"

She turned away from the window and surveyed their simple quarters: a bed in a room, nothing more. She sat on its edge. Lost in thought, she bit her nails.

"Don't bite them," Notté reprimanded her. He took the fingers she had gnawed and held them in one hand for close examination. He turned her wrist and ran his other hand along the scarred underside of her arm.

She pulled herself away and shot him a dirty look.

"I don't need you judging me," she said.

Turning back to the window, he said, "Let me tell you what I've learned since you've been gone. I talked to the ones dressed like me. They're called captains. I talked to them as well as some other…what shall we call them, prisoners? There is, indeed, no way out, they said. Henry's fort is surrounded by a great morass that cannot be crossed. It is a bog that allows no sure footing. To make matters worse, across the expanse up until these walls, he has cultivated more than 1,000 rose bushes. Whether this next part is myth or reality, I cannot say, but I have been told by no less than three people that those rose bushes were fed on human blood so they have developed a taste for it. A man tries to cut his way through there and sooner or later he is entangled and cut to death on their thorns, which are so sharp and strong, they are said to be able to cut through stone. Between the unsure footing and the threat of getting impaled on the thorns, there is no escape or easy access from the outside to the walls."

"And the castle?" she asked.

He said, "The castle itself is another ingenious stroke. No one knows what Henry made it from, but when its walls are attacked, they mutate."

"They what?"

"They change and adapt so they heal any breach," he explained. "They change to defend themselves once attacked. No way for those on the outside to reach us and break us out."

"So the only way in…."

"Is, I am afraid, the way we entered."

"With no way out."

"As you have seen, with no way out," he confirmed. "Did you find whatever it was that made that sound?"

Blythe crossed her arms and looked down to her left as if looking into the memory.

"I am sorry," Notté said. "I didn't mean to take you back there. From the sound of that animal, you are lucky to be alive."

She nodded, absently stroking her forearm.

"I am sorry to have gotten you into this," he said. She looked up at his pained expression. "I wish I had traveled through that passage alone. You should not be in here. You should be out there and free."

He turned back to the opening.

She rose and walked over to him. She rested one hand on his shoulder.

"It isn't your fault," she assured him. "Who would purposefully come into a place like this? You had no way of knowing. And remember what you said, I didn't have to follow you; I could have trusted my instincts."

"But you didn't," he said.

"But I didn't."

"And look at where you ended up. And with whom."

She squeezed him with both hands, "I could have done much worse."

Blythe

Without looking at her, he dropped his right arm and tucked it across her back so his hand rested firmly on her hip. He drew her in and for a long while they examined the square and the people who milled about. The light fell in on them as they turned to look at one another.

Notté came in and kissed her below her ear.

"We shouldn't," Blythe said.

His only response was to kiss her with a wider mouth farther down her neck.

"We shouldn't," she insisted again but still did not pull away.

"May I tell you something?" he asked then resumed his caressing.

Blythe paused for a long moment before answering, and, despite herself, enjoyed every conflicting way that he made her feel.

"I know you love that Aaron, Blythe," he whispered. "But ask yourself this."

He drew in even closer to her and whispered in her ear so close at times that the tip of his tongue touched her lobe, "Do you think he could ever truly forgive you for what you've done?"

His palm was tracing the outside of her hip, rising slowly to her waist. "Pardon me for saying so," he continued in his hushed voice, "but the moment before you crossed that threshold with me, you knew it would either be Aaron forever or me forever. And here we are. There is no going back to him. There is no forgiveness. There is only us now and forever."

His hand reached the outside of her breast and he let his fingertips dance softly there, tracing little circles on the side then racing back to her ribs. He kissed her deeply. His hand massaged her neck.

She leaned back and gave him one last conflicting look of wanting doubt. He closed the little curtains then lowered his hand and gently pushed her shoulder back. He plunged his mouth into her neck forcing her head back. His hands slowly lowered themselves tracing down next to her breasts, his thumbs extending to her ribs and glancing her abdomen as his fingers kept up pace. He reached her hips and began to disrobe her, to strip away any remaining resistance she felt. He continually whispered to her as they undressed, "There is no forgiveness anymore. There is only us."

Blythe laid down and watched how he looked at her. She wanted more than a look of desire. She received that from nearly every man who looked at her. What she wanted was a look from him that said this was going to be an equal act—something mutual in the taking and the giving. She did not want to be owned or to be made to feel that she owned him. He gave the proper look and she reciprocated.

She could not forgive herself for what led her to that moment because in her shame she felt unworthy of Aaron's forgiveness.

Afterwards, she rested into his right side as he lay on his back, her leg straddling his, her arm across his smooth chest.

She rubbed her fingers all over him as he lay perfectly still. He raised his free hand and began to run his fingertips in the little dimple of her elbow and on the soft underside crease. She looked down at the tender act.

"You have a scar," she said, taking his hand in hers. "How did you get that?"

He pulled away and said, "A childhood accident. I had been playing with a hunting knife and it slipped. I made the mistake of grabbing at it so it wouldn't drop."

She winced.

"You would have pretty arms if you didn't cut them up," he said matter of factly.

She didn't like how everything he said was focused on a fault or frailty. But she had no response for him. She went back to tracing her own fingertips along his chest.

"What was it like for you…growing up?" she asked him.

"Not as nice as you might expect," he exhaled. "I never knew my father, although my mother tells me he was very handsome. My mother was a beautiful woman with no income and no family and she didn't think much of herself, so she drifted from one bastardly man to another. She could never find a kind one, one who would make her happy. She said I was the only man who ever made her happy. Whatever she needed me to be, I tried to be for her. I would do anything, would be anybody she needed to make her love me. She died when I was twelve, and I have taken care of myself since then. I loved her very much."

Blythe

"That's so sad," Blythe said.

"It just is what it is," he said. "I don't think about either my father or my mother much anymore. I can still picture my mother, though. She was a beautiful woman."

Blythe rested with her ear against his chest.

She said, "I can hear your heart so clearly. It is so strong. It almost sounds like it is getting louder."

She raised her head. It wasn't just his heartbeat that she heard. It was a pulsing rhythmic beat that seemed to be pumping through the entire compound that perfectly matched the beat of his heart. It was the same rhythmic beat that nearly deafened her in the tunnel. Outside their window, Blythe heard a cacophony of loud shouts and people running back and forth.

She and Notté vaulted from their bed to their little vantage point to the courtyard. They slowly peeked under the curtain. Out in the open area, gates from within the walls above the archways lowered with fitful cranks of complaint, trapping all those unable to make it from the courtyard through the columns and into safety. As each door closed, people threw themselves through the narrowing gaps to find sanctuary from whatever it was that was to come. Those barred from leaving pounded on the doors and begged to be let in.

All the while, a nearly incapacitating pulsing sound resonated from every wall throughout the kingdom. Every archway door was closed, except for one. Blythe could see its side stairwell was barred. The only opening was deep into the surrounding ground through the passage Blythe had entered and returned through earlier that day.

The pulsing beat quickened and intensified. Blythe could feel her own heartbeat in her throat pump discordantly with the pump of the kingdom. Those who remained outside covered their ears in a fruitless effort to block out the crippling sound. A stiff wind swept in through the open archway whipping up a wall of dust in its course.

"It's coming," Blythe said.

Notté looked in every direction out the window and asked, "What? What is coming?"

She remained transfixed on the archway and announced in a flat, horrified voice, "The beast. It's coming."

What appeared was beyond even Blythe's experience or expectations. While the wind still swept through the piazza's floor, a hoard of the foulest creatures imaginable teemed through, pouring forth in every direction. Packs of misshapen beasts swarmed about descending on individuals and overwhelming them, tearing into whatever part they could lay their talons into. In only the most general way did these things resemble humans. Wiry, thick horsehair sprouted sparsely across their naked bodies serving as their only clothes but not so thickly that it covered the waxy white skin that lay beneath. Such hair erupted across the span of their faces right across their stout noses. Rather than walking erect, their powerful legs drove them along on their feet and knuckles thereby over-pronouncing the bony curve of their spines. This accentuated the beasts' ability to spring forward great distances ensnaring those who thought themselves out of harm's reach. A swiftly moving stream of these unwholesome bodies poured out of the archway by the dozens.

For those who remained in the square, there was no escape; there was only unspeakable death.

Civilized man had long discarded the ancient fear of being eaten alive. Yet, there it was, and on the wholesale: that very terror befell them all, a plague of gargantuan pestilence sweeping in on them to consume them while they still lived.

Once a body was down, the ogres toppled over one another like starving dogs tearing out whatever they could sink their claws into. The kidneys and liver seemed especially prized and once secured were spirited away to a corner where they were cupped to the beast's mouth in bloody hands of enormous proportions and equal strength then devoured with gluttony. Other beasts farther down the feeding chain settled for their leavings. One trailed along a string of intestine longer than he was tall. The animal sat in a quiet corner, squeezing the waste out of the long cord with both hands as he voraciously gobbled it down foot by foot, scarcely taking a bite.

The ill-shaped, ferocious beasts overwhelmed the human population until not a single soul stood. An eerie quiet fell over the entire

Blythe

square as Blythe watched in disbelief, unable to pull herself away from the scene. The animals gorged themselves until all that was left of the people were naked bones, and the flesh that covered only their hands and feet; everything else having been crushed or stripped clean.

During the attack, Notté had pointed out to Blythe one particularly heinous brute who dominated the others; they cowered before him as he took the best pieces of the bodies for himself. He was exceptionally fierce as well as strong. One beast who got in his way was left one arm shy of a set after which the others pounced on the defenseless thing and consumed him as they did their human prey.

This alpha beast, nearly sated, crouched on his haunches at the end of his meal near Blythe and Notté's window. His distended belly stretched out between his massive thighs as he worked over a solitary finger in his stained teeth, polishing it to the bone.

Suddenly, a ponderous gaze filled its face. A thought seemed to grip him.

"What could he be thinking?" Blythe whispered.

The beast raised his head and squatted with his back straightened. He sucked thoughtfully on an index finger—not his own. Blythe and Notté couldn't take their eyes off him.

The animal's face began turning crimson with intense concentration on something that consumed him or that he had consumed. At last he bowed his head and grunted and watched his own excrement fall to the ground between his feet. That finished, the beast stood erect, stretched luxuriously, then casually tossed the cleaned bone on a pile the other ogres had gathered beside the archway where they had first entered.

The alpha beast lurched on all fours back through the archway and disappeared. Transformed into docile beings by their meal, his kin followed him in kind.

The square was empty. The deep pulsing that permeated the very structure of the kingdom itself was quieted. It remained hauntingly quiet deep into the night.

Chapter 27

Sergio called out upon seeing Aaron, "No sign of Blythe yet, but I know who you pulled out of the water up at the bridge."

"The old man?" Aaron asked.

"The young man," Sergio corrected. "That was Stephen."

"Stephen?" Aaron asked. "Impossible. That man was in his seventies, maybe eighties. That couldn't have been Stephen."

Sergio said, "Stephen's father says it was him."

"When did he tell you that?" Aaron asked.

"Late yesterday, as they packed up his…."

"Wait a minute," Aaron said.

"Yes," Sergio confirmed. "Your father strikes again. Stephen's parents wouldn't talk about him. They were hostile…almost embarrassed by any mention about what happened to him."

Aaron asked, "How did you find out it was Stephen?"

"When his mother went into another room, his father shared with me that Stephen hadn't been himself; he went away and never talked to his father, which wasn't like him. He came back for one short visit and went away again."

"Did his father say where?"

"Stephen never told him, he said. The last time his father saw him, he said Stephen had wasted away to practically nothing. Those were his exact words," Sergio said.

Aaron asked, "My question remains: how do you know it was Stephen up at the canal?"

"Before his wife came in, he said that Stephen had died a few days ago. That someone pulled his body out of the canal up by the bridge. Who else could it have been?"

Aaron pressed him, "And who told him all this?"

"Duffy."

"Duffy?" Aaron repeated in disbelief. "And all the while he's telling me that I'm seeing ghosts. What else did Stephen's father say?"

"He said Duffy wasn't sure if Stephen's death was an accident or suicide, so they called it a drowning. That's how Duffy recorded it. Don't tell Duffy what you know."

Aaron asked, "Why shouldn't I?"

Sergio shrugged and explained, "That just seems like a card you hold close to your vest and play when the time is right. Why give it away and get nothing back but the smug satisfaction that you finally know what he's known all along? You should wait and lay that card down when the time is right."

Aaron considered Sergio's advice. "Stephen," Aaron muttered in disbelief.

"I saw a light on at Sasha's on my way over here," Sergio said.

"He must be back," Aaron said. "He made it back in time to play violin at Bruce and Gwen's reception. Blythe said he and her father nearly got into a scrap. You don't suppose...."

"A Troublesome One who went away?" Sergio cut him off.

"What else connects everyone who disappeared?" Aaron asked. "Either they themselves were one, or there was a close connection."

"Like Gwen to Bruce to Maddox...and the others."

"Exactly," Aaron said.

"How about Blythe?" Sergio asked.

"That's the one question I want to answer the most. The one in red pants.... Remember? The one I tossed out of the party?"

"Sure."

Aaron said, "He's wrapped up in this in some way. I'm sure of it. But all we can do now is draw a line from him to Blythe and maybe Parissa. We don't know where his line comes from or goes."

"What about Maddox?" Sergio suggested.

"What about him?"

"Doesn't he fit a description of one you should have your eyes on? He's the ultimate Troublesome One."

"He is," Aaron said, "and he might be messed up in this. I know my father is in some way. So Stephen's parents have already agreed to have my father sell his things?"

"That is what his father said."

"We'll have to find out how they're connected. My father told me to give him the benefit of the doubt, but it doesn't look too good for him. They die, he buys."

Sergio said, "He has to be piling up the lucre."

"That's the strange thing," Aaron told him. "I know all of his accounts, even the ones he thinks are hidden, and there is no extra money in any of them. We've got to find out what he's doing with it all."

* * *

Old Lucre and Duffy walked out of Sasha's home. As they shook hands, Lucre said to him, "Keep your mouth closed as tight as if you held a diamond between your teeth. Aaron's interference could kill our plans."

"It could kill much more than that," Duffy said. "Why not tell your boy what you're doing? He stands to benefit in a hundred different ways."

Lucre said solemnly, "Show me your friends and I'll show you who you are."

"You know how I feel about those poofs, Lucre, but Aaron is different from them. He's trustworthy."

"Well," Lucre said, "we don't know how he will act. The less he knows, the better."

"Fair enough," Duffy agreed.

"Fair has nothing to do with it, Duffy. What we're doing is necessary. I'm off now. Here is your share from Bruce's and Sundar's."

Duffy slipped the leather pouch deep into his inside vest pocket.

Lucre asked, "So you'll let me know if you want to purchase this one?"

"I will."

"The roof is sounder than yours, that's for sure." Old Lucre laughed with a silent shake of his shoulders as he walked off.

Duffy lingered, taking in the street, considering what he might do to Sasha's home. Aaron's and Sergio's conversation caught his ear as they approached. He took on his official bearing.

"Good evening, boys," he offered.

"Duffy," Aaron responded coolly as they passed.

As they walked up to Sasha's door, Duffy called out to them, "No one is allowed in there. I'm afraid your friend is sick. His mother is taking care of him now. She is the only one allowed inside those doors."

"What has he got?" Aaron asked.

"It's serious," Duffy responded gravely. "It is non nuff fyor."

"Non nuff fyor?" Sergio asked with equal seriousness.

"That's right," Duffy said, happy Aaron's friend had taken the bait. "Non nuff fyor business. The home is quarantined, so you are not allowed in, and they are not allowed out."

"Why haven't you posted it on the door?" Aaron asked.

"The decision was just made," Duffy responded as he wrapped his arm around Aaron's shoulder and led him and Sergio away. "The poof in there, what's his name, Sasha? He didn't take better care of himself."

"Like you?" Sergio asked bravely, patting Duffy on his "prosperity."

"Absolutely, absolutely. Just like...." he cut himself off, finally recognizing the barb. "Boys, there is right living and there is wrong living. Staying out until all hours of the night, sleeping with whatever will sleep with you, that's wrong living."

"Has my father been here yet?" Aaron interrupted.

Duffy responded honestly, "I can't say that I know."

"Sergio, let's walk up to see Augustus," Aaron suggested.

"You boys behave," Duffy called out after them.

Sergio followed Aaron's lead three-fourths around the block.

"We're not walking to see Augustus, are we?" Sergio asked.

Aaron shook his head.

"Back to Sasha's?"

Aaron nodded. He said, "I want to see what he can tell us before it's too late."

Aaron stood before the door with his hand about to knock.

"It works better if you make contact with the door," Sergio joked.

Aaron lowered his hand into his pocket and pulled out the knife he had taken from Notté. With a quick flick of his wrist, the blade popped out.

Sergio told him, "We don't need to pick the lock, Aaron. Knock and it shall be opened."

Sergio raised his own hand to knock but Aaron grabbed him by the wrist to stop him.

Aaron carefully held the blade up to a small cross that had been carved into the doorway's lintel. It fit perfectly into the slits. He pulled Sergio close to him so his friend could not be seen through the window. He knocked with authority, as he had heard his father and Duffy knock a hundred times before. Someone moved inside and the door creaked open a crack.

"I'm here to see Sasha," Aaron announced.

"But we are under quarantine," the woman informed him.

"It's all right," Aaron assured her. "Both Duffy and my father, Lucre, sent me."

She opened the door wide enough for them to enter then closed it right away.

Aaron asked as he entered, "How is Sasha?"

She looked at him worried, unsure if he should be there at all.

"An inconsiderate question." He held up his hands apologizing.

Unwilling to lose his momentum, he continued walking across the broad room where Sasha had so often performed his violin. He made his way toward the bedroom.

"This won't take long," Aaron assured her.

"Stop," she demanded.

They obliged and turned to her.

"He's not well," she told them. The voice of authority that commanded them to stop suddenly turned into a pleading, shaking voice. "You shouldn't see him, or you may risk getting what he has."

Aaron confidently lied, "I'm sure there is no worry about that. You stay here, Sergio. I'll be careful," he assured her, "and I'll be right back."

He walked on without waiting for permission. Once at the door, he opened it silently, slipped through, then closed it with equal care.

Aaron approached Sasha's bed on cat's paws. He looked down on his friend who was covered in perspiration, his eyes closed, his lips blanched with fever. Sasha's breath was labored and rattled around his lungs. Aaron thought back to Rashi's description of his son's final breath. Aaron assumed that Sasha was not far from that same experience.

He looked down at his friend's translucent skin, at the veins that bulged from his dwindling arms. A harvest of purple lesions in all levels of formation dotted every patch of skin that Aaron could see. Aaron wasn't sure if it was these wounds or his imagination that gave the room its heavy, earthy smell.

A floorboard creaked beneath Aaron's feet and Sasha opened his eyes, freezing Aaron without an infinitesimal movement of the sick boy's head. He remained perfectly still, his hauntingly vapid eyes seeming to stare through Aaron to the wall behind him.

"Sasha," Aaron whispered. "Sasha, I have a question for you."

Sasha's visage did not change.

"Sasha, where did you go when you left the valley," Aaron asked. "Where was it that you first got sick?"

Sasha looked through Aaron for another long moment, his glassy hollow eyes unblinking, before he turned them toward the ceiling and closed them without speaking a word.

Aaron stood over the sick body for as long as he could stand the silence. He reached out his arm and placed it on Sasha's thigh and shook him gently. The moist heat of the boy's fever seeped through the sheet.

Aaron looked down on Sasha's wasted frame. His eyes continued down to the young man's exposed feet. Something caught his eye. Aaron walked down to the foot of the bed and there, below Sasha's ankle was a raised cross—a scar—of equal sides.

"Sasha?" he whispered. "Sasha?"

Again the empty eyes opened and turned from the ceiling to Aaron.

"Sasha, I need to know where you were when you went missing," Aaron asked. "Blythe is missing. Remember Blythe? We're trying to find her."

Sasha's Adam's apple lurched up in a spasm. For the first time there was some human purpose around the eyes as he winced to speak. Little by little Sasha's face came back to life: first his eyes squinting, his cheekbones rising, his jaw pulling back with the greatest of effort. Sasha was ready to speak as Aaron leaned in as close as he felt safe to do.

"Henry," Sasha whispered looking up at Aaron with profundity. He repeated the name as if it held all the meaning in the world. "Henry."

"I don't know a Henry," Aaron told him. "Is he from the valley?"

Sasha sank back into his pillow. His eyes once again turned toward the ceiling, then closed. Sasha's breathing resumed its laborious tugs.

Aaron quietly walked out of the room and closed the door behind him. Sasha's mother cast aside everything she knew that was happening to her son and studied Aaron's face for some sign of hope, but seeing his grave response, she immediately reclaimed her worried wrinkles.

"You should go in," Aaron suggested. "He doesn't sound like he has long."

As Sasha's mother walked past, Aaron asked, "I noticed a small cross on the lintel of the door when we came in. Was Sasha secretly devout?"

His mother covered her mouth in a laugh that surprised her as much as anyone. "Sasha religious? I should think not. Perhaps it was there from the previous owner. Sasha has only lived in this home for two years."

Aaron shook his head. "The marks are fairly new. They don't have any stain or weathering over them."

"How is this important?" the woman asked.

"It almost certainly isn't," Aaron told her. "But I was curious. I wish

I had some words of comfort, but there is nothing to be said at a time like this."

"Thank you for understanding that." She managed to smile and turned toward her son's room.

Aaron and Sergio let themselves out. Sergio turned to look again more closely at the lintel. He asked, "What do you make of the cross?"

Aaron said, "Do you remember Red Pants?"

"The one you threw out the door?"

"He tried to cut me with this knife," Aaron said. "See the mark?"

"A cross."

"There was also a cross brand or tattoo on that man I found…on Stephen, down by his ankle." He slipped the blade gently into the crease and retraced the marks. He said, "Now we have a line from Red Pants to Sasha."

"And if that is a line, then it has to be drawn to…."

"Yes, to Blythe as well," Aaron confirmed.

Sergio asked, "Time to play your card?"

Father Philip walked down the hill past them as the two walked toward Old Lucre's. The priest paused as they all nodded at each other in passing.

"Aaron," Philip called out. "What's the trouble?"

"None at all," he insisted.

But the priest persisted. "Your expression says something else."

Aaron said, "I just have so much on my mind right now, Father."

Father Philip looked at him and asked, "What have I always told you in such circumstances, Aaron?"

Aaron thought for a moment, then responded, "God gives you everything you need."

"And," the priest asked.

Aaron concluded, "You just have to look around for it, and it will be there."

Chapter 28

"So you're certain?" Iris asked Duffy across their table.

"Absolutely, absolutely" he reassured her.

"You're sure of it?" she pressed him.

"Iris," Duffy laughed, "this is Blythe we're talking about. We would be more worried if she came home every night than if she didn't. I'm certain she's fine."

"It's just that I've been hearing so much about all these young ones disappearing and then coming back sick."

"Who's been telling tales?"

"No one and everyone," Iris said. "Everyone has heard a whisper about it. It has me worried for her, Duffy."

"Worry not," he said. "Those young men are in trouble for God knows what they've been doing with each other. You tell The Hens...."

"The Ladies," Iris corrected.

"Tell those Hens that whatever is happening to those young men is their punishment, but there'll be no punishment for Blythe, Iris. What has she done to be punished for?"

"But she's in their circles," Iris insisted. "She's with them and around them every day."

"You can't square things with circles; we're as close to their circles as she is, but you're not concerned about that happening to you, are you?" Duffy asked his wife.

"Of course not, but…."

He cut her off, "So don't be concerned about Blythe. No one will steal the cheese off of her plate. She'll take care of herself."

"I suppose you're right," Iris said trying to act comforted by what he said, but the worry lines at the corners of her eyes remained unconvinced. "So where do you suppose she is?" Iris asked. "Have you even looked for your daughter?"

"I haven't, but I don't need to, Iris. That is how sure I am that she is fine."

He looked across at his wife who stared down at the tabletop.

"Iris, I know more than you or your Hens of what goes on in this valley, and if I'm not concerned, you shouldn't be concerned, either." He kissed her head and gave her a hug around the shoulders. "I'm off to Lucre's. I'll be back in time for dinner. Set three plates. That is how certain I am that Blythe will be back tonight."

He slammed the door behind him in his customary manner, rattling the entire home.

* * *

Duffy stood before Lucre's desk and said in a confidential tone, "I'm concerned, Lucre. Blythe hasn't been back for two days. You don't suppose she could be up…. Well, you know."

Lucre looked at him skeptically. He asked, "Now how would that be possible? You yourself said he's only taken men in…and the Troublesome Ones at that, right? And you said Gwen might be with him, but we have no confirmation of that, do we?"

"Absolutely, absolutely," Duffy said most assuredly, but then added, "It's just that I'm having second thoughts about how we've been handling this. Maybe we were wrong to keep that place a secret."

Lucre gave him a skeptical look. "Well, that was your choice for your own reasons. You know my motivation. Are you now questioning your own?"

"You had no problem with my motives when you suggested we

keep this between us," Duffy shot back defensively. "Don't attack me for going along with your plan."

"Look, I know what we're going through now looks bleak, Duffy, but I'm sure that's the worst of it. We've made such progress and that couldn't happen if the entire valley knew what was happening up there; that whole place would be put on even greater guard. There is no success where there are no secrets. Don't give in now. I'm sure Blythe is fine. Stick to our bargain. Hasn't it made your life easier with those troublemakers too caught up in this to make trouble for you?"

"That's beside the point if Blythe is in there, Lucre."

"You know as well as I the chances of that are about as likely as you passing up Sasha's place," Lucre said, dangling the offer in front of him. "Have you made your mind up on that yet?"

In a rare act, Duffy reprimanded Lucre. "This isn't the time for that."

"I know, but you've been thinking about it, haven't you? You don't have to give me the full amount we discussed right now. Whatever I can quickly get for the place you know I can use. Let's take off twenty-five and we'll call it a deal."

"Twenty-five?" Duffy said surprised.

"I want you to have it as much as I want to get it off my hands," Lucre said. "We both win this way."

"Fair enough," Duffy agreed with a hearty smile shaking Lucre's hand to close the deal, but his expression quickly lost the thrill of the bargain.

"She's fine, Duffy," Lucre assured him. "You know as well as I that she's fine. You'll have your daughter, and she'll soon have a new house to call home."

"I didn't come over here to talk business," Duffy insisted, "but since you raised it, let me give you some earnest money so no one takes the house from me. I have fifteen; will that do?"

Lucre jibed, "You didn't come over here to talk business, but you're carrying fifteen on you?"

Duffy blushed and shifted uncomfortably.

Old Lucre reached out his hand and extended it to Duffy. "This alone would do, Duffy. A man is only as good as his word."

"That's fine, but my word and my fifteen will get me that house. Here it is."

The bell on the front door of Lucre's shop rang as it opened. Lucre and Duffy descended to find Aaron approaching the stairs as Maddox sat silently behind the counter.

"I've got some news," Aaron announced.

"So do I," said Parissa from the doorway.

Aaron spun around.

"Parissa," he exclaimed abandoning his father and Duffy. "Where have you been? You look like hell. We've been worried about you."

She said, "Well, no thank you for the first thought, and thank you for the second."

Aaron asked her, "Where have you been? Where's Blythe?"

Duffy looked at her, but Lucre held his arm to restrain him from speaking.

"Aaron, we need to talk," Parissa said, and she led Aaron by the arm just outside the door. "It took me two days to find my way home I got so lost. I slept in the woods last night. Can you tell?"

Aaron ignored her call for a compliment. "Where is she? Where did you two go?"

"Blythe and I went to another party after the one at Bruce's," she said. "That friend of yours, the one who left without saying goodbye to me, took us there."

"He's not my friend," Aaron insisted. "Where did he take you?"

"In the fog of that night, I couldn't honestly say," she said. "It was no place that I had been before. Some falling down house."

Aaron asked, "So Blythe is back, too?"

"Aaron," she said quietly, "I can't tell you."

"Are you saying 'I can't tell you' I don't know?" he asked, "Or 'I can't tell you' I shouldn't tell you?" Aaron asked.

"You decide," she said. She moved in closer to him and lowered her voice even more. "Aaron, as soon as we left the party at Bruce's, they clicked."

"Clicked?" he asked.

"Clicked," she repeated. "It was pretty innocent at first. Holding hands, too much laughing. But by the time we got to the bridge…."

"The old one?" he interrupted.

"Yes," she said. "We went way up there and beyond. By the time we crossed the bridge, Aaron, well…. I couldn't believe it."

"You're lying," he shot back, caught up in the moment. They both looked around toward the empty doorway.

"You're lying," he repeated in whisper.

"Aaron," she angrily cautioned him, "I would just as soon go to bed than be here. Do you want to hear what happened or not?"

"Parissa, I don't care about all the details," he said softly. "All I really want to know is, where is she right now? I want to know that she's all right. Is she back with you?"

Parissa shook her head.

Peeved that he had to play her game, he asked laboriously, "Well where is she?"

Parissa wouldn't let him off that easily. She walked past him to the door and as she did, she said, "You're asking the wrong person. Maybe you should ask your friend that she was with."

"Wait!" he ordered, stopping her at the door. He shouted at her, "For the last time, he is not my friend. He didn't wait for you because I threw him out the door after he pulled a knife on me. If this is the same one that Blythe left with, I have a right to know where he took her and where she is now."

Parissa looked at him dazed and asked, "He pulled a knife on you?"

Aaron led her through the evening. "He saw Blythe and me in the alley. He made some smart remarks and we nearly came to blows. He smarted off again inside about what he'd like to do to Blythe, so I took him on in a challenge and pinned him. He pulled the knife. Augustus opened the door. I tossed him out. Now I hear that he took you and Blythe to some abandoned home and you're standing here, but where is Blythe?"

Blythe

"Aaron, I had no idea," she confessed.

"Where is she?" Duffy shouted, pulling free of Lucre's grip.

Parissa looked down as she relived the evening in carefully chosen words, "She...they...they were getting so physical with each other, that I didn't feel comfortable. The two of them.... They...."

"What?" Aaron and Duffy asked together.

She said, "We were all playing a game where you had to take off an article of clothing every time you crossed a threshold. Remember, Aaron, we had had a lot to drink before we ever left, and we only drank more when we got there."

"So?" he asked, urging her to continue.

"So," she began, "it came down to one piece left for each of us. That's as far as I was willing to go, but Blythe took him by the hand and they.... Do you really need to know?" she asked Duffy.

"Tell me," he demanded.

"She took him by the hand and led him into a bedroom where I saw her take off her final piece of clothing then close the door," she cried. "I left right after that and I've been walking back ever since."

"Was he in a white shirt and red pants?" Duffy asked.

Parissa wiped her eyes and looked up at him, surprised by the specificity of his question. "Yes," she said. "Yes he was. How did you know that?"

Duffy turned to Maddox and asked, "Do you know the one Parissa's talking about?"

Maddox stared blankly at him.

"Answer his question," Old Lucre demanded.

Maddox remained silent. His father bellowed, "Answer the man's question."

"His name is Notté," Maddox said quietly.

"Is he part of...?" Duffy began to ask, but Maddox cut him off.

"Yes," he said. "Yes he is."

Before he could finish speaking, Duffy was out the door.

"What's going on?" Aaron demanded of his father and brother.

Neither said a word as Lucre looked violently at Maddox and

Maddox looked at the floor. Unsure of how this would play out, Parissa quietly slipped out the door.

"I need to know," Aaron demanded again. "What is going on, and where is Blythe?"

"We don't know for sure," Lucre said quietly. "She may be…. She may be in the kingdom."

Aaron looked at him nonplussed.

"Kingdom?" he asked. "What kingdom? Where Bruce and Gwen went? What kingdom are you talking about?"

"Follow Duffy up the hill," Lucre said. "You'll have no trouble catching him. He'll show you."

Aaron burst out the door.

* * *

Lucre turned to Maddox and said nearly breaking down, "This may be our last chance, son. Here is fifteen."

He handed Maddox the money Duffy had just given him.

"Stay out as long as you can and save this for when you're back in there and want to leave," he advised Maddox. "Get whatever intelligence you can from him and do your best with this. We have to recognize that once word gets out about the kingdom, there are no guarantees; you may be stuck in there until the end."

"But we know I can't stay out here," Maddox said.

Lucre nodded and pulled his son into his arms and hugged him close. "We've come too far to lose this now."

Lucre released him and pushed him toward the door. "Go and God bless," he said.

Lucre stood alone.

John E. Kramer   198

Chapter 29

Amid the valley's short grass, the earth's skin parted with a sensual sliver. The crease opened to a room lined with cords of innumerable passageways that connected every home and each person in the valley. The opening, and all it held buried below, was unique but by no means singular as many others could be found if one knew where to look. Entering any of them, however, was not to be done recklessly or without consideration of where they might lead.

Slip through one portal, wind along its way, and some kitchen may be the destination, with its comforting smell of bread baking. Take another route, connect to another byway, and end the trek where it began, achieving nothing more than the journey itself. Take a third path and the dense, confining dampness grows all around. Plunge deeper until two disquieting considerations must be confronted in that tight, dark space: the sheer mass of the earth that lies above, and the question of how long a ceiling can withhold such enormous weight before caving in. Squirm farther into that haunting internment and achieve the reward of growing room on every side until a crawl becomes an upright walk with arms outstretched if that is the wish. The archway ahead and the light beyond promise the lie of seemingly unlimited open space and a place to breathe, freely.

* * *

Blythe sat at the edge of her bed, her bloody arms resting in her lap when Notté entered. Even so slight a breeze as that caused by the door's opening created tiny fork points of intense pain across Blythe's face which had broken out with shingles. She cut short her wince because of the greater pain any facial movement caused the coarse net of bright red fishlike scales. Resting so much as a fingertip anywhere on them was agony.

"I brought company," Notté announced in a pleasant voice that immediately turned angry upon seeing her state. "What the hell happened to you?" he fumed.

Blythe twitched, realizing how she must look. She quickly covered her arms and carefully pulled back the curls that fell forward to cover her face. She raised her head and forced a smile up at him through her pain, hoping it might appease him, but the look of revulsion he returned blunted her brave effort.

"What did you do to your face?" he demanded to know.

"Nuh—ing," she said, trying not to move her mouth as she spoke.

"Blythe, this is Richard," Notté announced as he raised an arm for his acquaintance to enter. "He's brought us some food and some information about this place."

"Heh—o," Blythe said as warmly as she could through her forced and muted smile.

Richard stepped in, looked at her quickly as he returned her greeting, and then averted his eyes back to Notté.

"What do you have there?" Notté asked in an incongruously happy voice.

Richard handed him the provisions and said in the brief and uncomfortable tones of a man who did not wish to be where he was, "Some roast, some cheese, and here's some bread."

"Aren't things looking up, Blythe?" Notté asked.

Her bowed head nodded.

"Would you like to stay and join us, Richard?" Notté chirped.

Richard responded, "No...I...well," looking to find the words that could extract him. Notté flashed a sudden and severe look of disappointment at him that only exacerbated the man's stammering until he concluded, "I shouldn't. I came only to share this food with you and a little of what I know about this place." He spoke as if following a script he had not fully committed to memory.

"Well then, Richard," Notté asked in his high tones. "Why don't you start by explaining what happened out there?"

Richard struggled nervously, "Those animals that purged the kingdom . . ."

"Purged the king-om?" Blythe asked.

"Yes," Richard confirmed. "That is what it is called when they are set on us. They are the Mournex—Henry's henchmen."

"Mournex," Blythe repeated. "They live in the tunnels?"

"They are hidden throughout the walls of the tunnels that come in here. When Henry feels like his strength is weakening, he calls them to swarm out and purge anyone his captains trap in the courtyard."

"The captains are the ones dressed like Notté?" Blythe sought to clarify.

Richard turned his face away from both of them and nodded. "Yes, dressed like him," he repeated.

He said to Notté, "Your choice of clothing is fortunate. If they think you are one of them, maybe they will leave you alone. That is all any of us hope for. I know that is what I hope for."

"I'm sure they will," Notté assured.

Richard continued to Blythe, "The Mournex are the agents of Henry's strength. When they swarm out and eat those the captains trap, that somehow extends Henry's immortality and reinforces the kingdom's walls."

"You said something abou- Henry's immor-ali-y?" Blythe pushed the words out as best she could. "You can't be serious."

"Your name is Blythe?" Richard asked.

She nodded.

"Blythe," he explained, "Henry is alive and everyone who was out in that courtyard is dead. I believe in Henry's immortality. I think you would be wise to, as well. Never mock a king in his own castle."

"But immor-ali-y?" Blythe objected, "No one is immor-al."

Richard shrugged, "Listen and learn or don't, but Notté asked me in here to tell you what I know."

"Notté," Blythe said to herself. "His name is Notté."

Richard explained, "There is something about the Mournex consuming those bodies, drinking their blood that reinvigorates Henry, that strengthens the very walls around us. It is all connected, Blythe. And there are only two ways Henry allows a captive to die; either by his Mournex or he releases the person to die outside these walls by some other means after he's drained whatever he can from them. Suicide, murder or any death by any other means is not only not permitted, under Henry, it is impossible."

"And how do the cap-ains fi- in?" Blythe asked.

Richard said, "The captains themselves have taken a blood oath to Henry, spilling their own blood," he said, motioning with his right index finger across his left palm. Notté moved quickly to stop him from going on, but he was too late. Blythe looked up at him in disbelief.

Richard turned to Notté and studied his face. Abandoning his earlier self-consciousness, he concluded, "For that, they are promised a share in Henry's immortality, but I am less convinced of any promise made to the captains or any ones made by them."

"Thank you, Richard," Notté said coolly. "I think it is time you go."

Notté put his hand on Richard's shoulder and turned him to the door. "Why don't you thank Richard for the gifts, Blythe," Notté suggested without ever looking at her as he pushed Richard through the open door.

"Than- you," Blythe called out absently to the empty door, her head swimming with everything she had learned.

Dual distractions battled for her attention. In the hall, Blythe heard a quick, sharp whistle then Richard's voice protesting, "No! No! I did what you asked. I told her what you asked me to!" There was a thunder of many feet and the sound of scuffling, then silence from the hall. At the same time a crack at the opening to the courtyard turned Blythe's head. The madman who had accosted her in the courtyard had thrown a bone at the window and was yelling at her. His face and head were badly bruised and he shook as he stood there shouting, "I tried to warn you about him, and look at my reward. His men did this to me because I warned you… because I told you the truth. All I had left was my mind, and now they're taking that from me, too!" he bellowed. "I gain nothing by telling you, but I'm still speaking, so listen. You're with the devil. He's Henry's steward. Leave him. You can leave him before he hurts you anymore."

The madman fell to the ground in a convulsive heap as Notté returned and shut the door behind him. Seeing Blythe stare out the opening, he walked over and closed the curtains without looking out.

"You're one of them," Blythe stated, able for the first time to ignore the shingles and the thrush that had developed on her tongue. "You didn't bring me in here by accident. You knew all along."

Notté smiled warmly at her as he walked over. It was a smile that said he could explain. Without warning and without his smile dissipating, he slapped her across her shingled face with the full force of his hand. Blythe had never experienced such torture. She felt the searing pain shoot from the burning surface and explode in the very roots of her nerves. She let out an uncontrollable scream and threw herself to the bed using her arm to shield herself from the next blow.

Notté stood above her, unmoved. He said in a voice of controlled rage, "Don't you ever embarrass me like that again…with the way you looked…with the questions you asked. Whatever the hell you do to your arms, it stops here. You embarrass me again and you'll get worse than this. Do you understand me?"

She gasped for breath between her cries.

"Do you understand me?" he asked again in an even more intense tone that told her she had better answer.

She managed to sob out in four syllables without moving her mouth, "Yea-eh-ss-ss,"

"Sit up," he ordered.

She remained turned on her side, her arm still covering her face.

"I said sit up," he insisted.

She turned over and sat up, turning her shoulder away from him.

He walked over to pick up the food Richard had left on the

bed. She turned her shoulder in the other direction. He pulled out a replacement for the knife he had lost to Aaron and quickly fashioned her a sandwich.

"Here," he instructed. "Eat this."

He held the sandwich toward her face, but she would not look up or turn toward him.

"I said eat," he demanded.

She raised her hand and fumbled to take it from him, her hand flinching when it touched his skin then moving quickly to find and take the sandwich. Behind her curtain of curls she forced a small bite, breathing in with great sobs.

He walked back over to the window and opened the curtain. The madman was gone. Notté watched as people milled about the compound in a pointless danse macabre.

"You need to eat to keep up your strength," he told her. "I don't want to see you fade quickly in here. If you don't eat, you will. I'm tired of screwing twigs, Blythe. I want you to keep your curves."

She resented the sound of him speaking her name.

"I did take you in here on purpose, Blythe," he confessed. "It is a rule of the kingdom that when one is allowed out of the walls, he must take someone back with him. That is the only freedom you will find here, and once you take it, you will want to take it often to escape the thought of this place if only for a little while. That is how Henry can afford to make his sacrifices to sustain himself. You may not understand me now, Blythe, but soon enough you will. Do you feel that tightness in your lungs?"

She unwittingly took in stuttered steps of quick sighs to validate his point.

"There it is," he said. "That is what you will want to escape. Henry will get this place so packed the only hope for sanity is to leave these walls for some short time to breathe the outside air. But, again, remember: When one leaves, two must return. And two will stay inside until a Mournex purge or Henry releases them to the world outside to die."

He paced in front of her as she sat with the uneaten sandwich in her hands.

He said, "I believe in Henry the Fourth, Blythe. I believe in his promise of immortality. That is why I joined him as a captain."

He held out his palm to her unwatching eyes. "Oh, certainly, I did not ask to be drawn in here anymore than you did, but here we are. And if we are going to be in here, we might as well make it work for us, don't you think? Isn't it better to be counted among the living than to die?"

He looked at her for some response but saw only the top of her head.

"You don't have to die, Blythe," he said with new energy in his voice. "You can join us as a captain. You can join in his immortality. You can be free and even go out and bring that Aaron back with you to join you."

"Never," she croaked without looking up.

"That choice is yours, but here you are," he said. "Let me leave you now, but ask yourself this: What are you willing to do to live, Blythe? A small mark on the hand of an already scarred arm and a little promise to serve, and you can join him; you can live forever. I have never made that offer to someone so new to the kingdom, but I feel strongly that you have an important place here. That is why I felt inspired to draw you in. Henry has an answer for you, Blythe. He is god now. It is time you became a believer."

Notté walked to the door, but before he left, he offered her two more pieces of guidance.

"Before you attempt it, Blythe, let me warn you that suicide is an impossibility within these walls just as Richard explained," he said.

He paused. "Poor Richard. I miss him already."

Notté continued, "Henry sees all from his tower and knows when such attempts are made. He sends us to stop them, and we do. But there is always a price in terms of your own physical comfort that must be paid for such an unwise gesture. Trust me; you don't want to find out what that can be." He said by way of example, "Consider how your face feels now as a small warning, a pretaste, if you like. That is a gift from Henry to you with a warning from me that if you try suicide or murder in here, you will suffer a thousand times worse than that, Blythe, but not be permitted to find the sweet release of death. Do you understand me?"

Blythe

She became suddenly aware again of the throbbing, numb pain in her cheek.

Without warning, he struck her again across the same cheek. Her face exploded in searing pain. She threw herself on her bed and hid her face from him.

He let her screaming die down to crying and her crying die down to sobs before he continued. "No death occurs within these walls except for those that Henry desires; it is his plan that all those held within his kingdom grow weaker as he grows stronger, but, I promise, he will not kill you unless he wants to. He will release you before you die. So remember: Suicide is forbidden."

Then his tone became cavalier. "You need to get some air, Blythe. You need to get out of this room and walk around out there. The air will do you some good." He talked sweetly as if all conflict was forgotten.

His manner caught her so much by surprise that Blythe looked up with a deadened but no less incredulous expression. "How could he speak so cheerily to her after what he had done?" she wondered.

Seeing how she looked at him transformed his face from friendly sympathy to the narrow eyes and pursed lips of resentment; he was insulted that she had not accepted his suggestion in the kind spirit that it was offered.

As he left, he said, "Before you show yourself, though, clean yourself up. You're an eyesore."

Blythe cleaned up as best she could and plodded out. She knelt beside the stream and for a long time did not move. Her hands fell limp in her lap and her eyes held a dead expression that could not focus on anything around her. She felt empty in every way imaginable.

She leaned forward and raised a cupped handful of water and gently washed her one arm and then the other. The water was a salve to her hot skin and somehow she felt it begin to heal the wounds that lived for her whole life deep beneath the surface of what others saw in her.

Gaining confidence, she cupped her two hands together and drew up as much as they could hold. She raised them toward her face. Slowly she lowered her nose in to see how badly it would sting. To her surprise, it was soothing. One cheek and then another was lowered in, followed by the corners of her forehead. She scooted close to the water's edge and dunked her entire head below the waterline. She held herself under and turned her head back and forth, soaking in the coolness, drawing on its cleansing force not just for her body, but she could sense for her mind and spirit as well. It seemed a true baptism that worked to restore her to a state of grace.

"I will be restored," she promised in a voice that she didn't feel came from herself. It was something else, someone else speaking to her. "You will be better."

She bent deeply forward and submerged her entire head under the surface as long as she could, finally raising it straight out and letting the hair drip down in a cascade. She steadied herself and carefully raised her hands to either side of her face and in one smooth motion tossed the hair back into place. She knelt there for a long while, her hands resting on her knees, not looking at anyone and not considering for a moment whether anyone was looking at her.

At last she stood up and surveyed the entire courtyard. For the first time she noticed people gathered around barred openings throughout the outer walls. The people yelled out across the vast expanse surrounding the kingdom to those from the valley who had just learned of the kingdom's existence.

She walked to an opening that was not as crowded as the others and listened in.

One young man yelled out, "Well, this wasn't my idea. Do you think I'd choose this for myself? Don't be ridiculous."

A second kept on shouting, "How could you have done this to me? How could you have done this to me? I thought you loved me. How could you have done this to me?"

A third called out, "You've got to change. You've got to change the way you're living or you'll end up the same as me. Don't do that," he pleaded. "Change your ways and live. You've got to live for both of us."

As Blythe turned to walk away, she heard her father call out her name. She elbowed her way through the little crowd to the sound of his voice and looked through the opening.

Out beyond Henry's wall was the thick nest of rose bushes Notté had described to her. Beyond that was a morass no one could hope to cross without fear of being impaled on the sharp barbs and thus finding themselves dead or a captive of the kingdom. There Duffy stood, off in the distance where she now knew he and everyone else she loved would always be.

She called back to him as he stood with the others, just within earshot, "Father!"

He studied the structure looking in each opening he faced until he finally picked out her face and her waving hand.

"Blythe, oh, Blythe," he cried in horrible recognition. Behind him stood two silent twin figures that looked so much like Aaron and Augustus, but she couldn't be certain from the distance.

"Don't cry," she pleaded. "Everything will be okay," she promised him in the hope of stanching his tears.

"You don't understand," he said. "You don't understand what this means, Blythe."

"I do," she said. "But we'll find a way out. There has got to be a way out."

Duffy could not respond through his tears. He doubled over from the discovery and there it was—the movement that Blythe had expected. One of the strangers next to her father moved only as Aaron could move, comforted Duffy as she knew Aaron would at such a time.

She searched for the words to call out to him, but what could she say? How could she explain?

Duffy straightened up and called to her through his weeping, "I didn't want to believe it. I didn't want to believe that you could be in there, Blythe. That place was not meant for you. I am so sorry, my daughter. Forgive me. I am sorry."

He doubled over again as Aaron placed one hand on Duffy's back, the other on his shoulder.

Blythe called out to him and tried to reassure him, "You had no way of knowing. There was nothing that you could have done. I'm in here because…." she looked at the little figure of Aaron. "I'm in here because of what I have done, not because of anything you did. Please, don't cry," she pleaded.

As she spoke, Aaron raised his head to look at her when she gave that first admission of what drew her into the kingdom. It was that posture that made her stop and consider her words so carefully.

"Aaron?" she called out.

There was no response. The little figure did not look up.

"Aaron, is that you?" she called out, and Duffy stood up and turned to the other little figure and rested a hand on his shoulder.

"Aaron, I'm sorry," she called out to him, but there was no reply.

"Blythe," Duffy said. "I have to go home. I have to tell your mother. I have to go home and tell your mother what I've done."

"Dad wait," she asked. "Wait!"

He stood before her with his head bowed.

"Father," she said sternly. "I love you. I'll find a way out. I will."

Duffy did not respond to her, but slowly walked away and out of view. The figure she assumed was Augustus soon followed.

Aaron and Blythe looked at each other across the distance without speaking a word. They stood and looked at each other until everyone else had left.

"Aaron?" she called out, not expecting an answer.

"How I love you," came his reply.

It was her head that bowed in sobbing.

"Blythe?" he asked. Upon seeing her face again, he continued, "I don't know a lot about that place, but I know I can join you. We can be together."

"Don't you think of it!" she yelled at him. "If you even say such a thing again let alone act on it, I will never speak to you again. I will lose all love and respect for you, Aaron. Do you understand?" she demanded to know.

He remained silent and she repeated her threat. "I will lose all respect for you, Aaron. All love for you. Don't you dare. Promise me you won't. Promise me," she yelled to him.

"I promise, Blythe," he said. "But I also promise I will find a way to

Blythe

get you out. I give you my word."

"Don't," she cut him off. "Don't give your word on things you can't control, Aaron. You should know better."

"But…."

She said, "I know you want me free, and we will find a way, but to give me your word on something that you know you cannot control is lying. Please, Aaron, now more than ever, let's be truthful with each other. That is the only way we can win."

"I promise," he called to her.

"Aaron…. I'm sorry."

"Don't," he said.

"But, I…."

"Blythe?"

The directness in how he called her voice stopped her.

"Yes."

"I need you to say a prayer with me. The Lord's Prayer."

"Okay," she said hesitantly, not understanding why he chose this time for that prayer. They said together, "Our Father, who art in heaven. Hallowed be Thy name. Thy kingdom come, Thy will be done on earth as it is in heaven. Give us this day our daily bread, and forgive us our trespasses as…."

"Stop!" he yelled out. "Stop there, Blythe."

She was confused, but she followed his command.

"As," he repeated. "That is the most difficult word in a Christian's life. We must forgive *as* we want to be forgiven."

He let the silence of that moment settle in with her.

"I don't want to limit your forgiveness of me or God's forgiveness of me for all the times I failed you…for all the times I failed you both. And there were plenty of them. I forgive you, Blythe, as I want to be forgiven— and that is completely."

"But, I…."

"Don't, Blythe. We'll talk about that later. Let's find a way to get you out of there. Have you seen Henry? Is there some way I could speak with him?"

From the darkness within the walls, knowing laughter floated about at his words.

Protective of his pride, she tried to ease him off the subject. "Nobody sees Henry," she told him. "But if any sweet voice could talk someone to freedom, Aaron, yours could."

Disregarding the obvious impediments, he asked, "Are you all right in there?"

Again more laughter went up at the absurdity of his question.

"Everything is fine for me," she assured him. "Aaron?"

"Yes."

"Do you still love me?"

"Blythe, how I love you," he said in a statement, not a question.

A mocking voice from within repeated, "How I love you," but this was rebuffed by surrounding voices who certainly shared Aaron's emotion with someone outside.

She rested her chin on the back of her hands. "That's all I needed to know. Go home now. It's late. We'll talk tomorrow."

"Not yet," he insisted. "Tell me how it is."

Silence lasts longer in darkness.

At last she spoke. "It's lonely. It's sometimes dangerous, Aaron, I won't lie to you. There is every basic thing one needs, except hope. The men here seem no different than you. But I should be with you, Aaron. I shouldn't be in here."

Despite her best efforts, she broke down in a fit of sobs.

After another long, dark pause, Aaron called out to her again, "Walls alone don't make a person a prisoner, Blythe. I'm bound with you."

"I know," she told him, crying all the harder.

For another long moment there was silence. Then, Blythe called out again, "Aaron?"

From deeper in the darkness came his reply, "Yes, Blythe?"

"Always come to this window. This will be our window," she said.

He choked out the words, "I love you" loud enough only for himself to hear.

She called out, "I love you."

Blythe

He shouted in a reflexive tone that was both desperate and tearful beyond his ability or desire to disguise, "How I love you, Blythe."

Now as close as the voice had ever been, Aaron called back, "This will be our window. We'll talk tomorrow."

"Sweet dreams," she teased, as she always had at the end of their evenings.

He sniffed back a tear and laughed in surprise at the ridiculously positive wish.

"You will be free!" he promised.

"I am free, Aaron," she reassured. "You make me free!"

Without seeing the other, each reached out a hand across the distance. Their hands remained so far apart, but in their hearts, they touched.

* * *

On the other side of the camp, in a simple room much like Blythe's, a middle-aged man sat next to Maddox on the bed and whispered into his ear, "We'll follow our usual arrangement. Take your commission if you choose, although I say that each time and each time you decline."

He turned and let Maddox pretend to whisper for a while in his ear as well.

Back in Maddox's ear, he continued, "Bundle your clothes up on my pillow and when you get dressed, take the map that's under there and give it to your father. Leave with it immediately after we're through. It lays out nearly all of the kingdom's structure. There is still one area that I've not been able to see with my own eyes—in the tower in the center of the kingdom. I can't figure out how Henry gets in and out of it. Logic tells me there must be some substructure, but I can't seem to find the way to it. See to it that no one but your father gets that map. If anyone else sees it, it is certain death for you and me.

* * *

Duffy opened the front door to the sound of his wife's singing in the kitchen and the faint dripping of the water leaking from their bedroom ceiling into the pot. He closed the door behind him quietly, without his customary slam.

"Blythe!" Iris called from the kitchen, "Just as your father had promised! I can't tell you how glad I am that you're home, dear! I was so worried this time."

Iris rounded the corner to see her husband standing with his hat in his hand and a terrified expression on his face.

She took one look at him and began to cry, "Oh, no." She repeated the words, speeding up each time they were said, "Oh, no. Oh, no. Oh, no. Oh, no. Oh, no."

Strangely, she did not rush to Duffy as he had envisioned. Instead she retreated to her kitchen, standing before her stove although she did no work there. She no longer sang. She crossed her arms before her and rocked as she fought against her tears. "What was it?" she called over her stooped shoulders. "Tell me what happened to her?"

"How did you know...." he began.

"Duffy, don't toy with me," she shouted at him. "I've got eyes, don't I? Tell me what's happened to my daughter," she snapped.

Duffy walked in through the kitchen door. He looked over at the three plates arranged on the table.

Iris trusted him.

"Blythe had trusted me, too," he thought.

He began to blubber as he spoke, "She's.... She's...."

"Duffy, end this for me," Iris pleaded. "What happened to our Blythe?"

"Iris, she's been taken into a place called Henry's kingdom. It's a place ruled by...."

Iris whipped around. "She's alive?" Iris asked.

Duffy looked at her uncomfortably and stammered, "Well, yes, but...."

"You're telling me Blythe is alive?" she begged to know.

"Yes, but...."

"Oh, she's alive, Duffy," Iris exclaimed as she rushed to him and hugged him as she had never done before. "She's alive, she's alive, she's alive," Iris repeated, loving the sound of the truthful words. "Oh, dear God, when I saw your face, I knew the worst. I knew she was dead. But she's alive, Duffy. Oh, dear God, our Blythe is alive. Thank you, God! Thank you!"

It took Iris so long to compose herself that Duffy finally interrupted, "Iris? Iris, dear? I think the stew is sticking."

She gripped him tight once again and walked to the stove. She stirred the pot then took it off the heat. Iris let out another joyful yelp and laugh then asked, "So when will she be home? Will she be home tonight, Duffy?" wiping away a tear with her wrist.

Duffy suggested, "Iris, the news is not as good as it seems." He moved her toward the table.

Duffy proceeded to explain to Iris in the finest detail all he knew about Henry's kingdom, about those who had been taken in, about his knowledge of what had gone on before Blythe entered but his ignorance that his own daughter, or any woman for that matter, could be drawn into such a place.

Iris asked intelligent questions, most of which Duffy could not answer with any specificity. But the questions he could answer unequivocally, took away nearly all of Iris's hope.

Ashen, Iris asked again, "But can't you save her, Duffy? Can't we get her out? Is there no hope at all to spare her these things...to spare her that end?"

Wanting to give Iris hope, he began, "Absolutely, absolutely...." when Iris shouted, "Oh, not more of your absolutely, absolutelies," and she burst into tears.

Iris rose.

She could not look at Duffy.

Iris implored, "God save her. Please, God, save her," and left the table to make her way slowly up the stairs. She chanted, "My dear girl. My dear, dear, dear girl. What have we done, my dear girl?"

Duffy remained at the table. He echoed Iris's plea in a mumble. "Dear God, protect our Blythe. Forgive me for what I've done...for what I haven't done, and let me make it right, dear Lord. Please, let me make it right."

The ring of the drops of water in the pot carried down the stair. He waited well after the meal for Iris's call to him to change the pot, but Iris never called to Duffy.

Duffy wobbled to the stairs and climbed them with the greatest effort. He walked past his own door and into Blythe's studio. He lifted a match from his pocket and struck it against the wall to light a candle. He walked over to the painting Blythe had given him and Iris on the night she disappeared. He held the light close to the canvas to admire the work.

"We were happy," he whispered. "We were all so happy."

He looked at the crag of rocks and smiled when he thought of him and Blythe talking about how fearless she had been.

"You'll need that now, dear," he said.

Something amid the colors of the three of them reclined at picnic caught his eye and he stooped in to take a closer look. He cursed as the candle flame singed his cheek. He pressed the spot to take the sting away but it didn't help.

He stooped again, holding the candle more carefully.

Duffy gently rubbed the tip of his index finger along Blythe's arms on the canvas. The color was permanent but a few tiny flakes came off on his finger. He held it next to the light to examine them.

He stood back and held the candle up higher for better illumination on that spot. He had never noticed it before, but the color was so out of place, so dark amid the brightest point of painting.

"Why would she paint her arms the color of…." he searched for a description and finally settled on "dried blood?"

He tried in vain to flick the specks off his finger then walked away from the painting to comfort his wife.

Chapter 30

Henry's scheme was shrewd and well-constructed, beyond anything Duffy may have hoped or Lucre may have feared.

Henry positioned his initial agents at those cross paths of society rarely discussed in polite circles, but often traversed nonetheless. From there, new provocateurs—witting and otherwise recruited—extended Henry's web into the mainstream silently, without notice. His forces performed their work with the swiftness of human desire. Capture became an art form. The structure of his kingdom undetected, Henry tensely poised to strike even the most unexpected places, to take the most unexpecting people. Victims were mortally wounded even before they realized they were struck. Anonymity was Henry's strength.

As Gwen read to Bruce at their wedding:

"Be on guard if it gives you comfort, for all the difference it will make. I am patient and ever-watching. I live for that moment when you think yourself safe. It is then I will steal in and surprise you, when you thought you would be forever left alone and untouched by the mystery that sweeps in those around you. Hidden in love's plumage, I will descend upon you. Mankind's greatest desires—to love and to be loved—will find my way into you. Reason with such a power. It cannot be done. Predict its course. It cannot be done. Stifle its drive. It cannot be done. I will conquer with that force that conquers all. Your heart is not safe from me. So long as there is love, I will find you. So long as there is love, I will make you mine."

That was the promise of Henry the Fourth; that was the work of his agents.

Shrouded in ignorance, his kingdom was impregnable, impermeable, inevitable; his assault knew no retreat. Every hold was a stronghold; each man taken was clenched in a death grip.

To inform villagers of his capabilities, he sent down scores of fragile young men to haunt the streets, unrecognizable to their closest kin. Their eyes looked back with a fixed terror, like death was visible before them. Whatever it was that Henry was doing to them behind those walls, he dragged it out; he drew out as much from them as he could before tossing the husks away. With the return of each young man, and later older men and then women and ultimately children, those in the valley were reminded of a new proverb: lived in haste, died in leisure.

Seeing these wasted souls infused in the valley people a mindset of living under siege; trust, compassion and generosity—and with them so many of the once-natural social human tendencies—withered. A heavy yoke of shame bowed the heads of those in the kingdom as well as those who loved them. A psychological fever stifled the entire valley; it held each person rigidly in place with doubt and fear; doubt about what they had done that might take them away, fear that any misstep would lead to their own disappearance.

Henry understood that his forces must be widespread and entrenched before many learned of his existence because public awareness is the equinox of tyranny's rise; once one man learns of another's captivity, he will act to free him. It is the best and most certain part of man's nature.

Chapter 31

"Are you somehow surprised by this?" the old man shouted up at Father Philip. "What would be surprising is if God did not allow a Henry or his kingdom to be created to punish those who flouted His will."

"It may seem harsh," the man continued lecturing to the silent priest, "but I would not be truthful if I did not say it: stigmas matter. We must communicate to those who slouch toward the kingdom of Henry the Fourth that what they are doing is against nature and against God. And they are against us. This is not intolerance," he insisted. "This is love."

He said, as if looking down through the floor, "God has abandoned those sinners to live in a world created entirely of their own sin. God did not create that kingdom. Henry did not create that kingdom. Those inside did. They built those walls by their own actions, by pursuing their own temptations. They placed themselves on the cusp of their own ruin. These martyrs to faithlessness assigned themselves their own fate by their own sins, by their rejection of God's goodness."

He concluded, "It is an oxymoron of faith that to live freely we must remain held captive by God's will in our lives rather than by our own desires. This is their time for remorse. This is their time for atonement. This is their time for bowing before God and His will."

"Do you really believe what you say?" Philip asked.

"And what is that?" the old man responded.

"That Henry's kingdom is a judgment?"

"How does it strike you?"

"A test," the priest said, "but not of those in there but rather of us out here. To see if we listened when Jesus told us to love those we see as our enemy."

The old man grimaced, "That is not the message."

"But it should be," Philip insisted. "Even sinners have every right to self-determination."

The old man said, "You know the words: the wages of sin is death."

"Wages of sin?" Philip asked incredulously. "Death is a hell of a price for what could amount to only one mistake."

"Death and hell are often the price for rejecting God's way," the old man said dispassionately.

Father Philip asked, "So they should live and walk like you and your straight lines?"

The old man gave him a skeptical look and said, "You may have grown tired of my straight lines, but what is happening up there is what happens when man deviates outside the lines. God draws the lines. I live by them. It is not our place to question it. No one enters Henry's world sinless. From what we know they've each earned their punishment."

Philip countered, "No one enters this world sinless either, but that shouldn't make us another man's slave and his sustenance."

The old man shook his head. "If you're going to take a side, at least don't take the side of sin. It is unbecoming for a priest."

Father Philip laughed, "Perhaps you're right, but refresh my memory; who was it that ate with tax collectors and prostitutes?"

The old man carped, "Have you ever seen anything that was more clearly God's judgment than what is taking place right now on that hill? Look at who Henry has taken! It is not the little old lady making bread or sitting in our pews. It's homosexuals. It's fornicators. How can you think it is our place to criticize that? Stand aside and let God's judgment run its course."

"Every war, every plague is God's judgment," Father Philip said.

"But every man who rises up to stop the wars and the plagues is God's instrument. Human action is God's will, not blind indifference in the face of suffering. This is no different than any other struggle in the history of mankind. It is a fight between good and evil, between freedom and captivity, between life and death, and I will not stand idly by when I can help."

The old man finished as the priest walked away to prepare for the evening Mass. "What is needed is for those inside to repent and know God's mercy and for those out here to reform so they don't end up a victim of Henry's kingdom."

Soon thereafter before the congregation, Father Philip read from John's gospel. "Jesus crossed the Sea of Galilee and a large crowd followed him, impressed by the signs he had done in curing the sick. Jesus climbed the hillside and sat down there with his disciples. The time of the Jewish Passover was near. Looking up, Jesus saw the crowds approaching and said to Philip, 'Where can we buy some bread for these people to eat?' He said this only to put Philip to the test; he himself knew exactly what he was going to do. Philip answered, 'Two hundred denarii would not buy enough to give them a little piece each.' One of his disciples, Andrew, Simon Peter's brother, said, 'Here is a small boy with five barley loaves and two fish; but what is that among so many?' Jesus said to them, 'Make the people sit down.' There was plenty of grass there, and as many as five thousand men sat down. Then Jesus took the loaves, gave thanks, and distributed them to those who were sitting there; he then did the same with the fish, distributing as much as they wanted. When they had eaten enough he said to the disciples, 'Pick up the pieces left over, so that nothing is wasted.' So they picked them up and filled twelve large baskets with scraps left over from the meal of five barley loaves. Seeing the sign that he had done, the people said, 'This is indeed the prophet who is to come into the world.'"

Father Philip instructed the congregation, "This is one of Jesus' most important acts on Earth. How do we know this? Because it appears six times in the Bible. Once in John and Luke, and twice each in Matthew and Mark's gospels. Six references."

He asked, "But where was the miracle here? Did Jesus really turn

Blythe

five loaves and two fish into so much food that it could feed five thousand men, not including women and children? To understand God's miracle here, you have to understand the geography of that area. The Sea of Galilee was both very long and very wide. Its shore is a rocky, difficult terrain to travel. It is no easy walk. Where Jesus rowed off to, there were no shops, although if Lucre's ancestors had known this, they would have built one."

The congregation laughed.

"It was a remote and desolate wilderness," he said. "Now ask yourselves this: Would any of you travel to such a remote place without packing at least a few provisions? Some food? Something to drink? Even to follow Jesus, you would certainly take the most basic necessities. Of course you would."

He paused then asked in a deep and serious voice, "But what if no one else did?"

He let the words echo throughout the church so the parishioners might truly think about what he had asked.

"What if you were the only one prepared when it came time to eat, everyone around you turned to you with begging eyes and expected you to share what you had. Who would give up what is rightfully theirs—the very food you and your family are depending on after that long journey and before another one back—all for strangers who weren't as smart as you, who refused to think and follow the most basic rules of common sense? Why would you possibly risk letting a single other soul know that you had food when they did not?"

"So they hid their food, each of them," Father Philip said. "All those who followed Jesus to the other side of that sea hid it and played dumb."

He proclaimed to the congregation, "A call went through the multitude, 'Jesus wants to know if any of you have any food to share?' They all looked at each other: 'Food? What is food?'"

The congregation laughed perhaps recognizing a little of themselves in what he said.

"Food?" he continued, "Oh! *Food!* No, we completely forgot about food knowing that we're traveling so far away from home and knowing that there is no way any food would be over here. Even though my bag smells like barley bread and dried salmon, I haven't got a crumb."

He laughed. "Jesus must have looked out on all of them and shook his head and thought, 'Isn't any of what I'm saying getting through to you people?'"

"So what did Jesus do?" Philip boomed. "He gathered the bread and fish of those in his immediate company…that food that was in his possession, that he could have eaten and no one would have questioned him because he was the master. But he didn't eat it. He blessed it. He broke it. He shared it."

Father Philip guided them, "But look at how he shared it, because that, too, is important. He gave it all away to his disciples to eat or to distribute. And what did they do? They followed their Lord's example. They shared. Others who received that food from the disciples were so ashamed at how they acted after they saw the example of Jesus and his followers, that they not only repeated it, suddenly their memory was restored. Another miracle! They remembered they had actually brought some food along. So they took it out, kept what they needed, and passed the rest along. And those behind them saw that example, and they too pulled out their bread and their fish, and on and on it went until everyone was fed and they had baskets left over. That is the miracle Jesus performed: melting the otherwise hard human heart, making tightfisted men and women compassionate when it came to the wellbeing of their brothers and sisters…even the stupid ones who did not look out for themselves. What a miracle. What a God."

Father Philip continued, "When Jesus was done sharing his five loaves and two fish, they had twelve basketfuls of scraps from this gathering that supposedly had no food to start with. Yes Jesus prayed, but I believe what is more important is that he took action. Prayer is not enough when faced with crisis. It is easy to rest the problem in the hands of God. 'It's all yours!'" Father Philip called to the ceiling. "That would have been the easiest thing in the world for Jesus to do. I believe that Jesus showed us by his own example that hands that remain folded in prayer are idle hands. When there is a crisis, let your heart pray, but let your hands work."

Blythe

The priest reached what he anticipated would be his conclusion. He said, "The miracle of the loaves and fishes may have been divinely inspired, but it was manmade. It was the manifestation of man's goodwill for one another. It was human action. Human action that is compassionate in the face of human suffering is God's will."

He paused and looked over the little gathering and he questioned to himself whether he had said enough or if he should continue. The parish waited. The spirit moved him.

"I realize there has already been a call by many of you for condemnation of those up on the hill," he said. The many faces that looked at him throughout his homily now turned down and away. "Yes these individuals are being held accountable for their actions, but don't forget about the Golden Rule. What would you hope this church's reaction would be if you were sitting where they are? Would you hope for condemnation? Or merely for prayer? Or for a host of people to pray on your behalf and then to begin working for your freedom?"

He reminded them, "Whether each of us will fall is no longer a question. That question was answered by Adam. What remains to be seen in each of us is whether we will rise again, and whether we will help others to do likewise. If we follow Jesus' example—if this is indeed a Christian church and we are each a part of that Godly body—isn't it our call to help those who have fallen? To not wait for others and to be the first actor in the next miracle of human action? I encourage you to come to the aid of others who are isolated from their homes, who are in need of comfort. Act."

He told them in verse:

Dim light grows to sustain a steady flame
Tear-shaped radiance glows as to proclaim
That all shadows of the world will be tame
When man's wish and his actions are the same.

"We are that candle of hope I wrote about in that poem. We share that hope with the world around us by our mere presence. When the dark forces of evil see us so strong, they will retreat, but only if they know that our desire to rid them from our midst will be matched by our actions. That is what that poems means. That is what is needed now in this valley."

He said, "No doubt you are wondering, 'What can I possibly do? What can any of us do in the face of something so ominous, of something so overwhelming?' The answer is this: anything. That is what you can do: anything. If you can write, write about the injustice that is going on up there. If you know others who by their own actions may lead themselves to that place, lovingly counsel them to avoid it. If you have gifts of healing, find some way of directing them to those individuals. The smallest act of compassion can save a soul, perhaps your own."

He reached his new conclusion by saying, "Act to help raise them up even though we know they may someday fall again. We are all terminally mortal, but looking after each other will help us to become part of the immortal divine."

Blythe

Chapter 32

Henry was nothing if not ingenious. His labyrinth of tunnels had served him well, but when that entryway became well known, he adapted new means to bring in still more captives. Henry often heard it asked, "How many angels can dance on the head of a pin?" as well as "Can a camel walk through the eye of a needle?" Turning the point of each of those questions upside down, Henry himself wondered, "How many legions can I gain at the point of a needle?"

He answered that question in the days that passed.

* * *

Blythe's discovery that Notté was part of the kingdom, that he had purposefully brought her in so he could enjoy a little taste of freedom, poisoned her view of him. But that did not end Notté's efforts to recruit her as one of Henry's captains. Blythe, recognizing how dangerous he was, had no choice but to treat him with aloof acquiescence; she could not reject him outright.

"I want to show you something," he said to her. "Come with me."

Blythe had little choice but to follow.

Notté took her farther down the hall to one of the outer rooms. Once he opened the door, she realized it was not a room, as all the others on either side were, but a stairwell that led deeper in an ever-constricting spiral toward the center of the kingdom. She followed a few steps behind him, hoping she might have a split second to react should he suddenly turn on her. Her shingles had healed, but the memory of the pain he caused her would not leave. That hatred was reinforced every time she saw him across the courtyard.

The hallway they traveled went deeper in, ending with an elaborately carved stone monolith. Before they reached the end of the hall, however, Notté turned off into a recessed doorway and whispered, "Here it is. Stand back and watch."

Notté swung open the door to reveal an orgy of half a dozen men and women engaged in pleasuring themselves and each other. Upon seeing what was inside, Blythe averted her eyes looking back down the hall. These were the first women besides herself Blythe had seen inside Henry's kingdom, and it disgusted her that this is how they should be employed. Notté was captured by the scene and looked on in fascination. Finally, he whispered, "Look! Look there!"

She refused.

"Women never look," Notté said, his eyes never leaving the jumble of bodies. "Most men get drawn in and it becomes part of them, but women…women can somehow resist."

His eyes studied the room. "Look!" he insisted in a hush. "Look at the walls."

Blythe looked beyond the writhing trios to the walls that surrounded them. She noticed nothing especially significant about them and turned away.

"They're growing in," he whispered.

Blythe turned back and closely looked at the corners of the walls. Almost imperceptibly the corners were creeping across the floor toward the center. Even across the doorway, a thin, translucent membrane was stretching out from all sides, reaching toward the center. The men and women, distracted by their pleasure, never noticed.

Blythe took in a breath to warn them, but Notté's hand reached back and grabbed her behind the neck. "Do you want to join them?" he threatened.

She gave a truncated shake of her head.

"Then be quiet and watch," he warned. "I can still throw you in."

Cell by cell the translucent walls within the room pulsed and grew toward the center. Even those who were spent and laid back on the others were beyond caring about what was going on around them. They remained oblivious until it was too late.

Finally, Blythe sensed no more motion from the room. Everything inside was still but for the continuous pulse of the walls, a realization that disturbed her even more than when Notté had first opened the door.

"This is how he does it?" Blythe asked. "This is how he reinforces his walls?"

"This is one way," Notté told her. "He has many ways. Just your mere presence here is giving him strength. You sense that extra tired feeling you've had now for some time?"

In her own mind, Blythe attributed that to her feverish lack of sleep over the past few nights. She nodded.

"That is another way he sustains himself and his defenses," Notté said. "Come, let's go back now."

Blythe's stomach was weak. She took only a few steps when she had to lean against the wall for support and wretched. The sudden sickness made her dizzy; it drove her to her knees. She wondered if being so close to the center of the kingdom wasn't draining her at an even greater rate. Regardless, she lacked the strength to stand or to move on.

Notté stood above her.

"Congratulations," he said. "You've made me very happy."

Only half-listening to him as it was, his words confused her.

"Oh, dear God, no," she thought. "I can't be."

Notté had another jewel for his crown.

The mere thought that they should be connected in that way made her wretch even harder, but there was nothing more to come up.

Notté laughed as he stood over her and watched.

"This will only last a short while, I promise," he said. "I've seen it many times before."

She was certain he had.

He said, "This only makes my offer to you that much more important, Blythe."

She wished again that he would stop saying her name. She was certain he sensed that, so he said it again.

"Blythe, if you want to keep your health, you will need to become a captain. All that is required is a little blood as a bond. Let's face it, you will have blood to spare that you would have otherwise spilled over the next nine months, so it is no loss. Become a captain," he pleaded.

She remained silent on the cool floor and thought back to the morning after their first night together. She thought that would be the worst morning of her life. She was wrong. Every morning from that day on seemed to be a continuing downward spiral that left her dizzier, sicker, weaker.

"As a captain, you'll join in Henry's immorality," he said.

"That is what I'm afraid of," she said.

He stared at her, confused, having missed his own malapropism that was closer to the truth than he could have appreciated.

"I'll never join," Blythe insisted as she rose. "I'll never join you or Henry."

"I think you'll reconsider as time goes on, Blythe. And when you do, I promise you that we'll take you. You don't have to die, Blythe. I don't want you to die. You may not believe me, but I love you."

She reflectively cringed. "You're not capable of love."

"But I am," he said pushing toward her. He put his hand on her belly and said, "Look at what we produced, Blythe. That is the product of love."

"That is the product of sex," she said. "They are not the same. We had sex. We never had love, so don't call it that."

"Call it what you will, Blythe, but you and I are tied now. Come join me fully. Don't be foolish. Do you want to die?"

"I want to leave, Notté."

"That is the first time that you've said my name, Blythe. I like the way you said it."

"You'll never hear it again," she said as she walked away from him.

He pursued her as she walked up the hall and to the stairs.

"Henry promised that whoever offers their life for him, he will save it, Blythe. Like it or not, in here Henry is god. Who are you to go against him? Why would you want to fight him and lose your very existence? All you have to do is give a little blood and take a little oath. That's all. Then you can live."

"I would rather die than do what you did," she said.

"Do you want to leave here?" he asked as if making an offer.

She did something she never thought she would ever do again. She turned and gave him her full attention. She said, "You know that is what I want. How do I leave?"

"Forever? Is that what you want?" he tempted her. "To leave forever?"

"Yes."

"The only way that you can do that is to live, Blythe—to live long enough to find a way out," he advised her. "If you don't join him, you will die. I promise you that. Henry will kill you in here or send you back out to die in the valley by some other cause. But if you join him as a captain, you can live and perhaps find a way out yourself. If you want to live, it is the only way."

Her hands rose from her hips and crossed around her chest. She looked down and away from him to consider what he said.

"It is the only way if you want to live," he urged her. "Can't you believe that that is what I want, too? That is why I have accepted such a position—to bide my time. To live long enough to find that magic key. I, too, want to leave. But to leave, I must live. Join me, Blythe. Will you?"

She turned and walked away from him without answering.

Up in her room, she looked out her chamber's opening over the courtyard. As she scanned those who meandered, the madman walked by, lost in thought. She tapped on the bars with her rings and gained his attention. She asked him to wait and ran out her door.

As she caught up with him, he continued on his way.

"I owe you an apology and my thanks," she began. "I know you were trying to help me. I didn't know you well enough to listen. All I knew

Blythe

was Not…." She stopped herself. "All I knew was him. And I should have known better. I'm sorry for what they did to you."

"That's all right," he reassured, reaching out and patting her forearm. "In here, what they did comes with the territory. There is always something new they can do to you and always a new excuse why they can do it. I knew it would be something terrible, but it would be worth the effort. It always is. Haskel," he said, extending his hand.

"Blythe," she reciprocated. "Have you been in here long?"

"Longer than most," he said. "For some reason, I survive while so many of my friends have not. Some were sent out to die in days. Some weren't sent out for months. I'm beginning to worry that I'm immortal, too," he laughed.

"You're not?" she asked, unsure of the answer.

Haskel held out his pristine palm. "I'm not a captain, if that's what you mean. And I never will be," he said. "That one you're with…."

"Was with," she corrected.

"Congratulations," he continued. "The one you were with has tried to recruit me in many ways over the years. He's tried praise, punishment, bribes, pretty much anything he can offer or withhold, but I've turned him down all along."

"And why is that?" Blythe asked.

"Do you really have to ask?" he said in a sickened tone.

"No," she admitted. "I'm sure it's for the same reasons I did, too. I just wanted to know what your reasons are."

"They're the same," he promised. "So what questions do you have about this place?"

"I…." she began. "Can you…," but she lost confidence in her thought.

"No," he answered somberly. "That is not allowed. If you tried to kill Notté, Henry will only kill you or make you suffer in a worse way, and with all deaths and suffering Henry only gets stronger, you don't."

She looked at him skeptically and asked, "How did you know what I was going to ask?"

"That is everyone's first thought when they come in here," he said in a rounded professorial voice. "They want revenge. You'll come to realize that living as long as we can is the best revenge we can exact. Anything short of that is just a distraction, a trifle."

She asked, "So what were you thinking as you were walking along here? You looked lost in thought."

"One day you are living at home, enjoying warm buttered toast and ignoring the conversation coming your way. Then on some morning you couldn't predict, you wake up in here. You're confused. You're outraged. You explain, 'I don't belong in here.' And then someone pulls you aside and explains to you in chapter and verse everything you did to bring yourself to this end, and you think back to all those saving words people who loved you tried to make you listen to, but you wouldn't listen. You knew better. In truth we didn't know anything at all until we faced something like Henry. And now you know one thing…two…no, three things, perhaps."

"And what are those?" she asked.

"You know where you are and you know what's coming and you finally realize all that you've had but lost. That is suddenly the extent of your knowledge."

"How were you drawn in?" she asked.

"That is a question I don't answer," Haskel said. "There are some things for each of us that have to be left alone, and that, for me, is it."

"I apologize."

"No need," Haskel replied. "We are only just getting to know each other's limits. What day is it in here for you?"

"I've lost track."

"That's easy to do," he observed. "For me it is minus ninety-two."

"Minus?"

"I count down, not up. It is the only way I can preserve my sanity. I have ninety-two days to go before I'm released, one way or another. My work is nearly complete; I'm writing my memoir. I've learned what I'm going to learn. I might as well leave when it is done."

"You're not talking about…."

"No," he laughed. "Hasn't that one told you?" he asked, nodding

Blythe

toward Notté who walked on the other side of the courtyard. "Suicide is out of the question. It is either escape or release or the Mournex, I suppose. I hope it's the first or some other way rather than the latter two, but beggars can't be choosers. One way or another, I'm leaving."

"You make it sound so easy," she said.

"Every decision is easy once you make it. The important thing is to think carefully, make your decision, and then work to make your choice the right one. That is the secret to a happy life. There are very few wrong decisions in life, but very few people who are willing to make the effort it takes to make their decisions the right ones."

"Do you believe what they've told us?" she asked. "About Henry's immortality? About his captains' joining in that with him?"

"Who can say if it is true or not? I suppose you would have to outlive them to come to any definitive conclusion, but I do have two thoughts about that."

"And what are they?" she asked. She appreciated his fluid mind.

"First, for as long as I've been here, I haven't seen a captain die by Henry's hands or by anyone else's. They do survive. But that's quite beside the point. The other thought is this: Would you want immortality if it meant taking another's life to extend your own? Even if you do live forever, would that be a just price for what you gain? I think not. I think it is dishonorable to dictate to another man what his fate will be, especially when it is that end and for that purpose."

"I feel the same way," she agreed.

"So the answer to your question is 'a definite maybe,'" he said. "I suspect that the one you were with—Notté—speaks with all the sincerity in the world, but with no truth."

Blythe nodded in agreement.

Haskel said, "We have to remember, the devil is a fallen angel. All those people like Henry and his captains, they want good things, to live, for example. But they are willing to get those things at any price. That is what makes them evil."

"Do you think there is a devil?" Blythe asked.

"I didn't before, but now I know where he lives," Haskel said, pointing to the tower. "As for Notté's offer to make us captains…to join in Henry's immortality, I won't take that poison. We don't need Henry to make us whole and eternal. We are those things already. Henry needs us to achieve them."

"How are we eternal?" Blythe asked.

"We aren't born that way," he explained. "We become eternal by what we leave behind, I suppose. For me, I write. That may not make me eternal in the purest sense, but it is as close as a thinking person can get; to live on in words or some other art. You shouldn't bite your nails," he suggested.

She smiled and put them down. "A lady has to have some bad habits," she said.

"Bad, yes. But unsightly, no," he said. "I must say, those are pretty rings. Do you collect them?"

She looked down and admired them for the first time since Aaron had given her the last one. "Gold is cold," she said. "The only warmth it has, we bring to it."

"I like that. Did you write it?" he asked.

"Aaron did," she said waving around the rings. "He gave me the rings along with those words."

"Sage," Haskel said, and then asked, "But no ring to cover that last finger?"

"I think he had one for me before I came in here. I didn't give him time to give it to me."

"Well," he said cheerily. "All you have to do is make sure that someday you leave here in such condition that he'll still want to give it to you and soon enough that you can still enjoy it."

"I only have minus one hundred days to go," she said.

"That's the spirit," he laughed. "As for Henry and that other one," Haskel continued, "I think they are like every other false prophet. They promise a hidden path to our happiness in the name of some deity, some force, some human act, and we follow never seeing that they are just people with greater lacking than our own. That is what drives them. They don't have a vision; they have a greater emptiness and they draw us in to fill it."

Blythe

"We should know better but we don't and we follow," Blythe said.

"Exactly," he exclaimed. "And look at where we end up. They promise us so much, but in the end they always take much more than they give. I guess it's our fault for trying to achieve something great rather than just being happy with something that is good."

"What did you say?" she asked him.

"Rather than trying to achieve something great, we should be content with something that is good."

Blythe threw her face in her hands and began to cry.

Haskel gave her time to collect herself. She said through her hands, "Those are his words. Those are his words exactly. That is what Aaron told me after he gave me this ring. He said if I want someone great, I should find someone good."

"Well," Haskel said looking around the kingdom. "I tip my hat to Aaron."

"What else did he say?" she continued. "There was some other way he put it…. Pursuing goodness leads to greatness, but pursuing greatness leads to ruin."

She broke down again.

"Look around," she said. "Look around us. Here is where someone else's greatness leads."

"Blythe?" Haskel asked. "I told you, I am writing a memoir. I don't know if it will ever be published, but the important part is that I reflect on what I learn each day. I've learned from what I've written. Perhaps someone else will someday as well, and they can avoid the mistakes that I've made. I started it when I was on the outside, but even as a teacher I found I didn't know much until I was drawn in here."

"So what have you learned?" she sniffed.

"Many things, but recently I summed some of it up this way. Catastrophe alone sparks man's salvation. I don't mean in the religious sense, although I guess it is appropriate there, too, because believers agree that salvation comes only after death. It is part of the human near-tragedy that we learn more from loss than from gain. Gain binds us until we stumble and fall into that black pit then we find the spirit of understanding and truth. And if we fall far enough and still persist, we find our salvation."

"So you believe in salvation?" she asked.

"I believe in salvations," he corrected. "I think life is a series of catastrophes followed by salvations, if we are willing to learn, until that great final catastrophe."

"Which may or may not be followed by an even greater salvation?" she asked.

"Exactly. But I only believe what I see, so I'll have to wait to answer your question," he winked. "The key thing to understand is that there is no shame in ignorance and failing; there is only shame in not being willing to learn and repeating the same errors over again."

"Now that we're friends, Blythe, let me give you some subversive advice."

"What's that?" she sniffled.

"You'll find this place overly constricting," he said confidently. "But keep in mind we all feel that way. It is not unique to you."

"Why is that important?" she asked.

"Because if you keep that in mind, it means you haven't lost your compassion. That is part of Henry's goal: to get us so distracted with our own misery that we forget about the suffering of others. I've fought that instinct, and I think it is one of the reasons I've lasted so long. That is why I first approached you to warn you about that one you were with."

Blythe smiled, recognizing for the first time Haskel's effort not to speak Notté's name. "Thank you," she said. "I will remember that."

"He wants us to forget about kindness, about love and consideration, about honesty and truthfulness. But if we don't forget them, if we fight to preserve each of those treasonous ideals, it is a little victory for us and a loss for him. It preserves what power we have left and keeps it from him. That's why I said this advice is subversive. Do you understand?"

Blythe took off the last ring Aaron gave her and handed it to him. They smiled at each other knowing each was perfectly understood.

"I shall keep it warm," he promised and slipped it on his pinky.

Blythe

Chapter 33

"Duffy told you about the water?" Aaron asked Iris.

"We haven't spoken since I found out about Blythe," she said. "He always wanted a quiet house. He couldn't have a quieter one now."

"Let me tell you, then," Aaron said. "We've all been asked to use only well water for the time being. The canal water isn't safe."

"Was it because of Stephen?" she asked.

"That and some more of Henry's flotsam that clogged the stream."

"You don't mean other bodies."

"No," Aaron said. "I wouldn't call them that. People aren't flotsam…to you or to me." He looked over to Duffy's study and continued. "Until the canal is cleaned and we are sure the water is pure again, we should avoid it. I know you'll miss swimming as much as I will."

"More," she said. "That and my baking are all I have now."

"We each lost her, Iris," Aaron said kindly.

She agreed with equal kindness.

"They are closing the public baths, too," he said. "The stream fed them as well."

"We have our own bath here," she said absently, looking up the stairs to Blythe's door. Iris suddenly answered a question he had not raised. "I could never get her to believe in herself. I could never convince her to believe in her own goodness, in her own worth, even as a little girl. She put on such a brave face but was so fragile underneath, so needful."

"She was the same with me," he agreed.

Iris continued, "She bit her nails until they bled. She starved herself for weeks. She would cry inconsolably in her room."

"And her arms," Aaron added.

Iris looked up at him with hurt eyes. "You knew about them?"

He nodded. "There was something lacking inside of her that made her do it over and over again. I did my best to stop her."

"I'm sure you did," she said.

"At one point I found out she used the rings I gave her to cut herself, so I took them all away."

"I wondered why you did that," Iris said. "I always assumed it was because you two had a falling out. Thank you for trying, Aaron."

"I gave them back when she found something else to use. I thought at least the rings could remind her that someone loved her; that someone wanted something beautiful for her…someone in addition to you."

"We all did what we could for her," Iris sighed.

"She had to see it for herself, though. We couldn't convince her of how much she had no matter what we said or did. You know that, right?" he asked.

"I do." She sighed again. "I do. And now…Well, what difference does it make? We both know what lies ahead for her."

Aaron walked over and hugged Iris as she cried. She excused herself to return upstairs to go back to sleep again, as she had been when he first knocked. Iris's celebrated energy waned. Losing Blythe took the strength out of her knees, she said. She found she could stand for only short periods of time, no longer able to stand for hours on end as she once had.

"Promise me something, Iris?" Aaron called to her.

"What is it?" she asked, resting on the foot on the stairs and one hand on the banister. She did not have the strength to turn and face him.

"Promise me that whatever happens you won't sell Blythe's paintings to my father."

"Why would we do that, Aaron?"

"Iris, I don't know that you would, but if he asks, would you please turn him down?"

"I will, Aaron," she exhaled. "For you, I will."

Aaron walked into his father's store and saw Maddox behind the counter in a colorful vest that Sasha once owned.

"Is that a vest or a trophy?" Aaron asked him as he passed and walked up the stairs.

"Aaron," Lucre said in his office, "I need you to go over to Sasha's and bring his instruments over here."

"Doesn't any of this profiteering weigh on your conscience?" Aaron asked.

"What would you have me do?" Lucre asked in a mild and genuinely apologetic tone that surprised his son. It was a tone that actually invited a response.

Aaron answered his father's question with three questions of his own: "Why do you have to buy it? Why do you have to buy everything? Why prey on them?"

"Aaron," his father tried to explain. "I am in a unique position to create some good in an otherwise bad situation. I've told you before that these people asked me to take what they left behind and sell it. I didn't initiate this."

"So each of them, on their own, asked you to do this without you ever asking them?" Aaron asked incredulously.

"Well, no," Lucre said. "Just Bruce. And I did suggest it to the others. But the choice was still theirs to accept my suggestion or not."

"Your money or your life, but in this case they lose both," Aaron observed.

Lucre assured him, "Aaron, all I can tell you is that you can't understand it all. You're not seeing the entire picture and, as I've told you before, I cannot share any more of it with you."

"Well, Father, the picture I'm seeing right now is Blythe trapped behind the kingdom walls. She's there. Duffy and I confirmed it."

"I'm sorry, Aaron," Lucre said with the deepest sincerity. "I'm

Blythe

genuinely sorry to hear that. You know I'll do all that I can to...."

"To sell her things?" Aaron snapped. "To capitalize on this like you did the others? I can tell you're already thinking about it right now. Am I wrong?"

Old Lucre's only answer was to bow his head.

Aaron pleaded, "If you have any love left for me, Father, you won't. You'll leave her paintings and everything else she owns just where it is as a sign that we both believe we can find a way to get her out."

"Aaron, let me just say this: Whatever happens, don't be led by your emotions; be led by reason," he said. "That's how I raised you. You have to know in your heart I would only do what would be best for you and for Maddox and for Blythe, as well."

"Don't you dare say that," Aaron shouted. "Don't you dare tell me that you have the best of intentions for Blythe when I know that you have information that you are keeping from me...that you kept from her and everyone else. You knew about that place, but you said nothing and instead sneaked around behind the scenes to take what you could as quickly as you could, before anyone else could get there."

Lucre had had enough. "Then believe what you want," he said. "Believe everything you want despite everything I've told you, Aaron."

"You won't get them, Father."

"I won't get what?" Lucre asked.

"Blythe's paintings," Aaron explained. "I've already talked to Iris and I have her word that she won't sell them to you. She's made me that promise and I believe her."

"Well good for you, Aaron," his father said sarcastically. "You finally stopped me. You're finally a hero."

"You're just upset that I was one step ahead of you. That I had information before you did."

"Yes, that is exactly why I'm upset Aaron. Congratulations...you fool."

"There is no blessing like someone else's curse, is there, Father?"

Lucre was spent. He said, "Go and get the instruments, Aaron."

"I won't."

"Excuse me?" Lucre asked.

"Do it yourself, Father. Or have Maddox do it for you. He's wearing Sasha's vest. Why shouldn't he take care of his instruments, too? Take them and give them all to Maddox?"

Lucre demanded, "You'll do this, Aaron."

"I will not," Aaron insisted. "I won't have a hand in whatever it is you're doing. I won't help you anymore."

"So be it," his father said. "You no longer work for me. I'll send Maddox over to your home with what wages I owe you."

"Thank you for the warning," Aaron said. "I'll make sure to count it twice if Maddox is the courier."

As Aaron approached his new cottage, he noticed a thin column of smoke rising from the chimney. Outside, the litter of leaves that once tumbled about the slate walkway and remained pressed there by the recent rains was swept off leaving black, wet impressions as memories of where they once rested. He cautiously leaned over the bushes and peered through his kitchen window. Inside, Parissa hurried to set the table.

He entered. Fresh wild flowers in a vase decorated the entrance room table. The smells of burning wood intertwined with cooked ham made his mouth water.

"Welcome home, Aaron," Parissa said sweetly, resting against the doorframe that led into the kitchen. "With everything on your mind, I thought you might forget to eat."

"That's kind."

"Shhh," she insisted. "Sit. Eat."

She turned back into the kitchen to serve him.

Aaron sat as she set a hearty sandwich and a cup of lentil soup before him. He finished one serving and then another. Finishing, he wiped his mouth with the cloth napkin she laid out for him. He looked at Parissa.

"You look as if you've never seen me," she said playfully.

"Thank you for this," he said. "I didn't realize how hungry I was. That was very thoughtful."

Parissa declined his praise as she reached out and pressed his hand, "You have enough to think about. It's time someone thought about

243

you."

Aaron looked down at her hand on his. His bright eyes welled into an even more intense shade of blue. As one tear escaped, he looked up at her and asked, "Do you think I'll ever hold her again? It can't be as futile as they say."

Aaron's tears surprised him.

Parissa rose and stood beside him. She buried his face just below her chest and stroked his head. His big hands gripped the back of her thighs. She pressed him in, closer.

"Aaron," she comforted. "Keep up your brave face." She stroked his arm and pushed hard, encouraging him to hold her tighter. "Don't give up hope," she urged him.

Aaron pulled away from the tearstains he left on her dress. In shame, he looked away from the dark spots. He sniffed resolutely, "She's not lost until I say she's lost."

"You're right," Parissa said with genuine encouragement, resting her hand delicately on his shoulder. "You need to believe that. Keep telling yourself that."

She pinched the side of her dress and raised it to wipe a tear that clung on his cheek.

Parissa gently turned his chin up towards her. She said softly, "Whatever happens, Aaron, I'll be here to help you. I still feel sick about being the one to tell you about Blythe and that stranger. If I had known what would have happened, please believe me that I would have stayed. I would have stopped her."

"You had no way of knowing, Parissa," Aaron said as he rested the side of his head back on her again.

She closed her eyes at the sensation.

He said, "I know you and Blythe had your differences, but I know you would never have wished this on her."

"Never in a million years," she whispered.

He said quietly, "We both know Blythe can't be swept away like the leaves on the path, Parissa. She's not lost."

"Shhh," Parissa calmed him. "No one said she is. You're tired,

Aaron. Shhh. She'll never be lost so long as you keep hope."

Parissa soon released him. As Aaron sat alone in his thoughts, she cleared the table and squeezed his shoulder as she left.

"Thank you," he called to her, but she said nothing as she left.

Ignoring his own admonition to Iris about the canal, Aaron went up to the willow beside the canal and undressed. It was a warm early evening. He was exceptionally hot after the climb. The first dive in was every bit the shock he expected.

He allowed himself to drift down the canal and back in time to when he and Blythe were last under the bridge. He remembered the warm softness of her breasts as they rubbed against his arms, the cushion of her lips as they kissed, the salty taste of her neck. He floated past the turn and tested his courage and endurance by once again diving below the surface and pulling for the rock he and Sergio had dropped beneath the span. Pulling hard deep in the water with both arms and kicking with his legs, he felt he approached the spot. He dropped one hand to reach for the stone and there it was. His lungs burning, he sprang to the surface.

Swimming there wasn't the same knowing that Blythe would not soon join him. He hoped to be refreshed by the water and by returning there, but instead it left him feeling hollow and alone.

He pulled his way back up the canal to the willow and lifted himself out. Aaron sat there against the willow until it was dark, tossing pebbles in the stream and wondering if he wasn't kidding himself by keeping alive any hope that he could save her.

Blythe

Part Four

Chapter 34

Even in her captivity, Blythe had to seek out art.

Although she was not willing to pay the price Notté suggested for supplies he offered after hearing she painted, she found other means of securing what she needed. She palmed a piece of charcoal here. She tucked a discarded piece of colored chalk into a hem there. By every means imaginable, Blythe collected a wide variety of artistic materials and applied them to not only her own cell walls, which was the first room in Henry's castle to blossom with color, but she decorated Haskel's as well.

Such wanton consideration and its reciprocal appreciation were clearly beyond Henry's bounds of tolerance, but somehow the punishment for the crimes never came. If anything, their benevolence somehow pushed back the walls by many layers, giving Blythe and Haskel more room to move about. In that way, Blythe's art proved liberating on many levels for herself and for her friend.

But the tiny acts of kind rebellion Blythe and Haskel performed remained the exception in the kingdom, rather than the rule. Such actions require individual empathy, individual thought, individual initiative—the very traits abandoned when Henry's threshold was crossed, where group membership in the kingdom overrode each person's uniqueness. They were all captives quarantined in the same plague-infested city. That was their defining characteristic so that no one viewed another as worthy of any special sympathy. Henry's world depersonalized the person. One does not think of the individual log when it is thrown into the fire. It is all just fuel. That was Henry's view and the view he inspired in those he cut down and consumed.

It was clear from the valley's view that the kingdom continued to grow outward and higher. For the first time, the castle could be seen rising above the treetops as a warning to the village that Henry was gaining and they were losing. The fortress view reinforced the reality that those outside formed a stream of humanity that flowed backwards up the hill. By ones and twos, villagers drifted upstream and were not released until Henry had taken the best from them and then released them to die.

Beyond those women she witnessed get consumed by the walls of Henry's kingdom, Blythe presumed herself to be the only other woman held captive there. In fact, there were scores of other women in hiding, each cowered and tucked away, unwilling to show themselves for fear of what might happen to them. But seeing Blythe out in the courtyard gave them the courage to step out. Inspired by what to Blythe was an everyday act—merely walking around, talking to those she encountered—other women bound by fear took the first steps toward liberation and joined her in the open air.

"I seen you," a woman yelled at Blythe.

Blythe looked at the woman's enormous belly and thought of her own condition.

The woman continued at Blythe, "You strutting round, thinking you're queen of the castle. Well you ain't!" The woman let out a high-pitched cackle.

"You hear me? Oh!" the woman suddenly shrieked as she held her lower back. "I seen you walking around with that Notté thinking you all something special. Well, how...oh!" she yelled again in pain, "How'd you think I got in here?"

The pain was too much for her. She sat on the ground but continued to yell, "You're just another jewel he polished up. But he'll get himself another if he hasn't already. You can count on that."

The woman yelled in a grunt, "Oh, it's coming. Oh, dear gawd, dear gawd, dear gawd, dear gawd. It's coming."

Mab's baby would be the first born into the kingdom. Blythe along with a few other women rushed to her side.

"I don't need your help!" Mab shouted at them. "Oh, dear gawd, help me!"

Mab's labor was intense, as all labors are, but mercifully short. As Blythe extended her hands seeing the baby's head crown, a captain stepped into the group and knelt beside her.

"Let me help," he offered.

"Have you ever done this before?" Blythe asked.

"No," he said. "But I've been taught what to do."

Mab looked up at him untrusting and pleaded with the other women, "No. Don't let him. Don't let him in here. Please, don't let him."

But they felt powerless to usher him away so they hung close around her and watched.

"Don't let him," Mab pleaded with them. "Please get him out of here."

In a rush, the baby was out and in the captain's hands. He gently cradled it in one arm and took out his knife, which was identical to the one Notté carried.

Blythe's hands were tense and ready to lunge. She prepared herself to wrestle the knife away from him at the slightest threat to this child. But he gently rested the baby girl in Mab's arms and said, "Congratulations." He opened his knife, cut and tied the umbilical cord then tended to the mother.

Blythe felt ashamed of her assumptions. She relaxed and smiled at the innocent, freckled face of the redheaded captain who smiled back at her.

Blythe looked up and around, and nearly half the kingdom was there to witness the event. Even all the captains, it seemed, looked on, except Notté.

As things calmed down, one by one the crowd dispersed until all that remained were Blythe, who washed Mab and her baby with water

Blythe

from the stream, and the captains, who milled around talking to each other seemingly oblivious to the scene.

"What are you going to name her?" Blythe asked as she wiped Mab's forehead. Little trickles of water ran down Blythe's uncovered forearms. Since bathing in the stream, Blythe had experienced a kind of rebirth. She no longer cut herself. Washing her arms each day in the cool water, she no longer felt the urge to do herself damage. Blythe looked down at her arms as Mab spoke. Only vague traces of the former scars remained, and those, too, began to fade.

"I haven't decided," Mab said. "There are a few names I was thinking…maybe Viola, after my mother."

"Or how about naming her after mine, Mab?" Notté asked from amid the captains.

"See your baby?" Mab asked Notté with nothing but pride in her voice.

He strode in and gently ran the back of his fingers against the child's cheek. "She's beautiful like her mother," he said.

Mab beamed.

"I'll let you three alone," Blythe said coolly as she rose.

"What's your name?" Mab asked.

"Blythe," she said. "And yours is Mab?"

"Yes it is," she glowed. "Thank you for your help. I'm so sorry about what I was saying. I hope you understand I was just in a lot of pain."

"I do," Blythe said. "You rest now and we'll talk later."

Blythe had not made it halfway across the courtyard when Notté called to her, "Blythe, I need to speak with you."

"Shouldn't you be with your baby?" she asked, never breaking stride.

"I just was," he said. "Isn't she beautiful?"

Showing him no tolerance, Blythe asked, "What do you want?"

"I have an idea for you," he began.

"Not interested," she said.

"So be it," he responded, standing his ground. "If you do not want to leave, that is your business."

He turned and walked back toward Mab.

"Don't toy with me," she shouted at him, but he ignored her.

She ran over to him, grabbed him by the arm and whipped him around.

"What do you know?" she asked.

"I don't like the way you are acting," he pouted. "If this is the way you are going to act, I will not tell you."

"What do you know?" she asked again.

"Do you want to leave here?" he asked again.

"You know I do," she said. "But I won't become one of his captains."

"That is a matter still to be discussed," he said. "But I know of a way you can leave here for a while, not forever, but it is at least a temporary escape."

"How?"

"I can arrange it," he offered. "See me this evening in my quarters and I'll fill you in."

He turned to walk away but she held him in place with a single, softly spoken word: "No."

"No?" he asked.

"I won't see you there," she said. "I won't see you anywhere but here anymore. What we've done, we've done. I won't do it again."

He smiled at her, "But Blythe, tell me you didn't enjoy it. You can't, can you?"

She struggled to find words that conveyed her disgust but before she could speak he responded, "I thought not. Come by tonight."

This time she said the words so quickly that he didn't have time to turn. "I'll never go there. I will never be with you again. Now tell me how I can leave."

"So be it," he said nonchalantly. "I'll tell you now. I've had my fun," he said, looking at her belly. It was a look that turned her stomach and her face showed it.

He moved in close and said in a confidential tone, "There are passageways where the Mournex are not permitted. There are passageways where one can pass safely from Henry's kingdom to the outer world and

Blythe

back again."

"Where are they?" she asked.

"Here and there," he said. "I could show you."

She asked, "And what do you expect in return?"

"Me? Nothing," he assured her.

"I don't believe you," she said.

"I give you my word," he insisted.

"Your word means nothing to me," she snapped. She thought of how Aaron used that expression. Aaron truly was as good as his word. For him, uttering that phrase meant the world; it meant himself. The thought of Aaron compelled Blythe to preserve the validity of those words on his behalf. She said to Notté, "That turn of phrase doesn't serve you well. It only makes me instantly distrust whatever you said. If I were you, I wouldn't use those words again."

"You can believe me or not, but I gain nothing from you leaving."

"And Henry?" she asked.

"Well," he backpedaled. "Henry is a different matter."

"I should have expected," she said. "There is no way I'm sleeping with him."

Notté laughed in hysterics. "Sleep with him!" he repeated. "Is that what you think? Oh, Blythe you are funny. No one has ever seen Henry, let alone been his lover."

"Then what does he expect?" she asked.

"Tell me, would you like to sleep with that Aaron again? Is that what you want?"

"That is none of your business," she fumed.

"Excuse me for asking a stupid question. Let's assume you do."

"What is your point?" she snapped.

"You can, Blythe," he said. "You can sleep with him and in fact, that is all Henry would ask."

"What are you saying?"

"I am telling you that I can show you a passageway out," Notté said. "You can be free of this place for a little while. You can be with your Aaron again, and Henry would expect nothing more from you than that.

Of course you would have to return."

"Of course," she repeated, thinking about everything he had offered. "That's it? No tricks by you? Nothing for him?" she said as she looked up at the tower.

"That is it," he assured her.

"And what about Aaron?" she asked.

"Aaron would join you," he informed her.

"In here?"

"We would take him in carefully," Notté promised. "Nothing would happen to him and for the time that you are outside you would be perfectly free. You and he would be together again."

"But by sleeping with him, I bring him back in here?" she confirmed.

"No, not you," Notté insisted. "You don't have to be the one to bring him back."

"But he will enter the kingdom? He will be trapped in here like I am?"

"Yes, but he would have the same freedom to leave as you do," he offered.

Blythe had a revelation, "What if I didn't sleep with him?"

"Who would you sleep with?" he asked a little intrigued that there could be someone else to tempt her.

"No one," she said. "I would leave and be free for that time, but sleep with no one."

"Well, that is possible, as well, but then there are other tasks you must undertake."

"Such as?" she asked.

"Such as pricking someone with a special needle, perhaps. That is all."

"But to leave," she asked, "I have to draw someone else in? Is that right?"

"Exactly," he said, relieved she finally understood.

"And what if I don't?" she asked.

Annoyed at her analysis, he asked, "What if you don't what?"

"What if I leave but don't draw anyone else in with me?"

"Then there is a price to pay," he said. "You've seen the Mournex. You know the price."

"I could stay in my room," she said. "I could lock the door."

Notté said in a yawn, "Others have tried. They are simply dragged out and tied to the tower. It is not a pretty sight. But that is all beside the point. Tell me, would you like to be free, Blythe?"

"That's not freedom," Blythe said. "That's murder."

"Call it what you will. Would you like to leave? This place will get crowded enough that I promise you, you'll want to leave soon enough if only to taste again a little space and freedom."

She looked at him in disbelief and shook her head.

"What?" he asked waiting for her answer.

"Just when I thought you couldn't get any more revolting, you come up with something new."

Notté shrugged, "So be it. Let me know if things get so tight for you in here that you change your mind."

They turned from each other and walked away, Blythe back to her room and Notté towards Mab. As he walked, Notté let out a sharp whistle like Blythe had heard outside her doorway. Fearing the other captains would soon swarm over her, she turned to see what he was up to.

The captains did swarm, as Blythe had expected, but not over her. Rather, they descended on Mab and ripped the baby from her arms.

She screamed, "Don't let them take my baby from me. Dear gawd, don't let them take my baby!"

Notté continued his casual stroll through the middle of the melee where he was handed the baby. He pushed Mab to the ground and pulled out his knife. Blythe was halfway there when Notté carved a cross into the baby's sole, which sent the baby and her mother shrieking.

The captains formed a circle around Notté as he walked toward an arch. Mab found herself quickly outside of the circle on her side, reaching futilely for her baby girl.

Notté yelled to the mother, "Stop your crying. Babies are useless for the kingdom. They can't bring anyone in. They must be sacrificed.

Think of it as an offering to Henry."

Notté turned from the arch and held the baby up toward Henry's tower. Everyone but Blythe and Haskel were frozen in fear for what might happen to them if they moved to thwart the captains' plan.

Blythe and Haskel threw themselves simultaneously at the captains' perimeter in a desperate effort to save the baby, but they could not break through. They were each punched to the ground.

Blythe called out for others to act. She pleaded with everyone around her to help, but they looked away, their hearts hardened with fear.

The captains formed a semicircle around Notté as he lowered the child into his arms and cradled it there. He let out three more crisp whistles and a gust of wind blew into the courtyard from the archway he stood before. His hair blew about in the breeze.

Blythe looked around to all the archway doors to see if she, too, should flee, but they were opened with no other captains in sight. She looked back to Notté.

"Please don't be the Mournex," she prayed. "Please don't be the Mournex."

She heard Haskel say to no one in particular in a voice that made her blood run cold, "As flies to wanton boys are we to the gods; they kill us for their sport."

The alpha Mournex she and Notté had watched during the purge slothfully crept out of the shadows and went as far out as the arch. He sniffed the air as the baby howled in her father's arms. The captains and everyone else in the kingdom looked on, still and transfixed.

Notté clutched the baby by her feet and let her swing down to his side. The Mournex's head suddenly snapped in the baby's direction. Notté remained perfectly still and dropped the baby out of his hand to the ground. Behind the line, Mab screeched for mercy.

Slowly the Mournex advanced on the child. It skeptically sniffed the crying newborn, then gently took it in its mouth, turned and walked slowly back through the archway into the shadows. In a matter of moments, the baby's cry was suddenly cut short.

Blythe strained to hear it again, as everyone did. But it would not

Blythe

return.

Blythe was the first to move as she stood up and brushed herself off. Haskel, too, stood, and they walked over to comfort Mab who lay on her side staring at the empty archway beyond the disbanding captains. Blythe, too, looked over there. She saw that Notté had disappeared.

As she and Haskel helped Mab to her feet, Blythe looked up and saw the shadow of a figure thrown up against the wall up in Henry's tower. She adjusted Mab's arm more securely around her shoulders and when she looked back up, the shadow had disappeared.

Down in Mab's room, Haskel and Blythe gently laid her in her bed.

"You'll stay with her a while?" Haskel asked.

Blythe nodded.

Haskel slipped out as Blythe gently swept the hair away from Mab's forehead and neck. She blew a gentle breeze on her temple. Soon, Mab was asleep, holding Blythe's hand.

Blythe slowly extracted herself from Mab's hold and rested her hand on the bed. She continued to blow soft breezes Mab's way as Blythe took off one of her gold rings, the eighth one Aaron had given her, which circled her right index finger, and slipped it onto Mab's ring finger.

Later that night, Blythe pointed out to Haskel, "She hadn't even had time to name the baby."

"The baby's name was Mara," Haskel informed her.

Blythe asked him, "How do you know?"

Haskel simply stated, "Mara means 'one with whom God has dealt bitterly.'"

Chapter 35

The old man who had yelled at Father Philip was engaged in a heated discussion with another parishioner as they walked out of the church. He said, "Still, we should pray for those in Henry's kingdom. We can only hope that their misery will be a happy misery made meaningful by the spirit of repentance."

There was, in fact, little happy misery in the life, death and hope for resurrection of those suffering in the kingdom of Henry the Fourth. It is difficult to be happy when one is coughing up blood as they drown from the buildup of fluid in their lungs. People misplaced the spirit of repentance when Henry turned their brain to pudding because of dementia. What those in the kingdom of Henry the Fourth really wanted was out; they wanted out.

Blythe had scooped up a little boy during a purge. They arrived too late at every door they came to as the Mournex swarmed around. Blythe and the boy were the final two to squeeze under the last archway door open before it closed. For many nights later, Blythe would be awakened by the feeling of the hand of that person behind her, the one that pushed her in certainly with the hope that he or she, too, would follow. But they had not. Blythe had no idea who that person was who pushed her, but she was certain they did not survive. No one survived the Mournex.

On the other side of the door, Blythe held the little boy close. She felt the bones of his ribs in her hands. There was little left of him after the wasting Henry had put him through. She was sure that he would soon be sent out to die as was the fate of nearly all children inside the kingdom. The little boy screamed as much out of anger as from the agony of everything he had suffered. His twiggish limbs and bulging joints were covered with seeping purple wounds. The swollen glands in his neck were granite marbles. He had become blind through Henry's wrath.

In Blythe's room, away from the madness of what transpired outside, she rested the little boy on her bed and knelt beside him. He gripped her hand with improbable strength considering his condition.

"I want this place to go away," he said. "I want this whole place to go away. I want things to be like they used to be. I want my mother back. I want my father again. I want him to carry me around again on his shoulders," he said. "I just want this place to go away."

"Shhh," Blythe said as she stroked his hair. She could feel his fever before she ever laid a hand on him.

"Do you like rings?" she asked to distract him.

He didn't respond. Instead he continued his blank-staring cry up at her ceiling.

"Tell me," she asked again. "Do you like rings?"

"I never had one," he coughed. "My mother had a pretty one. My father had one."

"What was your mother's ring like?" she asked.

The boy's crying subdued as he thought about it.

"It was gold," he said with wonder. "It was gold with all these rays shooting out from one corner so it looked like the sun was rising on her hand."

"Was it square shaped?" she asked him quietly.

"Longer," he corrected.

"A little longer than a square so it stretched across her whole finger?" Blythe asked.

"Yes," he said, excited that she knew. "That's it!"

She pulled the ring from her right pinky, which most-closely matched the one she and the boy described.

"I've got one like that here," she whispered. "Would you like your mother's ring?"

"Yes," he said with all the tired energy he could muster. "Yes I would." The thought calmed him.

"Here you go," she said and lifted his skeletal hand and slipped it carefully on this thumb. Although it had fit snuggly on her pinky, it swam around his little digit.

"You be careful with that, okay?" she asked.

"I will," he solemnly promised, and slipped the other hand over it for safekeeping.

Blythe asked, "You keep that and give it to your mother when you are with her again. Would you do that for me?"

"I will," he promised, fading closer to sleep.

"You promise?" she asked him.

"I promise," he whispered back to her.

His cough gave way to a struggling sleep, and his sleep gave way to the unconsciousness that would prompt Henry's captains to slip him into the stream taking him out of the kingdom, where he would take his last breaths.

Blythe hoped to herself that the ring she gave him would soon be where it belonged, forever on the comforting hand of his mother's in the great thereafter.

Later that evening in the courtyard, Blythe, Mab, and Haskel sat around. Blythe was very quiet, she was so taken with the little one she had seen drift away only hours before.

"I'm tired of thinking about Henry," Mab said. "I'm tired about him being everything we think about."

"Same here," said Blythe. "Why don't those people out there do something to end this? Why haven't they busted down those walls and gotten us out of here? Don't they know what we're going through? Don't any of them care?" she cried.

Haskel let her cry for a while, but then said quietly, "If we tire of thinking about Henry, then there is no hope for us."

"Why's that?" Mab asked.

"Think about it," he said. "Here we are in the center of the storm, and if we grow tired of thinking about Henry and talking about Henry and plotting against him, how interested are those on the outside who are only grazed by his storm going to remain? If we remain vigilant, they will as well. If we get bored and go slack, so will they."

"I suppose you're right," Mab said. She asked Haskel, "Were you a teacher or something before here?"

"Yes. Yes I was," he said. "I guess that is why I don't mind thinking all the time about this man. I thought of something today that gave me some comfort and maybe it will do the same for you two."

"What's that?" Mab asked.

"The way I look at it, Henry is the one with the problem, not me," Haskel stated.

Mab laughed. "You hear that, Blythe? He said Henry's got the problem. He's got problems all right, but you ain't it!"

Mab coaxed a laugh out of Blythe.

"Well, the problem for Henry is that I want to live more than Henry wants me to die," he said. "I think that's the same for you two, as well. That's why we're all hanging on."

"Oh," Mab said seriously. "So that's why I'm still in this hell hole? I wanna live?"

They all laughed together.

"Let me ask you two something," Haskel said. "Have you noticed the captains have been a little more...tame...than usual?"

"Yeah," Mab agreed. "What've you been doing?"

"I worked up a little cocktail and when they are all in the yard, I add it to their drinking water. You can't taste it, but it carries a good punch. This way when they're not drunk, they're hung over, and when they're not hung over they're drunk."

"Either way, they off our backs," Mab bubbled. "You're brilliant!"

"That one you two came in with," Haskel observed. "He's the only one who resists it. He's shrewd."

"Well, we all thank you for taking care of the rest of them," Blythe said. "The women especially thank you."

"I know some of them have just given up," Mab said in disbelief.

"Some of them have just made their peace with things."

"We all know better," Haskel said. "There can be no peace, no easy compromise of coexistence. He means to end us, and therefore we must end him. It is that simple."

"It is simple now that you said it," Mab chimed in.

Blythe said, "It's not a fight we asked for."

"But it is a fight we've earned...at least I've earned," Haskel said.

"It isn't a fight my little girl asked for," Mab interjected.

A heavy silence held the little group.

"You're right about that, and perhaps that is Henry's greatest punishment for us all," Haskel said. "What can be worse than to know that someone who is innocent died for our misdeeds?"

Silence again.

He continued. "You asked before, Blythe, why those on the outside aren't breaking these walls down. Think of the world we left to come in here. Think about all the inhumanities that world is exposed to every day. I'm afraid it's worn away the heart's walls. They can't feel anything for anyone anymore because death has just become a way of life. All that inhumanity has murdered human outrage without them ever knowing. That's the greatest tragedy I fear in this whole mess: that we've stopped feeling for each other."

"Don't you think anyone cares?" Mab asked.

"I know some of them do, Mab," Blythe said surely. "I know for a fact some of them do."

* * *

Father Philip read from the Book of Luke. "For each tree is known by its own fruit. Indeed, people do not gather figs from thorn bushes, or grapes from brambles. The good man brings good things out of the good treasure of his heart, and the evil man brings evil things out of the evil treasure of his heart. For out of the overflow of the heart, the mouth speaks."

Believing that every good homily begins with a question, he asked them the obvious question. "What fruit are you bearing from your thoughts, from your words, from your actions? Is it a kind fruit? Is it a loving fruit?"

Blythe

They laughed, as he knew they would.

"These days we are all consumed with what is happening up on the hill, and rightfully so," he said. "What kind of a man is Henry, do you suppose, if those are the fruits of his heart? What a rotten, rotten man. Rotten to the core. His name is Henry the Fourth, which suggests lineage. But I am dubious that Henry had a father, if you get my meaning. What do they call a man without a father? That is what Henry the Fourth has proven himself to be."

Father Philip told them, "Earlier today, some in this church heard talk about the 'happy misery' those in Henry's kingdom are suffering through. Happy misery. Happy misery," he said again. "I shudder at the words. Rather than casually submitting these people to the happy misery of their deaths, wouldn't it be nobler to take some action to give those people the choice of whether they live or die? There doesn't seem to be too much choice for them right now. That is the evil here—that some authority other than these individuals themselves is making that choice for them. This is what evil does; it makes choices for others in the name of religion, in the name of government, in the name of community, in the name of personal gain, that these individuals are best able to make for themselves. You've seen it in your everyday lives. We are seeing it up on the hill. Someone claims himself or herself an authority and says, 'You are to do this,' or 'God wants us to do that.' Don't believe them. You are your governor. You are your faith. Think about what is best for you, and then do that. Short of harming another, what is truly best for you is what is best for God and government and mankind. Don't allow yourself to be blindly led. Grow and harvest a thinking fruit from your tree."

He said to them, "I spoke many days ago and told you praying hands are idle hands. I said that God would be happy if our hearts prayed but our hands worked to help those in the kingdom find freedom. Let me add to that today with some thoughts on other idle hands. Those are the hands that death has made idle. Those are the hands that Henry has left still, and how it affects us."

He urged them, "Consider for a moment the unanticipated legacy those in the kingdom leave behind. It is a legacy of half-done tasks abandoned because of captivity and then death. How much richer our lives would have been if those now lifeless hands had completed that manuscript and thereby given us a better understanding of who we are and inspired us to be the joyous people God envisioned. Rather, the scraps of notes and half-filled pages yellow. The ink of man's knowledge fades.

"How much healthier our lives could have been if those now still hands had had a few more days or months or years or however long the strands of their lives would have stretched but for Henry? They could have mixed those herbs and crushed those minerals and combined them to cure our malady. How much imagination we have lost because the hands that could have held that sustained note that confirmed in our hearts the certain joy God meant for our lives instead rest, crossed across a still chest in a grave dug equally by man's sin and the devil's delight? How much we have lost."

He concluded, "Let me leave you with these words of hope, however. The most frightening time of this crisis is behind us. That was when we knew nothing about who we were up against. He didn't even have a name. Now he does: Henry the Fourth. Three simple letters: H.I.V. Think about how important that is, that he has a name. It was no accident that one of the first things God asked of Adam was for him to name the animals he saw around him. Why do you suppose God asked man to do that? Because once you have a name, you have the beginning of understanding, and once you have understanding, you lose fear. God didn't want man to be fearful. He wanted man to be brave. So here we have Henry's kingdom. We know what it is and where it is. Now it is up to us to follow that first burst of knowledge we just experienced to see how this evil can be checked and ultimately defeated. There is no other course for man. When we see a wrong, we must correct it. When we see evil, we must conquer it with our own good. Yes, there will be delay. Yes, there will be angry words and fighting. But in the end, man must pursue the path of knowledge to some good end. We have choices in how we reach that end, but the outcome is never in question. Man must be free or he will not survive. All in this valley will be free, and we all will survive."

After everyone had left, Aaron asked Father Philip how God could allow evil, like Henry's, to exist?

Blythe

"It is not that complicated, Aaron," he said. "It is because God gave us the capacity for great intelligence then granted us free will to decide between good and evil. Some of us will use our skills to elevate man by freeing him; others will choose to elevate themselves by controlling man. In nearly every action we choose either the side of freedom or the side of control. There should be a constant tension between the two sides, but unfortunately, sometimes it is only those on the evil path that make the effort to draw people to them. Let's face it, there is more incentive to justify their actions by drawing more and more people to their cause. When you are absolutely certain of the purity of your quest, you will never force a person to join your side. You will assume people will see the wisdom of your way, and they will follow out of persuasion, not force. And they will. But when, at the base of your ideals, you are convinced that your ideals are not wholly pure, and others will judge them so as well, then you will conscript others to your cause, whether you're in the government, in the church, or in Henry's kingdom. You will supersede another man's free will and choice; you will wall him up; you will impose your choice upon him. That is the essence and outcome of every bad decision man has made. It takes away one man's free will by demanding that he follow another's. Most men lead average lives; they do this only in petty ways. But the most intelligent of our species can do this on a grand scale. For good or for evil. God doesn't will these things. Man wills them or wills them to end by his actions. God only gives us the intellectual capacity to choose which we want, then gives us the facility to accomplish that end through our own action or inaction."

"God gives us everything we need," Aaron said.

"All we have to do is look around," Father Philip added. "We are free to resist this kind of evil. But the longer we choose to do nothing, the more difficult it becomes to put it in its proper place."

"You still getting resistance from the parish?" Aaron asked.

"From some of them," Father Philip sighed while he shook his head. "They don't believe we can or should make a change up there. They think this is God's will and judgment. Some people are anchored to this world by their feet, others by their fears. I know we can make a change if we all contribute," he insisted. "God didn't create us to be spectators in our own lives."

Chapter 36

Aaron woke with a start.

He heard the question as if someone stood next to him and asked, "What makes you think that Henry started in your valley?"

Aaron looked around.

It was the middle of the night.

His mind wandered to Seguida Villa, the next closest village to his own. Anyone, including Henry, who came to Aaron's valley would by necessity have to go through there.

Aaron thought, "Could Henry have just passed through there, or did he murder that valley like he's murdering here?"

Aaron had to find out.

If those in Seguida Villa had faced Henry and run him out, maybe their lesson could be applied up the hill in time to save Blythe.

He rose and packed without hesitation. In a short while, he was out of the village and cresting the valley ridge.

There, in the early morning darkness, Aaron turned and looked down toward his home. The entire valley was his home. Henry's castle loomed above everything, massive with its eerie green glow at night. Somehow, even though Aaron knew it was there, it still surprised him. Its presence in this otherwise serene setting triggered a visceral and deep-seated resentment within him. He did his best to ignore it, focusing instead on the thin layer of smoke trapped by the cool night air. It hung suspended like a light blanket over the homes. Little yellow dots of light sparkled here and there in the hazy gray blackness. Aaron wondered how many more lights Henry would snuff out before he returned. He turned and walked on with resolve.

Later that morning, Iris knocked on Aaron's door. She wanted to ask if it was safe once again to swim in the canal. She also hoped he might join her. Now that none of her circle of friends came round to speak with her, what with the scandal of Blythe entering Henry's kingdom, she could use his company. But her knocks went unanswered, so she returned home.

As Iris changed into her swimming clothes, the bedroom ceiling no longer leaked now that the rains had passed, but instead complained with bitter creaks as it dried. She felt unsettled in the home's unnatural stillness and quickly made her way out and up to the canal's willow tree turn.

The cool stream transfused her with energy she sorely needed. Despite her recent difficulties merely standing, she remained the strong swimmer she had always been.

Iris let herself drift along with the current so she could rest and think. She missed Blythe dearly. She prayed to God that He might find it in His heart to forgive Blythe and reunite the two of them. She still could not find it in her own heart to forgive Duffy for what he had done—or not done—to protect not only Blythe, but those others who were taken into the kingdom. She realized he wasn't the brightest of men, but what he did went beyond questions of intelligence; it was a vengeful, spiteful thing. It shocked her still that he was capable of such passive deviousness.

She drifted under the bridge and turned over onto her stomach. As she did so, she took in a refreshing drink and continued with a breaststroke. She planned to pull for a while until she felt it time to turn back, but she became light-headed.

She dunked her head in hope that that might mitigate the shaky feeling that came over her, giving her a new transfusion of clarity.

Iris pulled for the right side, convinced the strain of everything she had been under finally caught up with her. Her arms and legs were limp strings. It took great concentration for her to continue clinging to the canal wall.

Suddenly she was in a shadow. She looked up to see if a cloud had passed overhead, but instead of seeing the sky, she saw a man's silhouette.

He asked, "Do you need some help?"

"I...I don't know what happened," she said. "I was swimming and all of a sudden I lost my strength. I got so dizzy I had to stop."

"Let me hold your wrists and see if I can pull you up," the stranger offered. "You can rest on shore. It'll be safer for you."

Iris thanked him and let him hold her by the wrists.

"Let me pull you up a little," he instructed. "You plant your feet in the wall and then I'll give a strong pull to get you out. Do you have the strength for that?" he asked.

"We better try it before I don't," she suggested.

The maneuver worked.

"Oh, thank you," she said as she lay on her back still looking up into his silhouette. "You did that so easily. Have you done that before?"

"No, ma'am," he said. "But I've been trained to do those kinds of things. Why don't you let me give you a hand up. There's a place not too far from here where you can rest up before you go home. I'd be happy to fetch anything you've left behind."

Iris rested for a while longer before she could finally take the kind young man up on his offer. Once up, she looked into his fresh, freckled face crowned with his carrot-top hair and said, "I don't know what I would have done without you. You're a godsend," she said.

"Well, ma'am," he replied. "You must have said the right prayer."

Farther down in the valley, Henry showed once again how diligent he was at infiltrating hidden pockets of society where no one might suspect: behind a perfect smile and a well-painted door, in a tastefully decorated living room on a well-upholstered couch.

"More tea?" the Hen asked.

"You're too kind," Notté gushed.

"I'm not surprised you couldn't remember me, but I couldn't forget

Blythe

you," she said. "I even remember what I was shopping for on that day. It was two loaves of bread, basil, five apples and two pounds of beef," she said to impress him. "My husband loves beef."

Notté smiled to feign interest and asked her, "Does he?"

"Of course he loves everything but eats a little too much of it all. I've tried to give him smaller portions, but he just goes back for seconds and thirds. You know how men like him are."

"I'm sure," he said, sliding over a little closer and instigating more flush in her cheek than even he expected. Every word she said captivated him. "You have children?" he asked.

"I do. But they're grown," she explained. "Now you're too young to have children."

She hoped the statement would elicit an answer—an unsuccessful effort on her part.

Notté continued to stare at her lips.

She slowly reached out and touched his warm arm. She couldn't believe she touched his arm. She was awestruck at her own audacity. It was a touch Notté knew well, but he looked at her squarely to make certain there was no misunderstanding.

There was not.

Within an hour, their sweaty, spent forms rolled off one another and lay back on the cool sheets.

She tried to speak, but as soon as the first few banal words left her lips, he silenced her with a long and hushed, "Shhhhhhhh."

She smiled and obeyed his command and snuggled close, drifting off to sleep.

When the Hen woke, she was alone, confused at being alone and uncertain of the wisdom of what she had just done. It certainly was the much-needed release she sought, but some foggy notion inside of her began to grow. She scolded herself—as she would have her children—with the thought, "There are prices to be paid for such things."

She hoped the price was only the little sum of money and jewelry she assumed—correctly—that he had lifted. But if life taught her anything, it was that people rarely get off with such a nominal fine for such a major offense.

The valley inhabitants believed that other villages, such as Seguida Villa, existed, but few possessed the physical bearing to make the arduous trip to confirm that with their own eyes. So harrowing was that expedition that, once concluded, it left the traveler resolved never to repeat it.

Yet Aaron trekked on until Seguida Villa stretched out before him, a quilt of green hues spread out across the broad valley, sown together by thin threads of rock walls that encircled each plot. Having moved stones himself to create such fields in his own valley, he marveled at the number and breadth of fields these people had created not only for themselves but for those who would follow. He could not help but stop and appreciate what they had achieved.

But something subtle was at play in the vista. What was it?

His heart sank.

The telltale signs of life—smoke from the chimneys, neatly growing rows of crops, dots of people venturing about—were all missing. Aaron knew at that moment that Henry had been there.

Seguida Villa was dead.

Aaron found the percussion of his shoes striking the empty lanes so unnerving that he slowed his pace. It was the only sound he could hear other than the faint beat of his own pulse. He peeked into windows hoping not to be startled with a face peeking out. He gently pushed open doors and peered in so see if anyone would return his call. He took a foray into a shop and picked up a muffin tin for Iris. Character, it is said, is best demonstrated when we know we are not being watched. He reverently laid down enough money on the counter to pay for it, then slipped out. Finally in the center of the village, he cupped his hands to his mouth and yelled in all directions, "Is anybody here?"

His echo was the only response, and it answered him but once.

Around the empty homes, rose bushes flowered brilliantly. Flower pots overflowed with treasures no eye appreciated until Aaron arrived. Aaron thought of the irony that something so delicate and temperamental as a rose bush should outlast something as substantial and permanent as a home, but if he came back in 50 years, the bushes, he was certain, would still be there; the homes, almost certainly, would not.

Aaron looked at the homes, the rose bushes and the grass that was already crawling over the walkway and he recited a poem that Father Philip once taught him about nature's victories over man's construction:

Nature seldom cleaves
Yet man's labor leaves
Right angles to repair.
We must be naïve
To build and believe
Nature won't strip it bare.

Man seeks to confine,
River banks define
To make straight water's way;
But streams will assign
Their own waterline
And flood our homes for play.

Consider the seas,
Each wave falls and heaves
In curves as waves of sound.
Just as snow conceives
Wind-blown slopes achieves
To mock the straight-plowed ground.

Each heightened skyline
Raises conceit a shrine
To pierce the heaven's dome.
If such is benign,
Recall Babel's fine
For lines drawn to God's home.

While he still had daylight, he began looking for anything that would confirm his suspicion that it was Henry who had done this. He didn't have to look long. Thinking back to what he had seen in his own valley, he spotted a dozen razor-thin crosses carved into lintels here and there.

"If the owner had only known what lay in store for them," Aaron thought. Then he answered himself, "If they had only known, they could have done nothing."

He came to realize the homes around him were no longer homes, they were monuments, museums. The possessions they contained had, upon the owner's death, transformed into artifacts.

This answered the question Aaron had wondered about when Henry might stop his killing and move on.

"When we're all dead," he answered himself aloud.

He was too angry to be shaken by the sound of his own words.

Aaron could not force himself to sleep in the empty village. If he had stayed there, he would not have slept. Instead he climbed over the ridge and slept out of this valley's view.

Seguida Villa was dead. He hoped he could return before the same fate befell his own village.

Blythe

Chapter 37

Duffy scraped the mossy green mold off his bread. He slathered on some butter and took a timid bite.

Nearly every cupboard door stood open, their interiors emptied of anything edible. The cloves he bit into earlier that afternoon stapled a bitter taste to his tongue. He hoped the buttered bread would remedy the biting residue. Dirty dishes piled high and deep to every side.

He set his plate next to Iris's cookbook on the table, sat and leafed through her collection to find something he could prepare. Page after page he turned, but it all looked so intimidating, so confusing.

Duffy cradled the book. As he flipped through, a faded, dried white rose fell out into his lap. He stared at it for a moment, unsure of what it was, but as the memory came back to him of that day when he and Iris and Blythe sat around the table, he slowly returned the book to the table.

His eyes never left the flower. Both portly hands reached down and picked it up with the greatest tenderness so he could examine it more closely. He turned its short-cut stem between his fat fingers. He brought the bud to his nose, closed his eyes and took in a deep sniff, but the fragrance along with the flower itself had faded. In his memory alone it bloomed.

Disappointed, he gently rested the flower behind the book's next page, closed the cover, and pushed it aside. He looked at the bread and pushed that away, too. Duffy sat at his quiet table, in his quiet home, and considered all he had lost. He looked around for anything to distract him, but nothing caught his interest. This was how every meal had gone for Duffy since Iris entered the kingdom.

His "prosperity" had faded. His shirt grew dingy and shiny from wear, his pants were matted and stale smelling.

With what passed for his supper completed, Duffy, as he did after every meal since Iris left, sat and watched an invisible play of memories unfold time and time again on his tabletop. He meets and marries a pretty girl. She makes him happy and secure. They buy a home. They have a child—a daughter—who adores her father. The father becomes preoccupied with his work. The little girl's affection first turns away to her mother and then to her beau and then to seemingly no one at all. The wife—older now, but still with a glint of her youthfulness he has chosen not to see for years—turns and walks away from him.

"Yes," he points out to himself, "She looked at you like you betrayed her. That was the look she gave you. Absolutely, absolutely."

He agreed aloud mournfully. "I should have looked out for you like you looked out for me, Iris. Can you forgive me?" he blubbered. "Please forgive me."

Again and again, Duffy saw Iris turn away with that same scornful look.

The silence proved too palpable for him, so he lifted his meaty paw and knocked three times on the hardwood table to break the silence's spell. Three knocks on the door answered his call.

He examined his fist in wonder.

He did it again and, again, three knocks at the door responded. A call of "Duffy?" finally awoke him to Lucre knocking at his door.

"Well I suppose you know why I'm here," Lucre said in his staccato.

"Do they know?" Duffy asked with a note of fear.

"Does who know, Duffy? Does who know what?"

"About…you know. What we did?"

Lucre looked at him with a pathetic grimace. "Duffy, collect yourself. I know you've been through hell, but get yourself together."

He put his hand on Duffy's shoulder to steady him.

Lucre said, "You've done nothing wrong. You did what you thought was best, so leave it at that. Nobody knows what you did or didn't do."

"And why should they?" he asked indignantly. "I've done absolutely nothing wrong. Absolutely, absolutely. Absolutely nothing wrong. Henry's the one who's done wrong, Lucre. Not me."

"You're absolutely right, Duffy," Lucre assured him. "How long has that been sitting there," he asked about the bread.

"Oh, I don't know," Duffy said. "Days, I guess. There was never moldy bread when Iris was in this house."

"I remember," Lucre said fondly. "Why don't we arrange for someone to come in and cook for you, Duffy? You've been through enough. You shouldn't be subjected to your own cooking," he said with a silent shake of his shoulders in hopes of getting a rise out of his friend, but the words missed their mark.

Lucre suggested, "Let's get you cleaned up. You look like hell."

"I've lost my wife and my daughter to something I can't begin to understand. How am I supposed to look?" Duffy asked.

"Just as you do. I'm sorry," Lucre apologized. "But you don't need to stay that way."

"I feel everything, Lucre," Duffy announced.

"What's that?"

"I feel everything. I feel nothing. I feel helpless," Duffy said. "Our separation…. It was so sudden. How can I begin to deal with it?"

"You can't," Lucre said.

"I need another twenty years to say goodbye to Blythe," he blubbered. "I need a hundred years to say goodbye to Iris. I can't say goodbye now."

"Maybe there are things we can do so you don't have to say goodbye," Lucre suggested.

Duffy said blankly, "I was supposed to be the one to die and give them a lesson on how to get on with life. Now they are the ones giving me that lesson, but I'm too dense to understand what I'm supposed to do, Lucre. I'm too dense to understand any of it."

"You're supposed to live, Duffy," Lucre advised. "That, and do whatever you can do to help them to live, as well."

"How could they want me to live after what I let happen to them?" Duffy asked.

"So you could turn all this evil into some good, Duffy. What did Blythe love to do most?"

"Paint," he said.

"That's right!" Lucre said excitedly. "She was a brilliant painter. You should do whatever you can do to help her paint again."

"But she's going to die," Duffy cried. "What difference is painting going to make for her if she's going to die in no time? Look at everything I've done."

"It is too soon to judge what any of us have done or when any of us are going to die, Duffy. This fight is not over."

"You want me to do what the others have done? You want me to sell what was hers and give you the money?"

"We could take the money and...."

"I know what you would do with it," Duffy interrupted. "What difference has it made, Lucre? What difference has all the money made to those who died? You lucred every last one of them and they got nothing in return. They're all dead or dying."

"What is that supposed to mean?" Lucre demanded to know. "What does that mean, I 'lucred' them?"

Duffy threw down his hands and said, "Let it mean whatever you want, but you know what I meant."

"I'll let it go, Duffy," Lucre said. "It makes no difference to me what any of you think about me. I know what I'm trying to do, and I thought you did, too. If we've done nothing else, we justified the dreams of the dead when they hoped that someone out here was doing something to help them. Fine, it's too late for them. But what about the living? What about those in there right now, like Iris and Blythe?"

John E. Kramer

"And Maddox."

"Yes," Lucre said. "And him too."

"How could you forget Maddox?" Duffy asked. "After all, didn't this whole thing start with him?"

"I know you're hurting as much as I am, maybe more because your wound is fresh, but there's no reason to be hateful here, Duffy. We both want the same thing. We both want the ones we love to be free of Henry."

"Why did we do it, Lucre?" Duffy asked. "Why did we just stand aside and watch?"

"We didn't," Lucre insisted. "Let the world think that if they want, but you know as well as I that we have one hope of beating Henry and to do that, we have to keep our mouths shut. If we talked before, if we talk now, all is lost: Iris, Blythe and Maddox. Everything we worked for, everything we've worked to, it is all gone. So ask yourself: Are you still committed to ending Henry's reign and freeing everyone in there, or are you going to cave and quit and let them all die?"

"I'm in it," Duffy said weakly. "What choice do I have?"

"The same choice as me," Lucre told him. "None."

Lucre took in a deep breath of air to broach the subject he went to Duffy's to discuss, but Duffy continued. "If I had known for a moment... for a split second that Henry would take Blythe and Iris, I would have stood up against him, Lucre. You know that," he said seeking Lucre's absolution.

"Of course I do," Lucre reassured him.

"I would have stopped him early and let everyone know," Duffy went on, reinforcing the foundation of his reinterpreted past.

"But you had no way of knowing," Lucre said in a conclusive tone, hoping to end Duffy's desperate display.

Lucre again sought to bring the conversation back to his business at hand by asking, "What difference does the past make, Duffy? If we can find the means to free them, the past will be buried along with Henry himself."

Duffy said, "Lucre, I couldn't sell everything Blythe took years to create. It would be like losing her all over again."

Blythe

"Even if that might free her?" Lucre pressed him.

Duffy said, "You want me to pay a ransom with no guarantees, with only hopes."

"What else do we have?" Lucre asked.

Lucre studied Duffy, and Duffy studied the tabletop.

Lucre broke their stalemate and asked, "How much do you want for the paintings, Duffy?"

"Nothing."

"Duffy," Lucre reproached. "With Iris in, you now have more to lose and more to gain than anybody. You can't just let those paintings sit there."

"I'll give them to you," Duffy clarified.

"Excellent," Lucre exclaimed. "You have my word I'll get the most I can for them, Duffy."

Duffy added coldly, "Blythe once told me that no one loves an artist until they die. She was wrong, Lucre."

"You love her, Duffy. I know that and so does Blythe. Don't give up hope."

"You can't give up something you don't have," he shrugged. "Let me show you what she has."

Up in Blythe's studio, Duffy explained to Lucre what little he knew about each piece. He begged him, "Sell them fast, Lucre. Every time I look at them, they remind me that her blood is on my hands. Take them and get them off my conscience."

There was a knock at the kitchen door. Duffy bellowed down for whomever it was to enter.

"Duffy?" Aaron called out.

"Aaron!" Lucre exclaimed. He vaulted down the stairs and threw his arms around his son. "Aaron, you're out." Then he looked at him in sudden recognition of his own words and asked, "You...you know the consequences of leaving the kingdom. Are you going to...are you going to pay Henry's price?"

Aaron looked at him confounded. "What are you talking about, Father? I'm back from Seguida Villa."

"Seguida Villa?" he repeated in disbelief. It would have been easier for him to accept that his son had escaped Henry's kingdom. "How can you be back from Seguida Villa?"

Aaron told him, "An idea came to me as I was sleeping that if Henry came here, he would have had to first come through Seguida Villa. Someone had to go there to find out if he had. If he had and they expelled him, there would be something for us to learn. If he had and they couldn't, I needed to know how far he would go."

"And how far did he go?" Duffy asked from the top of the stairs.

"Duffy," Aaron said solemnly, "there was no one left. The entire village is empty."

"All of them?" his father asked.

"Dead," Aaron confirmed. "I couldn't find a single person. And Henry's cross was all over the village, on homes and businesses, everyplace someone might hide. They were all gone."

"My God, Aaron," his father exhaled. "No one had seen you for so long. We were all worried you had been taken into the kingdom."

"Or followed Blythe in," Duffy added.

Aaron reached into his bag and pulled out the tin. He held it out to Duffy, "I brought this back for Iris."

Duffy and Lucre looked at it, then at each other.

"I'll be right up, Duffy," Lucre said. Duffy shuffled back into Blythe's studio.

"Where's Iris?" Aaron asked.

"We don't know how, Aaron," Lucre said, "but she's in the kingdom."

"Iris?" Aaron said in disbelief.

"It happened while you were gone, the day you left as best we can figure it," his father said. "She was in the canal and...."

"That's impossible," Aaron interrupted. "I told her the stream was closed. There's no way she would have gone in."

"And yet some of her things were found up by the willow," Lucre said.

"Is Blythe still...?" Aaron began.

"Still alive and from all we can tell doing well, considering," he told his son. "She's strong, Aaron. And from all reports, even stronger than she was before in some ways. That will help her."

"How is he taking it?" Aaron asked, nodding up the stairs.

Lucre shook his head. "Look, he and I have to wrap some things up. Why don't you go home, get cleaned up and you can come to my home for your fatted calf."

Aaron laughed, and the two men embraced with noisy slaps on the back.

Aaron paused as he turned to leave. He asked his father, "What do you two have to wrap up?"

"It can wait till tomorrow, Aaron," Lucre said, dismissing him. "I'll see you tonight. I'm glad you're home."

Aaron said in a sick voice, "Oh, Father, this isn't about Blythe's paintings?"

Lucre's face took on a disappointed look.

"Oh, you can't be serious?" Aaron demanded to know.

"Look, Aaron, let's settle this once and for all," Lucre said. "You go up and ask Duffy what he would like to do. I'll live with his decision to keep them or to sell them."

He motioned his son up the stairs and followed.

"You can't do this, Duffy," Aaron told him. "I had Iris's promise. She promised me she wouldn't sell Blythe's paintings to him or to anyone."

"Iris isn't here," Duffy mumbled seemingly to himself.

"But don't you see?" Aaron shouted at Duffy. "If you do this, you're giving up on her. How can you give up on her so easily?"

Duffy shook his head. He said, "I'm selling them for exactly the opposite reason, Aaron. I'm doing this because I haven't given up on her. I'm doing this because I believe she will be free again. I'm doing this because I want to see her paint again."

"And where does the money go?" Aaron asked as he and his father entered Blythe's studio. "To Maddox? You'll see none of it and you won't see her paintings ever again."

Duffy said, "It is the only thing to do, Aaron. The paintings are only collecting dust here. We need to put their value to use."

He swept his finger along a frame and showed the dirty results to Aaron to underscore his point.

"With your father, I can at least feel they're being put to some good use," Duffy said.

"And what would that be?" Aaron asked.

Duffy held up his hand to silence Lucre who had inhaled to answer. He said, "I'll be getting a new roof for my room. Unless I sell the paintings, I can't afford to do that or the other things I want. I know you're upset, Aaron, but this is settled. The choice is mine. Not yours. Not your father's. It's mine."

Duffy instructed Lucre, "All of them are going, but this one." He motioned to the painting of the seaside cliff. "Blythe gave this to us on the day she left."

Aaron warned his father, "You take them and I'll tell the world what you're doing. You'll never buy or sell another thing in this valley."

Lucre looked back at him unfazed. "Go ahead," he dared. "I could use the word of mouth. It's good for business."

Aaron stormed out and back to his own cottage. No sooner had he burst in than a small and threatened voice in the darkness called out, "Who's there?"

Aaron commanded with greater authority and outrage than the little voice, himself demanding to know, "Who's there?"

"Sergio," the little voice responded. "I heard you were lost. I thought you were in the kingdom. Everyone thought you had followed Blythe."

"And that explains why you're here?" Aaron asked.

"I came here to have a final drink with you…at least with your memory."

Aaron lit up the room as they spoke. He could not be upset with his friend now, despite his great desire to be exactly that. He took the drink from Sergio's hand and downed it. Aaron looked at the nearly empty bottle he recalled as full when he left.

"One final drink?" he asked Sergio.

Blythe

Sergio poured them each another and Aaron collapsed in his chair. It was good to be home.

"So where were you?" Sergio asked.

Aaron told him, "Seguida Villa."

"How is that possible?"

Aaron explained, "I had to go there to see if Henry came through there before he came here."

"And?"

Aaron consumed the rest of his drink, then answered, "He had."

"Anybody left?"

"No one," Aaron replied.

Sergio refilled Aaron's glass with the dregs of the bottle, then raised his glass, "To Seguida Villa."

"To Seguida Villa," Aaron responded. He dropped his bag on the floor with a rattle. "And to Iris," he added.

"To Iris," Sergio said solemnly. "You heard?"

"Yes. My father was over at Duffy's lucring him out of Blythe's paintings. He told me. Duffy is falling apart."

"You don't know the half of it," Sergio informed him. "Right after she went in, Duffy organized a frontal assault on the kingdom. Each time anything struck the castle's walls, they mutated to heal themselves. The more we threw at it, the better it responded. And the worse the people inside fared. That's where it gets its strength from, we figured. A dozen or more people were drained by Henry because of Duffy's Travesty. That's what we're calling it. After that, he's never been the same."

"He never was one for complex answers," Aaron observed. "That's no surprise."

Aaron downed his drink then stretched the glass to Sergio for another. "And how are you?" he asked.

Sergio looked at the empty bottle and informed him, "I am thoroughly whiskied."

"Next time you drink to my memory, would it be too much to ask if you brought your own bottle?" Aaron asked.

Sergio poured the few remaining drops of the bottle into his glass and said, "I wasn't worried about you missing it."

"So, how are you?" Aaron asked again.

Sergio sighed deeply and sat back in his chair.

"And how is Kagetsu?" Aaron correctly assumed.

"She is perfect," Sergio sighed again.

Aaron said, "And therefore you are not?"

"How could you know so much about me and still have me for a friend?" Sergio asked.

"Who else would drink my liquor?" Aaron asked.

"We work well together," Sergio said, raising his empty glass.

Each toasted the other and drank deeply into their empty glasses.

Sergio rose with a yawn and informed his friend, "Well, I have your room, so I'm not sure where you're sleeping."

Aaron pointed to the couch. "I've got the guest suite. Good night."

"Good night," Sergio yawned as he climbed the stairs. "It's good to have you back, friend," he called to Aaron.

"It's good to be back, friend," Aaron replied.

Aaron unpacked his bag and made up the couch. As he extinguished the next to last light and planned his walk across the room in the dark to his bed for the night, there was a knock at the door. Aaron fiercely swung it open ready for a confrontation.

"Well, hello," Parissa said, surprised. "I heard you were back, and by the way you answered the door, you came back stronger."

"Sorry," he said. "I thought you were my father."

"Trouble on the home front?" she asked as she entered.

"Nothing new there," he said. "Who told you I was back?"

"It's all over the village, about you...and Seguida Villa."

Aaron closed the door and offered her a drink, which she accepted.

"Welcome back," she toasted with a glass of his wine that she poured. "I was worried about you."

"About me in the kingdom?" he asked.

"I knew you would never do that," she said. "I was the first one to suggest maybe you went to Seguida Villa."

"And why did you assume that?" he asked.

"Because you're smart, Aaron," she said. "You're not going to waste yourself in a gallant and hollow gesture of self-sacrifice. If you're going to do anything, you're going to do something that makes a difference or discover something new. Seguida Villa and back," she marveled. "That is Aaron."

She toasted him again before she drank.

He eyed the pillow and yawned.

"You must be exhausted. Why are you sleeping here?"

Aaron pointed up to the ceiling and said, "Sergio."

"He's been like a lost puppy since you left," she informed him.

They both laughed quietly so as not to wake Sergio.

Aaron informed her, "I found him here, drunk and teary."

"Kagetsu," Parissa said.

He asked, "Who else? He said he was having a last drink to me, but I wasn't convinced that was the whole story. Why can't he go after someone he can catch? Sylvia is wild about him."

"I can understand," Parissa said. "I actually admire him for it. It shows he thinks a lot of himself. He aspires for something better than what everyone expects."

"But he and Kagetsu? I just don't see it," he said.

"And why not?"

"She's too cool…too aloof. Opposites attract, but there are limits to any truism."

"So people can't raise themselves if there is someone better they love?" Parissa asked.

"I think it's Kagetsu who is unrealistic," Aaron observed. "She's setting her sights on the impossible, shooting for the stars when she could easily pull in the Earth."

"The Earth being Sergio?"

"The Earth being so many men in this valley," he corrected.

Parissa looked at him squarely and asked, "Including you?"

He answered, "Excluding me. You know which star I'm under the spell of."

He yawned and said, "Oh, it's good to be back among the living. The whole place was deserted, Parissa. Not a sign of life anywhere."

"It must have been a nightmare."

"It was worse," he said. "It was a vision of the future if we don't do something."

"But what?" she asked.

He shook his head. "That was what I went there to find out. But all I learned is what Henry is capable of, not how to stop him. Do you cook?" he asked her.

"Yes," she answered tentatively, not sure how his question related to what he had just said. She reminded him, "I made you that meal before you left."

"Oh, that's right. I'm sorry. Here," he said reaching into his bag. "I brought this back from Seguida Villa."

"A muffin tin?" she said unimpressed.

"I brought it back for Iris, but…."

"What a tragedy." Parissa stopped him. "If anyone deserved to be spared, she's the one. What a wonderful woman."

"And she's already lost enough with Blythe."

Parissa stood up and gathered the glasses and bottles. "You must be tired," she said. "You get changed and I'll be right back."

She walked into the kitchen and clinked around. She returned a moment later without announcing herself. Aaron was already tucked under the covers.

"You're quick," she said.

"I need sleep too much to be slow."

She knelt beside him and pulled the covers up to his chin. She tucked him in and sat beside him.

"I'm glad you're back, Aaron," she whispered.

"It's good to be back," he said, his eyes closed, his voice falling off.

"Do you want me to stay?" she offered.

"Hmmm?" he asked, as if she had woken him out of his slumber.

"Or do you want me to turn off the light?" she continued.

"Thank you," he said, and nestled his head deeper into the pillow.

Blythe

Parissa rose and turned off the lamp. She stood there for a tortured moment. She walked over in the darkness beside the couch and bent over close to where she assumed his head must be. She gently rested her hands on his pillow and his shoulder to help her gauge her target. She stooped even lower and planted a long, firm kiss on his temple, then released.

Aaron did not respond.

Daunted by everything she had to lose, she quietly made her exit.

Chapter 38

The severity of Henry's rule intensified to a full-blown assault on every captive. Purges occurred more frequently, inflicting ever-escalating human destruction. Those who survived sacrifices to the death god by the Mournex were wasted away more rapidly to feed Henry's hunger for life. It was rumored Henry did this in hopes of cleansing someone or something that threatened him, but the Mournex had not yet devoured the source of his complaint. The idea that anything could threaten Henry buoyed Blythe and the others' spirits even as the increased punishment drained them of their strength.

The sense of confinement within the kingdom heightened as more villagers were drawn in to replace those who fell to Henry's binge of purges.

All the while in every place except where Blythe colored her bright murals, the castle walls grew stouter so that people could barely pass two abreast in the once-spacious lower hallways. Despite Blythe's offers to other captives to paint their cells, all refused with indignant hostility.

Her own cell was painted to replicate her long-since-lost room back at her parents' home, with conjured bas-relief renditions of her furniture, her window and her view beyond. Haskel preferred the natural beauty of a broad and tree-lined field in the height of summer. Mab's colorful abstract murals drew her mind away from the horrors of the world outside her cell's walls.

While the paints of each of these rooms held back the growing confinement Henry imposed nearly universally, all the other cells began to take on the feel of coffins to those who slipped inside for rest. Henry hoarded health and life while those below him slowly loosened their grip on those same attributes.

The pent-up rage induced by the growing sense of compression triggered two responses. One was outward, forcing captives who acutely felt this pressure to leave the kingdom for a time and experience again the valley's spaciousness. This, however, only exacerbated the overcrowded conditions because for every one that left, two returned. The other response was inward within the walls of their confinement, marked by sudden and violent confrontations erupting among the captives. These were often ignited by trivialities that would otherwise have been overlooked in anyplace except one so confined and pressurized. A weariness of unpredictable and irrational violence prompted many who might otherwise have remained within the kingdom walls to leave so they could find some peace, some tenderness, if only for a short time. One would leave; two would return. Henry's castle was by design a house divided among the inhabitants, pitting all against each other rather than on the source of their complaints.

This physical constriction drove the better parts of human nature—dignity, kindness, humor, affection, courage—out of their beings. The overwhelming number of captives deferred to Henry and his captains for definitions of what was socially acceptable and so they reverted to savagery and hedonism, bent on the immediate and the physical rather than the long-term and anything of some higher order. Whereas before the social pyramid was Henry, the captains, the Mournex, and the captives, the captives became stratified so that some were hyper-aggressive predators and most were prey who now fell victim to a new class made up of their own kind.

Beatings and theft became sport. Rape and slavery grew into such common pursuits that they lost any social shock or stigma. The humanity of each person was driven down and out and replaced by a ferocity rejected even by any higher level of beast in the wild.

This carnal savagery forced individuals who thought for themselves and who sought to preserve what makes up truly human nature, deeper and deeper into their cells for their safety and peace of mind.

The three free thinkers dashed from one painted cell to another. They ventured out into the courtyard only when it was absolutely necessary, and even then, it was usually Haskel who made the trip on the others' behalf.

"I knew I had to die, but I can't believe I actually handed myself over by my own actions to this kind of a tyrant," Haskel said. "Cancer or drowning I could accept, but to me, Henry is the worst end imaginable."

"Why?" Blythe asked.

Haskel said, "Because he doesn't just torture us. He doesn't just drive us to death. Henry thinks for us."

"Oh, heavens," Blythe mocked to Mab.

"But for me, as a teacher, that is what I've fought against all my life," Haskel explained. "Henry dictates the hours of our lives, how long we suffer and when we die and every single decision in between. I always stressed to my students the importance of thinking for themselves, of not being led solely by a book, or a teacher, or a ruler, but rather to take in all of these and more to make your own decisions. Every manmade disaster begins when one man thinks for another. However benevolent they begin, the ultimate outcome is tyranny."

Mab said, "And here we are."

"Here we are with a man who tries to make us believe that hatred, fear, greed, and lust should drive human action rather than love, sharing, confidence, and restraint," Haskel said with great dignity. "He already has so many believing that sacrificing another for their pleasure is rational. It's against everything for which I've ever stood."

"Have you two seen what Henry does downstairs?" Blythe asked.

Blythe

"The room," she asked knowingly.

"Downstairs?" Haskel asked. "I didn't know there was a downstairs."

"There is a room across the hall from mine and down a few doors that leads to a stairwell that goes downstairs," Blythe said nonchalantly. "There is another whole level below us. Nott . . ." Blythe stopped herself. "That one who brought me in showed me when he tried to convince me that I should become a captain." She said deliciously, "They have an orgy room."

"A what?" Mab yelled and covered her mouth as she laughed.

"An orgy room!" Blythe yelled back.

"Where?" Haskel asked.

Blythe said, "Near the center of the kingdom below us. You go down the stairs...."

"On the outside room," Haskel clarified.

"On the outside room just down from mine," Blythe said. "It takes you down to another level to some hallways. Down the center hallway that leads back to the middle there are rooms on either side. We looked in one near the end of the hall and these three couples were having an orgy."

"No!" Mab laughed.

"But as they went at it, the walls of the room grew in on them," Blythe said.

"Don't all the walls?" Mab asked.

"Not like the others in here," she said. "They grew in much faster. Before the people inside knew what was happening, they were trapped and then I don't know what. Crushed or suffocated or absorbed into the walls, I guess."

"Listen, Blythe," Haskel said. "You said the hallway led to the center of the kingdom. How do you know? You were underground. You couldn't see the tower to get your bearings."

"I just figured," Blythe said. She stood up to demonstrate. "We went down a level in this direction, turned, turned again and ended up facing this way, I'm pretty sure. It wasn't smooth corners; there was a curve to it all."

John E. Kramer   292

"What do you mean by a curve?" Haskel asked.

"I guess the more I think about the shape of the halls, it was more like spirals that circled in tighter and tighter the more you walk around."

"Like the inside of a conch shell?"

"Exactly. Then we walked down the hall about as far as we would go to be near the center of the courtyard…."

"Where Henry's tower is?" Haskel asked.

"Yes," she said. "Right around there. But we stopped before the end of the hall. That's when he showed me the room." She turned to Mab, "He threatened to throw me in if I warned them about what was going on."

"Hey!" Mab laughed, "If you've got to go, that's not a bad way!"

"What was at the end of the hall, Blythe?" Haskel asked.

"Just a wall," she said.

"Just a wall?" he repeated.

"It had some carvings on it," she said. "A crest."

"Really?" Haskel said. "That's what I'm interested in, much more than your orgy room."

"My orgy room?" she objected.

"I'm too old for such a place." Haskel laughed. "I'd be bored and would find out what they were doing right away. What did it look like… the crest?"

She looked down to remember as closely as she could. "It's hard to say. I only got a quick look at it. It was a shield in the back with two lines across that divided it into four fields. There was something in each field, but I can't remember most of them, if I ever knew in the first place."

"What do you remember?" Haskel asked.

She said, "I can only remember the lower right hand field. It had Henry's initial in a large capital with the Roman numeral four in little letters next to it: Hiv."

"Nothing else?" he asked.

"Why?" Mab asked. "Is this important?"

"It may be," Haskel said. "Do you remember anything else about the hall or the rooms or the wall at the end? Maybe the ceiling of the hall?"

Blythe said, "Everything down there was pretty much how it is up here. But the end wall....”

"Yes?" Haskel asked in anticipation.

She said, "It wasn't as much a wall…you know a flat square face…as an arch that was filled in on the sides."

Haskel asked, "You mean there was an arch and the tops of it were filled in and went back to form a dome, or that the wall had an arch in it, but the wall itself was flat?"

"The second," she said. "It was a flat wall, with an arch inside of it and the crest inside of the arch. Above the arch is a hole that seems to go all the way through."

"How large would you say the hole is?"

She made a circle with her index finger and thumb.

"Fascinating," Haskel said.

"Why?" Mab asked. "Why do you care?"

"Because I love to study and I love to learn," he said. "I've been in here nearly from the start and I've never seen that place. I never even knew another lower level existed. An outside room," he laughed. "What a simple way to hide it! So any more orgies in your future?" he asked.

"Not for me," she said.

"I don't know," Mab said. "Things get any worse around here and I might take two or three strapping men and do myself in. They can just put on my tombstone: She died with a smile on her face!"

"Well," Haskel announced as he rose, "It is time to break up this clandestine gathering. I'm fading."

"And I've got to go to my mother's," Blythe said.

"How she doing?" Mab asked.

"Not well," Blythe said. "Henry's hitting her pretty hard."

"Boils?" Haskel asked.

"Beyond that," Blythe said. "I better go see how she is."

"Send her our best," Mab said.

Haskel offered, "Why don't you go first, Blythe?"

Blythe poked her head out Mab's door but ducked back inside and closed it. She held her finger to her lips to silence them and they respected her command. She tried again and this time slipped through and disappeared.

After sprinting down the hall as fast and quietly as her feet would allow, Blythe quickly tapped at her mother's door. Blythe listened as her mother grunted to her feet and shuffled over to let her in. Blythe slipped through the crack and shut the door behind her without taking the time to look back to see if anyone had noticed her.

The walls of Iris's room were covered in bright pastels forming a garden of flowers around faux-framed reproductions—as best as Blythe could remember them—of famous paintings Iris had admired over the years. Alone on the back wall below the window, Blythe reproduced her own painting of their picnic by the seaside cliffs. The ceiling was covered in rich burgundy to look like fabric lined with gold cords. Iris called her room, "The Queen's Suite."

"So how is the queen tonight?" Blythe asked.

"We are regal," Iris said in her best false air and extended her hand for Blythe to kiss. It was everything Blythe could do not to cry looking at how her mother was wasting away. Blythe knew what her mother was in for.

"I'm sorry to get you up, but I wanted to look in on you before I went to sleep. What's that?" Blythe asked, at some scraps of paper that were half-hidden by Iris's sheets.

"Nothing," Iris said.

"Is it your will?" Blythe asked earnestly.

Iris laughed, "Oh, no!" She laughed again at the thought. "It's not my last will, but may be my testament."

"What do you mean?" she asked her mother.

"Oh, it's nothing. It's just something silly I've been thinking since I came in here that I wanted to think through…that I wanted to understand, so I wrote it down and rewrote it and rewrote it until it came close to what I was thinking."

"What is it?" Blythe pressed her.

"I don't know," she giggled. "Just some thoughts—some bitter thoughts, really. I don't think you'd call it a poem, but it's something close."

"Mother, I had no idea."

"What? That I wrote? I used to love to write. I used to write so much when I was young, but your father hated when I took any time away from him, so I stopped."

"Is this the first thing you've written since then?" Blythe asked.

"Oh, no. Your father was out more and more. So when he was out in the afternoons, I'd sneak into your room…the light was always best in there…and write down whatever I was feeling. Your father will find it under our bed if he ever looks."

Blythe leaned over to pick up the pages and asked, "So what did you write?"

"Oh, Blythe, no," Iris objected. "It's silly."

Blythe held the papers in her hands and asked before she looked at them, "May I?"

"Promise you won't laugh?" Iris asked.

Blythe crossed her heart so Iris nodded her approval toward the pages. Iris said, "This is how I always envisioned it after your father died, but here I am the one to go first."

"You can't say that," Blythe objected.

"Let's be honest with each other, Blythe. We both know we have so little time left."

Blythe stood there silently and read:

Duffy

I have too often felt your presence above me, Iris.
It is getting so you will beat a path between our home
And this plot.
It would be better for you to go about your other work.
There is nothing more to do here.
I cannot enjoy even one of the flowers
You rest above my head
Or hear your low whispers.
Besides,
Flowers are such impractical things,
And I have told you as much.
You, in life, were all I ever wished for.

Nothing more.

Iris
I promised I would never live like those
Who, out of repetition,
Beat a path through neighborhood grass
Turning it to dust—
Never venturing far beyond our home.
I would never live like them
Until I carried back the dust of a few continents
On the soles of my shoes,
Leaving it along my own well-worn local routes
As memories to sustain me.
But then I met you.
And I did not travel.
I never swam in the Nile nor sipped high tea
Blocks from the Queen's residence.
My memories are as domesticated as I have become.
And now I know that discontent comes from two sources alone:
Not having dreams
Or not pursuing the ones you have.
No one has ever died sorry
Who tried to turn a wish into a memory.

Blythe began to cry but Iris cautioned her through her own tears, "Don't you."

"This is beautiful," Blythe said. "You deserved so much more, Mother. You deserved so much better than this."

"And so did everyone in here, including you, Blythe."

"I know, but...."

"Blythe, I want you not just to hear what I said, but hear what I mean."

Blythe looked at her strangely.

Iris said, "You don't deserve to be in here, Blythe. All my life I've

Blythe

tried to tell you how wonderful you are, but I know I never got through. Now that you're in here, do you understand what you had, how much you had to offer?"

Blythe lowered her head and nodded, the tears falling as brightly and sporadically as raindrops at the beginning of a spring shower. They seemed strangely wholesome in that unwholesome place.

"Do you?" Iris asked. "Do you understand how much you deserve to be loved?"

"I do," Blythe said. "I do now. I wish I had understood before."

"That's not important now, Blythe. The important thing now is that you know it at last. You were loved, Blythe. And you were worthy of love."

Blythe knelt beside Iris. She rested her head in her mother's lap as each recalled at that moment how Iris always consoled her in just that way when she was a child. How many times had they done this? How long ago had it been since the last time? No matter. This time Iris's loving touch reached the depths she always hoped it would. They each wept so hard they shook the bed, which made them both laugh.

Blythe finally straightened up. "I'm making a mess of you," she said.

"I couldn't care less," Iris said, wiping away her tears of pain and laughter.

"Let me get you back into bed," Blythe said and she pulled back the blankets. Iris was tucked in and breathed a heavy cathartic sigh. "You needed that," Blythe said. "And so did I." She forced a deep stair-stepped sigh herself.

"Nice, isn't it?" Iris asked and Blythe agreed.

Blythe looked down. This time it was she stroking her mother's hair rather than the other way around as it had always been. Henry's stigmata were all over Iris. Her skin was hysterical with angry, open boils. Despite that, it was easy for Iris to drift in and out of sleep now that lethargy was her constant companion.

"Do you still like your paintings?" Blythe whispered. "Are there any you would like me to change?"

"I adore them," Iris whispered back. "I wouldn't change any of them. I still love that one," she said raising her hand to the seascape. "That's my favorite of them all."

Blythe took her mother's hand and started rubbing it against her own smooth forearms.

Iris said, "I'm so proud of everything you've become, Blythe."

"I'd like to give you something else, Mother."

"What's that?" Iris asked.

Blythe slipped off the band from her left index finger and gently slipped it onto her mother's finger.

"Oh, Blythe, I couldn't," Iris objected. "Please, no. You keep it."

"Please take it and love it, Mother. It will be a reminder of how much we love each other. Would you take it?"

"How could I not if that's how you ask?" Iris held it up and stretched out her arm to admire it. She laughed, "I'll need longer arms to really appreciate it."

Blythe kissed her mother's forehead. The ever-present fever had not relented a degree. Blythe tried to convince herself, "Maybe it's your own drained lips that made it seem so hot."

"Is there anything else you need?" Blythe asked.

"No," Iris said shutting her eyes and resting her hands on the blanket. Her fingers still played with the ring.

"Will you be able to sleep?" Blythe asked.

Iris said in a suddenly wide-awake tone but without changing her disposition, "Absolutely, absolutely," perfectly mimicking her husband.

She and Blythe laughed until they cried again.

The following day, Blythe noticed Notté with a flashy blonde on his arm. They tickled each other and laughed as they walked.

After they separated, Blythe approached her as stealthily as she could and asked, "Are you with him?"

The woman looked down with pity and contempt. She asked, "You're Blythe, aren't you?"

Blythe looked back at her surprised. "Yes, I am. I want to warn you…."

"About Notté, right?"

"Right," Blythe said. "You don't know it yet, but...."

"He's the devil," the woman said in a playful tease. "Or one of his assistants. Notté told me all about you, Blythe. I'm sorry it didn't work out for you, but that doesn't mean I can't tame him."

"Tame him?" Blythe asked. "This has nothing to do with that. You are with the devil. He said it."

"He said that is what you would say," the blonde snapped. "I like Notté. I like him just the way he is. Maybe he isn't what you were looking for, but he suits me fine. Why don't you run off with your old teacher friend, what's his name? Rascal?"

"Haskel," Blythe corrected and then nearly kicked herself for taking the bait.

"Haskel, right."

"Listen, I'm trying to help you," Blythe insisted.

"I'm sure you are, but I don't want your help, Blythe. Thanks," she said sarcastically and strutted off.

"What's your name?" Blythe asked.

"Tessie," she replied without looking back.

"You don't know what you're in for, Tessie. But when you find out, come see me. I can help."

Tessie gave her a wave without looking back and disappeared through an arch.

A sudden gust swept through the courtyard. Blythe spun around. It came from the far side. She had time to escape.

As she joined the other veterans making their way out, she did something that no one had ever had the courage to do before for the newcomers; she began to shout, "All of you, get out of here! Run to the archways, this way! Quickly!"

They moved slowly at first, but seeing the urgency in everyone else's action they picked up the pace until everyone was in a dead run.

Blythe passed a short, dark-haired woman who was hobbling along. Blythe took a sideways glance at her. She was very pregnant, near term.

"Do you need some help?" Blythe asked.

"Yes," the woman grunted as she ran to the closing archway door. "I'm going to have a baby."

"You need to get out of here," Blythe said as she passed her. "The Mournex are coming. You need to get out of the courtyard right now."

"I know," the woman grunted again. "But I'm going to have the baby...right now," she shrieked. She slowed down to a stop and rolled to the ground.

"No!" Blythe ordered and ran back to her. "You have to get up. You have to get out of here. Take my hand."

"I can't," the woman insisted.

But Blythe insisted more forcefully, "Take my hand or you and your baby both die!"

Beyond all physical constriction, the woman reached up and allowed Blythe to help her to her feet. Together they trotted and hobbled, pressing in and among the crowd that fought to get through the closing door.

"Let us through," Blythe demanded. "She's having a baby."

"But you're not," someone shot back as they pushed by her.

She wanted to correct them, but thought wiser of it. It was no time for arguments or confessions.

The press of the crowd carried her and the woman through the arch and they ducked under the doorway.

Blythe instructed her, "My room is this way. Is yours close by?" The woman held her belly and shook her head with a fierce grimace. "Mine is," Blythe said. "Follow me."

She led her by the hand down the stairs and to her room. No sooner had they closed the door than there was a frantic knock at it. Blythe opened it.

Mab pushed her way in and said, "I saw you two running. I thought you could use some help."

Blythe asked the woman, "Are you all right?"

"No," the woman moaned. "It's time."

"Oh, dear gawd," Mab said. "I didn't think you'd need help this quickly."

"Oh!" the woman screamed out from the edge of the bed.

"What are we going to do?" Mab asked Blythe. "The captains are going to find her. You know what they'll do."

Blythe and Mab sat to either side of her and took her hand. Blythe asked, "What's your name?"

"Maria," the woman panted, squeezing hard on their hands.

"Maria, listen," Blythe insisted, getting right in her face. "Have you been in here long?"

"Yes," she insisted through the pain.

"Have you seen what they do to babies in here, Maria?" Mab asked.

"Yes," she grunted again. "I don't want them to have my baby. This is my baby."

Blythe looked at Mab and said, "The purge is going to help us with the noise."

"Not for very long, thanks to you," Mab said. "You may have saved a whole bunch out there, but the shorter that lasts, the surer they'll be to find this one."

Blythe knew Mab was right.

"Listen, Maria," Blythe said, again getting very close. "If they hear a peep from you, they'll know you're delivering. Is there any way you can try to keep silent?"

Mab looked at her and laughed. "You've never had babies, have you? Of course not," Mab huffed. "Look at those hips."

"Maria, we're going to do all we can to help you, but you've got to be as quiet as you can," Blythe said. "Can you do that? Can you be as quiet as you can for your baby?"

Maria nodded violently as she slipped back to lie on the bed.

The cacophony outside was milder than it had ever been during a purge. The shouts for mercy were already becoming few and far between, and Blythe cursed her own goodwill, but then reconsidered. She wouldn't let Henry win this battle on any level.

"You're doing great," Blythe assured Maria.

Maria bit hard into the pillow with every contraction and with all the love a mother could muster, she remained nearly silent through the whole ordeal.

Finally, the baby was delivered.

Mab said in awe, "I've made more noise conceiving babies than you made giving birth to one."

All three women laughed.

"What are you going to name her?" Mab asked.

"Esperanza," Maria glowed. "It means hope."

"It better mean 'baby who cries quietly when she needs food,'" Mab joked.

"Maria, we can keep her in here until I color your room," Blythe said. "Something about the drawings blocks out Henry's force in the room. He can't sense what goes on."

"At least we hope," Mab added. "Seems to work, though. You listen to Blythe and me. We'll look out for you and this little one."

Maria thanked them as she looked down on her newborn.

"Don't you have a ring for her, Blythe?" Mab asked.

"I wish I had a whole jewelry box," Blythe said, slipping the ring off her pinky. "That was the most beautiful expression of a mother's love I've ever seen."

Maria simply smiled down on her child. "You're beautiful, Esperanza," she said.

Blythe took Maria's hand and slipped the ring on. "Oops, not that finger," she said. "Let's try that one."

"Oh, beautiful," Maria said. "I've always wanted a gold ring."

"Keep it warm," Blythe asked. "Keep it warm for Esperanza."

For the first time since she became pregnant, Blythe felt faint butterflies from the baby within her. She quickly sat up straight and moved her hand to her stomach to confirm the sensation, but it was over.

"You okay, Blythe?" Mab asked.

Blythe gave a fleeting smile.

With Maria and her baby soon asleep, and Mab keeping watch over them, Blythe made her way to Maria's cell. Blythe was so overwhelmed by what she had just witnessed with Maria that she didn't run or hide. She leisurely strolled down the corridor.

"What a lovely smile," Notté said as he approached.

Blythe was in too fine a mood for even him to spoil it. She smiled with a brief bow as she passed.

"Are you thinking about him?" Notté asked. "About that Aaron?"

"Why are you so obsessed with him?" Blythe spun around to ask as she continued on her way. "Are you in love with him as well?"

"And if you loved him, could you really joke like that?" he asked. Notté always managed to find the words to take a smile off of Blythe's face. "You reminded me of something as you passed," Notté said casually.

Still smarting from his last retort, Blythe asked quietly, "What is that?"

"I think it is time you brought that Aaron into the kingdom."

Blythe laughed to his face.

"No?" he asked.

"No." She laughed at him and turned to leave. She knew it was dangerous to turn her back on Notté, but the only thing more dangerous was remaining in his company.

"Come with me," he commanded as he walked in the other direction. "I have something I want to show you."

Blythe knew better than to disobey. She followed many paces behind him as he walked up to the courtyard giving herself a good running distance should he turn on her. As they turned the corner, she caught her first glimpse of what it was Notté had for her to see. Eight captains surrounded Haskel and held him bound.

"You have a choice," Notté announced in a loud voice. "Go out and bring that Aaron in, or my men will mark your friend here as an aide of Henry. You know what that means, don't you, Blythe?"

She stared at Haskel, unsure of what she could do.

"It means certain death," Notté said. "Haskel's life is drained in a matter of days so Henry can get that much stronger. Is that what you want?"

"Don't you dare," Blythe said without considering the futility of her words.

"Think I'm bluffing?" he asked. He let out a quick whistle and his men went to work over Haskel's screams. But Notté quickly followed it up with two more whistles, and his men stopped.

"Do you believe me now?" he asked. He whistled again and his men went back at it, until he whistled twice more to have them stop. Each time the blade drew closer to brand Haskel with Henry's cross. The entire time Notté remained transfixed on Blythe, a smile across his face.

"You know the consequences of this, Blythe, do you not?" Notté asked. "Once that mark is made, that is all for him. There is no turning back. There is no saving him, not even by Henry himself. Is that what you want for your friend, Blythe?"

"Don't you worry about your soul?" she asked.

"When you live forever, you don't have to worry about your soul," he said. "What is your decision?"

She hesitated and he whistled.

"I will," she screamed above the din.

He whistled twice again.

"Don't you dare, Blythe," Haskel insisted. "If anything we've ever discussed means anything to you, don't you dare."

"Oh, how noble," Notté said. "Release him."

"I will not," Blythe said.

Notté's hand quickly raised and his men held their grip. "Which will it be? Either you bring that Aaron in, or your friend here gets marked. The next time I whistle, Blythe, will be the last. I promise. Which is it going to be?"

"Don't you make that deal, Blythe," Haskel yelled at her. "Do it for Aaron, Blythe. Let love win."

"You can't do this," she screamed at Notté. "You can't make me make this choice."

Notté laughed, "And yet here you are making it. Hmm. I guess that means I can. That Aaron?" he asked sternly, "Or this one? I have other things I must do."

"Notté," Blythe said sweetly, breaking the promise she had made to herself never to speak his name again. She repeated it, "Notté," as she approached. "Please don't. For me? I'll give you whatever you want. I'll give you more than she could ever imagine."

"Surround yourself with your golden vanity, Blythe," Notté said. "*For me,*" he mocked her. "*Please don't...for me.* Inside the golden bars of your cage are iron and rust, Blythe. You've lost your luster. Your brave face is rotting away because there is nothing underneath it," he whispered. "It's all destroyed just like you are inside, Blythe. Don't you want to cut yourself? You've got the rings there. Do it," he urged. "Can't you feel your arms itching right now?"

She lunged at him with her fists out front, but he grabbed her and spun her to the ground. He looked down contemptuously.

"What a pity your mother never loved you," Haskel yelled to Notté.

Notté glared at him, looked toward his men and whistled. Blythe refused to watch their savagery as her friend was dragged down and tagged. Haskel wailed in protest, but Blythe kept her eyes locked on Notté, who stared at her with his contemptuous smile, disinterested in how his men, just feet away from him, carried out his command.

Haskel shrieked his pleas. "Please, Notté. No! Please. I beg of you. Show some mercy."

Notté never stopped smiling.

In a moment, it was over. The captains backed away with Notté, then disappeared through the archways while Haskel remained in a sobbing pile on the ground.

Blythe stood and walked over to offer him some help.

He looked up and said bravely, "I guess I don't have too much suffering left now." A surreal calm possessed him. "Would you help me up?" he asked.

Blythe obliged.

He steadied himself and looked around at all the people who hadn't come to his aid. None of them looked at him. Heads bowed, they dispersed. He casually glanced at his ankle, which continued to bleed.

"Let me help you to your cell," Blythe said as she moved to tuck herself under his arm as a crutch.

"No," he insisted without emotion. "This is my walk to make. You made the right decision. I'm proud of you."

Blythe watched him as he hesitantly moved in one direction and then the other. Halting steps ended in a confused shake of his head and then he returned to the place he started. Blythe saw an uncharacteristic uncertainty in his eyes as they darted about, unsure of what he must do at that moment.

Suddenly, a look of clarity possessed his face. He looked at her in recognition and said, "For my entire life I worked to write some legacy onto paper as if it were carved into stone, and now I know I will leave too soon to complete it. I will leave before I ever understand us, Blythe," he said as he looked around again and breathed in deeply. "Humanity is not that difficult to understand; it is inhumanity that I cannot decipher."

"Who can understand such people?" Haskel asked, and limped off in the evening's terminal light.

Chapter 39

Whether one lived as Notté, in the certainty of earthly immortality, or as Augustus who, upon hearing a rumor that Aaron willingly followed Blythe into the kingdom to be with her, abandoned himself for Henry's death, a certain recklessness took over. Men at either extreme lived to tempt fate. Faithlessness lurked in the margins while hope resided where it always had: in the center of all extremes.

Augustus knew he had to be with Aaron. He had to understand what his friend was experiencing inside that place. The only way to achieve that understanding was to follow him. If Aaron sacrificed himself for Blythe's love, Augustus would sacrifice himself for Aaron's.

At night in a corner of the village, shadows of hunched men scurried in from off the dark streets to a tavern that posted no sign out front. Unlike the others who stood erect only once inside, Augustus approached it with his head held high, looking around into the faces of people he passed.

He opened the door and looked in at the men who mingled, drawing not a few glances as he surveyed the room. With a drink in his hand, it was not long before he felt confident he had found the one who could transport him to the kingdom.

Augustus entered the kingdom that night. It was not until the next day that he learned of Aaron's return from Seguida Villa.

* * *

Kagetsu never looked more radiant to Sergio.

Still basking in the flawlessness of their last encounter, he was unwilling to approach her for fear of once again opening his mouth only to change feet. But as he watched her, something Sylvia said drifted back to him.

"She has all the warmth of moonlight," she had told him.

It was Kagetsu who approached Sergio. She did so with her customary tight smile and bow.

"Sergio," she offered.

"Moonlight has no warmth," he said, reconsidering Sylvia's words.

"Excuse me?" Kagetsu asked.

"Moonlight has no warmth, Kagetsu," he repeated, at last understanding the meaning of the words, freeing himself from her spell.

Chapter 40

Hope faded into anxiety, and anxiety into fear, and fear is as contagious and lethal as any disease.

It was clear that Henry was winning and all were powerless to stop him. This village would become Seguida Villa—another silent monument to Henry's efficacy. All that remained for debate was Henry's timetable.

It was in that disposition that Blythe called Aaron to the castle walls to talk one final time.

"Your voice sounds strange," he said.

"Hard to speak," she admitted. "Tongue has hard, white sores." She fought to pronounce each word, not to let each 's' lisp into a 'th' or each 'r' round into a 'w.' Even into this, the most important conversation of Blythe's life, Henry intruded. Her voice was drained of its energy and passion.

"Another of Henry's curses?" Aaron asked.

"Always something new," she answered.

Her tone became calm and commanding. "Aaron, this is the last time we'll talk."

"No," he responded, the words having barely left her mouth.

"It has to be, Aaron. I'm not doing well. I don't have the strength anymore."

"You'll pull through, Blythe," Aaron reassured. "You're strong beyond anything you know."

"Not anymore, Aaron. I don't want to be strong anymore. I'm tired, Aaron. I'm tired of all of this. I'm ready for the end."

"Don't, Blythe," he insisted. "Don't say that. I can't imagine how you feel, but you cannot give up. This fight has to turn our way sooner or later. I want you there when it does."

"No more, Aaron," Blythe said. "We have so few words left. No more talk about Henry or fights or freedom. I don't care about any of those things anymore. I only want to talk about you."

"There's nothing to talk about," he said.

"Listen," she commanded. "I love you, and you love me, but this is it, Aaron. This is how it ends. You and I won't be together again, ever."

"Blythe," he interrupted but she silenced him.

"Aaron!" her voice cracked.

He remained quiet.

"I don't have strength to bicker. Listen. We won't be together. And let me tell you, if you come in here, I will not love you. I will hate you for it."

The tone and substance of her words left no doubt to anyone, including Aaron, that she meant what she said.

She said, "You will live, Aaron. I know, somehow, you will live through this. And when Henry is done, I want you to love someone else who will cherish you like I never did…like I should have."

"I can't…." he began, but she cut him off.

"Aaron!" her hoarse voice cracked again to cut him off.

She said more calmly, "You will make me happy if you do that. Find someone, and find her soon. We both know now that life is short. Don't waste any more time here. I will not see you again."

"How I love you," he called out to her.

"Let those be the last words I hear from you, but not again. No more words," she insisted. "I can't talk anymore. And I don't have the strength to listen. Do what I ask, Aaron. Do that, and make me happy. I loved you," she said. "Goodbye."

Blythe walked away and stood out of his view beside the window until she was certain he was gone. She leaned back against the castle wall and sobbed.

Aaron stood outside hoping she would return. When it seemed clear she would not, he left and returned home.

"So that settles it?" Notté asked. "You will never bring him in?"

She turned and looked at him with her eye that wandered slightly to the outside and asked him through her sobs, "Now? You would set on me now?"

It was a look so genuine in its pity that even Notté could not pursue her. "No," he said. "I suppose not."

Just at that moment, Blythe's name drifted back through the window. It was the call Blythe had anticipated and poised herself to answer. She took a deep breath and turned away from Notté. She walked to the window.

Parissa called out again, "Blythe?"

Blythe spotted her but was overwhelmed by the thought, "How can I do this?"

She held up her hand to forestall Parissa's pleasantries. Parissa took it as a wave and waved back, only to see Blythe disappear. Blythe bowed and coughed violently to release the emotion that clogged her throat in a hard, tangible lump. All the while Parissa called out again without consideration, "Blythe? Blythe?"

Blythe took a moment and then stood. Parissa waved again in an overly friendly manner that Blythe knew was disingenuous. Blythe could not stand it any longer. She spoke, with her trying to ignore the deep sores on her tongue before Parissa could say anything, "He is yours, Parissa. Aaron is yours."

The words were sudden and blunt and on every level difficult for her to say. Parissa laughed uncomfortably, then responded, "You make him sound like a thing, Blythe, not a man."

"He might as well be," she insisted. "He isn't mine anymore. He is yours, Parissa. Aaron is yours."

The words seemed meant to inform not only Parissa of this fact,

Blythe

but Blythe, too.

"So you finally thought through what I said?" Parissa asked.

Blythe's mouth tightened. Even across the distance, Parissa saw this and knew her words touched a part of Blythe that was still sore.

"You dragged this on for too long, Blythe," Parissa insisted beyond any obvious need. "You didn't need to do that to him. But that's exactly what I expected from you."

Blythe looked up at the sky, trying to let the words bounce off her.

Parissa went on. "I'm glad that you accepted that he deserves someone who can love him…in every way, I mean."

Blythe responded before the words could sink in, but her hatefulness helped her speak more clearly beyond the physical pain, "That's why he's yours, now, Parissa. Don't speak to him for a few days. Give him time to settle into everything he and I discussed. After that, he should be ready for you, if you take things slowly."

"So you can change your mind?" Parissa laughed. "I don't think so."

"Move now, Parissa, and you'll lose him," Blythe said.

"Maybe you're right," Parissa reflected. "I do have time, don't I?"

Blythe had enough. She asked, "Why do you have to be so cruel about this?"

Parissa brayed sarcastically. Her thin veneer was peeled away. "How dare you ask that question," she shouted. "You never thought about that when you were the cruel one…when you were the pretty one. But look at you now, Blythe. You're not pretty. You're as ugly as you ever were on the inside."

Parissa pretended to cut her arms and wiggled her hips to mock her.

"Yes, I knew," Parissa said. "And I made sure everyone else did, too. I give Aaron credit for staying with you as long as he did, considering you had nothing to offer him but looks. And now they're gone, so you're giving him to me. Ha! Thanks for giving me something that would have been mine with or without your blessing."

"Something?" Blythe thought to herself, but she couldn't answer. Everything Parissa said was true.

Parissa pressed on. "You had everything, Blythe, everything, but that wasn't enough for you. Forgive me for saying so, but this is everything you have coming. How does it feel now that people look past you, Blythe? Does it feel like it did for me when you could not have cared less? I'll bet that dandy who brought you in doesn't even look at you anymore, does he? Well, don't worry. From the looks of you, you don't have too much time left to worry about it."

Parissa stood defiantly with her hands on her hips waiting for Blythe's response. It took a long time for Blythe to think of what to say, but finally in a calm and even tone, as if Parissa had said nothing, Blythe advised her, "When you can't stand to wait any longer to be with Aaron, tell him that you've always cherished him."

"What?" Parissa asked baffled.

Blythe said, "Tell him in just those words. But if he asks you whether I told you to say that, deny it, Parissa. Be careful and don't play too naïve or he will see through you and Aaron will never be yours. He must believe that is how you feel."

"It is," Parissa insisted.

Blythe concluded, "Then if you fold those words into your conversation with him—that you've always cherished him—Aaron will be yours."

"Why are you telling me this?" Parissa asked.

"Because if Aaron can love anyone, Parissa, it will be you. I hope you make him happy. If anyone can change you, can make you happy, Aaron is that man. But you already know that."

"I've always cherished him?" Parissa asked.

"Said naturally," Blythe guided her.

Parissa practiced in a lighter, more sincere tone, "I've always cherished you."

"Let him be a good man in the little things, Parissa, and he'll be a great man for you. I'm sorry for how I treated you. I wish you the best."

"I'll have the best," she said without really directing the words to Blythe. Parissa walked away preoccupied with her practice.

Notté said from off to Blythe's side, "I could make sure she never reaches that Aaron. I don't like that one."

"Who do you like?" she asked before she could restrain the words.

"I'm beginning to like you. Or at least feel sorry for you," he corrected.

Blythe walked off to return to her room, and Notté joined for part of the walk.

He asked, "Do you know what she told me the night she made sure you and I ended up together?"

Blythe thought back to that night. For the first time she clearly recognized Parissa's role.

"What was that?" she asked.

"She said, 'The only difference between lust and love is if you get what you lust for.'"

Blythe refused to comment.

"The only difference between lust and love is if you get what you lust for," he repeated. "I've told this to many others and they find it very amusing."

She turned away to go to her room.

"Do not listen to that one," he called after her. "I don't like her. And don't believe her; you are still beautiful, Blythe."

Later that day there was a light knock at her door. Haskel had become meek or perhaps just overly polite in his frailty and gently asked to come in. For the first time since they had met, Blythe thought he looked ragged and beggarly.

She offered him the bedside while she stood. He accepted.

"I get so winded now," he confessed. "Now that I'm an aide, though, at least I don't have to run in the halls anymore. They leave me alone. I laugh now when I think about it; me running in the halls. How many boys did I yell at for doing just that? Well, no more."

Fluid filled Haskel's lungs so that every time he exhaled, he unintentionally whistled. His failing liver only exacerbated this by allowing great quantities of fluid to accumulate in his belly, putting more pressure on his lungs, which forced him to take shallow pants of air to breathe. His belly grew so large, in fact, that he claimed to be pregnant. He laughed off these complaints by saying, "I now have a fluid body to go along with my fluid mind," but he repeated the line so often that Blythe and Mab recognized he was losing touch with the man he had once been.

He had put on a brave face until that day, but, hunched over his belly and looking at the floor, he admitted to Blythe, "I see what's happening to me. I see that terrified look in my eyes." He panted, "It tells me my body knows what my mind refuses to accept: death is coming soon, Blythe. I know that look. I've seen it in others. I promised myself I would look for it in my own eyes as a warning."

Blythe didn't protest. To make him speak any more than he had to would be a cruelty she did not want to inflict on him. So she listened without interruption as he spoke.

"Before that happens," he panted, "I want to have a party...a going away party for myself. Will you come?"

"I will," she said enthusiastically. "I wouldn't miss it."

"No gifts," he said. "I can't take anything with me." He whistled out a frail, shallow laugh. "This will take our minds off of all this for a little while," he suggested. "We all could use the distraction."

"Have you finished your writing?" she asked.

He stared up at her blankly trying to consider what she said then it finally registered.

"No, no," he said. "How can you explain this to the world? Besides, their emotions...the ones outside...have gone smooth with wear. There is too much horror in the world, Blythe...not enough beauty. Ease and profit, anger and hatred, yes, but they've forgotten about beauty. How pointless."

"We haven't," she said, waving to her walls, which brought her back to her old room at her parents' home.

The reminder made him happy for a moment. "Yes," he said. "You're right. All the better for us."

He said by way of conclusion, "If they want to understand about hell, let them read Dante. I won't write words for the sake of words or for my own vanity."

"You've said a lot," Blythe told him.

"Too much, maybe," he laughed in his whistle. "I always thought that terrified look came from knowledge, Blythe, but now I'm not so sure."

"What look?" she asked.

"Don't feign ignorance, Blythe. You know I don't like that. Look at my eyes. Look at the terror in them…at the shallowness…at the whites how they look out with such ferocious intensity. When I saw that look on others, I always thought that terror came from knowledge. Even if those people were beyond the point of communicating, there was a look of knowledge they had gained. I want that knowledge, Blythe. I'll take whatever comes with it, as long as I can, for a moment, glimpse into that world of insight."

"Give me blissful ignorance," Blythe laughed trying, unsuccessfully, to lighten his mood.

"I can't have that," he insisted. "I could never have that. My curiosity was my undoing," he said.

Haskel sat there trying once again to muster his breath. He continued, "Ignorance has one virtue: persistence. It will insist through dogged persistence on leading others to follow its vision no matter how misguided. Ignorance will drive the world to the brink of failure and catastrophe and beyond into the abyss with arrogance and anger because wisdom is often too polite to fight. Wisdom doesn't like to impose its will, but that is all ignorance understands—force over free will and choice. Sooner or later the world comes to its senses, but oh the damage that has been done.

"I used to mock those who meditated in the pursuit of total consciousness, but now I have a greater appreciation…maybe even an understanding of what they were after. Think of all the wars, all the conflict, all the misery we could avoid if we could tap into that Great Knowing and communicate without all the prejudice of the human mind and the shortcomings of the human heart to interfere? We would understand each other perfectly. We would know the magic words to speak that would cut through all the confusion and skepticism of our lives and raise us all to where we operate with a presumption of goodwill because we would know another's will and he would know ours. Imagine a world where we all operated with a presumption of goodwill? That would be a place of peace."

"It sounds like you have already seen it, Haskel," Blythe said with wonder.

"I've seen a glimpse of it, Blythe. Speaking to you now I got a glimpse."

"You amaze me sometimes, Haskel. I've never seen anyone so bent on learning, on challenging themselves to improve."

"You recognize that, Blythe, because you yourself are now doing the same thing," he said.

"Am I?" she asked.

"Surely you've felt it?" he asked. "When you entered this place, you were inert, drifting with the negative tide."

"I was frightened," she admitted.

"Beyond that," he said. "That was on the surface, but below, there was nothing within you to move you. But that has changed. Hasn't it?"

"It has," she said. "I know there is something better, and I want it. I don't just want it handed to me, I want to work for it first and then possess it, but only because I earned it."

The conversation engaged him, and he gained strength as they spoke.

"Exactly!" he said. "The journey and the destination. But you had to break from your comfortable flow to realize you were being dragged, let alone understand that it was in the wrong direction. Blythe, it takes a strong will to jump into that current then wade against it, but you are doing it and doing it well. I've seen it."

She reflexively felt the smoothness of her forearms as he spoke.

"You've grown kinder since I've known you. You've grown both more self-aware and yet more selfless at the same time. You've grown in your forgiveness of others. I've seen all that in the limited time that I've known you, Blythe. And I know from experience you can't help but continue this. The more you experience virtue, the more you will seek it out. Dine at virtue's banquet once, and you will resent having to eat at sin's trough ever again. I recognize what you are doing, Blythe, and I admire you greatly for it."

319

Blythe thought about how she had never met anyone like Haskel before, never heard such words directed at her. She flushed with joy.

Chapter 41

Wide swaths of the social fabric were cut away by Henry's ravages. Financiers whose loans provided the lubricant for economic growth were lost to the kingdom. Merchants were forced to close when they entered Henry's employ. Otherwise productive fields lay fallow after the farmers, who served as the land's stewards, were taken into the land of Henry the Fourth, leaving no one to plant the next crops. Once abundant food supplies ran low as the cold season approached. The print shop closed so quickly that there was not even time to print a notice to let its customers know. Scientific advancements were forestalled. Classrooms remained empty for want of educators. Physicians could not cure themselves of Henry's curse let alone others with more minor maladies. Civic leaders received no special civility once drawn in and they left behind a political vacuum filled by hacks and novices. There was less music, fewer books, no new works of art to enjoy. In many households, children were left behind to raise not only themselves but also their younger siblings. Stark questions arose about how traditional family life could return without parents to teach the next generation by their example. Individuals fended for themselves with no functioning magistrate to look over them. And as more parishioners became personally touched by Henry's plague of captivity, more took up Father

Philip's call:

Not by prayers alone will a captive be freed,
But by another man's prayers matched by his deeds.

Father Philip encouraged prophylactic safeguards to stem the flow of people entering into Henry's kingdom, and they were not altogether unsuccessful. He organized people to go out into the village and educate others on how Henry operated so no one could claim ignorance if he was taken in. He filled their days and nights with positive distractions to grow their faith but also to keep them close together so they would not fall prey. He was often spotted with Lucre tramping around the outside of the castle walls examining the structure and its surrounding environment looking for some flaw, some weakness to seize upon. It was in those moments especially that people took note because, as he had always told them, "How easy it is to act honorably when you know others are watching. Private moments, not public ones, display a man's true character."

Those walks around the kingdom displayed Father Philip's character as a priest who not only preached, but who acted.

Duffy had not been to church since Iris disappeared. He walked down the lane to his home. Entire blocks of houses remained dark day and night, their owners long since lost to the kingdom.

With great relief, he left the empty street and walked through his door closing it quietly behind him. Something in the rattle of the empty home frightened him when he slammed it, so he had amended his ways.

He pulled together something resembling a meal—this included the last egg in the home, which he fried without butter because there was none, the final crust of what passed for bread that he had tried to make for himself, served on a plate he had washed with his thumb.

He sat down heavily at the table, looked at this dinner and yelled at the top of his lungs, "Damn this silence!"

Duffy rose from the table and pulled himself up the stairs to Blythe's studio. The drip, drip, drip of the pot in his room overflowed onto the floor and began to compromise that level, but he ignored it.

Duffy picked up the charcoal sketch Blythe had made of Iris. "What was she looking at?" he wondered.

He walked over to the window and looked out at the trees and the horizon trying to find some meaning in what she saw, but if there was any, it was beyond him.

Duffy looked down through the lowest windowpane where a fly knocked up against the glass then fell onto the outer ledge. It perched perilously close to the edge and in a moment, Duffy expected it to fly away again. But the little creature turned on its front legs. It whirled away from the world before it and toward the corner of the window where a gossamer spider web clung, sheltered from the rain.

Duffy watched, hoping the fly would scoot off beyond the trap or would turn back in the direction it had landed. He considered knocking on the window to startle the thing before it turned anymore, but he felt it wasn't his place to do that. He watched as the fly launched itself into the corner of the window and onto the sticky net.

Confused by being trapped, it struggled to break free.

Again, Duffy thought, "I can open the window and free it." But he felt restrained. "It is not up to me to play God," he thought.

In the upper corner of the web, the spider sensed the change in tension below. It had captured something and descended quickly.

Duffy knew this was his final opportunity.

He considered his choices: open the window and shatter the web to free the fly, or let nature take its course even though it means the fly would die.

He watched as the spider tranquilized the fly with a kiss. The captive's hind legs twitched once, then once more, then the entire body laid perfectly still as the spider wrapped it up in its silk.

A creature of habit, Duffy turned from the window and rested the sketch of his wife back where he had found it.

He examined again the painting of his family reclining at picnic, but his eyes began to play games with him. He thought for a moment he had seen the figure of Blythe move. Had he?

He had.

Blythe

Blythe stood and brushed off her skirt. She looked at her parents, then at the sea and sky, and then walked off the canvas edge into nowhere. Likewise, Iris rose. The image of her looked down on Duffy and solemnly shook her head, then walked off in the opposite direction as her daughter, out of the painting and into the ether of whatever lay beyond. The back of his portly figure, his head drooped low over its prosperity was the only image remaining as the sun set and left the canvas in darkness. No more sea. No more sky. In the long time he stood there and looked at the painting, the canvas dimmed to black as he looked on with fascination.

Duffy withdrew to his fusty room.

He unbuttoned his wool shirt, which had become threadbare in spots, and draped it on his bedpost to be worn again tomorrow. His paunch had shrunken to half of what it had been. He was a man diminished, so much smaller than he had once seemed before the catastrophe began.

He kicked off his shoes, dropped his pants on top of them but kept on his socks as he collapsed wearily into bed. His socks added a pungent element—an essence of crushed corn—to the room's mélange of earthy smells.

Duffy looked to heaven and pleaded aloud, "Forgive me. Please, forgive me."

His words reminded him of prayer, and so he sought to pray.

"I must pray," he said aloud desperately. "Let me pray for forgiveness. But how? I've forgotten how to pray. A prayer, a prayer, a prayer," he struggled. "I've forgotten how to pray."

He fought to remember a single prayer that he had ever known, but in that moment's anxiety, none would come to him. Finally, he stumbled upon something. It was a prayer, he thought to himself. Yes, it was. He began unsteadily at first, but then grew in confidence and speed as he spoke the words without consideration, "Bless me, oh Lord, and these thy gifts which I am about to receive from Thy bounty, through Christ our Lord. Amen."

As his amen reached the ceiling, the ceiling gave way with a massive moan and creak. It crashed on Duffy, crushing him beneath its weight, either burying his prayerful plea or perhaps answering it.

Farther up the valley, Blythe sat on Iris's bedside nursing her through what was becoming increasingly clear to Blythe were her mother's death throes. Iris's fever spiraled out of control then relented into sudden grips of chills that overtook her, making her convulse in the frigid heat, her ashen fingers selfishly clutching the covers close to her chin.

Blythe felt confident the muraled walls would protect her mother from Henry's omniscience and allow her to succumb to the kingdom in the dignity of her own room with her daughter at her side rather than being sent out to wander and die alone. That is why over the past days Blythe had colored in every last inch of the room, including the back of the door and even the floor all the way below her mother's bed, with an explosion of designs. Blythe thought as she prepared Iris's room, if she herself could have one dying wish granted early to her, it would be that her mother passed peacefully—not as a victim of the Mournex, not as a lonely outcast or as sustenance for Henry.

Overnight, her mother's breathing had grown erratic. No longer could Blythe recognize the comforting deep melodic rhythm she heard for so many nights from the room next to her bedroom and studio. These were longer sequences of short gasps for breath accented with the wheezing howl of her laborious exhales as more and more fluid filled her mother's lungs. For two weeks, Iris had coughed incessantly. For five days and nights her mother found only the edges of consciousness as her breathing labored on, slowly unwinding like a clock winding down its last hours until its ticking stops. Blythe knew her mother had nearly run out of time.

"Shhh," Iris said thinly.

"What's that, Mother?" Blythe asked, hoping to coax her mother back.

The shock of Blythe's words startled Iris awake. She began to speak as if Blythe were Iris's mother, remembering pieces of some ancient conversation or perhaps manufacturing one with the feverish visions that crossed her mind with each synapse's misfire.

"It was warm there, Mother," Iris said. "Warm and just what we wanted. You have it, too. Oh, thank you, Mother. Thank you. I'm not feeling well, Mother. I better rest. I'll listen, Mother. I'll listen."

She drifted off again, laying still but for an occasional twitch. Blythe held her mother's hand.

Slowly Iris relented, winding down, until she was still.

Blythe studied her mother's face. It was over. The tension of life was released from Iris's whole being. She had passed in peace. Her mother slipped her worldly bounds with the perfect serenity she deserved, thus denying Henry something he sought.

For the first time, someone had defeated Henry at something. Blythe wasn't sure if it was she who had done it or her mother, but the answer to that question didn't matter.

Blythe sniffed back her tears and smelled how her mother's ever-sweet milieu had turned acrid. It was one more sign to her that this was no longer her mother who lay before her; her mother was elsewhere, and forever safe from Henry the Fourth.

A trampling of feet raced down the corridor.

Fists pounded on Iris's door, but when Blythe did not answer, the door was kicked in.

Notté marched in and looked around the room in shock at the elaborate drawings. Then he looked down at Iris. Blythe still held her mother's hand.

"What are you doing?" Notté demanded.

"Holding my mother's hand."

"And what is she doing?" Notté shouted at Blythe.

"Nothing," Blythe said calmly. "She's dead."

"Dead?" he yelled. "You know that is against Henry's wishes. You know you've taken life from him that wasn't yours to take."

"It wasn't his either," Blythe pointed out. "And I didn't take her life."

"How did this get here?" he asked, pointing around to the murals.

"I drew them," she said mildly. "I drew them then colored them in."

"Have these washed away," he ordered his men.

Notté pointed to Iris, "And have her taken away and given to the Mournex. If they won't take her then throw her in the canal."

"Thank you for taking care of her body," Blythe said sweetly. "She had such a peaceful death. Her spirit is safe now, and free."

Notté struck Blythe across the face. He turned back to the captains and said, "Check every cell and wash down any with these drawings. I want every wall spotless."

Blythe kissed her mother's hand and stepped aside. Two captains walked over and took Iris's body away as the others marched off to conduct their room-by-room search.

"You're foolish," Notté said, now alone with Blythe. "Henry will have some special punishment for you. I wouldn't be a bit surprised if you're the one he's been sensing all this time. I'll make sure he gets special word about you."

"But don't you pity me anymore?" she asked unfazed.

He slapped her again, but she only laughed. Iris was free of Henry's kingdom, and when her mother left, Blythe felt she had taken a small but important part of her daughter with her.

Chapter 42

As Blythe had done every day since that first baptism when she dunked her entire head into the stream to relieve her shingles' sting, she knelt beside the water, leisurely bathing. The water's soothing coolness had long ago cured the itching drive she once felt in the soft plains of her forearms. For those few moments when she knelt there, her mind was cleansed of all worry, all confusion, all pain.

She reached into the sack she had set down close beside her and pulled out a cloth and brush. She dried herself off then meticulously brushed out her proud mane. Although the rest of her may have faded, her hair remained lustrous and full. It was her last point of pride.

It went unnoticed by the captains and Henry's shadow, but each morning Blythe knelt closer and closer to the point where the stream finally ducked beneath the kingdom's walls and washed out into the valley. Not wanting to miss the obvious, she drew there in the hope of perhaps finding an easy out, a place she could dive through to be free of this place. She knew that if she knelt there on her first day or any day without first establishing her ritual, she would be pushed away by the captains, or worse. So little by little she made herself a fixture at the same time every morning. And little by little she inched her way closer to the water's end within the kingdom's walls.

As she brushed out her hair, she looked down through the clear water and her heart sank. It was too obvious an exit. Bars crisscrossed from wall to wall across the entire area. They were sewn so close together that no adult, not even one as wasted away as she, could possibly slip through.

Blythe flipped back her hair and looked above the stream where captains continuously stood sentry over a small walkway and opening that Henry used as his dumping place for those he was ready to jettison from his world.

"That would have been where Stephen was tossed out before Aaron and I found him," Blythe thought as she looked up at the opening.

Captives in their most weakened state were taken there, thrown out into the water and expected to sink or swim on their own; how they managed mattered little to Henry.

Blythe was so preoccupied with her assessment of the bars and the opening, dreaming of how she might trick them into letting her out before she was terminal, that she did not feel the gust of wind as it whipped across the courtyard. She had not heard the captives stampede their way to the archways before the doors closed them in, although not all were successful in that regard. By the time she turned around to see what all the commotion was about, the Mournex were already teaming out of the openings from the opposite side of the arena.

The doors were closed.

There was nowhere for her to hide.

She watched as the herd of Mournex spilled out, harrying Henry's captives, chasing them until they could be tripped up and consumed. Other captives were cornered and swung back futilely trying to defend themselves but were torn apart.

Blythe thought back to her first encounter with the beast in the tunnel. Why had it only pushed her limp body back rather than eaten her? And why did the alpha Mournex snatch Mab's baby from Notté's feet when it could have attacked and eaten Notté or any of the other captains in their semicircle around him? Why didn't it go for the man-sized feast rather than that flailing little baby?

"Limp body," Blythe thought. "Flailing little baby. The baby moved and Notté was still." She realized, "That is why he had the courage to stand there."

It was her only hope.

She saw the alpha Mournex leading the charge across the open space. It raised its snout into the air, sniffing briskly as it pounced around looking for prey. Hind feet, front knuckles, hind feet, front knuckles it skulked around in search of a meal.

Slowly Blythe lowered herself until her stomach and chest rested across her thighs. Her arms folded about her knees. She was a tight and still little ball beside the stream. She dared not look out from beneath her tent of hair but instead buried her nose between her knees.

The alpha slowly approached. She could hear its heavy breathing and the sound of its talons scrape against the piazza's hard surface. It stood right next to her.

The alpha pushed Blythe to watch her react.

Nothing.

It pushed harder, knocking her over onto her side, but the ball did not unwind and remained perfectly still. All around Blythe, she could hear the screams and pleadings of people as they met their horrible deaths, eaten alive.

The alpha drew in close and sniffed her hair. It sniffed so strongly that strands were drawn up into its nostrils causing a ferocious sneeze. The beast's spit and mucus covered her face, filling her own nose with its noxious scent and sending Mournex spittle into the slight gap in her mouth.

Blythe did not move.

To move was to die.

A lesser beast leapt over to join in the take just as the alpha, disappointed by his failed hunt, spun around to seek another victim. The alpha's sudden movement caught the lesser Mournex by surprise and rather than splitting open Blythe, its claws instead sliced clean through the alpha's belly. The alpha screeched in agony but instantly turned his anger onto the underling, which cowered and retreated, fortunate to have survived the encounter.

Blythe

The alpha turned back to Blythe to cover up its wound so the others would not see. Thick cords of dark blood pulsed out of the beast. The liquid ropes struck heavily onto the ground and squirted across Blythe's face, adding yet another odor she had to overcome. Its warmth and smell were about to make her wretch.

Blythe squinted up as the alpha remained transfixed on its leaking belly. Its fibrous intestine and other entrails began to slip out. To prevent them from falling any farther, the beast cradled them and hopped over her to hunker away in a corner.

Looking around to make certain that all the Mournex were fully engaged in their meals, Blythe slowly loosened up and turned to watch the alpha.

It was crouched down beside a door, its back to her, bowing its head most of the time, but every few moments looked over its shoulder to see if any of the other Mournex had yet taken notice of him. One who had been pushed away from three or four carcasses drew near, joined by another who had been similarly mistreated. They were lean, hungry, inquisitive.

They cautiously approached, lifting their snouts to whiff the air. On their hind feet and front knuckles they crept closer to get a better look at what the alpha was hoarding. The first one placed a paw on the alpha's shoulder to turn it around and have a look, but the alpha viciously snapped at him with his bloodstained teeth driving the lesser beast back. The other did likewise from the other side, but he, too, retreated after the alpha looked over the other shoulder and faced him down with a low, menacing growl. Whatever he was hoarding there, it wasn't for them. He ducked back down to his business, his head bobbing up and down; but starved, the two lesser beasts would not relent.

They each approached again, this time simultaneously. The alpha snapped again at the one who had touched his shoulder, then, catching a view of the other in his peripheral vision, spun around to make the other back down as well. The two beasts spotted the prize; the alpha cradled his guts in his paws and didn't bother to turn around before he went back to snapping at his intestines, gorging himself on what parts of the delicious mess he could draw up to his mouth. He never considered the consequences of his actions.

Seeing his weakness, the lesser two pounced without hesitation, the first knocking heads with the alpha sending him reeling on his back unconscious and laid out like a banquet. Neither of the two hunched homunculi wasted time in diving into the feast their master had spread out for them. Within moments, everything on the alpha was stripped, leaving his face, feet, and his bloodstained paws behind.

As soon as the two started eating, Blythe shut her eyes and slowly drew herself back up into a tight ball. She remained perfectly still until the purge concluded and the satiated Mournex retreated to their lairs. When the archway doors opened again and captives returned to walk about, Blythe scampered to the water's edge. She dunked her head to wash away the alpha's juices that began to dry on her skin. She fiercely scrubbed her face and hair, and rinsed out her mouth and nose to try to free herself of the awful smells and tastes. She washed her entire body free of what the alpha had left behind.

Satisfied at last that she had done the best she could, Blythe dried herself off, picked up her bag and walked back toward her crowded quarters.

Maria and the others rushed to meet her at the archway as she entered.

"You're lucky to be alive," Mab glowed.

"We watched the entire thing," Maria said. "No one survives the Mournex."

"I had a lot to live for," Blythe said.

"But how?" Haskel asked. "How did you do it?"

Blythe told them about her encounter in the cave with the beast and what she had remembered with the alpha Mournex when Notté had sacrificed Mab's baby.

"I lived because I didn't move," she said. "That's the secret. Let the others in the kingdom know so they have nothing more to fear from the Mournex."

"Henry is not going to like this," Haskel said with relish.

As Haskel faded, he lacked the quickness to slip his cocktail

Blythe

concoction into the captains' water. The sudden withdrawal made them all irritable, especially Notté, who only lately had begun to enjoy the water, but drank the most heavily. He became furious all the time. His head throbbed. His hands shook as he drank more and more water, but it lacked the kick it once possessed. For a time he even questioned his decision to live forever if that was how he would feel.

Brooding down the hall, Notté passed Maria's cell. A high-pitched sound caught his ear. It sounded like an infant's laugh. He stood outside her door and sneaked in close, listening for another sound.

Mab, on her rounds to deliver the news about the Mournex, watched from behind an arch. She had to act.

"Notté," she called out. "No more Mournex for us. Whatcha gunna do now?"

Notté turned from the door and asked, "No more Mournex? What are you talking about?"

Just then, another captain called to Notté from down the hall, "Notté, there's trouble downstairs. You better come."

Relieved at the genuine distraction, Mab yelled to him, "Now whatcha gunna do?"

Notté backed away from the door. Taking note of which one it was, he went off to see what was the matter. As soon as he was out of sight, Mab flew to Maria's door and knocked.

"Maria?" she called as loudly as she could in a whisper. "Maria?" she pleaded.

Maria walked around the corner from the stairs. "Mab?" she asked. "What is it?"

"It was Notté," Mab said. "He was outside your door listening in. I think he heard the baby."

Maria bolted by her and into the room. Mab followed. They closed the door, and Maria fell to the floor where she pulled Esperanza out from underneath the bed. Blythe had brightly painted the walls below the bed again after the captains had washed them clean. Had it not been for Maria's bold desire for Esperanza to take a secret adventure out into the plaza to get her first sight of sunshine, the baby might have been discovered when the room was washed. As Maria pulled Esperanza out, a little bell tied underneath the bed jingled.

"Oh, mi hija!" Maria said gratefully, clutching the child to her chest.

"That baby's not safe here, Maria," Mab said. "We got to get her out of here before Notté comes back. He looked real carefully at your door. He knows which one it is."

"Where can we hide her?" Maria asked. "With the walls washed, no place is safe."

"She can't stay here," Mab insisted. "This is the first place Notté's going to look for her. Let's take her to my room. We'll work something up."

Maria agreed. The two women wrapped Esperanza in a sack. They ran as silently as they could down the hall to Mab's room.

Notté understood the importance of washing the walls. The secrets the captives wished to share would remain unsaid if they presumed the walls would tell on them. That was one way Notté and Henry gained the power they craved—by imposing silence. The people's silence is a tyrant's greatest advocate. The less captives talked, the less they knew; the less they knew, the more they feared; and the more they feared, the more easily Notté and others could manipulate them to their own ends, the more easily the captives could be controlled.

Maria ran back to wash the walls before Notté could return. Just as she pushed the bed back to its place, Notté stepped in unannounced. Maria fell to the bed with surprise, ringing the bell beneath.

Notté looked at her flush and sweaty face but said not a word. She looked up at him with all the anticipation of a disobedient child. He dropped to one knee before her, his eyes never leaving hers. He swung his second knee down, continuing to stare directly at her. Finally breaking eye contact, he let himself fall forward in front of her feet catching himself in a pushup just before his nose would have hit the floor. He turned his head up to see what had made the noise. All that remained to be seen was a single bell hanging from a string.

"Move," he ordered.

Maria stood and walked to her window.

He reached in and plucked the string. He stood up and brought it

Blythe

before her asking, "What is this?"

She looked up at him, unsure of what to say.

"Is that your bell?" Mab asked from the doorway. "Did he take your bell?"

Notté spun around as Mab continued, "You bad girl! My aunt and uncle once hung a bell from my cousin's bed. He wasn't that dumb, but he was slow enough. He had the room above them and anytime he had a girl over, they'd know he's being bad when they heard that bell go off. Maria, I'm a little surprised at you. You don't strike me as that kind to be playing around!"

Notté looked at the bell and looked at Maria. Maria could only look up, smile sheepishly and shrug.

Notté held out the bell on the string and dropped it into her hand. He walked past Mab who curtsied as he departed.

Mab closed the door and the two women burst into contained laughter, hugging each other.

"I got Esperanza safe in my room," Mab whispered. "I even drew up some pictures for her, but I'm no Blythe. Baby'll probably wanna cry when she sees the mess I drawn."

They laughed again as they walked out to check on Maria's daughter.

* * *

When Parissa invited Aaron to the picnic, she left the distinct impression that they would be joined by a few other friends. Somehow those others never materialized, and so Parissa and Aaron were left to go it alone.

"More wine?" she asked.

"Please," he said. "Too bad for Sergio and the others. It's not like him to miss a free meal."

"All the more for us," Parissa said.

"Cheers to that," he said, holding up his glass.

"And speaking of us," she said after their drink, and then let the words hang out there by themselves. She put her wine glass down on a level spot in the hillside grass and began to look at him differently, in a more timid manner.

Assuming she was merely humoring him, he turned to her with a smile, but, seeing her expression changed, his look turned more quizzical.

"Aaron, I've always cherished you," she said, then nodded unconsciously, once for each syllable to the exact meter of the words she had said, making sure she got them right. Satisfied she had, she continued. "I know this is difficult for you and you would never raise this while Blythe is going through…well, everything she's going through, but I at least wanted to let you know how I feel. Where we go from here is up to you." She paused.

"No one else was invited to this picnic, were they?" he asked as he looked down at the wine glass he held with both hands. His tone made it clear he sought a straight answer.

"No," she said embarrassed. "I only asked you. But I wanted to do something special…something where we could be alone…to talk."

"Parissa, I…," he began to apologize, but before he could finish, she sought to salvage her opportunity.

"Aaron," she said, "I've talked to Blythe."

"You what?" he asked.

"I talked to Blythe about the two of you and where things stood and where they were going. I didn't bring it up, Aaron. Honestly, I didn't. She called me to the kingdom to talk."

"Parissa, I…," he began apologizing again.

"I know," she said. "This makes you very uncomfortable. But sooner or later it has to be raised, Aaron. And I didn't want to lose you to someone else. Blythe wanted to make sure you were taken care of after she left, and she asked me to be the one to do it."

"I can take care of myself, Parissa. No offense."

"The words are coming out wrong, Aaron. It's just that I have always cherished you."

He looked at her more closely. He was beginning to understand things better. "Yes," he said coolly. "You said that."

Parissa smirked. "You want a straight answer? Fine, Aaron. Here's your straight answer. I know you love Blythe, but it's time to face facts. She's not coming out of there, Aaron. At least not in any condition where she'll survive. Nobody does. You know that as well as I do. You're still here,

337

Blythe

Aaron. I'm still here. And while we're here...."

"Let's forget all about them?" he said to complete her thought more bluntly than she might have.

"Exactly," she said to his surprise. "Let's live while we're still free."

Aaron shook his head, but she insisted, "It's what Blythe wants. It's what she asked me to do for you."

"Just like the party with that one who brought her in? Did she ask you to do that, too?"

"What are you saying?" Parissa asked in her best insulted voice.

"You know exactly what I'm saying, Parissa. You're no friend to her. You've never been a friend to her. You're a second-class schemer. That's all you'll ever be even though you'll never admit it to yourself. And that's another reason I'll never trust you: You can't be honest with yourself."

He yelled at her. "Blythe and I might have said a lot of angry things to each other when we fought, but we were always honest with each other. We always told the truth about what we did and how we felt."

He yelled at her as she hastily threw the picnic into her basket. "That's something you'll never understand, Parissa. That's something you'll never feel—the honesty that true love is based on. The best you can ever hope for is some man who will at least smile at you when he lies; that way you can convince yourself that he's all right. But he'll never be all right, and neither will you," he yelled as she stormed down the hill. "You'll never be anything more than a miserable liar."

* * *

Notté did not return to Maria's room. Rather, he went back to his own quarters, placed a cold cloth across his forehead, and ordered that Blythe be brought to him.

She knocked gently, hoping that perhaps he would not hear her and she could walk away, but the captain who escorted her took the initiative to knock more loudly.

Notté groaned and ordered her in. From his bed he lifted the compress and presented a hateful look to the man who had knocked so loudly. The man shrank from the look, quietly closing the door in retreat.

Blythe looked at the floor rather than at Notté. "What is it?" she asked quietly.

He said with one hand bearing down on the compress, "I wanted to tell you that I was sorry we had to destroy your work...your drawings. They were beautiful."

She did not respond. Hoping he had said his peace, she turned and put one hand on the door handle.

"Where are you going?" he asked, peeking out from under the blindfold.

"I...thought that was all," she said.

He grunted out a laugh.

"I was thinking about those paintings...," he began.

"Drawings," she corrected.

"Paintings, drawings, whatever. I was thinking about whatever you call it that you put on those walls, and a question came to me. 'How would Blythe like to paint for a thousand years?' Imagine it, Blythe: having the life span to paint for a thousand years? What would you give for that?"

"Not what you're asking," she said.

"Wouldn't you? Have you really thought about what I'm suggesting? For a little oath, for a little blood and nothing more than that, you could put Michelangelo to shame. You could be the greatest painter of all time."

"At what cost? Murder?" She laughed at him. "Leave it to you to sell immortality by making life look cheap. Either all life is precious and should be preserved or none of it is. You can't have it both ways. You and Henry are obscene. You are evil and immoral."

"Morality, morality. Morality is dead, Blythe. You're living in a past age where such things mattered. But don't you understand? All that matters now is living and pleasure. What else is there?"

"Honesty. Truth. Freedom. Love."

"Don't talk to me about a unicorn's bones, Blythe. They never existed. They were dreams. Beautiful dreams, but that is all. Listen to me, Blythe. Enjoy yourself. Paint. Sculpt. Become the master of artistic masters."

"And serve your master?" she asked.

"Our master."

"Yours," she replied.

"You are being foolish," Notté said. "You give nothing and you get immortality…one hundred lifetimes if you wish, to do with whatever you want."

"Is that what you're doing?" she asked. "Is this what you want to do with your eternity?"

"Well, no, but…." he began.

"And how many lifetimes have you lived? Ten? Twenty? Fifty?"

"So far only one, but I have faith…."

"You have a scar on your palm and a power to kill. Nothing more."

"Sit down here on the edge of my bed," he ordered as he swung his legs around and stood up. "I've wanted to do this from the first time we met."

He forced her head down and cut off the last piece of physical pride she possessed. And as he did so, she watched her bright tears fall along with her hair. He left her with choppy, clumps of remains.

"There," he said. "That's better."

She flinched as he laid his hand on her head to wipe off the hairs that had not fallen. Once that was done, he kicked the clippings under his bed.

Notté circled her as she sat there, her naked head bowed. He admired her from all sides then ordered her to lay down with him as he held her and drifted off to sleep.

She lay there with her eyes open. Barely blinking, she was lost in a complex web of fractured thoughts. Unable to escape him, she drifted off to sleep. When she awoke, the evening light was fading.

She moved gently to get up without waking him. She noticed his knife on his nightstand. She picked it up. She examined it closely and thought back to the redheaded captain. She tried to think back to how he had moved his wrist to open the blade and remembered the sharp sound it had made. She did not want it to make that sound. She wanted it silent as Notté slept.

She reached her fingernails in and pinched out the blade, slowly bringing it all the way out. She rested it on the nightstand.

Blythe leaned over Notté without leaning against the bed, without making a sound and held the sharp blade so close to his skin that if he hadn't shaven that morning, she would have cut his whiskers.

She knew where the jugular vein was. Her father had taught her.

She held the blade confidently in her hand and prepared to plunge it down in one swift cutting motion—not a stab. A stab could be repaired; she was going to slice him as a sacrifice to the love she and Aaron shared.

Then she thought about Aaron.

And she knew that if she killed Notté, her punishment would be death in one form or another. Yes, she could outsmart the Mournex, but Henry had incalculable ways of killing people. And Blythe wanted to live. More than anything else she still wanted to live.

She would not give the one who drew her in or Henry such a cheap victory. Henry and he would die; of that she was certain, but not by her hand, and not at that moment.

She would live and somehow Notté and his kind would not. That would be her revenge.

She withdrew the knife and leaned the blade upright on his nightstand. Without a sound, she leaned on it and stuck it blade-first into the wood. She wanted Notté to know how close he had come to losing his life. That would be a measure of revenge for what he had done to her.

Blythe silently opened the door, slipped out, and returned to the stream where she washed away all memory of what he had done.

As she rested on her haunches there, a shooting pain cut through her abdomen. In agony, it forced her to lie on her side.

"The baby...the baby," she thought. "It's way too early, but the baby is coming."

Fighting with every fiber of her being not to scream in pain, Blythe stumbled off of the courtyard and onto the stairs. She rested there for a moment, covered in sweat. She leaned against the cold wall for support as she circled down the stairs, down the corridor and into the crowded walls of her room. She hadn't the strength to walk, so she dropped hard to her knees and crept along the floor. She could not lift herself up to her bed, not how she felt. She remained on the floor, her knees to her chin, pushing, pushing harder in her agony.

The contractions grew more painful and came closer together. She restrained every sound she wanted to make but still she had to pant for air; she had to grunt out with a gaping mouth each horrific razor of pain that shot through her stomach and into her back, sticking blade after blade through her.

"Oh, hurry, you," she urged in a cry, pushing mightily to be relieved of her agony. She pushed and pushed again; pushing well past sundown she pushed with everything within her to be free of this bond to that one who had drawn her in, who had lied to her. "Oh, hurry, you," she pushed again.

At last, the little one loosened his grip on her, and he was released.

With a small snip, the stillborn pile no larger than the palm of her hand was something a world away from her even as she could feel its diminishing warmth that she had provided. There was no movement from the mother or the child.

"I am free of him," she said as a prayer of thanksgiving. She chanted it as a mantra, "I am free of him. I am free of him. I am free of him. I am free of him."

In the emptiness of that moment, for part of a fraction of an instant of time, Blythe felt as if she had tripped across that cosmic cord Haskel had discussed with her. She felt connected, tied into all that knowledge he had promised, all that peace. In emptiness, she found the fullness of peace. In peace, the essence of the world. In that essence, she told herself, "There is only 'is'...that of being."

Blythe was at the center of herself looking out in all directions with absolute grace. She was one; she was one of many that made up the one.

She looked again down on the small, misshapen remains of what would have been her son. In that new spirit of peace came a recognition that what she lost was not only half his father; it had been half of her as well.

She gently cradled the little form, asked for his forgiveness and lowered him into the stream where he was carried away.

When she returned from that place to the awareness of her room, she began to chant a new, truncated mantra as she knelt, "I am free. I am free. I am free."

Henry's kingdom sought to destroy her. It proved, instead, the crucible that purified her. For good.

Chapter 43

"This is minus-one for me," Haskel announced to the little gathering in his cell.

It was an act of sheer will for him to stand, let alone with his typical poise. Everything about him had wasted away until all that remained was a flurry of energy: shaking hands, wobbling head, a twitching torso overtaken by uncontrollable and—for such a prideful man, embarrassing—spasms. Haskel's clothes draped off him and flowed all the more because of his constant motion.

"Because tomorrow is my last day in the kingdom, this must be our goodbye," he said.

Blythe smiled at him indulgently, knowing Henry alone controlled such decisions. She knew equally well that Haskel would never compromise his ideals for a conditional release.

"Don't be sad," he reassured Blythe, Mab, and Maria. "I intend to live, or to die trying."

They laughed at his turn of phrase, illuminating with appreciation his otherwise drawn face.

He said, "So before I leave, I wanted to share this last happy time together with my few friends. I also wanted to leave you with some thoughts and a gift to keep close when I am no longer here."

Haskel reverted as best he could to his professorial tone, and said, "Let me begin with the obvious; don't give into this place and your own apparent outcome. Death does not have to be a certainty here. Live. And live well. Continue to live each day in such a way that you rob Henry of the victory he would otherwise claim. Show by your example that the meaning of Henry's kingdom is not about his life by your death. He and his captains want you to believe otherwise, but that is a lie. The meaning of this place lies within the resistance in our hearts when we refuse to abandon our better nature, our kindness and goodwill, our love and friendship, our humanity. Those are the things Henry seeks to take from you as much as life itself. He would make us objects, not men and women. But hold onto them. They are the things we will remember and be remembered for. Keep alive those ideals in your actions and you will keep yourself alive. Keep them alive long enough, and you will find they form the key to open any door and lead you from captivity into freedom."

He let out a series of coughs that threatened to stop his speech, but he fought through them.

He continued. "You already feel this or you would not be in this room, but I must say it nonetheless: Fight Henry with everything you have left within you. That is exactly what I have done and what I intend to do in my one remaining day here. It would be easy to be tempted by death in such a place as this. We think how easy death would be once the hard part of dying is done: to lay down and have it all go away...to rest... to cast off whatever is now, and to become whatever will be. But death is a fraud. It draws us in, subtly, and lies to us when it claims to have meaning. Regardless of how much we may rationalize, there is no meaning in death; there is only finality. Life has meaning. What we do in life has meaning. Death ends all that. It cheats us of what should be...of what we could be. There is no victory in death. There is victory only in living, and that is why I intend to live."

He said, "Besides, I never did anything en masse, and I refuse to die that way—as merely one of hundreds or thousands or hundreds of thousands. I refuse to have people think of me and say, 'Oh, he was one of Henry's.' That would make me just one of the many who died in his plague, in his offensive, in his disaster. I want more than that for myself. When I die, I want my death to be significant because I died, because it was the end of me, not because I rounded off the digits to an easy ten or hundred or million. But, regardless, my death is a story for another day."

Blythe watched as Haskel's words strengthened him. Not only did his voice become stronger, but his hands steadied as he spoke; his hunched back straightened some.

"Let me say in conclusion, never forget that to be free, you must think," he told them. "There is no way to follow blindly and to be free. You know this now because each of you, like myself, followed someone in here by our own choice even when our minds told us to be wary. We didn't think. We followed. And here we are. But this does not need to be the end because we can think still. We can keep our eyes and ears and minds open and observe. We must continually challenge ourselves to learn even when we feel too tired to learn another thing. For me," he said as an aside, "that is when my breakthroughs have always occurred—when my body is too tired to fight my mind's questioning; only then is my mind finally allowed to work its magic unhindered. Let it be the same way for you. Think and be free."

He raised his glass and said to them, "Minus-one, my friends. To each of you. To the fall of Henry the Fourth. To our freedom."

They cheered him and repeated his toast.

As they began the meal, Blythe mentally withdrew from the festivities. She sat back and marveled at the animated joy reflecting on each of them as one does when considering a fond but distant memory.

The moment brought Aaron back to her. To be touching, to be planning, to be surrounding each other with the love they felt, to be, and to be with him. All of this Blythe relived in that instant. Likewise, her mother returned, comforting with her silly joy and quiet confidences, the unspoken expectations one held for the other, the solace of knowing one was perfectly understood even when all words had failed. Such moments between a mother and daughter are love lived. All those memories, considered in an instant, made Blythe stop and understand for the first time that all she would ever have from that point forward of Aaron and her mother were memories…no new tales to tell. They had said their goodbyes, but she hadn't understood what that meant. There, surrounded by the joy of that room, she finally understood what it meant to say goodbye forever to someone she loved. That thought—of never sharing another experience with them in anything but her memory—pushed her to the point of tears.

But her eyes came to Haskel's joyful yet tired face. She refused to ruin Haskel's party with that kind of display. And so she asked him in hopes of distracting herself, "How are you so sure that tomorrow will be your last day?"

He looked straight in front of him with a sparkling gleam in his eyes, but said nothing.

"Are you keeping secrets?" she teased.

"No," he said, with even greater delight on his face. "I am certainly not," then went on eating his meal.

Maria cradled Esperanza in her arms and asked, "I wonder if she'll believe me when I tell her how beautiful life was before we came into this place? I don't want her to think this is how life is supposed to be, living in fear of what's next rather than in hope."

"Or thinking the only way to live is to kill someone else," Mab added.

"Or to be free, someone else's freedom has to be lost," Blythe said.

Maria said as she rocked her daughter, "I don't want her satisfied with having to live in the kingdom her whole life. God willing, we'll find her a way out of here."

Haskel said, "God is only as strong and sure as the men and women who believe in Him."

"Then I'm sure you'll be freed," Maria told her baby. "My God makes me strong so I'll make my God stronger."

"He'll hear you, Maria," Mab assured. "I know gawd will hear you. I've got a gift for knowing these things."

"Well, I may not have that gift," Haskel said, "But I do have a special gift for each one of you."

He walked over to his bed and picked up a little cloth that covered three brightly colored packages and a scroll tied up with a white ribbon.

"First, for Esperanza, who has been such a wonderfully quiet girl this evening," he said handing Maria the baby's gift. "Go ahead. Open it," he directed.

Maria carefully tore off the paper, which was the only bit of color in the room. Within it were two little bracelets of white beads tied together with string. Each bead carried a different letter so one bracelet spelled out "ESPERANZA" and the other "LIBERTAD."

"Esperanza and libertad," Maria read aloud.

"Hope and freedom," Haskel translated. "One will lead to the other."

He lifted up another gift. "And now for Esperanza's mommy," he said, handing Maria her package.

Maria opened it. They were a matching set to her daughter's gift, only larger to fit Maria's wrists. She laughed with delight as she held them up to show the others.

"This way you two can wear them and always think of the other," he said. "You'll always be tied together in that very special way."

"Oh, thank you," Maria cried as she placed them on Esperanza's and her wrists.

"I hope you don't find this too gruesome," Haskel said, "But I pocketed one of the captain's knives and swiped a few bones from that awful Mournex who went after Blythe to make those. That's genuine Mournex bone," he said with delight. "I thought it was a fitting way to show how we can overcome anything with hope and freedom."

They all laughed and clapped their approval in an uproar.

"And now Mab," Haskel continued. "For you, my dear."

"It better not be the rest of that Mournex," she laughed shaking the gift. "Look," she laughed, pointing up to Haskel, "I even got some color back in those old cheeks!"

As she unwrapped the package, she asked Blythe, "You color this paper?"

Blythe nodded.

"I could tell," Mab said. "It's beautiful."

Mab drew back the paper to reveal Haskel's prized notepad. She held it up with wonder and looked at him.

"Yes," he confirmed. "It's mine. To be a good writer, you need to always be looking and seeing things differently than anyone else. You do that like no one I've ever met, Mab. I hope you write so much about what you see that you fill that and another hundred volumes. Use it in good health."

Mab stood up and gave him a big hug.

As she sat down, she said, "I'll use it so long as I don't have to use all of your fanciful words," she laughed.

Again, more color rose to his cheeks.

"And for you, Blythe," he said handing her the scroll tied with white ribbon. "Don't open this until you're free from the kingdom," he asked. "You won't understand it until then."

She thanked him and gave him a kiss on the cheek. It was his third hint of color in the night.

"I am happy tonight," he said with great satisfaction. "But how can anything seem awful to those who win?"

Part Five

Chapter 44

Aaron looked around Iris's once-spotless kitchen. The entire downstairs of the home was so dust-covered that it tracked his footprints from the door to where he stood in the center of the room. Pots, pans, dishes, the table, counters—everything was covered with a thick layer of grit.

Again he called up the stairs, "Duffy?" but again there was no answer.

He climbed the stairs, gripping tightly to the handrail so as not to slip. Aaron craned his neck as he climbed to see inside the open door that led to Duffy's room. Unusual light poured out onto the landing.

Aaron peered around the corner and only then pieced together what had occurred. All he could see of Duffy was his ashen gray, bloated hand and arm that extended palm up from the rubble. The rest of him, and most of the room, was covered in the ceiling's debris. Bright sunshine streamed in through where the ceiling should have been, filling the room with an incongruous atmosphere of natural beauty.

Aaron's first thought was to run up the hills to tell Blythe, but she made it clear that they had spoken their goodbyes. Besides, Aaron thought, Blythe didn't need her father's death to worry about with all her other struggles. He would let Father Philip know, who would tell Old

Lucre, who would arrange for Duffy's burial.

Aaron looked at the crushed pot and thought of Iris and how often she pleaded with Duffy to fix the roof, to no avail.

"She never asked much, Duffy," he thought to the spirit of the corpse. "She asked you to look out for what was yours. Now you've lost Iris and Blythe and yourself as well. You could have stopped this, Duffy. You could have made this all go away, but you chose to sit by."

He gazed around the fringe of the room at Iris's curios; once neatly arranged and meticulously cared for, they were so buried in plaster dust that no one could say with any certainty what any of them had once been.

Aaron's eyes wandered back to Duffy's outstretched hand.

"Serves you right," he said coldly.

* * *

The spy's entire body, including his shaven head, was painted with bright colors in abstract patterns. He strode out confidently from his quarters, a smile on his painted face.

He walked down the hall, bowing at all the doors of his friends and acquaintances as he passed, coming at last to the door through which he had never seen a captive or captain enter or leave. He did not bother to look to see if anyone watched him but rather stepped directly to the door, slipped his knife in its lock, artfully twisted his wrist, and then walked through. Once inside, he paused to catch his breath; it was only then he realized he had forgotten to breathe in the excitement of the past few moments.

He descended the stairs with a lurching gait owed to his failing health and unsteady balance. Once at the lower level, he walked the length of the hall until he faced a monolithic wall at its end.

He studied the structure pulling out from it all the meaning he could glean. This was what he had prepared himself for. Years of snooping, years of pondering, years of research all came down to this moment when the structure of the riddle he had sought to map finally unfolded in front of him.

He stood before the shield only for the briefest of moments examining each stone of the surrounding arch support, one on top of the other on top of the other. It all fit his calculations. It confirmed his every assumption. Satisfied he at last achieved the answer to the question he lived to solve, he strained to raise his hammer, his eye keenly fixed on the keystone.

* * *

Father Philip asked the congregation, "What is the nature of a true God versus a created god? It is the difference between divinity and tyranny. We have only to compare what is in our hearts and in this church with what is up the hill to come to that conclusion. Today, I would like to share with you what I call the Conflict of the Crosses: Christ's cross contrasted by Henry's cross. Let's consider those crosses and the differences between them."

He said, "In our church, you have Christ's cross, the earthly symbol of a heavenly redeemer sent here to save, while up the hill you see the same symbol used by Henry the Fourth as a marking for those he's targeted for destruction. In Christ's cross, you have the symbol of a man's willingness to sacrifice himself to save others and God's desire to save all humanity. With Henry's cross, you have the willingness of a man who would be a god to sacrifice all humanity to save himself. That is the principal difference between the faith of Christ and the cult of Henry, between any genuine faith and any genuine cult—who makes the sacrifice for whom; God for man or man for the man god?"

Philip let the words roll over the parishioners before he continued, "The Eucharist's cannibalism—consuming Christ's body and blood—sacrifices our Lord to feed others so that they may have immortal life with God in heaven. Henry's cannibalism—his consuming of human flesh and blood—destroys mankind to gain his own immortality here on earth. In Christ's cross there is self-destruction in the deepest charity while with Henry's cross you see destruction in the deepest cruelty.

"Henry's cross takes a positive—and think about that little cross he uses as his mark…does it not look like a little plus sign with its equal sides?—he takes that positive sign and makes it a negative. Now think about the suffering Christ walking through the streets of Jerusalem with that great cross beam strapped across His back; Christ's cross turns a negative

Blythe

into a positive because He alone turns death into salvation. Christ's cross establishes hope while Henry's cross seeks to abolish that grace."

* * *

The spy swung the hammer with everything he had left within him. He hit the keystone perfectly square. But it did not do so much as chip. It absorbed his blow. Something within its hollow structure, marked by a circular opening in the center, absorbed the compression.

He struck again.

And again.

And again.

"What is wrong?" he demanded to know.

He knew he had little strength left, but somehow he had to try again.

He backed up as he heard the shouts and stamping of the people on the floor above him.

He ran as fast as his dwindled legs would carry him toward the wall and he hit the keystone square in the center over the opening.

The keystone stood.

Exhausted in every way a man could be, the spy staggered up the hallway. He reached the stairs and began to ascend them, but he was overwhelmed by his exertion. His legs were on fire. So were his lungs. He coughed in a spasm and spat out thick balls of phlegm on the stairs.

More voices yelled out in every direction. He knew he had to move.

He reached the top of the stairs and pushed through the door. He was dead. He was certain this was the end for him. But how could he let this knowledge…everything he had worked for…slip away to be lost forever with his corpse?

A man approached. A tall, blonde man whose confidence remained apparent even amid the rage of shouts and alarms that rose up all around him.

"He is my only hope," the spy thought. He motioned for the young man to come to him. The stranger caught him as he collapsed.

* * *

John E. Kramer   354

Philip continued his homily, "Some have said that Henry and his captivity is a moral wake up call for those of us in this valley. He is a call to those of loose morals to mend their ways. And while that is certainly true, it is by no means the complete message that we must take away from Henry's rise. If we left the message as that alone, it would be of little help to those who must be reformed, those who have been taken in and whose destinies hang on Henry's cross. For all of us—both those inside and outside Henry's walls—there is a greater moral fight at play here, and it is simply this: that man should dictate his own destiny and not have his future decided for him by others without his consent. Some, bound by romantic nostalgia, boast that such an epidemic could only have occurred in this modern age, that the chastity of bygone generations would not have allowed Henry's rise. But the truth is as long as there has been man, there has been sin and ample opportunity for Henry the Fourth and his predecessors to strike. There has always been that chance encounter. Nature would take over from there and spread Henry's vengeance whether it is today or was yesterday or was a thousand years ago or will be a thousand years from now. Such epidemics will persist so long as man is social and has desire. As long as man is man."

* * *

"Listen to me," the spy gasped as the stranger held him. "Listen to me and find a way to share what I'm about to tell you. There is an arch below here through that door and down the stairs. The entire kingdom rests on that arch. If it can be toppled, Henry will lose. Do you understand me?"

The stranger nodded.

"Break the keystone...the top stone, and the arch falls," the spy gasped. "If the arch falls, the kingdom falls. I tried to destroy it, but I haven't the strength."

A march of running feet approached them.

"This is the end," the spy said quickly. "This has to be the end for me. Quickly, leave me and go farther down the hall. I will run your way when the captains approach. If they order me caught, catch me. Kill me. Deny Henry the death god the immortality he would draw from me.

355

Please," he pleaded, "help me keep it from him. They must believe that what I know dies with me. Do you understand?"

The stranger nodded.

"Then go!" the spy ordered.

* * *

Father Philip paused as he held up the host. He waited long enough that each bowed head turned up to look at him.

He said looking up at the wafer, "This makes no sense."

He repeated, "It makes no sense in the world to believe in this. A piece of bread...a flattened wafer is God? What are we thinking?"

He lowered his hands.

The members of the congregation looked at each other in confusion and doubt.

"And yet this very act—believing in something that makes no sense—defines faith, doesn't it?" he asked. "If we believe only what is easy and tangible and provable beyond a doubt, that requires no faith at all, doesn't it? Seeing is not believing; believing is seeing."

He said, "God is not always easy. God is so rarely tangible. God can never be proved by our own knowledge and earthly experience beyond a doubt. To know Him, we must find some mortal way of reaching out to Him as a sign that we hope to understand Him, that we hope to understand His will."

He held up the wafer again and said, "This is faith that I hold in my hand. This is my personal faith, my belief in God, and my belief in His love for me and for you. This is my belief that I am an instrument of God and will work to do His will to do good for Him and for my fellow man and woman. This thin wafer requires faith to work its wonders just as any symbol of love does. I believe," he told the congregation. "I believe."

* * *

The spy lifted himself from the floor and struggled to run. He could no longer breathe. His legs were stiff and unbending.

"That man there!" the captains shouted out down the hall. "Stop him!"

The spy ran into the stranger's arms. The stranger wrapped him in a ball as the spy pleaded quietly, "They must believe I died with the knowledge. Kill me!" he pleaded. The spy said those words even as he yelled for the captains' benefit, "Let me go! Let me go! They're after me! Please, let me go!"

"Hold him there," Notté ordered.

The stranger gripped the spy as hard as he could until he felt the distinct crack of the man's neck. The body in his arms went limp, no longer struggling with a will of its own to live. As the team of captains reached him, Augustus unfurled the lifeless body on the floor before them.

"He's killed him," one of the captains said.

Another knelt beside the spy and slapped him hard in the face to see if this was an act, but the man did not move. His eyes did not wince. His mouth remained slack and open.

"Good work," Notté told Augustus. "This is the one Henry has been searching for. We'll take him from here."

Notté looked down, considering the development. He studied the body with disappointment and then looked into Augustus's face, which held no remorse or fear. It was a face that held only anticipation and servitude.

"Well done," Notté said to the stranger. "You've killed the enemy of Henry. He will want to make you a captain. You will have eternal life as a reward for your heroism. Will you accept it?"

Augustus nodded with a tight smile of pride.

"What is your name?" Notté asked.

"That's Augustus," one of the captains answered for him. "He was one of the ones who came in willingly."

Notté smiled broadly. "Then you shall be a captain, Augustus. Welcome."

Notté looked down at the spy and commanded, "Have this one taken away and laid before the tower."

As they walked away, Notté placed an arm around Augustus's shoulder and began to explain to him the expectations, the obligations, and the many benefits of being a captain in Henry's service.

* * *

Father Philip continued in appreciation, "I not only believe; I

Blythe

believe I understand. I now at last understand the need, the genuine need, for all these symbols, all this apparent mysticism. God is the creator of this world, but He is also at war with this world. He needs those disguises so He may remain hidden from all except those on His side.

"The host, the wine, the code book called the Bible…they are all just part of His disguise for those drawn to His side to understand His plan for our own salvation. The world sees them and tries to convince us that they are as earthbound as a caterpillar because that is all they can see in them. But we know better, don't we? We know they will take us higher. Everyone sees what is there—words written and spoken by men—but those allied with God see through the apparent. We understand their message and their potential. I finally understand why I must believe, and I believe what I could not understand. I now see the need for and the power of God's disguise."

* * *

As ordered, all of the captives and captains of the kingdom gathered around Henry's tower. Notté motioned down to the body of the slain spy and said, "Henry's enemy—the one who caused you to suffer with all the purges—is now dead. In celebration, all purges will stop for the foreseeable future and your cells will be restored to their original size."

The gathering broke out in cheers.

Notté continued, "And now, for the man who killed this enemy of the kingdom, who killed the man responsible for all the purges you suffered through, I present to you Augustus."

All but Blythe and her circle applauded wildly. Augustus looked over the heads of all those gathered. He stared at Blythe who stood stone-faced staring back at him.

"In appreciation for his dedication to the kingdom," Notté said, "we shall now make Augustus a captain in the kingdom." Notté shouted over their obligatory applause, "He will share in Henry's eternal life."

Notté led Augustus to where the stream narrowed and directed him to stand astride the deep water. He held out his right hand for Augustus's left and pulled it toward him, turning its palm upright. Notté then pulled out his knife and showed it to the crowd and then to Augustus.

"The Blood Oath of Henry," he shouted, and then asked Augustus, "Do you swear by your life to uphold the laws of the Kingdom of Henry the Fourth and for your allegiance gain the immortal promise Henry offers in return?"

Augustus nodded.

Notté asked, "Do you understand that with this promise of life everlasting comes the obligation that, should you break this oath by failing to uphold Henry's laws, your life will be forfeited?"

Again, Augustus nodded.

Notté held Augustus's hand and cut a line deeply across the palm. He turned it sideways to allow the blood to trickle into the water as he said, "You and Henry the Fourth are thus bound. Your life for his life; his life for your life, forever."

Notté signaled another captain who stepped forward and handed him a stack of neatly folded clothes. He said, "Your captain's uniform. Let the red pants remind you of the blood oath you took on this day of your rebirth into Henry's kingdom. And let the white shirt—free of all stains—keep ever-present in your mind the honor and obligation of your position."

Notté tucked the clothes under Augustus's right arm, and then signaled for another captain who walked forward and handed Notté a knife. He held the knife up for Augustus to examine and said, "The captain's knife marked by Henry's cross of two lines. See how one line stretches from left to right just as Henry and his loyal captains will forever stretch across the years of time. And see how the other line stretches down and reaches up. We are the foundation of that cross reaching down. It is your obligation and the obligation of every captain to support Henry as he rises high above us. Keep that foundation sure, and you will receive Henry's reward."

Notté lowered his hand and said, "This blade remains hidden among friends," then flicked his wrist to open the knife, "and ready to strike when it is Henry's will."

He flicked the knife again, and the blade retracted.

Notté placed it in Augustus's bloody palm and closed his hand

Blythe

into a fist. He helped Henry's newest captain step back to the side of the square where the tower stood. He turned Augustus toward the crowd who cheered him as they were directed.

Blythe, Mab, and Maria waited until the gathering dispersed before they knelt before Haskel's remains. It was only then they confirmed that the friend they had loved and who had taught them each so well was gone.

Chapter 45

Aaron spread the last trowel of plaster across the newly repaired ceiling. Duffy had long since been removed and buried. Aaron stretched out the kinks in his back and neck as he heard Father Philip call up to him. He tossed his tools into the mix, happy the back-breaking work was at last completed. Aaron beckoned him up.

"Let me show you what Blythe will return to," Aaron said as he turned to see Father Philip enter.

"What a transformation," the priest marveled. "Wouldn't it be spectacular to bring home Blythe and the rest of the relic without losing anymore?"

"It's what I live for," Aaron said, looking around the room.

"God bring that happy day to us soon," Philip said. "We'll succeed in this, Aaron. I'm certain we'll stop Henry and do it soon."

"I agree," Aaron said. "But what makes you so sure?"

"Faith and reason," Philip answered. "Look at how we've stalled the inflow into Henry's kingdom. We're forcing him to work harder than ever before for minimal results. We've nearly quarantined him. We're succeeding in this because we're keeping our faith but still pursuing him with our reason."

"Why is that so important?" Aaron asked.

"Those are the two essentials in every great achievement. But they must be kept in balance. Too much reason limits man to the physical world and blinds his imagination to the greater things that may be. But too much faith blinds him from curing the human suffering in this world. Men with too much faith accept suffering; they expect it and even seek it out."

"I've seen that, too," Aaron agreed. "I can't imagine God wants Henry to be permanent—a terminal condition."

Father Philip concluded, "Anyone who believes that doesn't know God, at least the God I've come to know."

Chapter 46

Parissa removed the note that was tacked to her door. She looked around to see if whoever had placed it there might still be around, but the lane was empty.

She flipped the envelope over. There was no mark on it except for her name on the front and a wax stamp sealing the back. She cracked the seal. The envelope opened to become the note itself. It read:

Tonight at the moment when the last light has left the sky, come by my home and together we will make it bright again. Look for the ribbon on my door. Let's forget about the past. Let us build a future. I am here to be cherished and to cherish you. No words until then.

Her heart stopped.

She read the words again, "I am here to be cherished and to cherish you."

No one knew those words except Blythe and Aaron, and there was no way Blythe left the note.

She looked around the street and thought all at once, "How? Why? Who cares?!"

"I can't make it this easy for Aaron, can I?" Parissa wondered. How could she not, she concluded.

Parissa looked up at the late morning sun. She had plenty of time to prepare. She would use every moment of it to make the most of that night. She would have Aaron at last.

As the thin horizon of light vanished, Parissa strolled to Aaron's cottage door. The two ends of a white ribbon tied to the door played games with each other in the light breeze. There was another note pinned to the door. It read:

> *Thank you for coming, Parissa.*
> *Please leave this note on the stand inside.*
> *I await.*

She took the note from the door and looked around to see if anyone watched, a futile effort in the darkness.

Inside, the entire hall and the stairwell were illuminated with candles that had been freshly lit. A little heart-shaped note on a piece of parchment greeted her on the stand. It read:

> *Shh.*
> *Silence and the stairs.*

She walked over to the stairs where a second heart-shaped note rested on the first step. It read:

> *Drape what you have on over the chair behind you.*
> *You may pick them up in the morning.*
> *We are now so close.*

She followed his command and as she did so, looked to the third heart-shaped note on the next step, which directed her up the candlelit stairs. When she reached the top step, a fourth heart-shaped note lay for her on top of a red strip of cloth.

Raise this to your eye and tie it.

We shall start tonight and be forever blind to every distraction but each other.

No more notes; just me behind the door.

Walk to my whistle when you enter. It will guide you.

She lifted the cloth up straight as it was laid out for her and placed the blindfold across her eyes tying it so it would not come loose. Everything about her was piqued for the next moment.

Parissa gently rested her hand on the door, slid it down to the handle and slowly worked it. She pushed her way out of the hallway and into Aaron's room. Although she could not see, she could sense the room was filled with fragrant candlelight, the smell of lavender. He whistled lightly like a bird, and she reached out to him and began to walk, a cautious smile on her face. As she walked to him, cool rose petals clung to the soles of her feet and formed delicate slippers. He whistled again, guiding her in toward the bed and to him. They touched hands and she flinched from the surprise. He gently guided his hands up her wrists, up her arms and clenched her in the little crease at her elbow. He drew her up and into the bed and laid her down amid more rose petals on the cool silk sheets. His hands began to move on her. They were everything Blythe had promised when she spoke of Aaron; they were warmth and poetry.

* * *

Aaron called out to her from the darkness, "Blythe? Blythe are you there?"

A voice inside offered to fetch her for him without ever asking who he was. In a few moments a slender silhouette appeared at the window.

"Blythe? Is that you?" Aaron asked.

"Aaron!" she called out unable to control her excitement. "What are you doing here?"

"You called me," he said. "I was so happy to hear that I ran all the way."

"But I didn't, Aaron," she said. "I'm so happy to see you, but I didn't call for you."

"You had someone leave a note on my door," he said, holding up the evidence. "It said you changed your mind. That you wanted to see me tonight when it was dark."

"I don't care about the note, but whoever left it knew me better than I know myself. I love you, Aaron. I don't know how many days I have left, but I want to tell you that every day that I can. I love you."

"And how I love you, Blythe," he stated. "I can't tell you how good it is to hear your voice. I can hear you again," he gushed. "Promise I can hear you every day? Would you promise me, please?"

"Every day," she laughed in agreement. "How have you been?"

"Fine," he said. "But I need to see you. I'll be doing so much better now that I can see you again, Blythe."

"How is Parissa?" she asked.

"I knew you were behind that," he laughed. "I knew it when she told me that she cherished me. She would never say that…never feel that, like you and I do for each other. You told her to say that, didn't you?"

"I didn't want you to be lonely, Aaron," she said. "I wanted you to be loved."

"Well, you've made a wonderful love, you'll make a beautiful bride, but you will never make a good matchmaker," he laughed.

"That's the first time you've ever spoken to me about marriage," she said with quiet excitement.

"Can you see me?" he called out to her standing closer to one of the many fire rings that the villagers had built to encircle Henry's kingdom.

"Yes," she said. "I can see you perfectly."

He reached into his pocket and pulled out the final ring he had made for her. "Do you see this?" he asked, holding it out to her and looking through it with one eye so it encircled her. "I had this made for your final finger before you were drawn in, Blythe. I carry it with me always as a reminder that we'll be together again. Will you marry me, Blythe?"

He listened for her answer, which was long coming and in the darkness seemed even longer. For a full count of ten he waited there for her response, but there was only silence. A hundred thoughts flashed through his mind. "She's going to marry me. She's thinking about marrying me. Why is she thinking about marrying me? She's not going to marry me!"

Before he could accept this last thought, he began to shout to her that she needn't answer immediately, that she could consider it, but before he could get the words out she shouted her teary, "Yes. Yes I will, Aaron," as she bounced up and down with exuberance.

As they called across the expanse, they shared what they could about their hopes and expectations for their wedding day. But the night was drawing on, and—after hours of talk of the minutest of detail—Blythe began to yawn in her responses.

"You're tired now," Aaron said. "I can hear it in your voice. Why don't you go off to bed and I'll stop by tomorrow."

"If it's not already tomorrow," she said. "I'm glad you didn't go through with it with Parissa tonight."

"Go through with what?" he asked.

"Your plan...to be with her."

"What plan, Blythe?" he asked. "She and I talked once a few days ago and had such a falling out you wouldn't believe."

"But she came by here earlier this afternoon. She said she had a note from you inviting her over to your home so that you two could finally be together."

"Blythe, I never even thought of such a thing," Aaron said. "I have no idea why she would say that other than to make you jealous."

"It's certainly not beyond her," Blythe agreed. "So there was nothing to that?" she asked just to put her mind at ease.

"I give you my word," he said.

That was good enough for her.

"Aaron, it's late," she yawned.

"I know," he said. "I'm just so happy to be talking with you again. You'll have this ring soon enough, my bride to be."

"I love you," she yawned.

"How I love you," he yawned back.

Back at his cottage, Aaron looked suspiciously at the ribbon on the door. He stood back and looked around for any lights or sign of life from inside.

He cautiously opened the door and walked in. The house was dark, but a lingering smell of fragranced candles and the sulfur of quenched wicks hung about. He called out for Sergio. There was no answer. He demanded to know who was there, but there was no reply.

Aaron looked over on the stand and read the note that had been tacked to his door.

"Parissa?" he wondered. "What was she up to?"

He called out to her and waited, but she didn't respond.

Aaron picked up the notes and read each one. He looked for her clothes, but the chair was empty, if it had ever held what she was wearing.

He took a first, tentative step up the stairs and knocked over something. Still looking up to see if anyone was about, he stooped over and picked up a spent stump of a candle. He reached to the next step, and sure enough, there was another. He climbed carefully up the clear center of the stairs until he reached the landing. He picked up the heart-shaped note and read it in the dim light of the candle he carried.

Aaron looked to his shut bedroom door, unsure of what he would find behind it.

He took one cautious step and then another. He pushed open the door enough to see his open window and the breeze playing on the curtains, billowing them in a sultry dance.

He pushed the door farther and looked down at the dark circles that covered his floor. They moved occasionally in the breeze, but he could not figure out what they might be.

He swung open the door farther to reveal the end posts of his bed and as he did so, he anticipated seeing one or perhaps two pairs of feet. Instead, all he saw as the door swung open were his bed sheets tossed about and draping over the side.

Aaron pushed the door until he heard it hit solidly against the wall. There was no one hiding there. Still thinking there might be someone behind the bed, he carefully circled, his arms and neck taut with tension. As he walked around the foot of the bed, he stooped to pick up one of whatever was crawling about the floor.

"Rose petals?" he asked himself.

"Parissa?" he asked again. The far side of the bed was empty.

One large candle beside his bed remained lit, all the others having melted away.

As he turned to walk downstairs, a piece of red fabric across one of his pillows caught his eye. He put the candle on the nightstand, reached over and grabbed it by one end and then the other. He recognized it as a blindfold and smiled for a minute.

As he smiled, a gust of wind swept in and caught one end of the blindfold and plucked it from his hand. Still holding the other end secure, he snatched it and returned it back up for a final look.

Aaron was speechless and he felt a sudden chill, like all the blood had been drained from him; embroidered in the center of the blindfold was a thin, white cross of equal lengths.

He held the end of it up to his nose and breathed in deeply. That was Parissa's perfume.

It was unmistakable.

Aaron looked out his window up the valley hills. He was certain this had been Parissa's last night of freedom.

Blythe

Chapter 47

Certainly Blythe had wasted from the disease, but other changes, too, were manifest. Her arms were smooth and soft. Her nails grew to graceful rounded points. But those were only outward signs of an inward grace and strength. This was Blythe as Blythe had never been or known.

She eyed the scroll as she did every morning when she awoke, but dared not so much as toy with its ribbon or risk succumbing to its temptation. She knew that if she did even as little as that—merely touch the ribbon that held it rolled—it would be opened in an instant, and her word to Haskel would be broken as would the magic of what lay inside. She eyed it, but left it alone.

Leaving her constricted room for the courtyard's openness, however, Blythe suddenly realized what day it was. She sprinted past the open archway and down the other flight of stairs to Maria's room.

Blythe knocked. Mab opened the door and brought her in.

"Everything ready?" Blythe asked.

"Most everything," Mab said. "Except the baby and her mother and everything else."

"So nothing, then?" Blythe asked.

"She doesn't want to say goodbye, Blythe," Mab said. "She's having second thoughts."

Blythe knelt beside Maria's bed. Maria cradled Esperanza and cooed to her, ignoring Blythe's presence.

"Maria," Blythe said. "This is the day. This is what we've worked for. It's time."

Maria said in her sing-song voice, "I can't give up this little one. Not this little one."

"But if you don't, Maria, it's only a matter of time before the captains find her," Blythe said. "Before the Mournex get her. You want better for her than that, Maria. You want her to live."

Maria looked at Blythe, "But you can't understand. You can't understand what it would be like to give her up with no guarantee that she'll make it. How do you know she'll make it?"

"I don't," Blythe admitted.

"But we know what'll happen to her if she stays," Mab answered. "You gotta do this Maria, and you gotta do this today. This may be our only chance. Now let's get moving."

Maria continued to ignore them as they busied themselves with preparations for a plan they had no way of knowing would ever be put into action. Mab handed Blythe her sack, and Blythe opened it to inspect the inside. A bladder had been added as a lining. She took out a needle and thread and began to sew up the sack with fine stitches. When she got halfway through, she pulled the ring off her middle finger, one of only two she had left, and sewed it into the corner of the bag.

Mab looked at her and Blythe said, "For good luck and as a message to Henry," then went back to work.

Soon, there was only space enough remaining for the baby to pass through. Blythe looked up at Mab, each wondering who was going to press the matter with Maria.

Mab said, "Maria? You have them gifts from the Professor?"

Maria nodded.

Mab walked over to the corner of the bed and lifted the mattress. The two matching sets of bracelets for Maria and her daughter were neatly hidden there, each raising a circle in their original paper. Mab picked them up and handed them to Maria, who continued to ignore her.

"It's time, Maria," Mab insisted. "It's time to open these gifts and use 'em."

"I don't want to," Maria said, unwilling to look up. She played more intensely with Esperanza.

"Maria?" Mab asked until the pressure became too great and Maria was forced to look up with tears filling her eyes. "It's time, Maria," Mab said extending the packages to her.

Maria looked down again at her daughter, then reached up and took them. She opened the first and began to weep. And then the second, and she wept all the harder.

"You have faith?" Mab asked.

Maria nodded.

"Let's see it," Mab said to Maria.

Maria placed the bracelets on her daughter and then the others on herself. She kissed Esperanza on her forehead and on each cheek, gave her a final hug and without saying a word, handed the child, her daughter, to Blythe.

Blythe carefully lifted her and without hesitation placed her in the sack Mab had provided. She sewed up the rest of the bag, billowing it out so it held a little cushion of air around the sleeping child. She then carefully placed the sack in her own and placed her other articles on top of them.

Blythe stood and exchanged worried looks with Mab. They each looked at Maria who sat up in her bed, her arms still crossed as if they held her daughter. She stared blankly at the wall, empty, bereft.

Mab opened the door, and Blythe followed. They made their way to the courtyard and split up, Blythe strolling as she did every morning to her bathing spot and Mab drifting off to cause some trouble with her tongue.

As Blythe approached the stream, a captain called out to her from the catwalk. She ignored him and knelt down, gently resting the bag beside her. The baby and the bag started to stir.

"You're too close to the wall," the captain called down.

"But I bathe here every morning," she squinted up at him.

"Move or I'll move you," he ordered. The captain went back to his business certain she'd follow his order.

Blythe caught Mab's eye and nodded up to the catwalk where two guards busied themselves tossing out those whom Henry had exhausted.

She opened her sack and took out Esperanza's new womb. The little girl kicked and fussed as she prepared to cry.

"You up there!" Mab yelled. "That's right, you," she said to the captain from far on the other side of the stream. "How do you know Henry's through with those men? They don't look too close to dead to me. They still got weeks of life on those bones."

As Mab continued her diversion, Blythe slipped the baby's sack into the water and pushed it down deep into the undercurrent, nearly falling in herself. She recovered her balance and lifted her arms gracefully, rubbing them and washing them leisurely.

The guard yelled down to her, "I told you to move," and he made an effort to get past the other captain to confront her. But before he had time, Blythe lifted her sack and made her way back toward her room. Mab leaped over the stream and followed. They stayed true to a vow not to celebrate that moment for fear of drawing attention to the baby. The last Blythe had seen, the baby was still submerged and bumping through the bars beneath the castle walls.

Blythe could stand the suspense no more. She tossed the sack to Mab and asked her to put it in her room. She walked to an opening that overlooked the stream's descent and the valley below. Although these were the most popular openings to look out—framing memories of what life once held for those inside—Blythe had promised herself never to use them, for the pain of regret and separation she knew they would cause. But she had to look. She had to know.

There was the valley in its entire morning splendor. Still. Fertile. Serene. She tore her eyes away from it before it could sink in any deeper and looked at the stream as it made its way up from the hills and toward the kingdom. A woman stood at the first bend and helped one outcast after another out of the water. They made their way, hobbled on unsteady feet down the valley path to return to their homes and to die. But she had not yet pulled out Esperanza's sack.

Blythe stood on tip-toes to get a better look for some sign of the sack finally returning to the surface.

None could be seen.

Blythe thought of how carefully she had made the stitches, about Maria's trust in their plan to hand over her child, about the woman's promise to look for the child on that day from that location, and about the risk they took in finding someone trustworthy to leave the kingdom and find this woman in the first place. But why wasn't she pulling Esperanza up?

What Blythe saw next horrified her.

The woman turned and walked away.

Blythe looked up to the catwalk. The captains were done. They had already walked down the stairs and were returning to their quarters. This couldn't be happening, Blythe thought.

She looked frantically down the stream back to the woman. She felt the scream rising in her stomach, a plea to the woman to stop, to get in the water, to find what she had promised to find. The scream rose to her chest as the captains walked behind her, laughing with each other about the morning's work, mocking those they had cast off. The scream rose to her neck and caught there for a moment with the pounding of her blood that filled her throat.

"Turn, woman, turn! You promised us," Blythe readied herself to scream. And as the scream reached the back of Blythe's throat and the air with which Blythe had gasped to make herself heard began pouring out of her gaping mouth with her hands cupped to her lips, the woman spun around and bolted to the stream. Blythe saw the woman run without breaking stride and launched herself into the air then under the water's surface.

Then she was no more.

For a long while, Blythe watched as the woman remained beneath the surface. She thought back to Aaron scaring her in just the same way when he had discovered Steven's remains.

"How could this woman stay under for so long?" Blythe demanded to know. "Has she found Esperanza yet? Was the baby safe?"

A whitecap of water broke through the surface as the woman came up again for air and then returned below once more.

Blythe's spirit sank with the woman. She had not found the baby. Blythe would have to tell Maria that her baby was lost.

She studied the water's surface for some news, for some sign, but there was none. There was not even a sign of the woman splashing about in search of the sack. All that Blythe could see were the ends of the kingdom's walls, the stream and the valley. There was no sign of hope.

Blythe relaxed off of her tip-toes and stood flat footed. She remained where she was, her eyes stuck to the elbow in the stream hoping the woman would rise, but she did not. Long past the time anyone could hold their breath under water, the woman remained out of sight.

Tears streamed down Blythe's cheeks and onto the ledge where they were quickly absorbed by the porous surface.

Blythe lifted her hands and wiped them. She prepared to deliver the news to Maria when, at last, the woman emerged from the woods beside the stream and walked past the water's elbow to the path. She held a baby in her arms up at her shoulder. In her other hand, the woman held the remains of the sack.

"Was Esperanza alive?" Blythe wanted to know.

The woman turned so the baby and she could one last time face the kingdom of Henry the Fourth. She held up one of the baby's arms and waved, then turned and walked down the path back into the valley bouncing the baby as they walked.

Esperanza had made it, the first newborn to escape Henry's judgment.

Blythe spun around but then took control of herself. She must not be euphoric. She must remain steady. She could not dance. She must walk. She could not let loose that shout in the back of her throat that was now one of joy, not anguish. For the rest of her walk to the archway and beyond, the Blythe who could not contain her downcast beaming smile had to remain an outward captive even as her spirit soared free with little Esperanza—the first infant…the first person ever—freed from Henry's castle to live.

"TO LIVE!"

Blythe silently shrieked to herself as she ducked around the archway entrance and did a little dance down the stairs.

She could tell Maria, "Esperanza is free! Your daughter is free."

Chapter 48

Parissa glowered at Notté as he entered her cell.

"Oh, don't be so upset with me," Notté insisted warmly. "I only oversee things here. However it was you came in, it wasn't my doing."

"Then whose was it?" Parissa asked.

"Who do you think?"

"Blythe?" She sneered.

"And who else could it have been?" Notté smiled. "She hates you as much as you hate her. Maybe more because she had more to lose than you ever did."

Parissa spat at him.

"Charming," Notté said as he casually wiped the spit off his clothes with her bed sheets. "But that doesn't alter the fact. The question remains, what are you going to do to get back at her?"

Parissa crossed her arms and tucked herself into the corner unwilling to acknowledge him.

"Fine," Notté said. He added with a laugh, "Let her win."

"What can I do to her?" Parissa asked. "You yourself told me murder isn't permitted."

"No, it's not," he agreed. "But are you so devoid of creativity that you can't think of other ways to strike back at her?"

"What are you suggesting?" Parissa asked.

"Nothing. Nothing at all," he said. "But I'm just surprised that you haven't put two and two together yet."

"Meaning?"

"Ah!" he threw up his hands in frustrated disgust. "I will speak slowly, so you will understand. What does Blythe love most in this world?"

"Herself."

"Even more?" he prodded her.

"Aaron," she said with slow recognition.

"Very good," he said patronizingly. "Now how would Blythe feel if Aaron were somehow brought into the kingdom?"

"She'd be happy they were together," Parissa pouted.

"You are confusing your own emotions with hers," he said. "How would Blythe feel?"

"Destroyed," Parissa answered and began to smile. "It would ruin her."

"Exactly. And how would she feel if you got back at her for having you brought in here by bringing Aaron in?"

"She would want to kill me."

"But...."

"She can't," Parissa smiled more broadly. "And I'm permitted to leave so long as I bring someone back?" she clarified.

Notté nodded and smiled. He said, "Now you understand."

"But I've tried before," she said. "I've tried to...to be with him. He wants nothing to do with me. He still loves her."

"Yes, that would be the most pleasurable way to bring him in, Parissa, but there are other means."

He took a ring out of his pocket. On its black onyx face was a raised white cross. He slipped the ring on his index finger past the first knuckle and showed it to her, then turned it around so she could see all sides of it.

"Press the cross," he demonstrated, "and a little needle springs out back here."

He turned the ring over again to show her where the tiny needle had sprung out. "Henry is nothing if not adaptable. This is our newest means of drawing in captives. You merely shake his hand or pat him on the back a couple of times and he'll be in here before the next day. I will see to that. You just apologize for the sting and say that you've been meaning to get that ring fixed. Off you go, in he comes, and down Blythe falls. You don't even have to bring him in yourself. Just poke him one way or the other and we will take care of the rest. Simple enough?"

She nodded with a smirk. "And when do I have to return?" she asked.

"You will know when the time is right," he said. "I trust your judgment."

"And what if I choose not to return?" she asked.

"Henry has stewards across the valley. If you don't return, you'll be found and you'll be destroyed in the most painful way you can imagine, beyond what you could imagine," he corrected himself.

She took the ring from him.

"Go to him tonight," Notté ordered her. "We both want this done quickly."

"Why haven't you just gone out and brought him in here yourself? You could have done it a thousand times."

"I have one thousand lifetimes to live," he smiled. "I have to keep myself entertained somehow."

Notté left and returned to his quarters where he called for Augustus.

"You don't care very much for that Blythe, do you, Augustus?"

Augustus stood at attention and shook his head.

"I have an order for you I want you to carry out tonight," Notté said. "I've already spoken with Parissa. You know her, I'm assuming?"

Augustus nodded.

"She also hates Blythe, so to have a little fun at Blythe's expense, I'm sending Parissa out tonight to draw Aaron in," Notté explained. "Aaron was the one who chose Blythe over you, was he not?"

Augustus nodded, but this time Notté noted a clench in Augustus's jaw, and a pursing of his lips.

"That didn't sit well with you, hmm?" Notté asked rhetorically.

"Well, I don't blame you. Here is your chance to get back at them both. Parissa is beautiful, but more stupid than a round of cheese. She is going to attempt to bring Aaron in on her own, but if she fails, which I am confident she will, I want you there to ensure he is captured. I don't trust her judgment or her ability. Here is your ring. You know how to use it?"

Augustus nodded with a little smile turning up the corners of his lips. It was a look Notté fully appreciated as he handed him the ring.

"Well done," Notté said. "You know what to do. Parissa will leave sometime this evening. Make sure she doesn't see you on the outside. I don't want her any more flustered than she already is. Do this and I will see to it that Henry rewards you well. We could even have that Aaron as your personal...shall we say assistant?" he smiled.

Augustus smiled back.

"Very well then," Notté dismissed him. "You may go."

Out in the courtyard, Blythe approached Parissa. "I just heard you came in," Blythe said. "I'm so sorry."

"You're sorry?" Parissa spat. "You're sorry? You arranged to have me brought in and then you stand there and tell me you are sorry. You have more nerve than I thought."

Ignoring the affront, Blythe said, "I had you brought in? What are you talking about? I only just heard."

Parissa raised her hand to strike Blythe, but Blythe gave her a look that convinced her she shouldn't.

"I had nothing to do with you coming in," Blythe said flatly.

"I don't believe you," Parissa said. "That captain, the one who brought you in, he himself told me you ordered it."

"And you believe him?" Blythe laughed.

"Why shouldn't I?" Parissa asked.

"Because he does nothing but lie. How did you come in?" Blythe asked. "Who was it? Was it a person...a needle? How did you come in?"

"A person."

"Who?" Blythe pressed her. "Was it him?" Blythe asked, nodding to Notté, who had just entered the courtyard along with two of his underlings.

"I don't know," Parissa admitted.

"Was it any of the captains you've seen?" Blythe continued.

"I don't know!" Parissa shouted at her. Then controlling her temper said weakly, "I was blindfolded. I didn't see who did it. I thought it was…I thought I was sleeping with…."

"Aaron?"

Parissa nodded and Blythe could not contain her laughter. Parissa shot her a furious look.

"I'm sorry," Blythe said trying to collect herself. "I really am sorry. You don't deserve to be in here. No one does."

She looked at Parissa for some sign that she might accept the words, but Parissa only turned her shoulder away from Blythe.

"Look," Blythe said, trying to make amends. "I had nothing to do with you being in here." She slipped off her final ring. "I want you to have this, Parissa. I genuinely want to be your friend." She extended the ring to her and said, "We're both going to be in here, we shouldn't fight with…."

But Parissa slapped the ring out of her hand. It rolled off into the courtyard.

"We don't need to fight," Blythe said coldly. "We don't need to be enemies."

"That's where you are wrong," Parissa said under her breath as she walked away.

Blythe retrieved the ring and placed the smooth band back on her thumb.

It was past midnight when Parissa climbed the familiar stairs in Aaron's home. There were no candles this time, only the bare steps. She walked along the outside edges of the stairs to keep the creaking to a minimum.

At the landing, she turned the corner and opened Aaron's bedroom door slowly. With his curtains drawn, she could vaguely make out the outline of his figure in bed resting on his side. She took each step cautiously, silently, approaching his bed. She turned the ring on her finger so the cross was up and the needle down. She gently traced the cross on the ring in the dark as she looked down on him from right beside his bed.

She gently called his name, "Aaron? Aaron?"

"Mm-hmm?" came the sleepy reply as he turned over onto his back.

"Aaron?" she whispered again as she put one knee on the bed and leaned over him.

He answered again from his slumber.

"It's Parissa, Aaron," she said, expecting the words to shock him awake, but there was no reply. Knowing she had other options, she asked lightly, "Do you want me?"

She expected his indignation.

She expected a fight.

What she didn't expect was his sleepy but certain response: "Mm-hmm."

He slipped off the covers and drew her onto him. She swung her leg over and straddled him as he sat up and began to kiss her neck and undress her. In moments she was stripped bare and he was on top of her. No words. No fights. Just him. Just Aaron as she had always dreamed.

She circled her hands high above her head and clung to the headboard. Slowly, still watching his shadow, she drew her hands together and felt for the ring. She traced the cross again and straightened out her hand then pressed the cross down. She felt the silent spring action. She knew the needle was in place. As he reached his climax she clutched his upper thighs to draw him closer, tighter to her. She gripped him again as he shook, forcefully in her hands. He rested heavily back onto her, rocking and kissing her as he had begun, rocking, gently rocking themselves back into sleep.

Somewhere in the middle of the night, Parissa thought about Aaron's face, about the expression he would have when she would tell him it was time to go to the kingdom…that she was going to bring him in. It was an expression she did not want to see. Notté had promised her that all she needed to do was to sleep with him or prick him, and her job was done. She would have accomplished her revenge, and someone else could guide Aaron back in. And so while he slept, she quietly stood and dressed and left Aaron's home. She walked up the hill full of what she had done, wondering why it had to be this way, wondering why she couldn't have made love to him before there was a place called the kingdom and a man called Henry the Fourth. Aaron was amazing. She always knew he would be. And maybe this night would change him now that he had a taste of her. Maybe for what time they had remaining, he would choose to be with her over Blythe. If he did, she would let him. She loved Aaron. She had always loved him more than Blythe had.

As Parissa made her way back into the kingdom, Blythe lay awake, dreaming up at the moon. Its light fell through her curtains and cast its fractured light and shadows on her cell walls. She looked at the patterns and served it to her memory. She would have loved to paint it on that surface, just as it looked at that moment. The night was especially still and silent.

Then Blythe heard the tapping, off in the distance. It was faint, but consistent. Tap. Tap. Tap. Tap. Slowly growing. Tap. Tap. Tap. Tap. It was the sound of feet marching. Tap. Tap. Tap. Tap. Captains' feet on the floor. Tap. Tap. Tap. Tap. They marched in her hall. Tap. Tap. Tap. Tap. Reached outside her door. Tap. Tap. Tap. Tap. Then stopped.

Then the night was silent again as Blythe looked up at the moon and began to cry.

Notté opened her door and walked beside her bed. He looked down on her with a fearful expression.

She watched him lean over gently and press his hands on her covers, pinning her to her bed. He looked straight into her eyes and let out a sharp whistle.

His men marched in quickly and went to work as Notté looked into Blythe's eyes in the moonlight and she looked back at him.

Blythe did not struggle as the captains lifted the covers off of her feet but instead continued to stare with questioning disbelief up at Notté. She flinched when she heard the knife snap out of its casing. And when the cold, sharp blade suddenly turned white hot as it cut her ankle to mark her as one of Henry's aides, she flailed silently under Notté's grip and began to sob bitterly.

The captains marched out of the room.

Blythe

Notté looked down at her and released his grip. He rose and left her room and closed the door behind him.

Blythe listened as out in the hall the "Tap. Tap. Tap. Tap," grew fainter and fainter until it disappeared into the darkness.

She lay just as she had when they marked her, arms beside her, head crying toward the wall as she wept in the knowledge that soon she would be dead.

Chapter 49

It was midmorning when Augustus paraded out of his chamber. He was proud; he was upright; he was naked.

He walked without subterfuge carrying a hammer and chisel in one hand and a key he had hidden away in the other. He strode with purpose down the long hall, every eye watching him as he passed, acquaintances raising questions and exchanging comical looks. He slipped the key into the door on the outside of the hall and opened it, leaving the key within the lock. Outside in the courtyard, there was a din of shouting and orders being delivered in a high, excited pitch.

Augustus walked through the door and down the stairs. He marched down the hall and toward the monolithic crest. His eyes remained locked on the crest as he walked undistracted past the various rooms of temptation.

Augustus stood before Henry's seal and raised his chisel and hammer to the hollow stone that sat atop the arch. He placed the chisel's blade just below the hole and struck. The stone shook greatly from the force of his blow, but held. Again, he struck, but to no effect. Unflustered by the march of running feet behind him, he raised the chisel higher, above the hole, and struck again. But it was no use. The structure of the stone made it unconquerable. It absorbed the shock of every strike and held its place.

Undaunted, Augustus placed the chisel in the center of the hole and drove the spike through. He struck and struck again, but the stone held as his fellow captains finally reached him and dragged him down, the hammer still swinging in his hands.

Almost certainly to their great surprise, Augustus surrendered without a fight. He allowed himself to be taken down and beaten upon until they realized that he was already subdued.

They raised him to his feet and marched him back the length of the hall, up the stairs and out into the courtyard where an entire assembly of the camp awaited him. The crowd was kept divided by the captains who formed a passageway that led to the tower where Parissa was already chained by her feet.

Blythe stood amid the crowd and watched him as he passed, taller than the others, unapologetic in his posture and stride, while those who held him bound looked up to Augustus with the preoccupation of guilt showing on their faces.

As Parissa screamed at Notté, protesting her treatment, Augustus was marched next to her and similarly shackled by his ankles, his hands free.

He offered no resistance.

Notté stood before the semicircle of onlookers who comprised the entire kingdom and addressed them.

"Freedom is not free," he began. "When one accepts the privilege of leaving the kingdom, it is with expectation. There is an obligation to mark or to bring back another to join you. These two took advantage of that liberty, but did not fulfill their duty before their return."

Parissa listened to the words and shrieked at Notté, "I did! I did! I slept with Aaron. I pricked him with your ring! I followed your orders!" she screamed.

She turned her head to face straight up the tower wall and shouted up to Henry, "I did your will. I did as your orders demanded!"

All the while, Augustus stood unflinching, unapologetic, his head held high.

"Notté? Notté?" Parissa pleaded. "I did just as you had asked. Please don't do this, please. I slept with Aaron. You have to believe me."

"In a moment," Notté continued in his official voice, refusing to recognize her, "you will clear the courtyard and the Mournex will be released. Stay as still as you like," Notté challenged Parissa and Augustus. "The Mournex are trained to consume anything tied to this tower."

"No!" Parissa continued to protest. "You can't do this. You can't do this. I followed Henry's orders."

A gust of wind swept in from one end of the courtyard and the captives began to make their way out.

"I did it Notté," Parissa cried. "I did it."

Finally tired of her complaints, Notté turned to her and yelled in very distinct words that silenced her. "No you did not!"

Parissa sobbed and responded, "But I did. I did just as you had asked. I slept with him. I slept with Aaron."

Blythe, among those who remained in the front of the crowd, was among the few who heard Notté say, "You did not. You did not sleep with him."

"Then who?" Parissa asked befuddled. "Who?"

Augustus turned to her and winked.

The captives who had lingered in the courtyard made their way with haste back to the archway doors. Once closed behind the doors, they gathered at their openings to watch what would happen.

Blythe stood alone behind her opening and looked out as Parissa struck at Augustus. Despite her flurry of buffets, he stood unflinching. She beat at him as the Mournex, somewhat confused by her display, circled them, but approached no closer. Blythe watched as, exhausted at last, Parissa lowered her fists and stood with her head bent down, shaking as she wept. Spent, she swept her hair up and faced all of the Mournex who sat on their haunches looking at her. She stared at them then gave them a furious scream like Blythe had never heard another human being make. It was the final scream of an animal who knew this was its last exasperated act. With her head still thrust towards them, her face red with anger, her mouth agape, the tendons of her neck pulling her skin out into strings, the Mournex pounced on both her and Augustus. Parissa went down immediately, the beasts teaming all over her flailing body, each limb of which could be seen kicking or swinging for a few moments.

But Augustus, Augustus stood with his head remaining high, his arms at his side offering no defense as the Mournex scrambled over each other to get to him.

As they slowly dragged him lower, lower, lower to the ground, his head remained perfectly upright, his expression indifferent to their torture. His eyes stared into Blythe's as she watched in horror out her window, the stoic look on his face never changing as his head, at last, disappeared into the whirling waxy pile of Mournex spines that encircled him in their hungry fury.

Chapter 50

"So you kept quiet?" Aaron asked his father incredulously. "You kept quiet and knowingly sacrificed everyone else to save Maddox?"

Lucre looked across his counter and shook his head, Maddox at his side. He said, "I could tell no one. Yes, I was a father working to save his son, and I make no apology for that. But I was also the only one in this valley who had the wherewithal to find a way to end that place, Aaron. I hope you'll see that after everything I'm about to tell you.

"Father Philip?" Lucre asked the priest who stood beside Aaron, "Can't you explain this to him so he'll understand?"

Father Philip said, "What more needs to be said?"

Aaron asked his father, "But what would have been the harm in letting others know? They could have defended themselves against Henry. They could have changed their ways and protected themselves."

"Have they?" Lucre asked. "Have they changed their ways since they discovered his kingdom? Everything we set up to gain information so we could defeat the kingdom would be discovered once more people knew. And here we are. We could tell no one, including you, for risk of losing it all."

"But wait a minute," Aaron said. He turned to Maddox and asked, "If you were a part of that place and you were out here walking freely, then that means that you had to go back and forth in and out of the kingdom. You had to bring others in if you left? That's how it works, doesn't it?"

"Maddox never had to bring anyone in to come out," Lucre explained. "That's what I did with the money we made from all the sales. We bribed what captains we could and we bought information. For enough money, some captains would let him out and in without the usual demands; for all their vows of obedience and the promise of immortality, they wanted to see the place destroyed as much as any captive. They were all too happy to take our money and spend it on the outside when they took their jaunts. But it wasn't cheap. I spent everything I had for your brother's weekly freedom…everything I took in and nearly everything I had before then. This store is all I have left. Maddox was the only one I could trust to carry what information we'd learn from the inside and get it out. Nobody else trusted him; that's why I knew I could."

"Why couldn't you tell me?" Aaron pleaded.

"I could tell no one."

Maddox smiled back sarcastically.

"Aaron," Father Philip said. "Brow-beating serves no purpose here. It only delays us."

"That's okay, Father," Maddox said. "Aaron would rather be high and mighty than take care of business."

The priest held up his hands to stop the brewing battle. "Aaron," he said, "damn what they've done; it was murderous, even if that was not their intention. But as your father said, here we are; these two finally have something that might save those remaining captives, including Blythe; they have the information that will finally make Henry pay for what he's doing up there."

Aaron shouted, "And what do these two pay? Do they pay with their lives? Do they pay with their loves? They pay with their possessions; they pay nothing!"

"This isn't about revenge, Aaron," Father Philip said, trying to cool him. "Your father devised the only plan conceivable to defeat Henry. Was there a steep human cost? We all know there was. But we also must recognize that if his plan was compromised, there was no other plan with any hope of success. We either lost some with his plan, or we lost all."

"Then how about penance?" Aaron asked.

"Even Father Philip doesn't care about penance anymore," Maddox quipped.

"Are you a fool?" Father Philip asked Maddox, silencing him. "Aaron," he continued, "We can finally topple Henry's kingdom, but we need you; we need your help."

"So you'll do nothing?" Lucre interrupted. "You'll let Blythe die?"

"Don't you dare," Aaron warned his father in a steely tone.

"Lucre," the priest cautioned the big man.

But Old Lucre pressed on, challenging Aaron, "Is that what you're going to do? I doubt that."

"Lucre, silence!" Father Philip commanded. He asked Aaron calmly, "When was the last time you saw Blythe?"

"Why?" he replied.

"She was tagged last night, Aaron," Father Philip informed him grimly.

"What does that mean...tagged?" Aaron asked.

"She was marked as an aide of Henry now," Lucre said. "They cut her ankle like they did Stephen's when you found him. Henry is tapping her out faster than ever now until she has nothing left. She has a few days at the most."

"She's already coughing up blood," Maddox reported. "I saw it myself this morning. That's the last stage before Henry tosses her out. You either save her now, or never."

"You do it, Maddox," Aaron suggested. "You helped start all this. You save her."

"He can't," Lucre explained. "They know he's part of this now. If he goes back, they'll kill him. If they find him, they'll kill him. I'll hide him until this whole thing is done."

Aaron asked his brother, "Oh, you hiding until father has taken care of things? What a surprise."

He asked his father, "You have the information. Why don't you do it?"

Lucre admitted, "I don't have what it takes anymore, Aaron. I've lost the speed and stamina. I'm too thick for the job. You're the only one with the strength and our trust to do this and do it right." He looked at Aaron and said, "It's you or no one."

The room went still.

Aaron thought about Blythe and swallowed his anger. He broke the long silence. "What do you know and what do you need?"

Father Philip wasted no time. "Here's what we've been able to glean so far. We've long-known that there is a maze of passageways all around the kingdom leading in and out, but there is no safe and certain way in except for one."

Lucre continued, "The stream runs through the center of the kingdom and is fed by many little rivulets that spring up just above the castle. Some of them are large enough for a man of your size to swim through."

Aaron asked, "How do you know this?"

Philip said, "Lucre and I have been forcing these pouches down through into the springs until they get caught in the current," and as he spoke Lucre pulled one out from behind the counter and showed Aaron. The pouch was a little narrower than Aaron's shoulders and nearly perfectly round.

Aaron let it drop to the counter with its surprising weight. He shook it and it rattled. "What's in here?" Aaron asked.

"Rocks," Father Philip explained, "to make them sink under the water, but not so many of them that it wouldn't have a little buoyancy."

He continued, "We had to figure out which if any of the springs led to the castle's stream. Once we discovered the few that did, we timed each with Maddox's help on the inside to see how long it would take with a slow count to get in. He'd retrieve the balls, pop them, and send them on their way with the current."

"And how long does it take?" Aaron asked.

"Sixty," Philip said.

"Sixty?" Aaron flushed, thinking about all that time trapped underneath in the cramped darkness. "You're certain someone can get through...without getting caught up?"

"No, Aaron," Lucre said plainly. "To be honest, we are not. Some of the pouches were cut up badly on their way through and burst. Others came through fine in the same spring. We don't know what you'd be facing down there, but we haven't any other hope."

Father Philip said, "Once you're inside, the stream comes back above ground for a stretch before ducking back down below the castle wall again."

"How deep does it go?" Aaron asked.

"As tall as you," Maddox said. "Maybe taller. It narrows for a bit, but it doesn't get any shallower until it leaves."

Father Philip warned, "There's a grate there, Aaron, where it leaves, so you can't go through, but if you go that far, the captains of the kingdom are sure to find you and kill you. You have to find a way to surface before then."

"How do we know there's not a grate on the upstream side to trap me out, to trap me under the water?" Aaron asked.

Maddox answered, "The stream is too swift for someone to swim out against the current, so they haven't blocked it. That's why the balls can pass through." He smiled at his brother, "Henry must be confident no one is stupid enough to swim in."

"Is there anything inside the kingdom that sinks?" Aaron asked Maddox.

Maddox looked at him confused. "Sinks?" Maddox repeated. "What do you mean?"

Aaron clarified himself. "What can you pick up and drop in the water in the kingdom that would sink quickly to the bottom?"

"Bones?" Maddox answered unsure of himself.

"Do bones float?" Aaron asked looking around at the men. None of them knew for certain.

"Why?" Father Philip asked.

"If someone inside can drop in a sack of something that is sure to sink to the bottom quickly, I can keep my hand out for it as a marker," Aaron said. "When I reach that spot, I'll surface. I've done it before in the canal. But never after being under water for that long."

Blythe

"What's your best count?" Lucre asked.

"Thirty-five. Forty at best," he said.

"Can you stretch it?" Philip asked.

"What choice do we have?" he answered. "What do I do once I'm in?"

His father said, "You slip out of the water on the left bank as you go downstream. You'll be in the central courtyard. There is a tower in the center on that side of the stream. Go through the archway facing the tower opposite the stream. There are many archways…."

"Twenty-four," Maddox said specifically.

"Twenty-four," Lucre repeated, "But the one you want is on the left bank—the tower side of the bank—opposite the tower. Inside the arch is a tunnel that goes straight ahead. Don't go in there."

"That's where the Mournex are," Maddox said.

"Mournex?" Aaron asked with trepidation.

"We'll get to them later," Lucre insisted. "Inside the archway is a tunnel straight ahead and stairs to either side. Take the stairs to your left."

"Left bank, left stairs," Aaron repeated out loud for himself.

"Exactly," his father continued. "Circle down the stairs and turn left down a long hall. Count ten doors on your right. That is the door you'll need to go through. Maddox has a key for you."

Maddox handed him the key and began to say, "On the left side, three doors down that hall is…."

"Not now!" his father chastised Maddox. "He's got enough to remember. Let's keep him focused on only what he needs to know."

Lucre turned back to Aaron and continued, "Left down the stairs, left down the hall, ten doors down on your right is your door. Use that key to open it and you'll find another set of stairs. Go down them…."

"Which way?" Aaron asked.

"They only lead one way…down," Lucre continued. "Take the stairs down and they'll spill out to a hall. Go straight out the stairs down the hall and whatever you do, keep your eyes forward. Don't look left or right into any room until you come to the end of the hall. It will spiral around and take you in only one direction."

"Got it," Aaron assured him.

Maddox advised, "Aaron, there are rooms along that last hall that will be difficult for you to keep yourself from. They'll be filled with the most beautiful men and women you've ever seen. But they are traps, Aaron. If you look at them, you're lost. You'll lose whatever will and drive you have; whatever true love you have for Blythe will be diminished or lost entirely. They'll draw you in. Once you join them, the walls will close in on you. You'll be absorbed into the kingdom. In that hall, you must keep your eyes straight. Don't look to the side. Do you understand?"

Aaron nodded.

Lucre continued, "Here is where it gets into a gray area for us. We're certain of everything else up to this point. That hall dead-ends in a wall. The wall is embossed with Henry's seal. It has Henry's mark...."

"The cross along with his initial and the Roman numeral four," Father Philip interjected.

"All that is on his shield," Lucre said. "His crest is contained in an arch set within the wall. We're sure the arch is right under Henry's tower. That wall is also holding back the stream, so if you're able to knock the wall down, the tower will fall...."

"And the ceiling?" Aaron asked.

"Yes," his father said grimly. "I suppose so but we don't know for certain. The hall will start to fill instantly with water if that wall is compromised. You'll need to get out of there as fast as you can. But the wall is the key and the key to that wall is the arch...."

"And the key to the arch is the keystone, Aaron," Father Philip said. "The very top stone of the arch. If that stone is split, the arch will fall in on itself. If that happens the wall collapses. When the wall goes, Henry's tower falls and we hope so do all the walls in the kingdom that rely on that arch."

"How many walls is that?" Aaron asked.

"Every last one of them," Lucre said confidently. "The entire structure is keeping perfect pressure on that arch from all sides. So long as it holds, they hold."

"So what's the gray area?" Aaron asked.

"So far the keystone has been indestructible," Lucre said. "Men have taken chisel and hammer to it, but it won't give. It absorbs each blow."

Father Philip explained, "It has a hole in the center of it." He made a circle of his index finger and thumb to demonstrate. "We're not exactly sure of its size, but we know it is about this large. We've concluded that something about that structure—that hole—helps it to absorb the shock of the strike—to withstand each blow."

"So what do you plan to do?" Aaron asked.

Father Philip pulled out a sack tied with a string. He loosened the string and turned the sack over in his hand and allowed a perfectly round cone of stone to fall out into his palm. He showed it to Aaron.

Aaron said, "Plug the hole with this cone, and hammer away."

"That's the idea," Lucre said. "No matter how far you have to put it in, at some point it will have to fit. Once that hole is plugged, we think the keystone will lose its pliability…its resistance and will be as hard and rigid and vulnerable as any other."

Father Philip placed the stone into the sack and handed it to Aaron. Lucre pulled out a hammer and chisel from beneath the counter, placed them in another larger sac, tied up the ends and gave it to his son.

"No chance of me floating to the surface with all this on me," Aaron laughed. He was the only one to do so.

He asked Maddox, "How am I going to fit in inside? Will I be noticed?"

"Like a black fly on a white wall," Maddox said. "But someone was looking out for you."

Aaron looked at him confused.

"Aaron, where were you last night?" his father asked.

"I couldn't sleep," he said. "I hiked up to the ridge to look down on the village and think."

The three men looked at each other, then at Aaron. Aaron waited for them to share what was on their minds.

Old Lucre pulled out one more sack from behind his counter. It was tied up neatly with a leather strap of a belt serving as a ribbon. Lucre handed the package to Aaron who opened it.

"These are clothes identical to those worn by the one who took

Blythe in," Lucre said. "They are the clothes of a different captain of the kingdom, Aaron, left especially for you for this effort."

"They were Augustus's," Maddox said bluntly.

Aaron's head snapped up at him in surprise as Maddox continued. "Last night, Notté—the one who captured Blythe—ordered Parissa and Augustus to capture you one way or another. Augustus went to your home before Parissa could get there. He pretended to be you in bed and she slept with him. After she left to go back to the kingdom, he came by here and told Lucre everything he learned about the kingdom's structure. He dropped off his clothes for you to wear as a disguise so you could enter the kingdom undetected if his plan to strike and break the arch failed. It did. Parissa and he were executed for the crime of returning to the kingdom without bringing anyone back. Parissa thought she had drawn you in, and she would have one way or another, but Augustus made sure she didn't. Parissa had no idea until the last minute that Augustus had tricked her. She was screaming that she had captured you."

Lucre added, "There was no way of talking him out of going back, Aaron. I went through a dozen different options for him, but he insisted it was the only plan that would make sure you stayed free."

"He gave his life for you, Aaron," Maddox said.

Aaron stared down at the clothes and thought about Augustus's sacrifice. He placed the pants and belt on the counter and began to slip on the shirt when his father advised him, "You don't want to swim through the stream in that, Aaron, and come out wet. It'll be a dead giveaway that you don't belong in there. The sack I'll put them in should keep those dry until you surface. Let's tie them up until you need them."

Aaron stared at the bundle and asked, "You mentioned the Mournex. What's a Mournex?"

Maddox explained, "Those are Henry's henchmen. He pumps them out of the tunnels around the kingdom and into his courtyard to overwhelm and eat anyone who is trapped in there. Somehow that adds to Henry's strength and the life force of his kingdom. The trick with the Mournex, Aaron, is if you face one, stand perfectly still. They only attack those who move."

"What do they look like?" Aaron asked.

Maddox told him, "They're about your size but bigger legs and stronger arms. They have thick horse-like hair all over, but not so much you can't see their shiny leathery skin underneath. The things to worry about with them are their claws and their teeth. They've got plenty of both. If you play dead, though, they'll go right past you."

"Suddenly the idea of being trapped underground in the spring doesn't scare me as much as it had," Aaron confessed.

He and Father Philip made their way back to the church to sort out the final details. Once the store door closed behind them, Old Lucre wrapped his arm around Maddox and walked him over to the basement stairs where he led his son down. Along the back wall was a cedar door behind which was a large storage closet, empty except for some of Maddox's mother's old clothes that Old Lucre could never quite bring himself to give away or to sell. He opened the door. Maddox stepped forward to enter, but Old Lucre stopped him before he could. He pulled his son toward him and gave him a long embrace before finally patting him on the back and letting him walk in to hunker down in the corner. Maddox pulled the musty clothes about him for cover then gave a warm smile and confident wave up to his father before Old Lucre shut the closet door and returned upstairs for the night.

Chapter 51

"Such a cold morning," Aaron complained as he took off his shirt. He looked down into the churning darkness of the gurgling wide spring mouth. Galaxies of eddies swirled, catching the light of the setting moon. They spun around the surface then dissolved, another one taking their place.

"Tie this belt to your waist, Aaron," Lucre said, doing the chore for him. "We'll tie the sack of stones and the others to it. Your hands should be kept free and in front of you. Guard your face as you swim."

Aaron raised his elbows to give his father room. "Sixty?" Aaron asked them again.

"A full sixty," Father Philip confirmed. "Don't fight the current. Let it take you where it will just like the pouches we sent down. If this spring took them to the kingdom's stream, it will do the same for you."

Lucre looked into the water. "I feel like we're spitting into the darkness. I wish we could feel more confident about hitting our target."

Father Philip said, "Maddox got word to them inside, Aaron. They slipped a big bag of bones into the stream right after it surfaces inside the kingdom's walls. They said it clung tough to the bed and didn't move. Don't forget to reach for that marker, Aaron."

Another cold chill shot through Aaron as he nodded.

"You go in hands-first and once you're under, we'll push your feet from there," Lucre said. "It's nothing but under until you reach the castle floor, so hold your breath as long as you can."

"Don't forget," Father Philip advised, "God gives you everything you need."

"I only have to look around for it to find it," Aaron answered.

Aaron looked down to the castle walls and measured the distance to the kingdom in his mind.

"If you want to come right back up once you're in, shake your feet as a signal to us," the priest said. "But if you keep them still and hold them firm, we'll push for all we're worth."

Aaron stepped to the spring's edge and knelt on his bare knees in the cold mushy grass. He thought about the cool mud beside the canal the last time he surprised Blythe with this kind of trick. It would be an even more amazing feat this time if he could pull it off. He hoped to God he could.

Aaron took some quick, deep breaths to prepare himself for the plunge. Careful to keep his balance, he slowly raised his hands to a point above his head and announced, "Ready."

"Good luck, son," Lucre said.

"Godspeed," Father Philip said, "however fast that is."

As a final check off, Aaron recited, "Clothes, chisel, hammer, cone, left bank, door straight away, left stairs, left down hall, tenth door on the right, not third door on the left," he added for comedic release still not knowing what his brother had referred to, "down the stairs, straight out the hall, wall at end, don't look in rooms, cone in keystone hole, hammer, run like hell."

"Run like hell indeed," Father Philip confirmed.

"Ready, Aaron?" Lucre asked.

"Ready," Aaron confirmed.

"I love you, son, and I have always been proud to be your father," Lucre choked out.

A few more intense breaths in and out and one last long one that Aaron held, and he was under.

He plunged hands-first down into the cold darkness. He kept his feet and ankles intensely stiff as Lucre and Father Philip watched his white arms fish around for the feel of a path in the dark maze. The two men grabbed his feet, lifted him slightly, and then thrust him as hard as they could onto his course.

"Go, go, go," Lucre said quickly. "Go, go, go, go, go, go, go."

"Get there, Aaron," Father Philip urged him. "Get there."

Below in the black labyrinth, Aaron did his best to keep his hands in front of his face at all times, reaching ahead when he could. The swift current pushed him along. Sudden changes in the current's direction tossed him into sharp points on one side and then the other. They grated his back along the ceiling only to rise without warning and leave his belly pinned against the coarse little mountains of rocks along the floor. It was a constant centering effort for him as he pulled himself deeper and deeper through the watery vein. His elbows and forearms took the worst of the punishment with abrupt crashes into outcroppings he could neither anticipate nor fully grasp as he passed swiftly by. Deeper, deeper into the stream he went, feeling the pressure build in his ears and the burning just begin in his lungs as he wriggled his way along.

Only after going numb to the frigid temperature of the water did he collect his wits enough to start a count.

"One. Two. Three…."

A hard slope turned down and to the left. His entire right side crashed and stuck to the jagged points of stones that formed the walls all around him. To move at all, he had to lift and move his feet and legs off of the daggerlettes then slowly work that progress forward to his waist then to his chest then to his shoulders. In progress measured by mere hand lengths he inched along.

"Ten. Eleven. Twelve."

The current pulled him along again at last.

"Eighteen. Nineteen. Twenty…."

Blindness. Blindness from the eyes shut by his grimacing face. Blindness from any knowledge of where he lay, of how far he had fallen away from the world's light.

Blythe

"Thirty-six. Thirty-seven. Thirty-eight...."

Tiny effervescent bubbles shot by. They teased his lungs with air too small to breathe. The damp, dank smell of the aquifer crawled up and into his sinuses. It clung there heavily, making his nose run to evict the stench.

"Forty-five."

All air shot out of Aaron's lungs for an instant of ecstasy in release. But even before the last breath left him, his body craved the next one. His lips begged to open, trying to convince him to suck up the little bubbles he could hear pass. His lungs flexed to breathe in, pulling his chest down in sharp flexes. But Aaron refused to crack. He pulled himself along, guarding his face from the next invisible hazard, the next unseen turn.

With great force his entire body lurched to a stop. His hands flung far out into the open blackness before him, his head snapped down as an excruciating pain burnt up from his right ankle and into his leg. He felt the water rush by him more forcefully now that he was no longer being carried along with it. He was caught in a dead stop.

He lost all concern for more air and thought only about the mass of stones that surrounded him on all sides. He thought about how far he was from anyone or anything that could help him.

He had only one option open to him and before he even had given it a conscious thought, he tightened the back of his right thigh with strength that amazed even him and he began pulling himself back up against the irresistible current to the lodged foot. He stretched out and reached back and grasped one side of the crag that held him in place and let everything but that arm go limp. With all the power he could muster, his arm pulled his entire body back, back up the stream against the force and quickly pulled his foot to freedom. Aaron straightened out again, oblivious to any bodily concern, serene in the sense of what he had just accomplished. For a moment, he forgot about the pain in his lungs.

More tributaries cut into the channel or fell away from it. The chamber moved left and right, up and down with more cuts in each twist.

"What number?" he thought, trying to remember where he had left off. He guessed at how long it might have been since he stopped.

"Thirty? Forty? Had I made fifty?" he asked as the base of his throat began to pull fiercely and demand some passage of air.

Aaron snorted what air remained out of his nose to trick his body that it had missed a breath, which he had given it, but it was too slow, too preoccupied and had missed his gift. The trick worked for another few counts.

"Fifty-nine. Sixty. The bag."

The marker was in his hands.

Sensing the greater space around him as the hiss of the bubbles died away, he allowed his knees to tuck in underneath him as he held his spot above the bag and reached out for the left wall. It was beyond his reach, but he imagined it could not be too far. He vectored his way up to the imagined spot where the water met the courtyard's edge and his hand swept gently over the stones for a firm grip. He pulled himself up, kept low and took in a deep open-mouthed gasp of breath before he forced himself under again, lest he draw attention to himself.

The breath satisfied his body's aching need for the moment. He slowly blew it out with complete pleasure underneath the water's surface where it would make no sound. Aaron broke through again next to the water's edge and repeated that breathing-style another few times to let his lungs restore themselves.

He rose through the water one last time and held himself at the edge. His knees and feet bumped against the cold stones that formed the canal's walls. Aaron's mind leapt ahead for a moment and stood him on the other side of that very wall. He looked downstream to the tower. It was a good thirty paces, he thought, as he allowed his lungs to catch up to the rest of him.

He looked all around. Except for two men at the end of the stream looking out a window down to the valley, no one else was in sight.

He silently lifted his chest out and onto the courtyard floor, then swept his legs around. Without rising, he felt down for the sack of clothes and, with a quick tug, snapped it from his belt.

Still prone, he brought the bag up below his armpit and opened it, drawing out the shirt, pants and shoes. He wrestled to put them on while

Blythe

still on the ground.

Once dressed, Aaron tip-toed in an angle halfway between the tower and the wall, then changed his direction to walk directly through the arch before him. Conscious for the first time of how he might look to others in the kingdom, he slowed himself down, he forced himself to walk upright in a nonchalant air, relaxing what had been his suspicious hunch. He walked with unfounded and unfelt confidence to the opening. The shadow he so desired to walk into drew closer, closer, closer.

At last it was his.

Under the kingdom's walls, he descended the stairs and turned left down the hall. To humor his father, he nodded at the third door on his left and continued on. Until he heard her cough.

Aaron stopped in the center of the hall, returning again to a frozen pose of suspicion: elbows up, palm facing the ground, feet poised on their toes, his shoulders hunched.

He turned his head to face the door as he listened intently. That was what Maddox wanted to tell him, but his father dared not let him find out. She was there. She was behind the door.

Blythe coughed again.

Aaron vaulted to the wall and walked along it. He looked up and down the hall. He was alone. Blythe coughed again just beyond the corner of the next wooden door. He lowered his hand to the handle and lifted it up with surety. He ducked inside.

It took a moment for his eyes to adjust to the room's darkness after the relatively well-lit hall. He stood still. The door closed. Turning from side to side, his awareness of the space around him slowly grew from the barred opening outwards, to a wall, another wall, the ceiling, a third wall, the hint of something there in the remaining shadow, and then a cough arose from that blackness.

Aaron crouched to the bedside and knelt.

"Blythe?" he asked, his hands racing across the covers to feel for her. "Blythe are you there?" he asked.

A hoarse and weak but familiar voice answered him, "Aaron. Oh, Aaron you came for me. You came for me, Aaron," but then it sank back into the dark.

"Blythe, I'm here," Aaron said finding her hand and gripping it tightly.

A fearful coughing spell overtook her. She hacked, desperate to draw in another breath, but she could not as the coughs continued on and on. Aaron's eyes could at last make out her outline against the wall. After traveling through the stream, he knew how angry her lungs felt, looking for that next breath. He found himself drawing in shallow pants of air in his upper lungs to breathe for her, to will her next breath when the coughing would finally stop. But it would not relent.

She turned her head into the pillow, gasping for breath between each hack of the long jag. At last it released her.

Wearied from the experience, she breathed in and out unsteadily, as if breathing itself was new to her. She rolled away from the wall and back to where she had rested looking up at the ceiling.

Aaron's voice called out to her in the feverish darkness, "Blythe, are you better now? Is that better?"

Distracted by her fever's dream, she turned her head to him and looked up and smiled. He could see the faint glints of light on her teeth. She reached out her hand and let him hold it up to his cool lips. "I love you," she said in a voice that said she thought he should be no other place than there beside her.

"How I love you," he said to her and continued kissing the hand as he held it tightly, reacquainting himself with her familiar touch.

"I have something for you," he whispered.

"What?" she asked with the excitement of a feverish little girl who had just been woken up.

He reached his hand into his pocket and pulled out the ring. Pinching it in his fingertips, he placed it on her left ring finger, then kissed it and her hand. "How I love you, Blythe," he told her again, his eyes closed, savoring the sensation.

"How I love you," she responded sweetly, lifting her hand and running it through his hair as she had always done.

Spent by her dream, she pulled her hand away to return to sleep.

Blythe

She gently rested it with the other across her chest and drifted off. He stood, bent over and kissed her brow, then slipped out the door as quietly as he could.

Aaron blinked up and down the hall. Again, to his great relief, it was empty. He counted the doors from the beginning, "One, two, three." Even with Blythe's room. He made his way out and continued counting on his way.

At seven, he heard a door behind him open and the sound of feet shuffling out into the hall. He reverted to his suspicious pose and turned painfully to look.

It was Blythe.

She stood, squinting eyes, hand guarding her somewhat-open eye from the light, blinking to look at him. The other arm hung loose from the shoulder. She was the very countenance of a little girl roused from a sickly slumber.

"Go back to bed," he commanded her in a hushed order.

She stood there and blinked, her posture unchanged.

He ordered her again in a desperate whisper, "Go back to bed, Blythe" adding a wave to try to break through.

"You're here," she whispered back to him.

Still frozen in his spot, he said, "I am, and I'll be back for you, but you have to go to bed. Now go."

Oblivious to his commands, she said as she jerked towards him with unsure steps and nothing but happy recognition in her raspy voice, "You're really here. I thought it was just a dream until I reached out and felt the ring you gave me. I thought that was a dream, too. But you're really here. I didn't have that ring before. That's how I knew this wasn't a dream. You're here, Aaron," she said finally reaching him and raising her arms to be hugged. "You're really here."

Aaron wrapped his arms around her giving her a long, rocking kiss on her forehead. He released her and ordered again, "Blythe, I have to do something right now. I can't take you along. Please, go back to bed and I'll come back to get you. You have to go back to bed."

"No," she persisted. "I went away from you once and I'll never do it again, Aaron. I'm not leaving you again Aaron…ever."

The tone of her voice told Aaron that if he argued any more, this little girl would create a teary scene that would wake up the entire hall.

"Then, shhh," he insisted and he took her hand. She flopsed along after him as he looked back to restart his count of the doors until he reached the tenth.

His hand dove into his shirt and he pulled out the little sack that contained the key. He pulled it out and slipped it in the lock. He gently guided Blythe through and then followed.

She turned to him, roused again out of her dreaminess and put her hands up on either side of his face then drew close to him. She nestled in, rubbing his cheek against hers as she continued to say, "You're really here, Aaron. You're really here."

Conscious of the dangers they could face at any moment, he confirmed, "Yes, I am," as he turned her around and led her down the stairs that then opened to another warren of rooms and passages that stretched out further below the kingdom.

At the bottom of the stairs, the question that might have otherwise reached Blythe in her cell finally came to her. "But how can you be here, Aaron? How can you be here?"

"I just am," he insisted, leading her by the hand down the hall.

Blythe stopped him and demanded to know, "But how? How are you here?"

The realization caught her fully and she gasped, "You haven't! You haven't," she implored him. "Tell me you haven't let yourself be taken in, Aaron. No, Aaron! No!"

Her voice became louder as she pulled away from him in sleepy rage swinging her tired fists to hit him, "You haven't. You can't be here. You can't! Not you. You can't be here, Aaron."

"I'll explain later," Aaron begged as he grabbed unsuccessfully at her. "Please just come with me now and I'll explain later."

"No," she insisted. "You'll tell me now. Or you're not here."

Aaron finally secured her wrist and dragged her behind him as they walked. She fought him with increasing strength as something within

Blythe

him seemed to drain. Suddenly dizzy, he asked her as he let go, "Please, Blythe. Don't. We don't have time for this."

He bent over and rested his hands on his knees.

"The swim in," he thought. "It's finally catching up to me." Everything about him became bone weary. The walls, as well as the blood in his ears, began to pulse, stronger and stronger.

He looked up to grab Blythe and continued on his way, but saw that the sound wasn't in his ears alone. She looked fearfully up at the walls and ceiling. The entire structure around them was pumping with sound, louder and louder.

Aaron looked off through one of the doors. Maddox's warning came back to him. There were three of the most beautiful women he had ever seen, posing for him, calling him in. A tall blonde stood with her flawless back towards him, feet slightly apart and her head turned back to look at him with an alluring open mouth that grew into an open smile. A brown-haired beauty knelt beside her, knees spread wide, her back bowed backwards, resting on her hands as her hips rose to meet his gaze. To the other side lay an exquisitely dark woman who rested on her side, one hand fondling her breast while the other stretched out to play with the blonde's ankle.

"Aaron?" Blythe called to him, unsure if she would have the physical strength to draw him away.

Sure of his purpose, however, he turned with a half-laugh to Blythe. "There is nothing for me here."

They again made their way down the hall when a gust of wind swept down the stairs and raced along the hall toward them.

"The Mournex!" Blythe yelled.

Aaron grabbed her hand and sprinted to the end of the hall. The percussion of the Mournex stampede above them made the ceiling shake as the sound of their screeching nails against the stones and their terrible howls could be heard throughout the castle.

"They're coming, Aaron!" Blythe screamed at him. "They're coming for us!"

Aaron and Blythe ran the remaining length of the hall and stood before the monolith while Aaron reached into his shirt and pulled out the hammer and chisel. He handed them to Blythe as his hands thrust back in looking for the sack with the cone.

The wind grew stronger as did the sounds of the animals. Unlike earlier purges, Blythe knew this one had one target—two, to be precise. It was Henry's swiftest and most massive outpouring as hundreds of beasts poured out of the tunnels and in through the open archways.

"They're coming, Aaron. We should get out of here," she insisted, finally looking around to where he had led her. "Aaron, we must get out of here."

"Where is it?" he shouted looking down at his waist. He tore off his shirt to see his belt more clearly.

Aaron saw the frayed tassel of a leather band where the pouch once hung.

"Damn it!" he shouted.

"What is it?" Blythe asked, finally drawn away from looking down the hall.

"I need to fill that hole," he shouted nodding up to the hollow keystone. He reached for chest pockets that didn't exist. "I had a stone for it, but I lost it. I must have lost it swimming in." He felt every inch of himself hoping beyond hope for a miracle, for something to replace what he had lost.

The first Mournex fell down the stairs with a shriek of surprise that echoed down to Blythe and Aaron, with many more right behind.

"They're here!" Blythe screamed.

"God gives you everything you need," he chanted low to himself. "God gives you everything you need," he said over and over again.

Blythe looked down at her hands and pulled off the two remaining rings from her shaking hands, first the ring Aaron had just given her, and then her last remaining ring, one that circled her thumb. It, too, was a smooth band. It was the first band he had ever given her.

Aaron and Blythe looked away from the sound of the marauding band of Mournex to the rings she placed in his hand.

He closed up his hand and bunched the rings together, one on top of the other. He snatched them between his fingers and one snapped inside the other so they formed one perfect circle within another.

With the Mournex halfway down the hall and closing fast, Aaron raised the rings as Blythe raised the hammer and chisel. He popped the rings into the gap—a snug fit. Aaron reached down to Blythe's waiting hands and took the instruments from her. The Mournex were approaching, nearly within lunging distance.

He drew back the hammer as the chisel fell into place in the small cross just below the ringed hole.

The lead Mournex compressed itself for its leap just as the hammer flew forward and struck the chisel, cracking the stone in two. A tremendous tremor rippled throughout the entire structure and something within the Mournex, too, seemed to break. At the moment the hammer hit the chisel and the chisel dug surely into the stone, the Mournex were tossed to the ground as so many flailing masses of tortured beasts, convulsing and writhing around one on top of the other, their jaws opening then clenching shut, their heads shaking wildly. Blythe heard the clack of their teeth as they struck smartly together. Their muscles shuddered with wave after wave of convulsion.

But neither Blythe nor Aaron concerned themselves with the Mournex's demise; their eyes remained fixed on the two rings as they tumbled out of the split keystone. Once the chisel struck its mark and the stone split, the rings sprang out and separated and tumbled through the air.

The wall shook and began to crumble as the rings tumbled and descended. What the wall did at that moment was beyond their concern they were so transfixed by the rings. Blythe and Aaron each reached out and grasped one band and then the other before they fell to the floor. The first gush of water spouted from the breach as Aaron and Blythe looked down at their possessions. They extended their hands, one to the other, and there placed and accepted signs of their love for each other. The water poured in more forcefully as they finally turned hand in hand to make their escape.

Aaron and Blythe sprinted down the length of the hall, hurdling over the still-twitching, groaning remains of the failing Mournex. The torrent grew behind them and seemed intent on washing away the entire kingdom with everyone in it.

The Mournex, in the final throes of their abject agony, clogged the stairs, forcing Aaron and Blythe to clamber over them. The fallen bodies proved firm and spongy beneath their feet. Halfway up the stairs, Blythe's foot slipped, and Aaron could not restrain her fall. She found herself astride one of the beasts, looking into the fearsome gape of its mouth, its tongue still moving, still sensing something before it, and its mouth gave a little clap, closing just shy of her nose. She screamed from the bottom of her lungs and lunged for Aaron's extended arm to help her up. Stepping anywhere on the Mournex they could find a foothold, Blythe and Aaron scrambled up the remaining stairs and out into the hall.

Captives teamed down the hall and up the stairs into the courtyard, wailing and shouting in confusion and fear, presuming this was their moment of death, not their moment of liberation. Dead Mournex littered the floor and were trampled into bloody mats.

Aaron and Blythe held firm to each other's hand as they made their way to the stairs just below the courtyard. They reached the base when Blythe tore herself free from him and stood fast. Aaron looked at her in disbelief.

"We have to go, Blythe," he yelled above the noise. "We have to get out of here."

Restrained by some thought, she said distantly, "No. No, Aaron. I have to go back. There is something I have to get."

"No!" he yelled to her as loud as he could but the sound was absorbed by the rest of the cries in the hall.

She tenaciously fought her way through the current of people, past one door and then another, finally reaching her own. She clenched one hand to her doorway and pulled herself in. Aaron watched her disappear. He clung hard to the wall so he would not be swept away by those rushing by.

In no time she emerged with a white scroll in her hand, which she held aloft, and allowed herself to be swept along with the human stream.

Blythe

Without warning, the ceiling to the hall dropped down as far as the top of the doors and those that were not opened shattered into splinters, impaling anyone unfortunate enough to be caught in front of them at that moment.

Up the stairs, Aaron and Blythe flew and out the archway.

The tunnels that once had been the pathways each captive had entered through collapsed, releasing great billows of dust that clogged the courtyard air. A dirty coating covered everyone, ghostlike, filling their mouths with the taste of raw earth.

The kingdom, from its floors to its walls, seemed bent on shaking itself into oblivion. The world became a blur of motion, a shaking whirl of action. Unsure of where was safe, Blythe and Aaron stood clutching each other just outside the archway as people tore about in all directions seeking refuge. They watched untrusting of their own eyes as great strips of the courtyard that once served as a ceiling to the structure below, gave way, taking many captives down as the trusted earth evaporated beneath their feet.

"Blythe!" a voice called out. "Blythe, help me!"

It was Notté. He called up from between two bars in a gap at ground level.

"Please," he begged. "I'm trapped. Please, Blythe, please help me. Forgive me!"

"Let him die," Mab shouted.

"We can't," Blythe insisted. "Not even him."

She took Aaron's hand and ran over toward the wall. "Save him for me if you can, Aaron, but stay on guard."

"Never!" Aaron protested. "We have to get out of here, and we have to do it now."

He turned to her and placed his hands on her shoulders to spin her away from Notté's half-submerged cell. Despite her emaciated frame, she was strong and resolute. She would not be moved.

She swung her hands up and freed herself from Aaron's grip.

Ignoring the madness around her, she sat down in the dust.

"Either we forgive," she said, "or we die."

Blythe refused to look up at Aaron. Her jaw set itself stiffly, the muscles taut.

He recognized he had no choice.

"Get away from the opening," Aaron instructed Notté. The curtains fell. Notté disappeared behind them.

Aaron kicked with all his strength against the bars, tearing one after another from their anchors. At last there was room enough for Notté to pass. Aaron one last time instructed Notté to stand clear. With both feet, he knocked the frame free from the wall, and it fell with a rattling crash to the floor.

Aaron stood up then hunched over and extended his hand. "Come on!"

Notté seized it and pulled with all his might not to raise himself to Aaron's level, but, rather, to drag Aaron down into the cell.

Aaron was ready for the betrayal. He planted his foot above the opening as he lunged forward and held himself fast. With one swift tug, he freed himself from Notté's grip and leapt back into the courtyard and out of reach.

No sooner had he done this than a great gust of wind pushed forth from every opening of the kingdom's cells as the structure above the rooms collapsed an entire story, and then another, and another. Notté and his cell and all the other cells around the courtyard disappeared in descending debris and dust.

The compromised outer walls of Henry's kingdom undulated wildly in curious, sick waves performing a lewd and frantic dance. Quick flashes of light within the walls' now-translucent structure glowed with arcs of dazzling brightness in veins of lightning that pulsed across the surface and deep below. An explosion of sparks shot out here and there and fell like showers of tiny stars into the courtyard. Some fell on Blythe and Aaron, stinging their skin with pinpricks of pain. A massive and tangible current of energy coursed through the walls, so strong it made the hair of all those who stood nearby stand on end.

Aaron, Blythe, Mab, and Maria clung together in a tight circle as cries called out from all around them. Screams for mercy and for help

Blythe

shrieked across the courtyard while the kingdom's walls continued their grinding collapse with sickening groans.

More captives joined the clutch as they held together and prayed with everything within them, knowing with certainty that the next moments were their last. They held to each other with all their might, their heads bowed, the ground shaking beneath them until as last the world around them seemed to explode.

And then there was nothing.

Not a sound. Around them was something more than a sense of total stillness. There was a vastness, a feeling of light and space spreading out around them in all directions such as they had never felt inside the kingdom before.

One by one, awed faces rose to look out at the brown scorched field that surrounded their once-prison and the green grass beyond that and the trees and valley beyond that and then the sky.

The kingdom of Henry the Fourth had vanished.

Each man and woman—they were indeed men and women again and no longer merely captives—rose up and walked in a daze to the streams of villagers who approached.

One by one they walked away, back to their old homes and the world they had known but never allowed themselves to dream they would ever see again until it was too late.

Blythe and Aaron took it in, unable or unwilling to move.

It was too much to understand. It was too much to appreciate.

Jostled by a passerby, Blythe at last returned to animation. She blinked and looked around, looking finally down to her hand, which held Aaron's in her own. There was a look of wonder on Blythe's face as she looked down into the valley; overwhelmend by a feeling of awe and appreciation that she had never known.

Aaron released her hand, and gently sweeping up her frail frame into his arms, they made their way back into the valley and into freedom.

Chapter 52

Lucre stood before the closet door and knocked again. He called out once more to his son, "Maddox, it's safe now. You can come out. Maddox?"

Lucre's hand was unwilling to pull the knob to open the door for fear of what he might find.

He knocked once more and called out sweetly, "Maddox? Are you still in there, Maddox? It is safe to come out."

He felt he no longer had a choice. Lucre pulled open the door. He showed no sign of emotion as he saw that there, in the back wall of the cedar room, beyond the pile of old clothes that held his son, a hole had been punched through from the outside leaving shards of wood and splinters around its edge.

Lucre slowly entered, his eyes fixed to the hole as he knelt beside the heap.

Piece by piece he removed each article, his eyes remaining on the opening as he waited for some sense of movement, for some sign of life to rise from where his son had hidden himself away.

At last, the veil was raised, and there laid the withered remains of Maddox, a grotesque reminder of what the boy had once been. In that final wild frenzy before the collapse of the kingdom, Henry's men had found him and exacted their punishment. His cheeks were hollow, his mouth agape and on his face was not the slack release of death but the grimace that held the pain of his last moments of life.

Lucre moved from his knees to take a seat resting up against the wide wall and, as he did, he gathered his son up in his arms and wept over him.

* * *

Aaron ever so gently rested Blythe onto her bed.

In her room.

In her home.

In her valley.

He walked to the footboard and retrieved a small blanket, which he unfolded and draped over her wasted frame.

Blythe barely blinked as she looked up, stunned by the world around her.

"Aaron?" Sergio called from downstairs.

Aaron quickly tiptoed to the landing and whispered down, "Not now, Sergio. She's just in bed."

Sergio and Sylvia walked hand-in-hand to the base of the stairs and looked up at him.

"We just heard," Sylvia whispered. "We wanted to congratulate you both."

"I'll pass it along," Aaron said and waved goodbye.

Quietly he returned to Blythe's bedside and looked down on her. The blanket had only made it as far as her waist so he stooped to finish the task. As he bent over, he noticed that still gripped in her hands was the scroll she had gone back to retrieve. He gently dropped the blanket and pulled the paper out from her fist and laid it beside her bed atop a chest of drawers.

"Let me hold you, Aaron," she whispered. "Let me hold you again."

As Aaron kicked off his shoes, she slid toward the wall to make room. Aaron laid down beside her on the bed and pulled up the covers on them both. Blythe nestled in on top of his arm and rested her head on his chest.

Blythe stroked Aaron's hair and looked around the room that she never thought she would see again. All her paintings were gone and the walls held a fresh coat of paint that smoothed out all the imperfections and marks that had once scarred them. It was a clean and wholesome place for her to begin her life anew, free from the burdens and distractions she once felt. She took in a deep, satisfying breath.

At last, Blythe's eyes came to the thin, white scroll, one end of which pointed toward her.

She reached gently across Aaron so as not to disturb his quick sleep. Her fingertips gently coaxed the very ends of the scroll toward her, leaning it closer and closer to the edge until it at last fell into her hand. She brought the paper back to her. With what little strength she had remaining, she struggled to sit up and press her back against the cool wall. She crossed her legs and untied the cord, gently laying the tie on her knee. Blythe quietly unrolled the scroll and read the words that were written for her.

She considered the words and so much beyond the words. She knew for certain she understood them and that she would live them for the rest of her life. She had become everything the words and the promise of the words could inspire.

Forgiveness—given and received—is the most powerful force for peace known to each person and to the entire human race.

To know forgiveness is to know love, to know love is to know joy, to know joy is to know forgiveness.

Achieve any one of these three, and you will know them all.

Blythe

John E. Kramer

About the Author

John E. Kramer directs the award-winning communications department at the Institute for Justice, a public interest law firm that litigates for liberty nationwide. He directed the media relations in six landmark U.S. Supreme Court cases, always fighting on the side of greater individual liberty. *Blythe* combines the two core elements of Kramer's personal life: libertarianism and his Christian faith, each of which, properly pursued, should advance respect for the individual, as well as human freedom and flourishing.

Find out more at www.BlytheBook.com.

Freedom Forge Press

About Us

Freedom Forge Press, LLC, was founded to celebrate freedom and the spirit of the individual. The founders of the press believe that when people are given freedom—of expression, of speech, of thought, of action—creativity and achievement will flourish.

Freedom Forge Press publishes general fiction, historical fiction, nonfiction, and genres like science fiction and fantasy. Freedom Forge Press's two imprints, Bellows Books and Apprentice Books, publish works for younger readers.

Find out more at www.FreedomForgePress.com.

Blythe